MURDER
IN THE
OVAL LIBRARY

Books by C.M. Gleason

Murder in the Lincoln White House

Murder in the Oval Library

MURDER IN THE OVAL LIBRARY

C.M. GLEASON

KENSINGTON BOOKS
http://www.kensingtonbooks.com

KENSINGTON BOOKS are published by

Kensington Publishing Corp.
119 West 40th Street
New York, NY 10018

All Kensington titles, imprints, and distributed lines are available at special quantity discounts for bulk purchases for sales promotion, premiums, fund-raising, educational, or institutional use.

Special book excerpts or customized printings can also be created to fit specific needs. For details, write or phone the office of the Kensington Special Sales Manager: Attn. Special Sales Department. Kensington Publishing Corp, 119 West 40th Street, New York, NY 10018. Phone: 1-800-221-2647.

Kensington and the K logo Reg. U.S. Pat. & TM Off.

Library of Congress Card Catalogue Number: 2018941296

ISBN-13: 978-1-4967-1021-5
ISBN-10: 1-4967-1021-5
First Kensington Hardcover Edition: September 2018

eISBN-13: 978-1-4967-1022-2
eISBN-10: 1-4967-1022-3
First Kensington Electronic Edition: September 2018

10 9 8 7 6 5 4 3 2 1

Printed in the United States of America

To MaryAlice and Dennis Galloway
For over twenty years of friendship, support, food, and love

ACKNOWLEDGMENTS

With this second book in the Lincoln's White House Mystery Series, I have an ever-growing list of people to thank for their support and efforts in bringing the story to life, and the books to the stores!

The team at Kensington—especially my editor Wendy McCurdy and her brilliant assistant Norma Perez-Hernandez—has been a pleasure to work with, and I'm grateful to be in such expert hands. Vida Engstrand, Lauren Vassallo, and Claire Hill round out a great team of thoughtful, savvy, and enthusiastic publishing professionals.

My long-suffering agent (though a big part of me hopes *she* doesn't think of herself in that way), Maura Kye-Casella, has, as always, been a firm guide as well as an energetic and savvy advocate for me, my books, and my career overall.

Gary March, D.O., continues to be my number-one go-to for all things medical. Between his wry sense of humor, creativity, and careful explanations and responses, I'm always confident the medical aspects of my books are both accurate and interesting.

Special thanks to Jennie Ross and Bruce Miller for their help and expertise related to Civil War-era firearms. I really enjoyed Bruce's willingness to let me see the actual revolvers and shotguns used during the time period—because no book or photograph replaces the ability to actually hold and examine the authentic items from the era.

I am so very grateful to my friends, family, and readers who've supported this series from the very first book—especially Darlene Domanik, Gary March, MaryAlice and Dennis Galloway, and Donna and Bob Lorenz for sharing their time, talent, and creativity during the release of *Murder in the Lincoln White House*. Also a special thanks to MaryAlice, Erin Wolfe, and Tammy Kearly for doing an early read-through under a tight deadline.

I know I wouldn't be where I am today without the love, support, and guidance of my mother, Joyce, and my stepfather Larry. Thank you for the infinite ways you've supported me and my career over the years.

And finally, as always, my thanks and infinite gratitude to my husband Steve and my three amazing children—all of whom have been subjected to the various requirements of being close to a working author: last-minute pizza-delivery meals (if that), acting out the choreography of crimes, dinner discussions over the distribution of clues, listening to me ramble on about fascinating (at least to me!) historical facts, and so on. I love you all!

—CM Gleason, September 2018

CHAPTER 1

"At 5 o'clock in the afternoon . . . the telegraphic wire brought the long looked-for intelligence that WAR HAS BEGUN, and that the forces of the Confederate Traitors have struck the first blow . . . Many had hoped the contest might yet be avoided. Others thought the Federal Government would back down rather than shed blood; and others were certain that a Divine Providence would interfere to prevent so fratricidal a strife.
. . . The feeling of rejoicing was everywhere to be met: that Major Anderson had not lowered his flag, and that President Lincoln had determined to sustain, even at so fearful a cost, the honor of the country."
—New York Times, *April 13, 1861,*
reporting on the firing upon Fort Sumter

April 14, 1861
Washington, D.C.

*T*HE CAPITAL WAS HARDLY MORE THAN A BEDRAGGLED SWAMP LINED with muddy, unpaved roads and studded with a few stately buildings: the Capitol (appearing half-dressed with its unfinished dome), the President's House, the Treasury, and the Smithsonian Institution. Despite all the grand plans of its American forefathers from less than a century before, Washington City remained the ugly, simple stepsister of Philadelphia, New York City, New Orleans, and Charleston.

Today, a mild Sunday in mid-April, the unpaved streets were thronged with people crowded around bulletin boards. Some were clustered in the drinking rooms of the largest hotels, worrying, arguing, or celebrating—depending on the side with which each sympathized—for word had come via telegraph late yesterday and news was still trickling in: The war had begun.

Adam Speed Quinn, a new and reluctant resident of the small, muddy capital, had no need to stop and read the notices on the boards, to try and buy one of the few unsold newspapers, or to crowd around the bar counter at Willard's to get updates on the news. He'd just come from the Executive Mansion and the private office of Mr. Lincoln himself. Because of this, Adam, at least, knew what was just beginning to dawn on the people of Washington: their city would soon be invaded by the Confederate army.

"Mr. Quinn!" Birch, the elderly Negro doorman at the Willard Hotel, greeted him as he stepped aside for Adam to pass through to the lobby. His rheumy eyes were watery but sharp, and he stood erect in his uniform and spotless white gloves. "You done seen the president, sir? Is he well?"

"I've just come from his side. I reckon he's the least rattled of anyone in the city right now. Which ain't sayin' much." Adam gave Birch a grim smile as the man touched his hat in greeting, then went on into the lobby.

Though the roar of conversation and debate spilled from down the red-carpeted hall where the bar and men's restaurant were located, the fancy, chandeliered lobby was nearly empty. Its lone occupant was a tall, lanky man of forty-seven with weather-beaten, sun-brown skin. He was dressed in a manner similar to Adam in black trousers and a homespun, double-breasted cotton shirt with a creased leather vest over it. He held a wide-brimmed black hat in one hand, and from the looks of his messy dark hair, it appeared that he had just recently removed it.

Adam knew better. Jim Lane never combed his wild mop of hair, and shaved only when he had to—that is, he claimed, when the stubble became too itchy. Thus, Lane always looked as if he'd just come in from one of the wild winds that stormed across the Kansas prairie. That appearance contributed to his reputation of being a brilliant war general who was more than slightly mad.

"Senator," Adam said as they embraced, clapping each other on the back vigorously. "Glad to see you made it in one piece. And congratulations. If I'd still been in KT for the election, you'd have had my vote."

"Thank you—and what's this senator nonsense?" Lane said. Though at six foot four he towered over most men, he was just above eye-level with the younger Adam. "You leave Kansas Territory to travel with the president, and you get all formal and citi-fied?"

Adam grinned. "I reckon if you take a better look, you'll see I ain't been citified yet." He gestured to his scuffed, worn boots and the loose, knee-length frontier coat he'd not given up since coming to the capital.

Lane laughed. "You, me, and Abe Lincoln—we're proof you can't take the frontier out of the man once he's been there, I reckon." Then he sobered. "Does he have any good idea what we're all up against?"

The moment of easy humor passed and Adam shook his head. "Hell, no one here does, Jim. No one who wasn't in Kansas knows how bloodthirsty and violent the pro-slavers are. The people here—no matter what side—are saying this'll be over by end of the summer, tops." Adam gave a bitter laugh. "You and I know better'n that."

"I'll do whatever he needs," Lane said simply. "You tell him that."

Lane and the president had become friends during Lincoln's speaking tour in Kansas only eighteen months ago, in December 1859. At that time, Adam was barely recovered from the injury that took his arm, but he'd been with the future president while he traveled through Kansas and had introduced the two men.

"That's why I'm here—besides that I needed to shake my new senator's hand." Adam's quick smile faded. "I heard most of your speech last night—out there on the Avenue. The crowd was too thick for me to get to you."

"They had me standing on a rickety dry-goods box out there on the street, and one of those bastards got close enough—tried to set me on fire." He flapped the back of his battered coat at Adam, displaying a coin-sized burn mark near the hem. "Damned near fell on my arse because the crate tipped on the cobblestones."

"Damn." But Adam wasn't surprised. The pro-slavers he'd encountered in Kansas were vicious and didn't hold back from any sort of violence. "Better cobblestones and a rickety crate than standing in that swamp out past the President's House, or in mud up to your ankles."

"Thank God for small favors. Although I reckon I didn't expect to see a pair of pigs walking along the street in the middle of the capital city."

"That happens," Adam said with a quirk of his lips. "They like to wallow behind City Hall in the square there." When Lane looked at him as if he wasn't certain whether to believe him, he added, "God's truth. Sometimes there are even chickens gathered on the National Mall, there."

"Well I'll be damned," Lane muttered. "Lawrence is still more civilized than Washington. I thought that might have changed since I was here last."

"Anyway, I reckon your reputation preceded you here to the capital. All of those Southern rebels know who you are. And they're telling tales." Adam had been at the outskirts of the crowd who'd gathered around Lane last night on the street shortly after word had come of the fall of Fort Sumter.

The new Kansas senator was nearly as well-known nationally as the new president—and was equally feared and hated by the pro-slavers. He was legendary for being a little mad and very bold when it came to battle. Adam had seen his friend acting with both strategic, calculated moments as well as in a sort of feral, berserker sort of mood—both of which had sealed his reputation.

However he'd come away victorious, Lane was a national figure. He'd been called the General Washington of Kansas because
of the way he'd successfully led a small number of frontier freedom fighters in months of battle against a large crew of Southern
soldiers, as well as much of the federal government—both of
which wanted to make Kansas a slave state. The Free Staters had
finally won at the ballot box in 1859, but only after much death
and bloodshed.

Hatred for the man from Lawrence had followed the senator
here, and last night during Lane's impromptu speech, he'd nearly
been mobbed by Southern sympathizers and other pro-slavers
who knew Lane from Kansas. These antagonists threatened to
hang him. But Adam and a dozen or so other Loyalists put their
hands on their revolvers, clicking the hammers in a sharp warning to those who wanted to start a riot. The troublemakers who
were interspersed among the crowd realized suddenly they didn't
know exactly *who* was standing next to them: ally or enemy. The
cries and threats for hanging went silent.

For the moment.

"They're going to take the city, you know, Jim. The Confederates. As soon as Virginia secedes—and that's going to be any day
now, I reckon. If Maryland goes too, there's no hope for Washington, caught as we are between the two states—and the city already mostly Southern. All the Rebels have to do is come across
the Potomac. They're eight hundred feet away. Eight hundred
feet from taking the damned city."

Lane swore under his breath. "How many Union men you got
here?"

"Lincoln's calling up the city militia, but dammit, they're most
of them Southerners themselves. And none of 'em are experienced in any sort of battle fighting. Half of them are older and
fatter than my Aunt Gertrude. Even so, I reckon you ask if they'd
actually fire on the Confederates, and that'd be like asking them
to fire on a brother. Most of 'em surely *are* brothers—or cousins.
This is a damned thing. A *damned* thing." Adam had kept these

thoughts to himself when in the president's office, but they'd
been haunting him for weeks.

The whole country knew the war was inevitable—ever since
Lincoln had been elected. Once that had happened, there was no
turning back.

Though the new president clearly and repeatedly stated he had
no intention of freeing the slaves in the South, people in those
states didn't believe him. Even more than that, they wanted assur-
ance that the "peculiar institution" of slavery could expand west
along with the nation. That, however, was where Lincoln drew the
line. He would not see slavery expand into any more territories or
states—on that he'd been clear.

That was how he'd been elected. And that was why he'd been
getting death threats—both openly and secretly—since the votes
were counted.

"There's no one here to protect the city, then."

"Not enough, anyway. Not until more troops get here from the
north—which could be a week or more. He's expecting fifty thousand or more—he'll be publishing the official proclamation calling up the troops tomorrow. But who knows when they'll get
here."

Lane looked grimmer than ever. "And in the mean time, those
damned pro-slavers won't hesitate to shoot and kill anyone—
brother or no."

Adam didn't need to verbalize his agreement. He was person-
ally acquainted with violent pro-slavers like John Atchison and
John Stringfellow. And it was Orin Bitter, his red-headed cohort
Leward Hale, and their small gang who'd taken not only Adam's
arm from him, but also the life of his best friend . . . and more.
Tom, Mary, and little Carl Stillwell.

He tamped back the rise of memory, the grief that still hadn't
gone, and returned his clear-eyed gaze to Lane. Both men—and
many of their friends and cohorts—had experienced deep losses
on the Kansas prairie. Because of that, they knew what to expect
in a battle against Southern rebels who were determined to protect their way of life. There would be no quarter given. The Se-

cessionists would fight like savages. The rest of the country had no idea what they were about to face—but Adam and Jim Lane, and the other frontiersmen who'd fought with them, did.

"The Confederates won't wait. They'd be foolish to hesitate from attacking Washington. Everyone knows the city's not prepared and hardly protected. And when they take the city," Adam continued, speaking his worst fear aloud for the first time, "they'll go for the President's House right off."

He and Lane looked at each other. There was no need to say anything more. They'd both seen what the pro-slavers had done to the men they hated and considered their enemies. It wasn't just simple killing. There were tar-and-featherings, beatings, cuttings, hangings, and more. More often than not, those horrific actions had been unprovoked and retaliatory—not even taking place in the heat of battle.

"Then they ain't gonna take the city. And they sure as hell ain't gonna take the president or his house," Lane said flatly. "I reckon Mr. Lincoln needs a special guard, and I reckon we're the ones to do it."

"There's some good Free State Kansas fighters already here in Washington. I reckon they're ready to fight for the Union again."

"Then let's rally up those frontiersmen to that big white house." Lane extended his weathered hand.

"I already told Mr. Lincoln you'd say that." Adam shook his friend's hand firmly, feeling as if he finally had a true ally in town. "He's hesitant about garrisoning soldiers at the 'people's house'—doesn't want to upset the public—but I'll talk him into it."

"I don't see how the president has any choice."

"I don't reckon he does."

Thursday, April 18

It wasn't until four days later, when word came that the Confederates had attacked the Union armory at Harper's Ferry less than seventy miles away, that the president was convinced to let Jim Lane bring his frontier fighters to the Executive Mansion. Although the outnumbered Union troops had done their best to keep the federal arsenal and weaponry from the hands of the Rebels by setting fire to the Harper's Ferry armory, that small town was now in the hands of the Confederates—and far too close to Washington for comfort.

Nearly five hundred troops from Pennsylvania had arrived in the capital on the seven o'clock train, and they'd be stationed at the Capitol and Treasury Building. The colonel from Kentucky, Cassius Clay, had gathered a small group of a hundred or so staunch Union men, and they were garrisoned at the Willard Hotel.

Colonel Stone assigned Clay's men to patrol the streets, but Lane and Adam—along with Major David Hunter—had convinced the president he needed more security in the presidential residence. They all feared the Confederates would not hesitate to storm the Executive Mansion and kidnap or assassinate the president.

"It's a damned thing," Lincoln said as he, Hunter, and Adam greeted Lane at the main entrance to the house. "Having soldiers garrisoned inside the White House."

The president squinted a little and seemed particularly grave as he looked out over the motley troop of sixty soldiers assembled on the Ellipse—the oval-shaped drive on the north side of the mansion. The men had just marched loudly and conspicuously along Pennsylvania Avenue from Willard's. Their shadows fell in long swaths behind them, for the sun was low to the horizon.

"Half the city's evacuated itself. The streets have been clogged with people taking all their belongings and getting out of town," said Adam, wondering about young Brian Mulcahey and his family.

The Mulcaheys were poor Irish immigrants who lived in the mean, primitive alleys in the First Ward, just north of Lafayette Square and the President's House. Would they have left too? Did they have any means or money to travel? Adam reckoned he could make the time to check on them tomorrow.

"We all know the Rebels are coming. Word is, they might be coming even tonight. But they won't take your house, Mr. President. Not while we're here," Lane said in an uncharacteristically formal manner.

"From your mouth to Heaven's ear," replied Lincoln.

The president stood in the grand foyer, just past the wizened Irishman Edward McManus—the doorman who'd worked for seven presidents—and greeted each of the frontier fighters as they came in.

Lincoln's hand was just as callused and weathered as those he shook from the men determined to guard him, and though at six-foot-four, he loomed taller than all but Jim Lane, he was as informal and relaxed as they were in dress, manner, and words. To a man, each one greeted him with a steady gaze and a firm shake, expressing his honor at being called to this duty.

"I'll sleep outside your bedroom door," Lane said to the president when all his men had trooped through. He adjusted the rifle he held over a shoulder and pulled back his coat to reveal the revolver tucked in a holster.

"I'll stay in the East Room with the rest of the men," Major Hunter said, and Adam, who considered himself an unofficial member of the Frontier Guard, as Lane had dubbed the men, agreed he would do the same.

"No uniforms," Lane replied when Secretary of War Cameron broached the subject of clothing and weapons for the Kansans. "If they're in uniform, it's too easy for the enemy to count the exact number. Let the men stay in their own clothing so no one knows just how many we have. That's going to be important—we've got to give off that there's more of us than there are. As for rifles and bayonets, we'll take as many as you can give us."

While the Frontier Guard was armed with rifles, bayonets, and ammunition, Adam took Lane to the second floor so he could get the lay of the land there.

Though he didn't point it out, Adam was certain Lane saw in what disrepair the president's mansion was. Carpets were worn and threadbare in places, painting needed to be done most everywhere, and there were random water stains on the walls and ceiling. Some of the wainscoting was missing, and in other places it was coming loose. They didn't go into the Green or Blue Rooms on the first floor, but Adam knew how sun-faded the draperies were, and that the rugs were frayed. Mrs. Lincoln had created a mild scandal because of the cost of some furnishings she'd ordered from New York even before the inauguration, but the actual refurbishment had hardly begun.

As they ascended to the second level, Adam and Lane passed a long line of men that led from the main floor up the stairs and along the hall. The line ended outside the waiting room to the president's office with three chairs pushed up against the wall, where they were occupied by those who'd been waiting the longest.

"Job-seekers," Adam explained when he and Lane were alone in the oval library. An overturned pile of blocks indicated that Tad and Willie, the Lincolns' young sons, had been there recently. "There've been men lined up here since the day he moved in, and they stay till he meets with them or sends them home at night—then show up first thing at dawn the next day. Old Ed—you met him, the doorman—has been told to let them all in, no questions."

"These people just walk into the President's House without a by your leave? And without any security? And they stay all day? What is he thinking? We're at *war* for God's sake."

Adam shook his head. "Nicolay and Hay—the two secretaries—and Ward Hill Lamon, who was his bodyguard until just recently—and I and Mrs. Lincoln and everyone else who has his ear says the same . . . but he won't have any of it. 'It's the people's house,' he says."

Lane muttered something foul, then sighed and looked around as if seeing the place for the first time. "Never seen an oval-shaped room before. Especially one this big."

The large room was outfitted as a library, but the Lincolns used it as a casual family room. Shelves lined the curved walls, and the last bit of light from the sunset filtered through the large windows and over the hundreds of book spines. Adam knew more crates were coming, for Lincoln, who treasured every book he'd ever owned, had spent over a thousand dollars on new volumes for the library.

A large sofa and two comfortable armchairs had been placed in the center of the room, flanking a low table. There was plenty of floor space where Tad and Willie could play while their parents sat and talked, or while their father met informally with friends or advisors.

"Me neither," Adam replied. "Abe likes it because it's quiet and the boys can run around. They're a couple of ruffians," he added with a grin. "Willie, he's ten, and Tad must be eight by now. I'm surprised we haven't seen—or heard—them yet; Mrs. Lincoln must have them occupied somewhere. Abe's office is down yonder, and the two secretaries, Nicolay and Hay—you met them, and Hay's the younger one—are next door to it. They bunk across the hall, and the family bedrooms are behind those doors we passed at the top of the stairs. There's that screen that blocks the hallway from the private side to the public, but you still walk past the bedchambers at the top of the stairs."

"We'll be putting a guard at that screen," Lane said firmly. "And sending all those job-seekers home. Abe'll do it for Mrs. Lincoln's sake, and the boys, if no other reason. She's the wife—I reckon she's got something to say about it."

"Speaking of wives . . . how is Mary? And the children?" Adam asked with some trepidation, knowing that Lane and his wife had not only gone through an estrangement some time ago, but had even divorced in '56. They'd remarried two years later, but he knew things remained very tenuous between them. One thing he did know, however, was that Lane was very attached to his children, and had especially grieved over the death of his daughter Annie—who had died in Kansas.

"We're still married, but that's about all I can say on that," he replied brusquely. "The children are well, growing like weeds. Healthy so far." He looked at Adam and, lifting one of his thick, bushy brows, quickly changed the subject. "What exactly is your position here? You never did say."

Adam gave a rueful laugh. "That's because I reckon I don't

quite know. Abe asked me to stay on once my uncle Joshua left after the inauguration—the two of them are old friends, and Josh gave him a place to stay when he first came to Springfield. I've known Abe nearly twenty years since I came to live with my uncle, so I was asked to be part of the bodyguard team when he traveled from Illinois to here. Then I got caught up helping with a situation a few weeks ago—"

"That man who was murdered at the inaugural ball." Lane shook his head at Adam's surprise. "It was in the paper—even out to Lawrence—and so was your name. I reckon that makes you the president's personal investigator now, doesn't it?"

"Well, I'd've said that job belonged to Allan Pinkerton, but he's gone back to Chicago, so I reckon you might be right. But I can't say I'm interested in doing much more investigating of anything, to be frank. I'd've left Washington weeks ago, but Abe asked me to stay."

The president—who was like an honorary uncle—said because he'd known Adam since he was a boy, he knew could trust him, and since he didn't have even a whiff of political aspiration, that made Adam even more valuable to him. "You're the only person in this city who doesn't want anything from me," Lincoln told him.

Adam still wasn't certain how he felt about being cornered into staying in the city and dunked all the way into politics and formal gatherings and tight shoes when all he wanted to do was get back to the wide open space of the frontier, but he was here, and here he'd remain, to serve and protect a man he loved and respected.

"I suppose now that war's officially on, I'm going to be enlisting pretty damned soon," Adam said, wondering if they'd even take him with his missing arm. He gritted his teeth. Probably not. "Unless the Rebs come in and end things quickly."

Lane, who'd been looking out the windows at the last bit of the sun setting over the marshy ground beyond the house, turned back. "The way I see it, our entire concept of democracy is at stake. If Washington falls, the American experiment of democracy does too."

"We're going to have to put on a big show for the Rebs," Adam replied. "Scare the wool out of them. At least they know Jim Lane's Jayhawkers aren't afraid to pull a damned trigger. They'll think twice about attacking us."

"That's right. If we make it through tonight, I'll recruit more men tomorrow, and we're going to do whatever we can to put out the word how many troops we got here. At least three hundred. Probably up to four hundred by now." Lane grinned darkly, pursing his lips.

"I'll drop a few hints here and there at the bar counter at the St. Charles too. That's the hotel where the Southerners mostly stay, and word'll easily get back to the Confederates there's hundreds of angry Free-Staters here at the mansion, experienced and ready to fight."

"For now, we've got the sixty—but we'll make it look like more. Whether they invade tonight . . ." He made a thoughtful sound.

Adam pointed out the window. "Just yonder, down the hill there and across the National Mall—you can't hardly see it right now in the dark—but the Long Bridge is there over the Potomac. That's where they'll come."

Eight hundred feet away, across the river.

As he looked out into the twilit night, squinting to determine whether there was any sign of enemy troops gathering in the shadows, he saw the faint glow from a tower of the Smithsonian Castle. The sprawling, gothic-style building made from red-orange brick—so different from all of the other white marble government structures—was right there, at the end of the Long Bridge.

The fingers on Adam's real hand tightened. That building was the first place the Confederates would see when they came across. Though the president would be their ultimate target, the Rebels could easily be distracted by the stately castle.

And the occupants therein.

But surely Joseph Henry, the director of the Smithsonian, had evacuated with his wife, daughters—and niece.

But why was there still a light in one of the towers? In the East Tower, where the Henry family lived?

Adam checked the revolver holstered at his waist and then his pocket for ammunition. He'd grab himself an Enfield on the way out. "I'm going to take a few men down to the Long Bridge—it needs to be guarded. Maybe we'll make some ruckus too—give those Rebs something to worry about."

And while he was down there scouting, he'd find out who had a light on in the Smithsonian tower.

CHAPTER 2

*D*ESPITE THE RUMORS RUNNING RAMPANT THROUGH THE CITY, Sophie Gates wasn't particularly worried. At least, that was what she told herself.

Even if the Confederates *did* cross over the Long Bridge and end up right in the shadow of the castle-like Smithsonian building, that didn't mean they'd have any reason to come inside it. And even if they did, Uncle Joseph was a Southern sympathizer—so he'd probably welcome the soldiers inside with open arms.

If he ever came back from wherever he'd been for the past several hours, that is.

Sophie considered turning down her lamp so as not to attract attention *should* the Rebels make an appearance, but that would mean she couldn't write.

And a journalist had to write.

Here she was in the East Tower apartments of the Smithsonian, with a bird's-eye view of Washington. The city was holding its collective breath, surely soon to be invaded. She'd have the most unique and broad perspective of whatever happened, and her report would be filled with important details and news. She'd telegraph the information up to New York, and then, finally, Horace Greeley and his *Times* would have to take notice of her stories.

Of course, the reports would have to be submitted under her nom de plume, Henry Altman, because most people didn't think a woman journalist could write about anything other than gossip, fashion, or—she shuddered—housekeeping. But Sophie was bound and determined to prove them all wrong, and this could be her chance.

If she had a quiver of nervousness about what might happen if the soldiers did come tonight, she refused to dwell on it. A newspaper correspondent had to take risks. And besides . . . she knew how to shoot the rifle she had loaded and rested against the wall behind her desk.

She wasn't a fool.

Nevertheless, Sophie couldn't completely quell a twitch of nerves about being alone here in the castle when or if the Rebels invaded.

So she forced herself to focus on the words she'd written so far. She planned to prepare two versions: a brief report with the most pertinent information, short and sweet, that could be telegraphed for instant receipt.

And she'd also write a more detailed story to be sent by mail, to be printed in full later. It was that version to which she now gave her attention.

As the sun sets on a chill, rainy April day, all ears are turned toward any sound that might herald the arrival of the Confederate Traitors on the banks of the Potomac. If they dared cross the Long Bridge, the Union men of Washington City would meet them on the springy turf of the National Mall and—

Sophie stilled, tensing. What was that noise?

Her gaze went to the window, which faced northeast, over the mall. Heart thudding, she rose and, taking care to keep herself from being silhouetted by the lamp, peeked out from the edge of the glass.

There was no sign of movement below, but she was looking toward the Capitol building. If the Rebels came, they would cross the Long Bridge, barely a spit away to the south and west of her— everyone said so, and Sophie had been listening to the rumors and arguments for days.

The view of the Potomac and its bridge was from a different window than the one by her desk. Even though the night was cloudy from a day of rain, she might be able to make out some shapes and even count them. That would be good information. She started out of the room, then spun and came back for the rifle. Just in case.

As she hurried across the hall to the south-facing chamber—her aunt and uncle's bedroom—she heard the definite sounds of movement: thumping, clanking, thudding. It sounded like a massive army was marching over the wooden slats of the bridge. Inside, her stomach dropped and squished like tub of wet laundry.

The Rebels are coming.

Sophie gripped the rifle and tried to decide what to do. She was a woman alone in this huge building—which gave her many places to hide, if necessary.

But she was also a journalist.

It was her task to get the story. She would be the first reporter to see the Confederate troops; she could get their numbers, perhaps identify and even count their weapons—even follow them and watch as everything played out. Though her heart was thudding wildly, and her knees were a trifle weak, she knew this was her best chance to get a real story. She could be the first to get to the telegraph office and send word up to Mr. Greeley.

Fired by determination, she began to make her way down the stairs of the tower, rifle still in hand. In the past when seeking out a story, Sophie had often dressed as a man in an effort to be taken more seriously—and to keep from attracting attention as a woman, particularly if she was going to places women generally weren't supposed to go. But tonight, she didn't have time to change out of the simple shirtwaist, skirt, and subdued crinoline she wore at home.

She wasn't certain whether her obvious gender would help or hinder her if she came face to face with the Confederates, but she would surely find out.

She was nearly to the bottom of the dark stairs when she heard a sound at the exterior door. A thunk, as if someone was trying to open it.

Her heart skipped a beat and she paused, holding her breath, feeling the sound of her pulse ramming inside her ears. Uncle Joseph, finally returning? Maybe he was drunk, and was fumbling for the latch in the dark outside.

Or was it the Rebels, already determined to take over one of the government buildings, as they had done all over the South? The sounds of marching over the bridge were louder and steadier now that she was on the ground floor and closer.

Thud, thud, thud . . . How many *were* there? She swallowed hard.

The door clunked quietly again.

Surely if it were the Confederates trying to get in, they'd be louder and bolder. Of course Sophie had never experienced a war before, or seen an army in action—unless you counted the gangs in New York, but she expected if a group of invading soldiers wanted access to a building, they wouldn't be particularly polite about it. They'd pound on the door, demand entrance, even break their way in.

Maybe it was someone else who just needed a safe place to hide now that the Confederates were crossing into the city. Maybe Mr. Stimpson, or another of the young naturalists who boarded at the Smithsonian in exchange for doing cataloging, had returned from their evacuation. Those men, all of whom she knew, lived in the North Tower. But maybe someone had been locked out, not realizing everyone else had left the building—and the city.

These realizations emboldened her, and Sophie went to the door. She'd left a lamp on the table in the entrance, turned down just to the lowest glow to light the way for her uncle's return. Now she regretted it, for the light would give whoever was outside the advantage of sight inside.

Holding her rifle at the ready, she called, "Who's there?" as she peeked through the glass sidelight.

It was too dark to see more than a silhouette, but there was only one. The man's shape was too long and slender to be her rotund Uncle Joseph, though.

And it was holding something else long and much more slender. A rifle.

"Who's there?" she called again, edging to the window on the other side of the door to try a different angle.

"Miss Gates? Is that you in there?"

Sophie frowned. The voice was familiar. "Who is it?"

"It's Adam Quinn, miss. From the President's House. Is that you, Miss Gates?"

Adam Quinn? Sophie lifted her brows, frowning into the darkness. What on earth—?

But she was already undoing the locks, ridiculously relieved that it was him and not the Rebels. Unless he was with the Rebels—no, of course not. He knew Mr. Lincoln, and he said he'd come from the President's House.

Maybe he was trying to hide from the army that seemed to *still* be marching over the bridge.

She shivered. Just how many men were there on Long Bridge, coming to take the city? Her knees wobbled a little.

"Come in." She stepped back as soon as the locks were undone and raised her rifle . . . just to be certain.

When Mr. Quinn opened the door to reveal himself, he stilled at the sight of the barrel pointing at him. "Well, I reckon I wasn't expecting such a warm greeting, Miss Gates."

His drawling comment nagged a smile from her, and she lowered the rifle. "Are you alone? Come inside. What on earth are you doing out there? Don't you know the Rebels are coming across the bridge? Did they see you? Did you see them? How many are there?"

Still holding his own rifle, her visitor closed the door behind him. Along with him came the brisk chill of the damp spring night and the faint scent of wood smoke and tobacco.

In the soft golden glow, Sophie looked up at the man she'd learned was a close friend and confidant of the president during a recent murder investigation. He was nearly as tall as Mr. Lincoln, which she personally had cause to know, having once been in the same room with both men. That had been the most exciting day of her life, standing in the president's office and being commended by him for helping to catch a murderer. Her alter ego, Henry Altman, had written that story, and it had been Sophie's second published piece. Not in the *New York Times*, unfortunately, but in the much smaller, less prestigious *Washington Republic*. Still. It had been published.

"Where's your uncle? Surely you're not here alone, Miss Gates." Mr. Quinn set his rifle against the wall and swept off his unfashionable, wide-brimmed hat, spraying her with a soft rain of water from the drizzle that had been falling all day.

"I don't know where he is. He's been gone for hours. What are you doing here?" She went to the sidelight to look out, unable to see the Long Bridge from this view. "Did you see the soldiers? How many are there?"

"He left you here *alone*? With the Confederates coming?"

"Not exactly," Sophie replied, still contorting herself to look out the window. "I can't see the soldiers—"

Mr. Quinn sighed. "I reckon I won't get any straight answers from you until I give you what you want. Those aren't the Rebels crossing the bridge, Miss Gates."

"They're not?" She pulled away from the window and looked at him curiously. He was really quite tall, and somehow the only part of his face that was caught by the lamplight was the nice little cleft in his clean-shaven chin. The rest of him was mostly in shadow, though she could see a hint of unruly dark hair and long, straight nose.

"No, they're my men. From the President's House."

"*Your* men? How many do you have out there? Two hundred? Three hundred?" Sophie had heard enough buzzing rumors to know that when Mr. Lincoln had called up the city militia over the last three days, barely half of the men had signed on. They weren't willing to actually shoot at their Southern brethren, and some of them had even left the city to head south and enlist with the Confederate Army. But the troops she heard marching over the bridge sounded far more numerous and impressive than the low count that had been mustered.

Mr. Quinn chuckled. "That's what we're trying to make everyone think. There's only a doz—well, now, if I'm talking to a reporter, I best be careful what I say."

But Sophie caught on quickly. "You mean you're creating a lot of noise to make it sound like there are more men than there are." She grinned. "That's smart. The sound carries across water, too, so the Confederates on the Virginia side of the river will hear all the noise. Maybe they'll think twice about coming over here tonight."

He looked down at her speculatively. "Now, you're not going to be telling your Southern friends about that little trick, are you?"

"My Southern friends? I'm from New York City, Mr. Quinn. I don't have any friends in the South."

She felt his eyes fasten on her. "But your uncle does. And he's made no secret where his sympathies lie."

"I am not my uncle, Mr. Quinn. I form my own opinions."

"I reckon you do at that, Miss Gates." His voice wasn't quite as slow as a Mississippi drawl, but it took its time and had a low, rough edge to it.

She knew he'd lived on the frontier, in Kansas, for a while—which explained his informal manner, unfashionable clothing, and sun-browned skin. And she suspected—though she didn't know for certain—that it was during the Free State battles that he'd lost his left arm. He wore a prosthetic instead of an empty coat sleeve, and he was so comfortable manipulating it that Sophie wouldn't be able to tell which was the false one if she didn't know it was his left arm.

"Is it true there are soldiers at the President's House?" she asked. "I saw them marching along the Avenue."

"Yes." He looked at her with consideration, as if still questioning where her loyalties were. "Maybe you'd want to tell your uncle about the hundreds of men you heard marching across the Long Bridge tonight."

"Maybe I do. If he ever comes back."

"You don't know where he is? When did he leave? How *did* you come to be here alone, with the Rebels at our shores?"

Sophie still kept peering out the window. "Are you sure those are all your men—and what do you mean by *your* men?"

Mr. Quinn sighed again. "I reckon you've taken up the right vocation as a newspaper reporter, Miss Gates. You're more full of questions than answers. But I'm not answering any more questions until you do some of mine."

"I suppose you have a point. Yes, I'm here alone. Uncle Joseph didn't exactly leave me here; he doesn't know I'm back."

"Back?" It only took him an instant to catch on. "So your aunt and cousins evacuated, and you sneaked back. Is that how it happened? Your uncle was supposed to be here, and now he's gone. Probably at the National or Willard's, drinking with his friends and waiting for the invaders to come."

She frowned up at him. "Why are you asking me so many questions if you already know the answers?"

He shrugged, his wide shoulders shifting in the golden light. "I reckon I might have made a good reporter myself if it didn't require talking to people."

Sophie choked on a laugh. "Well, you're an honest one, aren't you, Mr. Quinn? You don't like talking to people."

He shrugged again. "Most of the time, I'd just as soon be in a quiet location with my own company."

"Then what are you doing living in Washington City?" she couldn't help but ask.

"I ask myself that nearly every day, Miss Gates," he said. There was a touch of levity in his voice, but it evaporated when he changed the subject. "What about the others—the Megatherium Club? Did they evacuate too?"

The Megatherium Club was the name adopted by the group of naturalists who boarded in the North Tower. All in their twenties and thirties, the men were hard workers during the day, but acted like a wild brotherhood at night. A few weeks ago, Sophie had infiltrated one of their nighttime club meetings as Henry Altman—and Mr. Quinn had been present as well. She supposed she still owed him a favor since he hadn't exposed her real identity to the men who worked for her uncle. Or to her uncle himself, for that matter.

That realization caused her to temper her tone into a more conciliatory one. "Yes, they're all gone as well. Uncle Joseph was going to stay because . . . well, you already know. He wasn't afraid of the Confederates, but he also wanted to make sure nothing happened to anything here at the museum."

"And you sneaked back so you could be here to report the story. What on earth did you tell your aunt?"

"I gave a note to one of my cousins to give to her later. We were all riding in a long caravan with some other friends in their carriages, and Aunt Harriet won't even realize I'm missing until they get to Baltimore."

"Baltimore! They're threatening to close the railways there and not allowing anyone to go north, or to come south from Delaware or Pennsylvania. I don't know how far your family is going to get." Mr. Quinn sounded concerned.

"My aunt has family in Baltimore. They're Confederate sympathizers too," Sophie admitted dryly. "Yet another reason I didn't want to go with them. I've heard arguments on both sides about this conflict, and I can see the perspective of both the Union and the South. But I don't think war is the answer, and states just can't decide to leave the country if they don't like who gets elected president. That's not the point of our democracy, is it?"

"I reckon we can't be the *United* States of America if those states can come and go as they please. Not to mention the issue of enslaving other men."

The bite in his otherwise relaxed drawl alerted her to his change of mood. "Are you an abolitionist, Mr. Quinn?"

"I reckon I am, Miss Gates. I lost property, peace, blood, and a limb fighting to keep Kansas free because I don't believe any man has the right to keep any other man like a possession."

She crossed her arms over her middle. "And does that belief include not treating a woman—a wife, a mother, a sister—like a possession as well? Like a half-wit, or less of a person than a man? Unable to make her own decisions?"

His eyes widened. "Well, now that's a sharp turn of conversation, Miss Gates."

"I merely ask because I suspect the next thing out of your mouth is going to be an admonishment to me about being here—a female alone—when the city is about to be invaded by an army."

He took his time answering, and for some reason, that annoyed her a little. "In my mind, it's not advisable for anyone to be alone when an army is about to invade a city—man or woman. Even if they do know how to hold a rifle."

"And load and shoot one."

"Even if. I saw the light on in the tower, and as I know Dr. Henry lives here with his family, I thought it would be a good idea to check in and make sure everyone was all right when we came down here to march on the bridge. And," he added a bit more firmly as she tried to speak over him, "I had a sneaking suspicion that a young woman who fancies herself a newspaper writer might have decided to investigate the situation."

"Well, now that you've proven yourself correct, I suppose you'd best see to your 'men,'" Sophie replied. *This* man was far too clever for his own good. No wonder Mr. Lincoln had put him in charge of investigating the murder of Custer Billings last month. "Does that mean you've enlisted then, Mr. Quinn? In the Union Army?" Then she could have kicked herself. Of *course* he couldn't enlist with a missing arm!

"Not yet," was his rumbling response. He didn't seem to notice her *faux pas*. "Not officially. But it's only a matter of time, now that things are going the way they are. But for tonight—and for the foreseeable future—I'll be guarding the president in his house, along with the other men of the Frontier Guard."

"The Frontier Guard. So that's who was marching to the mansion today. They said it was General Lane—do you know General Lane?" Sophie couldn't keep the light of admiration from her voice. The heroism of Jim Lane during the Mexican War, and then during the Bloody Kansas conflict, had been all over the papers—which of course she'd read avidly, as a hopeful journalist as well as an American.

"Fought with him in Kansas."

"You were a Jayhawker?" Sophie tried not to sound too impressed, but it was difficult not to. The stories that had come back to New York about the fierce frontier warriors led by the wild General Lane were both thrilling and terrifying. He was a national hero, despite the nasty business related to the death of one

Gaius Jenkins. Some said Lane had murdered him in cold blood, others said he'd been provoked—but the courts had ruled the case self-defense. "So it is true—there are soldiers garrisoned in the Executive Mansion."

"For the foreseeable future. The Confederates will come—if not tonight, then tomorrow or the next day. They'd be fools not to act quickly, before reinforcements come from the North. And God knows how soon they'll arrive." He reached over to take up his gun. "Miss Gates, I reckon one rifle ain't going to do much good against a whole army—whether it be a man or woman holding it."

She understood his point. "Uncle Joseph should be back soon."

"There's no telling when—or if—he'll be back. For all you know, he might have decided to follow your aunt and cousins to Baltimore. Why don't you come on back to the President's House with us. At least for tonight."

"I don't—"

But he kept talking in that easy drawl. "More important, Miss Gates, I'd consider it a personal favor. If my mother ever found out I left a woman by herself when an army was coming to invade the city, I wouldn't have enough skin left on me to hold my bones together. Not to mention what she'd do to my ears and the rest of me."

Sophie couldn't hold back a laugh—mainly because he sounded deadly serious. "Well, I suppose that would be a waste of a good Union soldier then." She drew in a deep breath in an effort to settle her pulse. *Stay at the President's House?* What better place for a news correspondent to be? "All right, then. I'll just go up and get a few things."

"Yes, ma'am," he said gravely. "I'll be right here, waiting."

And watching.

He didn't say it, but he didn't have to. And as Sophie dashed up the stairs of the East Tower, she could admit to herself that she was relieved not to be left alone when the invaders were coming.

It wasn't until she was on her way back down the stairs that she realized the President's House might not be much safer.

But at least she wouldn't be alone.

* * *

To everyone's surprise, the Rebels didn't come that night.

Dawn broke over a tense, half-empty city like a sigh of relief, revealing silent streets under a wash of pink.

True to his word, Jim Lane had slept at Lincoln's second-floor bedroom door, his long legs stretched out in front of it. He'd kept three weapons with him through the night: a bayoneted rifle, a revolver, and his "Arkansas toothpick": a long, slender, wicked-looking knife.

Located on the main floor, the East Room—which was the largest and most updated chamber in the entire mansion—was occupied by the men of the Frontier Guard. Two massive fireplaces cast dancing shadows over the occupants while keeping the April damp at bay. When not taking turns at guard duty, each man slept head-to-wall on the red velvet carpet. Their feet faced the center of the room, and they lined their Enfield rifles and bayonets in a long, metallic row down the middle.

"No pillows," Lane said. He wanted everyone to sleep, but to sleep lightly enough to come awake at the first sound.

It was nearly ten o'clock by the time Adam turned Miss Gates over to the other females on the second floor—some wives of Frontier Guard members, Mrs. Lincoln, and her relatives. Then he left the mansion to once again march two dozen men back and forth across the Long Bridge—creating as much noise as possible—before returning to the mansion just after eleven o'clock.

In Lincoln's office with General Scott, Jim Lane, the president, and Hunter, Adam shared the news of several Confederate campfires along the Virginia shore of the Potomac, but in the dark it was impossible to see how many troops—if any—there were.

This worked to the advantage of the Frontier Guard as well, and Lane and Adam agreed that their tactic of making so much noise on the bridge might have contributed to the hesitation of the Rebels to attack. Neither side could know how many men the other had.

Lincoln went to bed at half-past eleven, and Lane took up his post outside his bedchamber door.

Nevertheless, when the morning dawned without an invasion, the relief was tempered. If not last night, then tonight. If not tonight, then tomorrow night.

Meanwhile, they tensely waited for word of reinforcements from Massachusetts, New York, and Ohio.

Several hours after the peaceful dawn, the small Frontier Guard was eating eggs, dried apples, and ham in the East Room. Lincoln was meeting with his advisors. The women were dressing in the bedchambers.

And then someone screamed.

CHAPTER 3

Friday, April 19

BREAKFAST DISHES AND WEAPONS CLATTERED AS THEY WERE DROPPED and snatched up respectively, and every man in the East Room was instantly on his feet. They rushed to the windows, to the door, spilling out into the hall, ready for any threat.

Adam, who'd been halfway down the stairs—passing the ever-present line of jobseekers, who'd *still* showed up this morning despite the tensions in the city—spun around and bolted back up. The scream had come from the second floor, past the offices.

By the time he got to the top of the stairs, the feminine screaming had stopped and the sounds of rushing footsteps had ceased.

A small crowd—Mr. Lincoln's two secretaries, General Winfield Scott, Secretary Cameron, and the president himself—stood in the doorway of the oval room, where Adam and Lane had spoken yesterday. A young maid was sobbing hysterically into the bosom of another maid—older and sturdier, but wearing her own silent mask of shock and horror. The women who'd bunked on this floor—which included Mrs. Lincoln, her cousins, Miss Gates, some of the soldiers' wives, and more servants—had clustered in the corridor just past the screen that separated the offices from the family's residence.

Adam smelled the blood before he got to the door. It was so thick and heavy on the air, he wondered how he'd not scented it earlier. Probably the door to the room had been closed, locking in the stench. The others moved aside so he could pass through the doorway—actions he didn't realize the significance of until later—and he stepped into the oval-shaped room.

He took only two steps over the threshold, then paused to take in the scene.

The man was dead; there was no need to get close to him to make certain. The gaping wound where his throat had been sliced from one side to the other left no room for doubt.

Adam murmured a prayer and closed his eyes for a moment, asking for peace, guidance, and safe passage for the soul of the dead man. Then he opened his eyes and, before taking any further steps into the chamber, looked at what lay before him.

The young man had crumpled to the floor onto his back with limbs splayed and blank eyes open in shock. His face was splattered with blood, and his mouth smeared with what looked like fingerprints. More blood, dark and congealed, soaked the front of his shirt and worn coat, along with the rug beneath him. His head tipped backward so that the gash across his throat resembled a dark, horrible mouth. A few dark flies buzzed near the opening.

No wonder the maid had been screaming.

Lincoln was the one to break the taut silence. "Adam."

With a numb sort of acceptance, he turned to meet the president's sober eyes. Adam exhaled deeply and nodded at the question in his friend's gaze. Lincoln didn't even need to speak; his request was clear and Adam understood: *Another one. Tend to it, please, my friend. I place my trust in you.*

Adam stifled a ripple of frustration that mingled with pity and horror from the scene before him. He wasn't an investigator or a detective like Allan Pinkerton. Yet here he was again, faced with a seemingly insurmountable task for which he was unschooled and unprepared.

But when his attention returned to the dead man, a wave of sadness suffused him. Another death, another body, another violent scene . . . and surely there would be more to come.

But this one wasn't on the battlefield.

"I need a lamp or candle," he murmured, for the curtains on

the window near the body were still drawn, and the maid had obviously been interrupted in opening the others by her discovery. There were two lamps that had been turned on by the door through which Adam had entered, and where everyone currently gathered.

The smaller doors on either side of the chamber, near the rear curve of the room, were closed.

Someone thrust a small lamp, turned up bright, into Adam's hand and he murmured his thanks. He stepped closer, careful not to disturb any marks or bloodstains on the rug or floor and staying away from the area where the killer had moved—he could read the tracks even from the doorway. He bent to close the man's eyes with the fingers of his right hand. Then he stepped back to give himself space so he could look down once more.

Somehow, even before the president spoke Adam's name in that silent request, the others gathered in the doorway seemed to understand he would take the lead on this new and terrible problem. Adam supposed it was the least he could do, when there were so many other things for the president and his staff and cabinet to worry about. And yet there was a sense of fury and frustration simmering beneath his skin. He knew how to fight, how to soldier, how to protect what he loved and believed in, how to track and farm and build.

He *didn't* know how to find and catch a murderer. He'd barely managed it the last time he'd been set to this sort of task—and some of that had been pure dumb luck.

Yet, despite the fact that the Confederates were breathing down the neck of the city, this poor, murdered man—a very young one, by the looks of his unlined, untanned, hairless face—deserved justice for whoever had taken his life. At least on the battlefield, the reason—if not the culprit—would be obvious.

"Who is it?" Adam spoke at last. Had any of the spectators come close enough to get a good look at the man's face? "What's his name?"

"I shook his hand yesterday," said Lincoln quietly.

"He's one of the Frontier Guard," spoke up Cliff Arick, who

was responsible for keeping the roster of members and schedule of their duties. "He joined up with Dan Clayton. Name's Johnny—or maybe it was Jimmy?—Thorne."

"I reckon I'll need to talk with Clayton then," Adam said.

By unspoken agreement, the cluster of men dissolved from the doorway in order to get back to the business of running a country and blocking an impending invasion, leaving Adam alone to examine the scene.

Though he brooded that he wasn't able to contribute to that sort of wartime work at the moment, he understood that Johnny Thorne's death must be attended to.

The weight of his responsibility settled over him, and he took it on—if not happily, at least readily. He reminded himself, in a mental voice that was very like his mother's, that he was a tracker. An excellent one, in fact. That he read markings and residue left behind by any number of creatures—man or animal. This mansion with its oval library was an unfamiliar terrain, but the process, the discernment, the *translation* of his observations into facts, was still the same task.

He needed to know who the young man was—his name, his identity, what sort of person he was—to keep in his thoughts and heart as he attended to this terrible, impossible task so he could live the tracks.

That was what Ishkode had called it. And his grandfather Makwa as well: *living* the tracks.

So, for the time being, Adam stepped mentally out of the moment of horror over a young man's violent death—and the fact that a murderer was quite possibly among them even now, here in the White House—and began to read what he could from the signs left behind.

A spatter of blood arcing over the wall, window curtains, and bookshelves.

Adam had butchered and seen it done often enough to know how, when an animal's throat was slit, the blood squirted in a certain direction and pattern.

And how, though the wound was a lethal one, it didn't cause instant or even immediate death. Adam's fingers tightened as he imagined those last few moments of pain and fear, where Thorne's hands would have scrabbled at his throat as he staggered in shock and disbelief. The dried blood on the man's hands told the story, along with pools and smears all over the floor.

He thrust from his mind the horror Johnny Thorne must have experienced and forced himself to absorb the marks—the tracks, the footprints, the beginnings of the story—without emotion or pity.

Thorne was facing this direction, toward the door left of the window. Maybe he was walking out of the room. The killer hadn't been facing him, slicing out toward him with a blade, for the blood wouldn't have splattered as much.

Yes. It would be easier to come up behind a man—take him by surprise. Grab him by the hair, and bare his throat to slice it open from the rear—rather than strike out toward him with a blade and hope to catch him straight across the throat.

Adam tested it himself then, with an invisible knife and imaginary victim, and compared his movements to the wound. The gash over Thorne's throat wasn't straight across but angled down on one side, so Adam tried it again, quickly and then more slowly, and noticed that his own slicing movement started slightly higher than it ended, as his arm drew back. He was right-handed by birth as well as happenstance, and when he compared his practice motion to the angle of the cut on the man's throat, he concluded the murderer was also right-handed, for the cut angled in the same direction.

Johnny Thorne was a slight, skinny man; he'd have been easily overpowered by nearly any of the men currently barracked in the East Room. So whoever did it wouldn't have had to be very large or strong. *Young*, Adam thought as he looked down at the boy's smooth jaw. Maybe sixteen or seventeen? *So young.* Too young to be a soldier.

Was he someone's brother? Son?

He gritted his teeth and curled his lips, for he knew Johnny Thorne wasn't going to be the only too young soldier lying dead before this conflict with the South was over.

Adam forced his attention from those unpleasant thoughts to the rug beneath his feet, and what the shoe marks and blood smears on it and the uncovered wooden floor around the perimeter would tell him about the movements of the people in the room. He'd have to talk to the servant who'd found Thorne to learn how close she'd come to the body—there was a partial footprint near the edge that looked small enough to be hers.

There were other bloodstains as well. They were soaked into the wool of the frayed rug, which made their shape and any movement more difficult—but not impossible—to discern. Taking care to place his feet where they wouldn't disturb any marks or splatters, Adam crouched next to the body and impatiently waved away the flies. His nose was filled with the scent of death: blood, raw internal organs, bodily fluids and waste.

The boy was clothed like most of his Frontier Guard counterparts: in heavy Levi-Strauss trousers like the ones worn by the goldminers, a simple white cotton shirt that had turned dingy with age and overwashing and was now colored with blood, a striped vest of chocolate brown, and battered boots that showed feet the rest of him hadn't yet grown into. Over all of it, he wore a long, weathered coat of canvas, also marked with bloodstains.

He slipped his fingers into one of the pockets in Thorne's coat, pulling out the few contents inside: a penknife, a piece of paper, a large button that matched those of his coat, and a few pennies. The small knife was unremarkable, with its bone handle and sharp blade, if not fairly ineffective. It would hardly be good for anything but whittling a stick or stabbing a piece of meat to eat.

The paper, though only a scrap, was of fine quality and appeared to be from a piece of formal stationery. A number was written on it in pencil—430—then another word beginning with L or maybe I. Adam might not have found the origin of the stationery of interest if he hadn't recognized the portion of printed letterhead: *les Hote.*

Stationery from the St. Charles Hotel?

Hmm. He looked back over the young man, noting the worn boots for his too big feet, the frayed hem of his trousers and the patch on one knee, the loose button on his coat.

The St. Charles was a fancy, expensive establishment. And it was preferred by those who sympathized with the South.

Adam was lying on the ground, cheek and temple flush with the rug so he could discern the way its nap had been disrupted when a dainty buttoned shoe and the edge of a pale blue skirt came into view in his peripheral vision. He looked up and was only mildly surprised to see Miss Gates.

No, come to think of it, he wasn't surprised at all to see her.

He *was* surprised he hadn't heard her gasp or make any other sound of horror or shock.

However, even from his awkward position on the floor, he could see that her creamy skin had turned bone-white as she looked down at the remains of John Thorne. The fact that she hadn't spoken was a testament to the set of her mind. He heard her swallow hard and saw the slight tremble of her fingers hanging by her side, next to the skirt.

"Miss Gates," he began as he rose, thinking not only of the propriety of the situation, but also, as always, what his mother would expect him to do. "I don't think—"

"I've seen dead bodies before," she said. "I saw Mr. Billings, remember? And even ones . . . even as b-bad as this."

"That doesn't make it any easier."

"No. I—"

"Miss Gates, I commend you for your—uh—dedication to your vocation, but I don't think now is the time for you to be investig—"

"*No*," she said. More firmly this time; with a hint of outrage. "No, you misunderstand, Mr. Quinn. This isn't about me being a journalist and trying to get a story. Not this time. I . . . well, you shouldn't do this alone. And the rest of them . . . they all—left. I'm here only to help you."

He might have been more surprised if she'd begun to sing and dance in Ojibwe, but probably not much. "I see."

Before he could think what to say next, she spoke quietly. "Whoever would do this must have been desperate. Very desperate. And very bold. To cut a man's"—her voice wavered here a bit, then steadied—"throat in the middle of the President's House, when it's filled with soldiers and people . . . during a war. . . ."

Adam nodded. Yes, whoever had done this had taken a great chance. And one of the first things he needed to find out was *when*. Then he could begin to fill in the pieces, ask the questions, better read the signs. He hoped.

He wished suddenly that his Ojibwe friend Ishkode or his grandfather were here to help guide him. They knew so much more than he did.

"I'd like to cover him up," he said after a moment. "Could you find something? A sheet? And would you speak to Mrs. Lincoln and ask her if she's expecting Mrs. Keckley today? Or if she knows whether she's left town?" There were other ways to get in touch with Dr. George Hilton—if he hadn't evacuated along with half the city—but at least this would keep Sophie Gates busy for a bit while he finished examining the body and the area around it.

Adam was certain his mother would approve of this strategy.

"Mrs. Keckley is already here," she replied. "I just saw her. What does she have to do with any of this?"

He didn't have the time—or energy—to wonder how Miss Gates even knew who Mrs. Keckley was. The free colored woman was a celebrated seamstress in Washington, creating clothing for many of the rich and powerful. She'd become a regular visitor to the President's House since outfitting Mrs. Lincoln for her first levee.

"Please ask her to send for Dr. Hilton—if he's still in town. Mrs. Keckley can go with one of the soldiers or tell him where to find him."

After Miss Gates left on her tasks, Adam continued to examine Johnny Thorne's body and the bloodstains around it. He considered the fingerprints over the boy's mouth. They were smeared, but blood splatters formed the *outline* of the prints. They were from the killer's left hand as he held it over Johnny's mouth, obviously muffling him as his right hand wielded the knife that slit his throat.

Grimly, Adam continued his initial examination. He didn't

move the corpse other than to lift the head and examine the blood-crusted hands to see if there were any other cuts or injuries. He didn't find anything that appeared recent enough to have been inflicted during a struggle before he was murdered, but he was saddened to notice that beneath the rusty stains, Thorne's hands were not the callused, work worn ones of a manual laborer.

Yet another sign of his youth and inexperience.

Adam was digging through the remainder of the young man's canvas coat pockets when the soft swish of footsteps had him looking up.

"Hilton," he said in surprise. "That was a mighty quick trip to fetch you here from Ballard's Alley." He smiled as he stood to greet the man who'd been instrumental in helping Adam to identify and catch a murderer last month.

He offered his hand to the doctor, and after the briefest hesitation, Hilton took it. They shook firmly.

George Hilton was about the same age as Adam—thirty or so—but barely reached six foot. His springy hair was cut very close to his scalp, as were the beard and mustache he wore. Hilton had broad shoulders and a muscular build, and skin the color of rich walnut. Though he had been convinced of the doctor's abilities during the previous murder investigation, Adam still found it extraordinary that a black man somehow managed to practice medicine in Washington—in an area where Negroes weren't allowed to go to school or to be taught to read or write.

"I brought Miss Lizzie to see Mrs. Lincoln today," replied Hilton simply. "She thought she might need someone to talk to. The city is tense with fear and waiting." Then his attention went to the scene on the floor and he made a quiet sound of remorse. "So young. And the war ain't hardly started yet."

"Mr. Quinn, Mrs. Keckley is here—" Miss Gates had returned, and she stopped herself when she saw that Adam wasn't alone. She was carrying a folded sheet. "Dr. Hilton. You're already here."

"Yes, indeed, Miss Gates," he replied with a little bow. The two had met briefly during the events of the investigation into Mr. Billings's murder in March.

"What are you going to do?" she asked, coming into the chamber. Her gray eyes were alight with interest, though Adam noticed she didn't allow her attention to linger too closely on the body of Johnny Thorne.

He took the sheet from her while debating whether it was worth the effort trying to convince Miss Gates to leave, but in the end decided to save himself the breath. Instead, he unfolded the cotton cloth and, waving the flies away again, began to draw it up over the body. The doctor bent to assist, but held up a hand for Adam to pause in his task.

"Well, miss, I suppose that depends on Mr. Quinn," replied Hilton, looking down at Johnny Thorne from where he squatted next to the body. "He don't need me to tell him the man is dead, and that he's surely past any saving."

He lifted the man's arm and examined the cold fingers, testing their flexibility and that of his elbow, then allowed the hand to rest back on the floor. After a prolonged pause that might have been a prayer, Hilton began to drag the sheet up over Thorne's torso and face.

"I reckon I want you to . . . uh . . . do what you did before," Adam said, helping with the shroud. "Look over the body. It seems obvious how he died—name's Johnny, or maybe Jimmy, Thorne, by the way—but as you know, last time the obvious wasn't the whole story. If you're willing, that is."

"I'm willing."

"Much obliged, Hilton." Adam hesitated, then went on. "But weren't you meaning to evacuate with all the rest of the city?"

He didn't want to keep the man here if he'd intended to leave—a free man, whose independence could easily be "overlooked" by an invading pro-slavery army. God knew he'd seen it happen more than once in Kansas. And why *wouldn't* Hilton have intended to leave? Damn. Adam realized he'd likely put the doctor in an untenable position, and now the man's pride wouldn't allow him to renege on his agreement.

"I could have gone yesterday," Hilton said in that low, steady voice of his. "But I chose not to. I'm a doctor. If war's coming here, the Good Lord knows I'll have plenty of work."

Adam gave a short nod. He wasn't completely convinced he hadn't backed Hilton into a corner, but admittedly, he couldn't argue with his statement. "Again . . . much obliged. And, much as I wish it weren't true, you're right."

He gestured to the shroud-covered figure. Dark blood had already stained the white sheet. "I don't know whether you can tell how long he's been dead, but that would surely help."

"Full rigor hasn't set in yet—the small muscles have stiffened pretty good, which happens early on, but the large ones are still moving. No more than eight, nine hours dead, I'd say. I may be able to give you a better estimate, once I get him back and . . ." Hilton glanced at Miss Gates and didn't finish his sentence.

Adam nodded. "You got your wagon here?"

As the doctor replied in the affirmative, a creak in the floor drew their attention to the doorway.

"Cliff Arick said you wanted to see me." Dan Clayton was short and stocky, with a weathered face and a sun-bleached beard. He was speaking to Adam—though his attention slid to the blood-stained shroud. Behind him were two other men, crowding into the doorway. "Benson and Timmons knew him too, a little. Johnny Thorne."

Adam arranged for two of the men to help Hilton get the corpse to his workshop, several blocks away beneath a church in Ballard's Alley. He was about to leave with Clayton to interview the man, so to speak, when a thought struck him.

"Miss Gates," he said, "would you remain here at the door—close it behind you so no one's gawking in at it—and don't allow anyone to enter until I get a guard sent up?" He hadn't had the chance to look as closely as he wanted to at the scene of the murder and all the marks that had been left. He didn't want either of the Lincoln boys (especially Tad, the eight-year-old scamp)—or anyone else—to come in and disrupt anything before he had a chance to fully examine the room.

Miss Gates seemed disappointed—he reckoned she might have thought she'd be able to accompany him while he was questioning Clayton and the others—but she didn't argue. Although the look she gave him was a measured one, as if she wasn't certain whether he really wanted her help, or if he was just trying to get her out of his hair.

It was, Adam thought to himself, a little of both.

"I only met him two days ago," said Dan Clayton. "It was Wednesday, I guess, almost night, and I was coming out from Willard's to go fetch Benson and Timmons from their boardinghouse. Lane was wanting to get a count of who'd join up to protect the city and the president, and I knew how they'd want to be in on it.

"Johnny—he was there, standing on the street, and he musta recognized me as one of Lane's men, because he come right up to me and said how he wanted to join up." Clayton grimaced. "I asked him how old he was—damned kid didn't look hardly old enough to sprout whiskers—and he said eighteen. Which I knew was a lie, but . . ." He shrugged, and Adam nodded in commiseration.

Yes, there'd been youngsters fighting in Kansas too. And in the Mexican War. And probably in every other war. Hell, Andrew Jackson had been only fourteen when he fought the British in the War for Independence. Didn't make it right, but there you had it.

"But now he's dead." Clayton's expression tightened. "Who'd do such a thing?"

"That's what Mr. Lincoln wants me to find out. I need to hear everything you know about Johnny Thorne—where he's from, where he's been, and anything else he ever said so we can try to find his family."

And his killer.

Clayton shook his head again. "I ain't gonna be much help there, Quinn. The kid didn't say much a'tall. He sorta stayed in the background and did what he was told, but he didn't say much. I guessed it was because he didn't want to draw attention to himself 'cause he was too young to be signing up."

Adam couldn't help wonder if there was another reason Johnny Thorne didn't want to be noticed. Had the young man already known he was in danger when he signed up to be a Frontier Guard, and was using the troop as cover for himself? A place to hide, or get lost in?

Or had he seen or heard or done something that put him in danger *after* he'd joined Lane's guard? If that were the case, Adam reckoned the implications of that scenario were far less comforting, as that would imply someone in the guard was a cold-blooded murderer.

Either way, Miss Gates was right: whoever had killed Johnny Thorne had been desperate. He reckoned that also meant Thorne would have known at some point that he was in danger.

What was he even doing here, on the second floor, in the middle of the night?

He pressed the men further. "Thorne didn't mention anything at all? Or anyone? You've got no idea where he's from, his family? Wife?"

Clayton frowned as if he felt Adam's frustration. "The only thing was he had a Southern accent. I think he tried to hide it, but it was there. Kinda faint."

That, Adam supposed, was something—although it might not mean anything. A man joining up to fight for the Union might not want to draw attention to his Southern roots. Especially among the rough, experienced Jayhawkers.

Although, curiously enough, the scrap of paper he'd found in Thorne's pocket was from the St. Charles Hotel—the establishment preferred by Southerners over Willard's. Adam tucked that bit of information into the back of his mind as the two other Frontier Guard members, having returned from helping Dr. Hilton, entered the chamber.

"We only knew him a day or so, but he kept to himself, Johnny did. He was a shy one too—didn't like to be talking much. Sat in the corner and ate and drank mostly alone while we was waiting to see whether Mr. Lincoln would have us come here," said Timmons, looking around at the room where Adam had decided to do his interviews. It was the Green Room on the main floor, straight down the corridor from the East Room.

The carpet and walls had seen better days, and the furniture puffed out a musty smell when they sat down. But the wooden table in front of the sofa gleamed from being polished, and a vase of fresh flowers—some fragrant white ones that Adam didn't recognize—sat in the center. They were probably from the huge conservatory, located off the west wing of the mansion. It was obvious Mrs. Lincoln had high standards for keeping up the mansion, even if it was shabby and worn in areas, and one of her favorite places was the warm, fragrant greenhouse attached to the west side of the mansion.

"Did you see Thorne last night at all, once you got barracked in the East Room?" Adam asked

"He was out on guard duty at eleven o'clock and was on until two," replied Timmons.

"Do you know who relieved him? Where was he stationed? Upstairs?" That could explain why he was on the second floor.

"No, he was outside, assigned to the northwest corner of the house, near the conservatory. I was on the southwest side and we went out together. Lane come out and walked the perimeter, talked to each of us just around midnight, make sure we had what we needed before he took up at Mr. Lincoln's doorway. Hattenshier would have relieved Johnny at two, but I was on the other side of the house so I didn't see what time he came out."

That was helpful. If Thorne was relieved at two o'clock, and Hattenshier had seen him, that helped narrow the time of his murder. But that still didn't answer what he would have been doing upstairs on the second floor. Could he have had news to report to Lincoln or Hay—something from his shift? Or a message to deliver?

"Was anyone else up and moving around after the Guard settled in the East Room? You weren't on guard duty. Did you see anyone?" Adam asked, looking at Benson.

Everyone in the entire mansion would need to be interviewed about their whereabouts last night—not to mention who else they might have seen while up and about. He sure as hell hoped Hilton would be able to narrow down the time of Johnny Thorne's death.

All that questioning was going to be less than fun, collecting and then organizing all of that information. He wished Hobey Pierce was still here to help because he was good at talking to people, but the red-headed Pinkerton agent had left with his boss and gone back to Chicago.

Adam reckoned he could ask Miss Gates if she wanted to assist. After all, the woman sure as hell knew how to ask questions. But it wouldn't be seemly for a woman to be involved in a murder investigation, and especially if she helped interrogate a slew of men.

Although, he considered, maybe she could at least talk to the servants and the other women in the house. That would keep her busy for a while—and under the circumstances, he thought it would be an acceptable occupation. He had a feeling she'd find a way to get further involved even if he didn't ask.

"I got up to take a piss a little before midnight," said Benson.

"How did you know what time it was?"

"Well, that's because I laid there for a while contemplatin' whether I wanted to git my arse up to go. But when I remembered I didn't have to go *outside* to piss, I decided to git up and go. Why not, eh?" He grinned. "And I know what time because it was after the clock struck fifteen till midnight, but before it struck twelve. Cuz I was tryin' to decide if I could wait till mornin'."

Adam nodded. "All right then. Did you see anyone else around?"

"I was half asleep, Quinn, but I don't remember seeing anyone. I got a little turned around though—this house is so damned big! And it was dark and all. But I finally found the water closet—fancy having one inside!—took a piss, then came back," Benson said. Then he frowned. "Wait. Maybe there was someone going up the stairs—right, there was, now I'm thinking of it. On my way back, it was. I was more awake by then. And I heard two people talking. I think I did see someone, just a shadow from outta the corner of my eye, up the top of the stairs. Mighta been a skirt." He screwed up his face as he attempted to remember.

"Before midnight, then. Or maybe a little after, because you'd already gone to the toilet? Did you hear the clock strike twelve?" It probably didn't matter, as Johnny Thorne was on duty until two o'clock . . . unless he wasn't there when his relief showed up. But Adam knew he had to be thorough and clarify the details.

"The clock. Yes, it struck midnight while I was standin' and leakin'," Benson replied with a quick grin that displayed tobacco-stained teeth.

Adam wrote down all of the names and information, scant as it was, then dismissed Timmons and Benson and went in search of Hattenshier—who'd supposedly relieved Thorne—and Jim Lane.

He found his friend first, with Lincoln and several other advisors—including General Scott and Secretary Cameron, along with Major Hunter—in the president's office. Also present were Nicolay and John Hay. The grim expressions on their collective faces made Adam grit his teeth in expectation of the worst.

At first no one spoke, and that gave him the impression there was so much bad news they didn't know where to begin. His heart sank, but he exchanged resolved looks with Lane. They'd been outnumbered before and had emerged the victor.

Cameron broke the silence. "Virginia voted to secede a few days ago—in secret—so they could take over the public buildings and other federal property before we could stop them. Not a surprise, but if Maryland follows . . ."

"And there's been another riot in Baltimore," Lincoln said, looking at Adam. "The Sixth Massachusetts tried to pass through, and a riot broke out. They were attacked like the Pennsylvanian regiment was yesterday. This time, the mob stopped the troops from getting through. They've cut off the railways and roads going through the city." He gestured to a telegram on the desk. "I'm waiting for more information—in particular, how many dead and injured—but the telegraph lines aren't working too well. We don't know whether the Massachusetts troops are on their way again, and how many can travel."

"There's rumors that Baltimore mob's heading here to Washington too," said General Scott in his thready voice. The man was over seventy—older than Washington City itself—and though he'd attracted the nickname "Old Fuss n' Feathers," he moved slowly from gout and his generous weight, and certainly didn't seem terribly fussy at the moment. He was, however, one of the few men tall enough to look Lincoln in the eye.

Adam swallowed a curse and glanced at Lane.

His friend's expression was resolute. "I'm just about to leave here for a bit. There are more Union loyalists in this town. I'm going to find them and we'll get them signed up." A brief, hard grin flashed over his face. "Your ploy of marching across the bridge last night seems to have worked, Adam. All the ruckus left the Rebs wondering how big an army we got here, and they held off coming in so they could wait for more reinforcements. That bit of news is from two loyalists who made it in from the Virginia hills, sneaking through the backyards and forest while the Rebs sat by their campfires scratching their arses and watching us from across the river. Those two men are downstairs now, getting armed up and something to eat." He crossed his arms over his middle. "While I'm out, I'm going to be dropping plenty of hints about how many men we got here."

"We can see the glints from the spyglasses across the river," said John Hay. "They're watching us."

"And waiting for more of their own reinforcements. Our only hope is to make certain our numbers look much bigger than they are, and to hold off till the New York and Ohio troops get here. Are Cash Clay's men still over at the Willard, Major?" When Hunt nodded in affirmation, Lane continued, "With your permission, sir, we can march together and make ourselves look even bigger."

"I reckon I'll be out on the Avenue a bit today—probably need to go to the St. Charles. I'll manage to seed a few rumors myself," Adam said, thinking about that scrap of paper in Johnny Thorne's pocket. "I might scare up a few more recruits myself—though not likely at that hotel. But I also need a list of the regiment here, Lane, and the schedule of guard duty as well so I can account for everyone during the night.

"And, Mr. President, with your permission, I'll need to speak with—or have someone help me to speak with—the staff and Mrs. Lincoln, as well as the other women."

He didn't need to explain why, and the president, clearly dis-tracted by the impending invasion and other problems related to running a country, nodded vaguely as he stared down at some pa-pers. He didn't seem to be reading them, for he was shuffling through them aimlessly. "Yes, yes, whatever you need, Adam. You have that endorsement card; use it. My cabinet's going to be here at three, and I hope to have news from Baltimore by then."

Adam nodded. The endorsement to which Lincoln referred was a placard of thick, ivory paper stock. It was approximately the size of a party invitation and engraved on it were the words: *Office of Abraham Lincoln, President of the United States of America.*

Beneath it, Lincoln had written: *Please note that Mr. Adam Speed Quinn acts with all authority of the Office of the President of the United States, and that all due courtesies should be afforded to him in any request or action he takes.*

This was the second such card Lincoln had given to Adam; the first one had been ripped to shreds by an angry Southern sympa-thizer when Adam presented it as his credentials. Though he kept it on him at all times, the card felt unusually heavy in his shirt pocket—weighted down by the trust and responsibility implicit in the endorsement.

"Cliff Arick's got the list of everyone in the Frontier Guard," Lane told him—unnecessarily, as Adam had already gathered that information, but Lane hadn't been around when the body was found. "And he's got the duty roster as well." He made as if preparing to leave, setting a hat on the wild waves that were his hair and picking up his rifle, which had been leaning against the wall next to the window.

Despite the awkwardness of the situation, Adam spoke quickly and plainly. "Before we all go off, I reckon I need to ask where each of you were last night, and whether you saw anyone up and about from midnight until, say, eight o'clock."

He reckoned Johnny Thorne was killed before dawn, because there had been far more people moving around after that. But until he heard more from Hilton and found out whether Johnny had been relieved at two, Adam wouldn't have any better idea about the time of death. From the way the blood at the scene had begun to congeal and darken, however, he knew the death had to have been well over an hour or two before the body was found. Hilton had said maybe as long as eight or nine hours ago, which would put the time between midnight and six o'clock.

Every man in the room with the exception of Lincoln stared at him. Adam kept his expression blank and watched the array of emotions cross each face: surprise, confusion, gravity, and, in several of them, flickers of affront or insult.

Lincoln made a muffled noise that sounded like an abbreviated laugh and looked up from his random perusal of papers. His eyes were light with humor—not related to the subject matter, Adam knew, but due to the shocked reaction of his advisors.

"Gratefully, I was in bed by half-past eleven, which is where I stayed until just before dawn. Mrs. Lincoln was with me," he added unapologetically. "Our slumber was only disturbed once— by John here. I woke at half-past five to get shaved and to the news that there had been a plan to blow up Willard's"—Adam's eyes widened; for this was news to him—"but the plot was foiled. And so was the invasion of the city—so far, anyway. Since then, I've been here." The president spread his long-fingered hands to indicate the office. "In meetings," he added with such a grave tone that it was almost edging into self-deprecating humor.

Adam gave him a grateful look, and though he wished he didn't have to do so, pressed further. "Mr. President, as your bedchamber is only two doors from the oval library, I reckon I should ask whether you heard any sounds from that room during the night."

Lincoln thought before responding, tilting his head as he seemed to mentally review the time in question. "I couldn't say for certain, but I reckon I might have heard a small thump or thud sometime in the night. It would have been after you woke me, John. What time was'at? But it wasn't loud enough to cause alarm—at least, it didn't sound like an invading army." His dry attempt at humor produced a short, dutiful bark of laughter from Scott.

"Thank you, Mr. President," Adam said formally. He turned to the others with an expectant look.

As their commander had so willingly answered the questions put to the room at large, the rest of them could have no hesitance in responding.

"I was awake—writing in the diary I started just last night," replied John Hay in a rueful tone. "Near midnight, Thomas Burns came up to this floor. A visitor had arrived downstairs and wanted to speak urgently to the president. Instead of bothering him, I had Thomas bring her into the anteroom up here and spoke with her there, then relayed the message."

The anteroom was the waiting room situated between the president's office and the oval library. This was a spacious chamber where Lincoln generally met with people like job-seekers or others who weren't particularly distinguished and didn't need to be seen in his office.

"Her? The visitor was a woman?"

Benson had mentioned seeing possibly a skirt at the top of the stairs just around midnight, so that fit. But he'd also heard people talking.

Hay nodded, and, as there often was, a little sparkle of pleasure glinted in his eyes. His normal mood was one of cheer and charm, though today he sported circles under his eyes—as did everyone else in the chamber. "It was Mrs. Jean Davenport Lander. The famous actress, and wife of Colonel Lander."

The woman's name didn't sound familiar to Adam, but he reckoned he wasn't all that up on the names of such people. "What did she want?" he asked, even though he didn't know that the content of her message would be relevant to the matter at hand. "And how long did she stay? Who came with her?"

"She brought word of a plot to assassinate—or capture—the president. Six or so Virginians, collected by a man named Ficklin. One of them was bragging about it when he came into town to buy a horse, and made the mistake of saying so to Mrs. Lander. We've already sent someone to Richmond to find Ficklin," added Hay. "As to who else . . . well, Mrs. Lander had a maid who came inside with her. She must have wanted to see the inside of the President's House," he added dryly. "Only I guess the colonel wasn't with her, or surely he would have come in and left the maid at home.

"Mrs. Lander left about twenty past midnight, I'd say, and then I went in and woke up the president to tell him about it. After that, I wrote some more in my diary and then went to bed. I believe I slept because I woke up at five when Nicolay banged on my door. Been here in the shop almost ever since except to use the water closet or get more coffee."

Adam nodded his thanks and tried not to allow his attention to fixate on the news Mrs. Lander had brought. Assassination attempts and threats had been being made to Lincoln since the election and, he wagered, that wasn't going to end anytime soon.

"I left here at half-past ten last night," said General Scott with an air of irritation. "Came back this morning at seven. I didn't see anyone coming in or out of the library."

Similarly, Secretary Cameron hadn't spent the night in the Executive Mansion, but had left with Scott. Major Hunter, who was managing the two corps of soldiers between the White House and the Capitol, also was gone overnight, leaving well before eleven.

Even though Adam glanced at Lane, who'd seemed anxious to leave, it was Nicolay who spoke next with his story. He was the son of German immigrants, and tended to be far more sober and brusque than the younger, assistant secretary John Hay. "I worked in my office until about half-past eleven, then went to bed and attempted to sleep. I stuffed two handkerchiefs in my ears and pulled on a hat so I didn't hear much of anything, but I didn't get a damned wink of sleep. Didn't leave my room until five o'clock when word came about the ruined plot to explode Willard's. I woke the president then."

"All right. Thank you." Adam looked at Lane, the last one to speak.

"As you know, I slept on the floor across the president's doorway. I spoke to John when he came with the news from Mrs. Lander. It was almost half-past midnight. I left my post when the president left his bedchamber at half-past five to go to his office."

"Timmons mentioned you did a perimeter walk around the

outside of the mansion at midnight to speak to your guards," Adam said.

Lane seemed a bit taken aback. "Yes, of course I did. I spoke to each one of them to make certain they knew their area of responsibility, give them the new password, and to confirm the end of each guard duty. I was back at my post by half-twelve, and that's when I saw Hay coming out of Mr. Lincoln's bedroom after waking him."

"Then you must have seen Mrs. Lander and her maid," Adam said.

"Yes, I reckon I did. Her hackney driver had parked under the portico and was waiting there when I walked out to make my perimeter. She and her maid must have already gone in and upstairs, but when I finished my walk around the house, the carriage was just driving away."

"Was there anyone in the corridor during the night other than Hay when he woke the president?"

If anyone had seen or heard the murderer, it would have been Lane, sleeping in the doorway of the chamber two doors from the oval library. Adam knew from experience that his friend, when on guard duty, woke at the slightest sound or disturbance.

"No."

"Did you hear any unusual noises in the night?"

"Nothing unusual." Lane gave a wry smile. "But there were fifty soldiers sleeping on the floor downstairs, and who can say what's unusual. I didn't hear anything from the library overnight, if that's what you want to know."

If Lane didn't hear or see anything, he didn't. But how could that be? At least two people—Johnny Thorne and his killer—had to have gone into and out of the oval library sometime in the night.

Unless the murder had happened much later than Adam believed . . . but even then, after five o'clock in the morning, people were up and moving around on this floor. Someone would have seen something. Especially with all the blood that would have been on the killer's hands and clothing.

"There's a door connecting the library and the president's waiting room. And that door on that wall there," said Hay, pointing to a small, unobtrusive door at the back of the room, "leads from this office to the waiting room. So someone could move between all these rooms without going through the corridor."

Lincoln added quietly, "And there is a door connecting the oval library to Mrs. Lincoln's bedchamber . . . which then connects to my bedchamber."

Adam stared aghast as Lane choked back some noise that sounded like an outraged, disbelieving curse.

"I believe it would be prudent," Lincoln continued in his understated manner, "to move a dresser in front of Mrs. Lincoln's bedchamber door that leads into the library. Under the circumstances."

Lane still seemed to be struggling with his outrage and frustration, but he merely nodded. Then, after a moment of taut silence where everyone seemed unwilling to criticize the president for a lack of care for his own safety, the Kansas senator passed his rifle from one hand to the other, leaving his right hand free to shake that of Lincoln's. "I'll return as soon as I'm able—with as many men as possible."

"Thank you, Jim. God willing you'll scare up a passel of them, and that we get word from somewheres up north that the troops from New York and Ohio are near. And that the Massachusetts has passed through Baltimore." Lincoln glanced out the window, where he had an unobstructed view of Confederate tents just across the river.

Eight hundred feet away. Adam could hardly credit the situation. *If Maryland secedes . . . and even if it doesn't . . . Washington is caught in a trap.*

Let our troops come soon.

As Lane went to leave, someone knocked on the other side of the door. It was William Stoddard, the youngest and newest of the president's secretaries. "Chase and Seward are here," he said, referring to the Secretary of the Treasury and the Secretary of State, respectively.

Lincoln looked as if he were about to say something, then clamped his lips closed and nodded.

Adam could have spent a few moments bringing the president up to date on his investigation, but there was so little to tell as yet that he couldn't bear to burden the man with any more unpleasant information. Instead, he shook his honorary uncle's hand and merely said, "I'll be on my way as well. When there's something important, Mr. President, I'll report."

He wasn't certain Lincoln even heard him, for Chase and Seward entered the room, and talk immediately swung to armies, edicts, and strategy.

When Adam came out of the president's office, he turned in the direction of the oval library. The ever-present job-seekers were still there, lined up along the hall . . . but Miss Gates was not, as he'd expected, at her station outside the oval room.

Instead, the door was ajar—and, as he strode down the corridor, he heard voices coming from inside the chamber.

Precisely what he had been trying to avoid.

Where the blazes was Miss Gates?

CHAPTER 4

*I*N SOPHIE'S OPINION, THE OPEN AND EASY ACCESS TO THE PRESIDENT'S House was both distressing and shocking. She stood at her post outside the oval library and tried to ignore the line of people—mostly men, attired in all manner of clothing and aroma—who were apparently waiting to see the president without an appointment.

Aside from that, she could hardly believe they'd come *today*, with the Confederates breathing down the city's figurative neck—and that they'd actually been *admitted* to the house. Not only admitted to the house, but allowed on the second floor where the family lived and the president did his work!

But tension and nerves abounded, even among those seeking something from Mr. Lincoln—a job, a pardon, or a commission. Everyone throughout the mansion was on tenterhooks as they waited to see whether the city would be invaded tonight or not.

Every time a door opened on the east end of the corridor—where the president and his secretaries apparently had offices—those waiting in line jolted to attention and began to call out to whomever had appeared. Heaven forbid Mr. Lincoln himself should show even a whisker or the toe of a clunky shoe; she could only imagine the riot that would break out.

Sophie was torn between reluctant admiration for the tenacity of the job-seekers and irritation that they would dare to bother him or his staff during this anxious, dangerous time.

Thus, she intended to take no notice of them, even though she stood in the corridor and was facing the line of people (which, unbelievably, stretched along the wing where the family's bedchambers were located—what would happen if the president should walk out of his bedchamber in a night robe and slippers?). But it became difficult to ignore the queue, for she found herself drawn into listening to the soupçon of conversation rattling along around her. She'd always found people—what they did, why they did it, and how they went about doing so—fascinating and instructive.

That was, in part, why she wanted to be a journalist. Wasn't that precisely what the news was? Reporting on what happened and why and how, and the effects on people—along with the motivations of the people behind those actions.

"Is it true there's a dead body in there?" one of the men finally asked her. He was dressed in the clothing of a middle-class man—likely a tradesman of some sort: clean and hemmed trousers devoid of patches or mending, a crisp, white cotton shirt, a dark blue waistcoat, and over it all he wore a greatcoat that went halfway to his knees.

"No," Sophie replied truthfully.

"But there *was*," said another man with a bald head and bright red beard, clutching a silk top hat. "I heard them!"

"Who was it?"

"Was it one of them damned—pardon me, miss—Rebels, and got what he deserved?"

"Did he try to sneak in to kill the president?"

Suddenly she found herself the center of attention of a dozen pairs of eyes. Their owners shifted closer as if preparing to receive a confidence, and the line adjusted to snake in a delicate curve closer to her.

"I'm sure I don't know," Sophie replied, then swiftly took control of the conversation, redirecting it back to the curious. "And you're all waiting to speak to Mr. Lincoln? What do you hope he can do for you?"

To her mild surprise, as a group, they seemed eager to tell of their hopes and intentions. Perhaps they believed she might be able to help their individual causes in some way.

"I reckon I'm here for a position at the Treasury," one of them told her. He was short and wiry with gray threading his dark beard and sideburns. "I got some news for him about them Rebels too, and when I tell him, he's going to *want* to hire me."

"I want a post office commission," said a different one, dressed in slightly newer clothing. He had a shiny black walking stick with a silver knob at the top, and a matching tip at the bottom.

"I've got a letter from my cousin, who's married to Mrs. Lincoln's sister's nephew, says I'm the man for a job at the patent office." The man brushed his hand down over a dark beard, and she noticed he was missing part of a finger. "Got the letter from Mr. White right here!" He tried to hand it to her, but she avoided taking it.

"I'm only here to tell Mr. Lincoln I'm loyal to him, and to the Union," said a tall man dressed in shabby clothing that exposed bony wrists in the same way the president's clothing did to his long arms. "And I'll fight for him!"

She looked at him. "I believe he's going to need all the help he can get. But perhaps you'd be better served by speaking to General Scott rather than waiting around to speak to the president."

"Them Rebels—they tried to blow up Willard's last night," said Mrs. Lincoln's cousin's nephew—or whoever he was with the letter he'd shoved at her. "Need to have their arses—er, excuse me, miss—need to send them packing!"

The non sequitur drew Sophie's attention. "Someone tried to blow up Willard's? The hotel?"

"Sure was. They found a bunch o' piles o' rags hidden throughout the hotel. Looked like they was going to light them on fire and let it go."

"I heard about that too," said another man further up the line. "About Willard's. That black doorman found it all—and I'm here to tell Mr. Lincoln I'm going to sign up for helping keep him safe." He sported a dark mustache that drooped so far over his lips he appeared to lack a mouth.

"Do they know who did it?" Sophie asked, already thinking of the headline for another speculative news article: *Willard's Nearly Blown Sky High by Sneaky Sympathizers.*

Of course, she didn't know for certain the culprits were southern, but considering the fact that the Willard Hotel was where Colonel Clay's small troop was garrisoned, and also that Mr. Lincoln had stayed there before his inauguration, it made perfect sense.

Before either of the men could respond to her question, Sophie noticed one of the maids. She was peeking out from the luxurious bedchamber named after the Prince of Wales's visit last year, across from Mrs. Lincoln's bedroom and just down from the door Mr. Quinn had asked her to guard. Sophie recognized the maid as Leah, the woman who'd discovered the body of Johnny Thorne. Leah's eyes darted nervously between Sophie, the lineup of job-seekers, and the door to the library. She was carrying a broom and what appeared to be a dust cloth.

Speaking of people and their reactions and motivations . . .

"Leah," Sophie called, and smiling, beckoned to her with what she hoped was a comforting smile. "May I speak with you for a moment?"

Aware of the prying ears and eyes of the people in line, Sophie made another snap decision and opened the door to the library as the maid walked toward her. Leah stumbled to a halt, her eyes widening and her broom tipping when she realized the other woman wanted her to accompany her inside the terrifying room, but Sophie gave her an implacable look and gestured her inside.

Taking care to keep the view from the corridor as obscured as possible, Sophie slipped inside the room after the maid and pulled the door nearly closed behind her.

"Oh, praise Heaven, it's gone," Leah whispered. Her eyes were only a trifle less wide and horrified now, for her attention had gone to the bloodstains on the floor, then to the splatters over the wall and spines of books. The dark, floor-length curtains over the window nearest the body were still closed, and Sophie was certain they too had splatters of blood on them—though it was difficult to tell from where she stood.

They were at the base of the oval, standing in the main doorway. Across from them were two tall, wide windows that looked out over the National Mall and the swampy canal below. Between the windows were two armchairs and a small table that held a lamp, an ink pen, and a bottle of ink. There was a drawer in the half-moon table that presumably held paper and a sharpener.

On either side of the windows, on what would be the rear of the side walls if the room had been rectangular, were two narrow doors that Sophie thought led to either closets or possibly through to the rooms on either side.

In the center of the room was a collection of furnishings: a sofa that might have been long enough for even Mr. Lincoln to lie upon, two large chairs facing it, a low table, and some small side tables. The curved walls were filled with built-in shelves, stocked with books. There were two tall-backed chairs arranged at a small table between the windows.

The body had been found near what would be the back left corner of the room, and would have been hidden from view of this main doorway by the sofa and the gas lamp on the table next to it.

"Yes, miss?" Leah was clearly uncomfortable both being in the room, and with Sophie's request to talk to her.

The maid was in her thirties, and she wore a neat white pinafore over her gray dress, with a matching cap and shiny black shoes. Like all of the colored servants Sophie had encountered in the President's House, Leah had light skin and a polished demeanor. From what she understood, all the White House servants—black or white—were the best of the best in the city.

In fact, she'd heard that Mr. Lincoln's valet, a young black man who'd come with him from Springfield, had had such an awful time of it from the other servants because his skin was so much darker that the president had found him a different position as a messenger with the Treasury and War departments. But Johnson, as was his name, still came every morning to shave and dress the president.

Hmm. Sophie wondered what time Johnson had arrived this morning, and whether he had seen or noticed anything.

"I'm sorry to bring you in here," Sophie said, turning her attention to the other woman. "I imagine it's not a good memory for you, Leah. But Mr. Quinn has been asked to find out who did such a horrible thing—and I'm helping him," she added blithely. He *had* asked her to watch over the room, so that counted as helping. "Has he spoken to you yet?"

Leah shook her head mutely, her gaze continuing to slide toward the location where Johnny Thorne's body had been found.

"Very well," said Sophie, edging to one side so as to block some of the maid's view of the bloodstained carpet. She wanted to open the curtains, but that would require her to step through the area of where the body had been, and she didn't know whether Mr. Quinn would like that. "Could you tell me exactly what happened when you came into the room?"

"I . . . I always clean the library after I do Mrs. Lincoln's bedchamber." Her voice was soft but clear. "I used the door between the two rooms to come in here."

So the door on the right near the back of the room led to Mrs. Lincoln's bedroom, Sophie realized. And the door opposite, near where the body had been found, led to the president's office waiting room. She nodded to herself as Leah continued.

"It's . . . easier to come that way, through the side doors, with the hallway so full of people. The same people come back every day, some of them. And wait and wait." She trailed off and looked over at the stained carpet.

Sophie saw how it must have gone, for with the way the furniture was arranged along the center of the room, the tall-backed chair would have blocked the maid from seeing the dead body when she came in from the connecting door of Mrs. Lincoln's chamber.

"It smelled in here, but I didn't take notice right away. I only thought—well, I didn't give it much thought. All I can think about is them Confed'rate soldiers coming in here at night, and burning the place down, and taking Mr. Lincoln away—"

"When did you see the body?" Sophie asked, gently returning her to the story.

"I-I was tidying up the books on the shelf there—that little Tad, he likes to use them to build towers and mountains—and then I went to open the curtains. When I got over there to the windows, I—I saw it. I seen the flies, and came over a little to look . . ." Her eyes darted to the area in question, then back to Sophie.

"What did you do then?"

"I—I tried to scream. But nothing came out, miss. Not at first. I just stood there, looking down at it—him—and then it all came out."

Sophie nodded encouragingly. "I can't imagine what a horrible shock it must have been. Did you touch the—er—him?"

"Oh, no, miss, no. I saw him—saw what had been done—and I didn't go no closer. I didn't want to. I knew . . . I knew . . . he was dead."

"All right." Sophie tried to think about what else would be useful for Mr. Quinn to know.

The bloodstains on the floor . . . were any of them the footprints of the murderer? Or someone else? It was difficult to tell, the way they'd soaked into the rug in indiscriminate blobs.

"Leah, can you show me where you were standing when you saw him?"

Still holding the broom and dust cloth, the maid walked slowly to a position between the far ends of the two sofas and the exterior, curved wall of the chamber. "Right here, miss. I was just done pulling open these curtains."

"And you're certain you didn't move any closer—"

The door to the hallway suddenly opened wide, and Sophie spun around to see Mr. Quinn. He looked rather disgruntled, and when he saw the two women in the room, his expression became even more irritated.

"Miss Gates, I was under the impression you'd agreed to stand at the *outside* of the door—and keep everyone out—until I found someone to relieve you."

The maid seemed even more discomfited by the appearance of

the tall and imposing Mr. Quinn, who, although he wasn't strictly *rude*, he also wasn't attempting to hide his annoyance.

"I was just speaking with Leah, Mr. Quinn. She was showing me exactly where she was standing when she saw Johnny's—Johnny. I thought you would be interested in hearing her story," she added smoothly.

"I see."

Sophie could almost hear him grinding his teeth as his jaw shifted jerkily. She continued before he could say anything else. "Leah didn't touch or move the body, and she didn't get any closer to it than those sofas there so none of the footprints would be hers."

He directed his next words to the maid, clearly making an attempt to soften his tone. "All right." He paused as if to collect his thoughts, and Sophie, who'd been thinking about all the things she wanted to know, took the opportunity to jump in.

"Leah, did you notice anything unusual or out of place here in the library when you were cleaning? Anything that didn't belong? Anything that wasn't right or out of place?"

"No, miss. Not that I can think of."

"How often is this room attended to? Cleaned or straightened up?" Sophie asked. "Are you the person who always cleans this room?"

"Yes, miss. It's my morning duty every day. And at night I come in after the wall lamps is lit to close the curtains, straighten the cushions, and tidy the books. Us'ally there's some playthings left over from the boys."

"What time did you tidy up last night, Leah?"

"It was . . ." Her eyes darted about as if looking for a clock. "Half-past eight or thereabouts."

"And did you come back in afterward?"

"No, miss."

Sophie nodded with satisfaction, then looked at Mr. Quinn, who'd, surprisingly, remained silent during her interrogation. "Do you have any other questions?"

His eyes glinted with irritation, but he smiled reassuringly at the maid. "Not now. Thank you, Leah."

The young woman fled, exiting through the door to Mrs. Lincoln's bedchamber.

"Miss Gates," began Mr. Quinn in a stiff voice, but she forestalled him.

"Yes, I'm aware I left my post, but I thought it might be easier for me to question Leah instead of you."

"Why? Did you reckon I would terrify the woman that much?"

Sophie sensed a trap, but she barreled on courageously. "Well, you can be rather intimidating, Mr. Quinn. You're very tall, and broad—and . . ."

For once, words failed her. She couldn't *tell* him how a chamber seemed to get a little smaller whenever he entered one. It was his wide shoulders, and the confident way he moved with long, easy strides that transported him across the room with far more speed than it appeared. And there was his imposing but quiet demeanor, the sharp, contemplative look that always seemed to glint in his dark eyes, and the fact that he just seemed, well . . . *more* than the other fancy, well-dressed, perfectly-groomed dandies Sophie was used to seeing. He was bigger, rougher, darker. . . .

"I reckon I'm not the tallest man she's seen in this house," he replied dryly. To Sophie's relief, he didn't pursue the topic but instead went on to another. "You made certain no one disturbed the area over there?"

"We only stood just here, past the doorway. The farthest we came in was there. I know better than to walk all through the— the murder scene," she replied a bit frostily.

Mr. Quinn nodded. Before he could speak, she said, "Did you know they—some Secessionists—tried to burn down Willard's last night?"

"Yes," he replied, but his attention was on the stained carpet and floor. He glanced at the scene of the crime, then walked carefully past it to finish opening the curtains on both windows. Immediately, the room was much lighter, for it was a sunny day.

Though she was filled with questions and thoughts, Sophie decided to remain silent for the moment as she watched Mr. Quinn lower onto his knees and bring his face very close to the marks, resting his cheek on the floor. He favored his right arm and side, using his intact limb to hold his weight and the prosthetic hand merely to help balance.

The false hand was carved from wood, and appeared to be covered by some sort of supple leather. It fascinated Sophie the way Mr. Quinn slightly shifted his shoulders, upper arm, or torso, and the faux digits moved to open or close mechanically, or the wrist and arm twisted in an almost natural fashion. It was amazing what modern mechanics could do for someone who'd lost a limb.

She remained silent for what seemed like hours as he examined the bloodstains and, it seemed, the floor of the entire room, inching his way around. He spent a good amount of time near the door that led to the waiting room to the president's office, even opening it for a moment. At last, impatience had the better of her. "Well?"

He rose gracefully despite his handicap. "Johnny Thorne was standing here, probably moving toward that door to leave the room. His attacker came from behind—I think from behind this curtain, where he was waiting for some time—grabbed him with a hand over his mouth, and sliced." He demonstrated with a short, effective movement as Sophie swallowed hard.

"I reckon he held poor Johnny right there, from behind, to keep him from stumbling around and making noise that might have alerted General Lane—who was sleeping in the corridor just yonder. He held him there, hand over his victim's mouth—and all the while, blood was pumping out of Johnny's veins and he struggled to save himself. He held him there, torturing him, until he died."

She said nothing as he lapsed into silence, contemplating the floor with horror and fury mingling in his expression. She felt the same emotions, but she was also stunned by what Mr. Quinn seemed to know just by looking around the chamber. How could he know all of that? But she waited to ask.

After a long moment, he spoke again. "The killer was right-handed, taller than Thorne, and he took the knife—and a candle—with him when he left the room." Mr. Quinn pointed, not to the hallway door through which Sophie and Leah had come, but to the door opposite the one that connected to Mrs. Lincoln's bedroom.

"Where does that door lead?" Sophie asked, although she was sure she knew.

"Into the president's antechamber, which also has a door leading to the hallway—as well as another one leading to the president's office. All of these chambers are connected by doors."

"How do you know the killer went out that way?" was the first of many questions she had for him. But Sophie managed to contain them so she could dole them out one by one.

"Tracks."

Sophie looked down skeptically at the smudges, splatters, and streaks of blood on the carpet and wooden floor. "None of the footprints lead toward the door," she said. "So how do you know he went out that way?"

Mr. Quinn's mouth relaxed a trifle. "A trace of blood on the floor there—beneath the door. So someone with blood on them walked through and closed the door—and I reckon it wasn't Johnny Thorne."

With some difficulty, due to the inflexibility of her corset and the volume of her skirts, Sophie lowered herself into a crouch to see for herself. "That? You mean *that* tiny drop?" Was that even a bloodstain? She looked up at him, and, perched on her toes as she was, nearly lost her balance.

Mr. Quinn offered a hand—his flesh and blood one—and Sophie allowed him to help her upright. As neither of them were wearing gloves, a rare informality, she felt the unfamiliar texture of long, callused fingers and the warmth of his broad palm as their hands slid against the other.

"Yes," he replied. "That tiny drop. And the other one there," he said in a dry tone, gesturing with a booted toe to a slightly larger stain—still hardly the size of a pea.

"I daresay I wouldn't have noticed either of them if you hadn't pointed them out," Sophie admitted—privately rebuking herself for not being as observant as she should have been, and then promptly deciding that she would *learn* to be more observant about small details. "What about the candle?"

"Wax drips."

She shook her head. "How do you know the *killer* had a candle? Wax drips could be from anyone."

He gave her a small smile. "Some of the drips are on top of the blood drops or stains."

Sophie was fascinated. "How can you tell all of that—everything you said? How do you know he hid behind the curtain?"

He hesitated, then spread his hands in a gesture of nonchalance. "I reckon it comes from the five years I spent with my Ojibwe friend and his grandfather in Wisconsin. We were fur trappers, and Ishkode and his grandfather taught me how to observe and read markings and signs in the wilderness. Most every living thing leaves some trace of its presence and actions, and if you know where to look, you can see what and how."

Sophie nodded and surveyed the room, trying to imagine the horrific event. "But . . . wouldn't there have been more . . . more blood . . . if he—the murderer—was holding poor Johnny from behind while he bled to death?" She had to swallow hard again, and she clenched her stomach to keep a swish of nausea at bay. "He would have gotten it all over him—his sleeves, his hands . . . How could he keep it to such a few small drops?"

Mr. Quinn nodded. "You're right, Miss Gates. The killer most likely wiped his hands off on Johnny's clothing—he couldn't be walking around the President's House with bloody hands or clothes. Or he brought something to wrap his clothing and the knife in, and if he did that, that means he planned to kill Thorne in this room. Or he found something in here to wrap them up in. I reckon he also took off his shoes, which is why there aren't any footprints leading to the door."

"But . . . how can you know all of that? Where he stood? There are marks everywhere, and they're all jumbled up." She was fascinated, yet a trifle skeptical.

He sighed and crossed his arms. "I'm a very good tracker, Miss Gates. I've been doing it for ten years, and I was taught by—by a very smart man. Two of them, in fact. I've been taught to follow the tracks of an ant across a bed of stones."

She narrowed her eyes. "That's impossible."

Mr. Quinn shrugged, and a faint smile touched his lips again. "Not if you know what to look for." He scanned the room with sharp eyes. "The maid didn't mention that anything was missing or disturbed, did she?"

Sophie wanted to know a lot more about his claim to be able to track an ant—across anything, let alone stones!—but she controlled her curiosity. "I don't know how closely Leah looked at the room, to be frank, Mr. Quinn. She was, understandably, upset."

"Yes, I reckon that's true." Then, as if having spent his allowance of words but still had more to eke out, he pushed on, "If you want to be helpful, Miss Gates, you could talk to the women—Mrs. Lincoln and the others—to see whether any of them heard or saw anything last night."

"I'd be happy to do that, Mr. Quinn," she replied calmly. But inside, she was elated.

He gave a brief nod, then looked around the chamber. "I reckon there's no reason to keep the room closed off any longer."

"I expect the maids will want to remove the rug to . . . er . . . clean it. And the curtains too. Is that all right for them to do?"

He hesitated, then nodded again and made a gesture toward the door for her to precede him.

"Mr. Quinn," she said with her hand on the door latch, and looked up at him. "Do you have any idea who might have done it?"

His face was sober. "Not yet. But you're right about one thing, Miss Gates: whoever it was took a big risk. So it must have been for something very important, and very close."

Very close.

Sophie shivered, then opened the door.

Someone in the President's House was a murderer.

Even Pennsylvania Avenue seemed abandoned. Instead of wagons and carriages clogging the cobblestone street, and pedestrians navigating past each other on the walkways, the main thoroughfare of Washington was so empty Adam didn't have to slow or divert his path as he strode toward the St. Charles Hotel. He didn't see even the snout of a pig anywhere, nor the tottering sign of a chicken.

As he walked east from the White House, toward the half-finished Capitol with its scaffold-draped dome looking forlorn in the pale sunshine, Adam passed more than a few men. Whether dressed in the fine attire of the likes of merchants, bankers, or lawyers, or in the clothing of laborers or farmers, they stood in clusters talking earnestly. Southern accents prevailed, but Adam heard enough snatches of conversation to recognize representatives from both sides of the conflict.

However, he noticed, hardly any women or children were out today, even though the weather was fine and it was after noon. Either they were hidden away behind shuttered doors and windows, or they'd been part of the mass exodus that had clogged the roads out of Washington over the last two days. Those whose only means out of the city would be by train, however, had been forced to remain, due to the destroyed railway.

These observations explained why he was so startled when he heard a feminine voice exclaim, "Why, Mr. Quinn . . . what a pleasant happenstance to encounter you on this fine day."

It was a dulcet voice, smooth and sweet as honey, and dripping with the South.

"Miss Lemagne." He made no effort to hide his pleasure and surprise, smiling as he greeted the lovely young woman. "Good afternoon."

She had just emerged from a small shop—an apothecary and general store—and was holding a paper-wrapped parcel along with a small handbag. With her was an attractive woman in her forties that Adam didn't know.

Constance Lemagne was dressed, as she'd been every time he'd ever encountered her, in clothing that looked very expensive and was far fancier than anything he'd seen on the frontier—or even back in Springfield. Today's dress was light green with white polka dots bumping all over it, and a cascade of white lace dripping from her sleeves, hem, and around the bodice. The skirt's underlying cage of hoops and crinoline was not only as wide as a doorway, but also far too impractical for simply wearing about the house.

Her hair, the color of fresh honey, was arranged in some complicated twist beneath a dark green bonnet trimmed with pink roses, a whispery white feather, and more lace. The hat's brim rose high above her hair, creating an oval frame for her face, and did little to hide the delightful sparkle in her eyes and the attractive shapes of her dainty mouth and nose.

He'd met Miss Lemagne at Mr. Lincoln's inaugural ball—an event that had catapulted Adam into this strange new vocation of solving murders. As he'd done that night, today Adam found himself wondering why a woman from the Deep South—specifically Alabama—remained in the city.

"Good afternoon," Adam said to the other woman.

"Mrs. Rose Greenhow, may I introduce Mr. Adam Quinn." Then Miss Lemagne added with a wry smile and an exaggerated pout, "Mr. Quinn has the misfortune of knowing Mr. Lincoln personally."

Mrs. Greenhow gave Adam a very warm look as she raised her gloved hand. He knew enough to take it in his, lift it, and bow briefly. "It's my pleasure, Mrs. Greenhow."

"Mine as well," she said in a voice that reminded Adam of a feline purr. Her dark eyes gleamed with interest. "So you're likely a Loyalist then, are you, Mr. Quinn?"

"I reckon I am, ma'am."

"What a pity, Constance, dear," she said. Then, with a little laugh, she inclined her head toward Adam, then kissed Miss Lemagne on her cheek. "Good-bye, darling. I'll see you and Althea soon, I hope. And with any luck, Varina as well." Then Mrs. Greenhow turned away to a waiting carriage and was assisted inside.

"Why, Mr. Quinn, I can't think of *anything* that's been so delightful in the last *week* than this very moment." Miss Lemagne said with a warm smile of her own. "Fancy meetin' you right here on the way to my hotel."

Before he could think better of it, he said, "You're still here in Washington. What are you—what a surprise."

She patted his arm with her gloved hand. "I declare, Mr. Quinn, if I didn't know any better, I'd think y'all weren't nearly delighted enough to see me."

He'd already recognized his error and grinned at her unabashedly, appreciative of her good humor. "I reckon it's always a pleasure to see you, Miss Lemagne. But the streets are so empty, I thought for certain you and your father would have returned to Mobile." *Weeks ago,* he added privately.

The flirtatiousness disappeared from her demeanor and she became more serious. "My daddy wouldn't leave Althea," she told him. "And of course, she's not strong enough to travel. So we're still here in Washington. Staying at the St. Charles, of course. You can walk me there, Mr. Quinn, if you like." She dimpled up at him again.

Although Adam didn't know all of the details, he was aware that Mr. Lemagne had recently reunited with a woman he'd loved many years ago. Her husband had been murdered at the inaugural ball, and it was his death Adam had been charged with investigating.

"I'd be honored to escort you to the hotel—and not only because I was already heading there myself," he said with a smile as she tucked her gloved fingers into the crook of his false arm. "But surely you know the city isn't safe."

"Oh, yes, I've heard all the rumors. Mrs. Greenhow knows *everyone,* and they're all talking about how many soldiers are coming, and that the invasion is going to be any day now. This morning, right at dawn, we heard the sounds of loud thudding, marching, and rattling over the bridge, and Daddy and I were certain it was the Confederate Army. We were all gathering in the hotel lobby, waiting to welcome them in . . . but it was only the barrels of flour being brought over the bridge on those wagons." She smiled up at him. "But what have I to fear if our Southern boys take the city?"

Adam was torn between exasperation about her naiveté and

frustration with her father for risking her safety. He'd seen first-hand how wild and vicious men could be when caught up in the passion of battle. The fact that she had the accent and demeanor of a Southern belle wouldn't necessarily protect her—from either side of the conflict.

"I reckon there's no telling what might happen, Miss Lemagne. I would urge you to take no chances and don't go about alone—even during the day. And," he added, thinking of Lane's strategy to impart exaggerated information, "I wouldn't be so certain your Southern boys will even take the city. There's a fierce army of frontier fighters at the President's House and another at the Willard. Still more at the Capitol. Those men are used to violent conflict, and I reckon you wouldn't want to be caught in the mid-dle of it."

She seemed to take his warning seriously, for the challenging light faded from her eyes. Nevertheless, she replied airily, "There's not so many men there, from what I've heard. Hardly a hundred. Not nearly enough to stand up to the Confederates."

Adam knew he had to play his cards delicately, so he kept his expression sober and spoke as if choosing his words with care. "Miss Lemagne, the last thing I want is for you to be taken by sur-prise or be caught up in a dangerous situation, so trust me when I tell you: there's a far sight more barracked in the Executive Mansion and Capitol than your Southern boys know. And more signing up every minute. If the Confederates try to invade, they'll be unpleasantly surprised. Which is why I urge you to convince your father to leave the city. Today if possible."

She managed to hold his gaze for a long moment, even as they continued walking along the Avenue. When she turned away, he saw that the fine muscles of her face had tightened in a grave ex-pression. She believed him.

Adam pressed a bit harder. "If you need help with the evacua-tion, I'm certain I can arrange for a comfortable carriage for your father and Mrs. Billings. And any of your other friends," he added, thinking of Mrs. Greenhow.

"I'll speak to Daddy," said Miss Lemagne as they approached

the door to the St. Charles. "Now, Mr. Quinn, you never did tell me why you were visiting my hotel. Sadly, it appears it wasn't to call on me." She lifted her face and though she smiled and fluttered her lashes, he saw with some regret that her expression wasn't as soft and flirtatious as it normally was. There was a layer of worry in her face that hadn't been there before.

He reckoned that was because she really did believe him about the great army lodged in the mansion. He didn't want to be too specific by giving numbers for fear she—or, more likely, her father—would realize he was planting the details, but if given the chance, he'd feed her more wrong information. He was certain it would get to the right ears through Mr. Lemagne, or even Miss Lemagne herself.

"Had I known you were still lodging in town at the St. Charles, I certainly would have," he replied gallantly. "But I was certain you'd already left to return to Alabama."

"But Mr. Quinn . . . surely you didn't think I'd have gone without saying good-bye," she replied. "After everything that happened after Mr. Billings's murder." What pretty, clear blue eyes she had. With long, dark lashes and black flecks in the irises, and a depth to her gaze that threatened to distract a man.

"I hoped that would be the case, but I reckon it's best not to assume, Miss Lemagne. After all, many people have left the city very quickly in the last few days."

He gestured for her to precede him through the door into the hotel lobby, then nodded to the doorman who'd opened it for them. Once inside, Miss Lemagne turned to him.

"Mr. Quinn, rest assured I wouldn't leave Washington City without bidding you farewell. And I thank you for your warning. I'll—I'll speak to Daddy about it."

He tried to appear hesitant, yet grave. "I only gave you that information for your own benefit, Miss Lemagne. I wouldn't want anything to happen to you."

"Thank you, Mr. Quinn." She smiled at him and, to his shock and pleasure, used his forearm for leverage as she rose up on her toes to kiss his cheek. The edge of a feather from her bonnet brushed his temple, and she brought with her a wave of floral sweetness and the rustle of skirts, but it was the soft buss of her lips on his skin that made the strongest impression.

"Thank *you*, Miss Lemagne," he said, smiling back at her, then sobered once more. "Please be safe."

She looked up at him as if loathe to let him go. "Do you intend to be here long? Perhaps I could—perhaps Daddy would be more apt to listen to you if you told him directly."

Adam wasn't certain he agreed with that, but he was too polite to say so. Hurst Lemagne had been the one to tear up his authorization placard from the president. "I'm not certain how long I'll be here, but perhaps you could be of help. I'm looking for information about a young man named Johnny Thorne. He had a piece of stationery from the hotel here in his pocket, so he might have been staying here, or visiting someone here."

"*Had* a piece of stationery? You're looking for information *about* him, not looking *for* him?" Miss Lemagne looked up at him with narrowed eyes. "Mr. Quinn, are you investigating another murder?"

He exhaled a surprised laugh. "Well, I reckon there's not much I can put past you, Miss Lemagne. I'm afraid you're right. Johnny Thorne was murdered last night, and I'm looking for information about him so we can notify his family, and try to find out who would want to kill him."

"I'm sorry to hear that. I hope . . . I hope he didn't suffer too much."

"It was very quick," was all he said.

"Where was he killed?" she asked.

Adam hesitated, but decided it was best to answer truthfully. "At the President's House."

"Oh, my goodness!" Miss Lemagne's face was a picture of horrified shock. "How terrible."

"It was indeed. I'm hoping to find out who he was."

"Of course. So . . . Johnny Thorne. I don't believe I've heard that name, but we can ask the manager—no, perhaps *I* should ask the manager," she said swiftly. "I suspect I'd have better luck getting his assistance."

Adam looked over and recognized the haughty desk clerk who'd been here on his last visit. He was still wearing the same South Carolina palmetto cockade, proudly displaying his sympathies. Although Adam had no qualms about wresting cooperation from the man—however he'd have to go about doing so—he was forced to agree that his feminine companion would probably get the information he needed far more easily than he could.

"I reckon you might be right."

"Now what else do you know about him? This Johnny Thorne? What does—did he look like? In case the manager doesn't know him by name," she added unnecessarily.

"He was young. No more than seventeen. Clean shaved—no beard or mustache. Medium brown hair. This tall." He measured a height just below his shoulder. "Thin. I don't know much else about him except he was quiet and shy, and when he did speak, he seemed to have a Southern accent. Big feet. Small nose. Eyes were brown."

"All right, Mr. Quinn. That could describe quite a few men, but I can't say I recall seeing anyone around here who meets that description. Anyone that young . . . What was he wearing?"

Adam described Thorne's baggy, worn clothing, and though her brows rose at the description of someone who didn't seem able to afford the St. Charles, Miss Lemagne nodded. "Very well. I'll speak to Mr. Perkins, but . . . perhaps if you stepped over here," she suggested with a smile, gesturing to a location out of sight from the front desk.

With a wry grin, he did, taking a seat in one of a pair of high-backed, mahogany chairs upholstered in gold brocade. Perfect for a private conversation, they were screened from the rest of the lobby and the front desk by a thick plaster column, a man-sized potted fern, and a discreetly positioned spittoon. While he waited, Adam pulled the scrap of St. Charles Hotel stationery from his pocket to take a closer look.

430.

The numbers were neatly written in pencil. A room number, perhaps? Here at the St. Charles?

Or an address. But there was no street, unless it had been torn off.

Or, he reflected, it could be a time. Half-past four. Most often a man would write out the words, but he'd seen it noted with numbers as well. He peered at it closely. Was that a comma between the four and the thirty? Or simply a stray mark?

It could be a date. April 30—that was in less than two weeks.

What about the page number of a book? But what book? The Bible?

Shaking his head—for any of those possibilities, and probably more that he'd yet to think of, could be correct—he turned the paper over in his hands, looking for any other sign that might give him further information. But the reverse side was blank and clear of stains or smudges.

The rustle of skirts and a waft of sweet scent announced Miss Lemagne's return before he saw her.

He stood politely, then sat back down when she took the chair opposite his and waved him into his seat.

"There was no one here registered under the name of Thorne—Johnny or anyone else. I tried to describe him to the manager, but it was difficult. I think we need a likeness of him; then I can show it around and—"

"Pardon me?" Adam wasn't quite able to keep a crack of surprise from his voice. "Miss Lemagne, while I'm obliged for your assistance just now, I don't see any reason for you to involve yourself in this matter."

She merely reached over to pat his hand. "That's very kind of y'all to be worried about little ol' me, Mr. Quinn," she said in a voice that didn't sound as if she really meant it. Adam knew that kind of tone, and it usually preceded something unpleasant when it came from his sisters or mother. "But there's absolutely *nothing* for me to do in this empty, barren city right now—I've no friends, no parties, no luncheons . . . and, alas, not even one charming, handsome beau to keep me occupied. Therefore, I'd be very *grateful* to have something to do. And showing around a picture of a young man is the least I can do—especially since someone *murdered* him."

"We don't have a painting or photograph of Johnny Thorne," he said in what he knew would probably be a vain effort to stifle her interest.

"Not to worry, Mr. Quinn," she replied with a bright smile. "I'm quite handy with a pencil. In fact, Daddy has a collection of pencil sketches I've done hanging in his office. I'm particularly good at likenesses, as a matter of fact." Her smile became even brighter. "I can draw two or three images of Mr. Thorne's face, and then you and I can show it around to see if anyone recognizes him."

The way her eyes—the color of cornflowers—narrowed on him told Adam he'd walked right into a pile of pig muck. If he stayed in, he was going to be stuck, and if he walked out, the muck would stick with him. There was no clean way out of the mess.

Still, he protested, and rightly so. "That's a very kind and generous offer, Miss Lemagne, but I don't reckon you'd need to draw a portrait of a dead man."

"Whyever not? How on earth do you expect to identify him if no one knows what he looked like?" She reached over and rested her hand on his false arm, giving it a little pat. He had a flash of regret that it wasn't his real limb. "The description you gave me could fit any number of men in the city."

"Miss Lemagne, I'm very appreciative of your offer, but I reckon your father would have my head if he knew you were consorting with dead bodies—even for such a well-intentioned reason."

She withdrew her hand and gave him a considering look, then curved her lips into a sweet smile. "You're very kind to be so concerned about little ol' me, Mr. Quinn. And quite stubborn as well, I see. Very well, then. I suppose there's nothing I can say to change your mind." She tilted her head and the feather arching from her bonnet wafted delicately above her forehead. "At least tell me whether you have any suspects—or any ideas why he might have been murdered."

When he opened his mouth to speak, she held up a hand to

forestall his negative response. "Mr. Quinn, *do* have a heart! I'm *utterly* bored with nothing to do, locked up in this stuffy hotel and nowhere to go! At least you could tell me something interesting."

"The fact that the war will likely be coming to your hotel's doorstop isn't interesting enough for you?" he replied mildly.

She folded her arms beneath the sleek curves of her bosom, forming a moue with her lips. "I declare, I thought you were a gentleman, Mr. Quinn. And a gentleman," she continued in a steely voice, "never leaves a lady in distress."

She looked about as distressed as a cat who'd just discovered an unattended dish of cream, but of course Adam couldn't say so. Fortunately, before he could reckon a way out of the pig muck, the choice was taken from him.

"Constance! What the devi—what are you doing?" The booming voice had Miss Lemagne's eyes widening, then her expression shifted into exasperation as she looked between the palm fronds.

Nonetheless, as her father stalked into view from where he'd entered the lobby, she rose, smiling prettily at her parent. As if to head off any of his bluster—or worse—she rustled to his side, skirts swinging, and tucked her hand into the crook of his arm.

"Daddy, you remember Mr. Quinn," she said in a firm voice.

"Of course I do," replied Hurst Lemagne with a trace of grudging civility that Adam was certain had been prompted only by the presence of the man's daughter.

Lemagne was a stocky man a full head shorter than Adam, and he wore a set of thick and neatly trimmed sideburns that grew into a combed, graying beard. His brown hair had begun to thin at the crown, and his cornflower blue eyes were only slightly less vibrant than those of his daughter's.

"Good morning, Hurst," Adam said, purposely choosing the informality of the man's Christian name. After all, he'd helped to clear the man from suspicion of murder only a month ago. "I was just telling your daughter that I was surprised to learn you were still in Washington."

Bushy brows rose, crinkling his forehead, as the older man replied just as evenly, "One could say the same for you—and for your president. From what I hear, he's little more than a sitting duck for our boys." He glanced meaningfully toward the front window of the hotel, through which the hilly Virginia shore was almost discernible beyond the Smithsonian towers. "The boys'll be here tonight, I hear tell—and they're not in a very cordial mood. You still have time to get out of the city, Quinn. You and that rail-splitter—and the few old men you've got guarding him. They're outnumbered and will soon be outfought."

Adam only smiled. "I reckon we'll see about that." Then, with a deliberate nod toward Miss Lemagne, he allowed his smile to fold as he continued, "If it were me with a daughter here in the city, I'd be more concerned about her being in the middle of an invasion than what anyone else is doing. I reckon you're right things'll be getting ugly pretty soon in Washington, and I'd want my womenfolk to be somewhere far from it, and safe."

Lemagne's eyes went flinty. "Speak for your own boys, Quinn. But no Southern man I know would lay a hand on a woman, even in war—"

"Then you ain't ever been in a war, have you? I have. I didn't take you for being such a naive fool, Hurst." Adam made no attempt to hide his disgust even as he blocked horrific memories from his mind. "If Beauregard brings his men across the Long Bridge tonight—or tomorrow, or ever—he's going to find himself outnumbered and outmaneuvered. Jim Lane is here, and he's leading the troops. Ask around to your Southern friends what they've heard about how the Grim Chieftain fights a war. So if I were you, I reckon I'd do everything to make certain my daughter was somewhere safe. As soon as possible." Worried that he might have said too much, Adam gave a brief bow and set the hat back on his head. "Good day, Miss Lemagne."

As he stalked out of the hotel, Adam heard Miss Lemagne's hissed rebuke of her father for his rudeness. But it was the hint of shock and wariness in the other man's expression that had Adam feeling the most satisfaction.

The seeds had been planted, as Lane had intended. Adam hoped they took root and the rumors somehow kept the Rebels from attacking.

He turned off Pennsylvania Avenue onto L Street, heading to

the boardinghouse where Adam had taken a small room for himself.

Originally, Adam—who had been part of Lincoln's security team during his journey from Springfield, Illinois, to the capital—had had no intention of remaining in Washington once the president was inaugurated and settled into his new position. He disliked the city—any city—for its hordes of people, vehicles, buildings, and activity; not to mention the formality and societal expectations. At the same time, however, Adam no longer had any real home to which he could return—having left Kansas after the brutal anti-slavery battles there, grieving and injured in both body and mind.

He'd readily agreed when his uncle, Joshua Speed, suggested he travel with him and the president-elect. But after the events related to Mr. Billings's murder, Lincoln had asked Adam to stay in Washington. And Adam, filled with both patriotic duty and concern for the health and mental well-being of his friend and mentor, had agreed.

However, he'd declined the president's offer for him to use a room in the White House, as Nicolay, Hay, and Stoddard had done, knowing he would require some peace and quiet to himself at times. Thus, as he was barracked for the foreseeable future in the White House, Adam had to retrieve some fresh clothing from his rooms.

As he made his way down the street, Adam noticed a trio of men standing on the opposite side. One of the men was blond with a beard and mustache, and another taller with a full, dark beard and a long coat whose hem buffeted in the breeze. But it was the third man, who wore a wide-brimmed hat, who caught Adam's attention. He sported a beard the color of copper, and his barrel-shaped body was clothed in rumpled, serviceable frontier clothing just like that of his companions.

Adam stopped short, his pulse spiking, and the rush of anger causing his fingers to curl.

Leward Hale. From Orin Bitter's pro-slavery army from Kansas. One of the men who'd been in the mob that set the fires which killed Tom, Mary, and Carl—and who'd put the bullet in Adam's arm, shattering the bone and crippling him permanently.

His heart thudded and his mouth dried.

I've waited too long for this.

Without another thought, Adam pivoted and started into the street toward them, hand on his pistol and fury surging in his veins.

CHAPTER 5

"W HY WE GOING IN HERE, MISS CONSTANCE?" ASKED JELLY, HALT-ing at the mouth of the dingy alley. She looked around, up and down the street on which they'd just walked, which ended several blocks south at Lafayette Square. In contrast to the sunbathed, whitewashed houses on the well-trafficked road, the cluttered, shadowy alley was hardly wide enough for a single horse or a woman in full hoopskirts. "I don't think your Papa's gone like it, us going in *dere*. Not at all, Miss Constance."

Taking a step into the alley, Constance waved impatiently at her maid, who was fifteen years older and possessed of far less deter-mination than she—until it came to dressing Constance's hair or cleaning a spot from one of her skirts. Then Jelly was more stub-born than a fly on honey.

"How's Daddy going to know? *I'm* certainly not going to tell him," she responded primly, lifting her skirt hem as she avoided a pile of something . . . sludgy. And horribly smelly. Greasy.

She averted her eyes, afraid she might discover exactly what it was. Perhaps she should have taken off her big crinoline and hoop cage and put on a simpler dress, but she hadn't wanted to take the time to change after Mr. Quinn had left her at the hotel. (It had been an unexpected boon that she'd been wearing such a fetching dress and bonnet when she encountered him there on the street.)

She didn't change because it took forever to undo all the tapes that held the skirt's cage in place, and then she'd have to change her crinoline and petticoats for shorter ones . . . and she didn't want to waste any time. For this was the most interesting and exciting thing Constance had done for weeks, especially since the war had actually started—finally!—and so many people (Southerners) had left Washington.

Daddy was determined to remain in the city, mostly because of Althea Billings, as Constance had confided to Mr. Quinn. But he also stayed because, as he'd told her, "When the war's over, there'll be lots of opportunities for a Southern man like me here in the capital."

Constance knew the Confederate Army would take Washington, and it wouldn't be long until they did. Perhaps even as early as tonight.

She felt a thrill of excitement whenever she thought about it. In fact, Mrs. Greenhow had shared with her an invitation from Varina Davis, the First Lady of the Confederate States, to a fête she was going to hold at the White House here in Washington on May 1 for all of the ladies in society who were Southern sympathizers. That was less than a fortnight away, and Constance was *really* looking forward to it.

Washington had become morbidly dull in the last few weeks. And now, because of the evacuation, many of the shops were closed—including those of the seamstresses and milliners that would make her attire for the party. Constance decided she'd hire Mrs. Keckley to do her frock for the reception, since the black seamstress had worked for Mrs. Davis before the Southerners began to leave the city during the great Secession winter, just a few months ago. Right now, Mrs. Keckley was apparently working for the current First Lady.

It would be just perfect for the Negro seamstress to keep her same position once the Lincolns were run out of the President's Mansion.

She smiled at the thought, then gave the lagging Jelly a pointed look. The older woman sighed and muttered under her breath, but she came along as they ventured farther into the narrow throughway.

Constance had been here once before—the place was called

Ballard's Alley—and it was a muddy, bumpy footpath between two rows of decrepit buildings. The structures were shacks or lean-tos where, she'd discovered, people actually lived.

Many of them were blacks—both free and slave—but she understood there was a good number of Irish immigrants and some Germans as well. The ramshackle buildings faced each other on this back alley, hidden from view by the large, straight, well-appointed homes lining the broader roads that boasted street lamps and a width designed to accommodate carriages and wagons, two wide. Those homes had actual street addresses and front doors and, sometimes, even a tiny patch of grass in front.

Constance felt rather than saw several pairs of eyes watching her from behind cracks in the wooden walls, sagging doors, or fluttering blanket entries. Wood smoke filtered through the air, weaving between the putrid smells of rot and waste. The path of packed dirt was decorated with dark puddles and suspicious looking piles.

Nonetheless, Constance marched along, keeping her chin up and her eyes focused straight ahead unless they were checking to make sure she didn't step in anything. With her Swiss-dotted green skirt and white ruffled petticoats currently hiked a little too high for strict propriety, she nevertheless managed to keep most of her hems out of the muck. Prickles scuttled over her shoulders and down her spine, but she ignored them. It was daylight, and she wasn't alone. She told herself she had nothing to fear as Jelly ambled reluctantly behind her, carrying the small satchel Constance had packed.

They passed a pair of Negro women scrubbing laundry in small tubs. Both wore faded smocks of some indeterminate color, though one had gray streaks in her hair and more lines on her face. A tribe of children played in a patch of dirt, using sticks, stones, and a cracked cup for their toys, while a slightly older girl with light skin and hair watched over them. She held an infant in her arms and watched the two newcomers with dark, curious eyes.

Constance couldn't quell a stab of pity for them, living in such mean conditions: leaky roofs, warped doors, cloth-covered windows. If this was how free blacks lived, it was a disgrace. At home, in the Lemagne household, their darkies were kept in clean, neat quarters. They had plenty to eat, and each slave received a new set of clothing at Christmas and on the first of June, along with one pair of shoes every year.

She glanced back at Jelly, hoping her maid was noticing the rough lives of these women and comparing it to the clean, safe one she and her fellow slaves had back home. Not that Jelly was unhappy with her life—of course she wasn't. She'd been caring for Constance since she was born, and she loved her. Jelly was like a mother to her in some ways—which was nice, because Constance's mother had died when she was ten.

After what seemed like forever, she saw the building she'd been looking for. Her stomach gave a little leap of relief. She'd been certain she could find it again, but until she'd done so, there had been that little niggle of worry.

But there it was: a relatively solid structure, its walls white-washed and clean. A small cross hung over the door, and a neat sign was posted: Great Eternity Church.

Constance drew in her breath (as much as she could, laced into a corset as she was) and squared her shoulders. "This way," she said to Jelly, and started around to the back of the church.

The entrance she sought was a door leading to the cellar, which was partially belowground, but it had a row of short, squat windows that looked out over the grass. One of them was propped open with a short, fat stick. The steps that led down to the door were narrow, and Constance needed Jelly's help to maneuver her way between the brick walls.

Her maid grumbled about the way the pale green skirt scraped against the sides, all the while taking care to keep the ungainly hoops from tipping up in a scandalous fashion. Not that anyone was around to see.

There was another small sign next to this door, and it said simply: Doctor. The door was open a crack, and Constance squared her shoulders once more, then opened it and stepped inside—or, at least, attempted to.

But the entrance was narrower than the stairway, and her hoops didn't want to cooperate. So she had to squeeze her way through while keeping her skirt from popping up. Jelly's sharp intake of breath and muttered grumble were surely related to the sound of delicate lawn fabric brushing over the dirty, rough bricks. Constance hardly noticed, for she found herself the object of arrested attention—from a young man and woman sitting on chairs along one wall, from an elderly man who'd just emerged from behind a privacy curtain, and from George Hilton himself.

It was the doctor's attention that drew and kept hers: the dark-as-night eyes that revealed an instant of bald shock, then shuttered like a house against a storm. His hand fell away from where it had provided support to the elderly man, presumably a patient, and began to immediately unroll the shirtsleeves that revealed muscular arms as dark and strong as polished walnut. As he swiftly fastened his cuffs in an obvious attempt to put his informality to rights, she noticed that his facial hair—mustache, sideburns, and beard—had recently been trimmed and shaped.

"Miss Lemagne," he said, breaking the awkward silence that had surely stretched for hours. "How may I help you?"

He spoke like no Negro she'd ever met: with precise, smooth inflection. He met her eyes like no Negro she'd ever met: boldly, with something almost like challenge in them. And then suddenly that flicker of emotion was gone and his expression was blank as a schoolroom slate at the end of the day.

Before she could think how to reply—for all words had deserted her in this strange, strained moment—Jelly stepped forward.

"You's really a doctor, sir?"

Dr. Hilton (Constance found it difficult to think of a black man with a title) transferred his attention to Jelly. "I am. Do you have a complaint, ma'am?"

"Truth be told, I got plenty of 'em—but only one I 'spect you can do anything about," she drawled, and Constance saw a flash of humor in Hilton's eyes as his full mouth twitched.

"Well, I'll be happy to see what I can do about the one, then," he replied. He turned to his elderly patient, who'd joined the other two people waiting as they stood to assist him. They were younger than the patient, but all three were tall, leaning toward gaunt, and wore clothing that had seen better days. Probably a decade ago.

"Mr. Hodge, remember what I said about putting on that unguent. Two times per day, and change the dressing when you do."

"Yassir, doc," replied the man in a voice that sounded like rock scraping against rock. "Lissie here'll help me."

Lissie, whom Constance surmised was Mr. Hodge's daughter or some other relative, stood and handed the old man a smooth, gnarled cane of some syrup-colored wood. "Thank you doctor," she said, straightening her tentlike shift that had never seen a crinoline, and probably not a petticoat either. Then, her eyes flitting briefly to Constance, she leaned closer to the doctor and said something in a low voice.

"Don't you worry about it, Miss Lissie," he replied quietly; though the timbre of his voice carried a bit more. "You just take care of your papa. *And* yourself," he added with a meaningful look.

"Yessir." When Lissie brushed a hand down over her torso, Constance noticed the slight swell of her belly rounding beneath the loose shift. And the dark bruises on her slender arm that looked like finger marks. Her eyes jerked toward the third person there—a young man—and wondered if he'd put the marks there. And if so, was he Lissie's husband.

But it was none of her business.

Still, Constance found herself watching the trio as the two younger persons assisted Mr. Hodge in a labored shuffle toward the narrow door.

When she at last turned back to Dr. Hilton and Jelly, Constance found herself once again the object of his attention.

"What can I do for you, Miss Lemagne?" he asked. "Surely you didn't find it necessary to come all the way to Ballard's Alley to seek medical treatment."

From the likes of me. Although he didn't speak the words, Constance heard them as clearly as if he'd done so. Nonetheless, his expression was properly blank and respectful. "Jelly, my maid," she explained, "apparently has need of your medical treatment. As for me," she continued blithely, "I'm here to help Mr. Adam Quinn."

For the second time, that flash of bald shock flared in his eyes and was just as quickly subdued. "Quinn sent you here? Why?"

At that moment, Constance was struck by the possibility that she'd made a mistake coming to this place.

After all, she had no reason to believe George Hilton was in possession of Johnny Thorne's body. Just because he'd examined a dead body the last time Mr. Quinn had been involved in a murder case, that didn't mean he would do so this time. In fact, now that she thought about it, Constance realized it was a foolish assumption that a Negro doctor would be involved in such a delicate, important matter. She didn't know what had caused him to be involved the last time, but surely there were other doctors in Washington City who would be better suited to such a task.

However, she needed to make certain, and bluffing her way through seemed the best option. "I'm here to draw a likeness of Johnny Thorne so that Mr. Quinn"—she purposely left out mention of herself doing the same—"can show it around in an attempt to identify him or learn more about him."

Hilton assessed her in a way she was unaccustomed to being read by a black man—making her skin prickle—then gave a mild shrug. "Very well. If you'll give me one moment to prepare, Miss Lemagne."

As the doctor disappeared behind a blanket hung from the ceiling, Constance sat primly on one of the chairs, battling her crinoline and hoops into submission while ignoring Jelly's muttered comments. She took the satchel from her maid's grip and positioned it on her lap, curling and uncurling her gloved fingers over its handle as she considered the fact that Mr. Quinn hadn't told her how Thorne had been killed. She didn't know what condition the poor man's body would be in, and whether his face would show signs of trauma or injury.

"Miss Lemagne." Hilton swept the curtain aside and gestured. "I've lit the lanterns and lamps to give you as much light as possible. Don't touch anything, miss."

Constance bustled past him, aware of the way he stepped back to give her plenty of room. Even so, his words hung in her mind: *Don't touch anything.* She wasn't accustomed to that sort of impertinence from a nigger—even a free one.

Those jumbled thoughts dissipated as she saw the body of Johnny Thorne lying on a long table. He was covered by a dark blanket from chin to foot, with only his pale, dirty face revealed.

She swallowed hard and set her satchel down on a nearby table. As she withdrew a piece of paper—stationery, ironically, from the St. Charles Hotel—and a pencil, she looked at Thorne's white face. Dark smudges and speckles that looked unpleasantly like blood streaked his cheeks and chin. His eyes were open (she wondered whether Hilton had done that for the purposes of her sketch or whether they'd simply been left unseeing), and his mouth was slightly ajar.

She'd noticed the scent of blood and other unpleasant odors since coming through the door into Hilton's office, but now the smells were stronger and more astringent. It reminded her of butchering day at home—an event that happened monthly, and one she usually avoided by remaining in the house on the far side away from the barnyard. Still, the smell of blood and flesh was impossible to avoid, and Constance's belly wavered for an instant as the images of the slaughter at home mingled with the cloaked figure on the table in front of her.

"Miss Lemagne?" Hilton had come up behind her, and the rumble of his voice startled her back into the moment. "Do you need something?"

"No, no." She hoped he couldn't see her gripping the edge of the table in order to steady herself. She swallowed hard. "I was just looking at the—at him, to decide whether it would be best to draw him with his eyes open or closed. I think open is best, so we can see the shape of his eyes better," she rushed on.

"That was my thought as well. I'll be happy to close them for you when you've finished with that part, if you like."

"I'll let you know," she said, forcing dismissiveness into her tones. "Now, I'd like to get to work."

Hilton took her comment to heart and she heard the soft scrape of his shoe over the gritty floor as he turned to leave.

Constance picked up her pencil, and, blocking out the smells, the location, the doctor and his uppity ways, focused on the shape of Johnny Thorne's face. She realized yet another inconvenience to the wider hoops she'd eschewed changing: it was impossible to get very close to the object of her attention without bumping her dress against the table and tilting the skirt up in back.

Nonetheless, she could do what needed to be done—albeit from a greater distance than she'd like. Constance sketched the basic oval shape—which would be adjusted to show his narrow chin as she refined it—then drew light guiding lines: one down the center, bisecting the face from forehead to chin; then one each across in a smooth arc for eyes, nose, and mouth. Eyes were always set exactly halfway down the front of the skull, and nose and mouth half again from there. Focusing on these simple drawing rules helped Constance to set aside the difficulty of her subject and relax into the process itself.

With any luck, she'd be finished with her sketch before Mr. Quinn showed up—as he surely would do.

Adam stepped into the street, his attention so focused on Leward Hale and his companions that he barely stopped in time to keep from being trampled by a pair of horses pulling a large wagon.

"Watch where you're going!" cried the driver as Adam jolted back, shocked that he'd done something as foolish as rushing into the street without looking.

He waved his apology to the man and was forced to wait as the wagon rumbled by. By the time it passed and Adam was able to start across the street again, Hale and his friends were gone. He hurried to the other side and stood for a moment, looking up and down the Avenue and around the corner onto L Street. Adam cursed under his breath. Where had the man gone to?

Had he seen Adam? Was that why he'd taken off so quickly? Surely Hale knew what would happen if Adam got his hands—no, his single, solitary *hand*—on him?

Adam realized he was clenching and unclenching his fist, and that his muscles were quivering so tight that his prosthetic was trembling against him. His mind wavered, threatening to send him back to Leavenworth, back to the blazing fire that wanted to peel the skin off—

"Mr. Quinn!"

The sound of his name penetrated the haze of memory, and Adam turned blindly toward the sound. When he blinked and his vision cleared, it was to see a boy of about eleven running toward him. Apparently Brian Mulcahey hadn't left Washington during the mass exodus.

"There's gonna be a war," he said breathlessly as he stamped to a stop next to him. The youth's milky Irish skin was plastered with coppery freckles and his cheeks were flushed from the exertion of running. Over the last month, his missing tooth had begun to grow back in.

"There already is," Adam replied. He looked down automatically and was pleased to see that Brian was wearing the new boots Mr. Lincoln had "bought" for him a month ago. They were mud-stained but looked a far sight better than the boy's previous footwear, which had allowed for a toe to protrude.

"I'm about hearing the Rebels are coming tonight." His eyes flashed with excitement, and Adam had to tamp down the desire to lecture him about the hell of war. Every young boy—himself included—romanticized soldiering and fighting. And every young boy, if he made it through the battles alive, learned how unromantic it was.

"How's your mama?"

To Adam's knowledge, Brian had no father, but he had two younger sisters—one an infant—and his small family lived in mean conditions in Ballard's Alley not far from George Hilton's office. Adam used all of his ingenuity to create ways to help the family with food, clothing, and other needs without appearing to be offering charity. He was usually hungry whenever Brian was around, then proceeded to order far too much food for himself to eat, so had to send it home with the boy.

"Mam's got your coat mended," Brian replied, falling into step with Adam as he began to walk down the street. "And your socks, too."

"That was quick work, but I hope she didn't stay in the city because of that."

"She ain't afraid of them Rebels. The Irish been fighting wars and beating back the English and Scottish for centuries, she said. Me grandpappy's grandpappy's people even painted 'emselves *blue* sometimes."

"Is that so? I reckon that would scare anybody, seeing a wild man with his face painted blue."

"Not just the face," Brian said. "Everywhere. They weren't wearing no clothes."

Adam winced at the thought, then stopped at the meat pie shop. But when he pulled on it, the door only rattled in its frame. Closed. That wasn't a surprise. Half the shops were, with everyone gone.

"Och, and it was Dr. Hilton sent me," Brian said suddenly. "To fetch you. He said to come urgent."

"All right, then." Adam adjusted his hat, gave one last look in the direction Leward Hale had been, and made an about-face on the street. He could go to his boardinghouse later. "Let's be on our way. I reckon I've got a rumble in my belly for the sausages they have at the Willard. You mind stopping there while I get some for the doctor and you and me?"

"No, sir, Mr. Quinn. But the doctor seemed like he was wanting you to come on the way. It took me a long time to find you."

Adam quickened his pace, his long legs leaving the boy hustling to keep up, and wondered what had George Hilton up in such a dander.

* * *

George Hilton was in more of a fix than a dander. Where the blazes was that boy? He'd sent that scamp Brian Mulcahey off an hour since past. And when the door opened ten minutes ago, he'd expected it to be Quinn. Instead, it was Miss Constance Lemagne who'd made her elegant—and terribly inappropriate—appearance.

Now that she was here, he had even more of a reason to require Quinn's presence. What the hell had the man been thinking, sending the likes of her here? Besides the absurdity of the situation—a young lady in what amounted to a morgue—the last thing George wanted was to be alone in a cellar with a white woman.

Praise be to God she'd brought her maid with her so it wasn't just the two of them.

Her *slave* maid, he reminded himself as he gestured for the older woman to go behind the curtain that cordoned off the examining area. George cast a quick look behind the other dividing blanket, but he was only able to see the edge of Miss Lemagne's teacuplike skirt and her shadow spilling over the dirt floor.

"All right, then, Mistress Jelly, why don't you tell me about your ailments." As he spoke, his physician's eyes naturally assessed the woman and her physical state. "At least the ones you think I can attend to," he added with a smile.

By all accounts, the maid looked to be about the same age as his friend Mrs. Keckley—in her middle forties—but as George knew, looks could be deceiving. From what he could tell from beneath her neat and simple cotton clothing, Jelly was neither too plump nor too slender. Her eyes were keen and the sclera were milky white. There were no obvious lacerations or abrasions, and she seemed to move with the appropriate agility for a woman her age. He observed no tremors in her limbs or fingers, and her breathing seemed regular and unhampered. And when he reached for her wrist to take her pulse, it was steady and solid and her skin's temperature felt normal.

By all appearances, she was healthy as a prime hog, as his friend Dr. Gaspar would have said—though George would never dare utter such a comparison aloud. Apparently, the Lemagnes were a family who took care of their human chattel. At least, those who worked in the house. Sometimes the ones in the fields fared differently—especially in the Deep South, where work in the cotton fields was long and difficult. He steadied himself and forced his thoughts to remain here in his office, instead of on things he could do little about.

But what little he could do, he did.

"I got an ache in my toe," Jelly said. "The mid' one."

George released her hand slowly and looked at her. "Your middle toe?"

"Yessir. That's the one." Her gaze was steady as it met his.

"I see." He pursed his lips and said, "Well then, I suppose you'd best show it to me." He glanced toward the curtain separating them from Miss Lemagne. The quiet scritch-scratch of pencil over paper indicated she was hard at work.

"I don' know as you can help me, young man, but mebbe you know someone who can." Seated on the high table in front of him, Jelly was already unbuttoning one of her shoes.

George didn't mind being called a young man by a woman nearly old enough to be his mother instead of by the title for which he'd worked and bled and risked his life. In fact, her matronly attitude made him want to smile.

"You got yourself a man, Mistress Jelly?" he asked as she rolled off a cotton stocking that was neatly darned, but clean and didn't smell more than was normal. "Any children?"

"My man's dead. Goin' on seven years now. About the time my son was sold to another master, down to Mobile. He was eleven." Her words came out matter of fact—like she was talking about a bale of cotton taken to a merchant—but George saw a flash of raw emotion in her dark eyes. Then, as one would expect, the flare died away and her expression became bland, almost cheery, once more.

"I'm sorry about your man," he said. Her foot was bare: callused and ugly, but broad and sturdy. As he'd anticipated, no bruising or injuries there or on her ankle and what he could see of her calf and shin. "And about your son."

"He my only one lived past a year. Had two others died."

"I'm sorry for that too, Mistress Jelly," George replied, though he spared a thought that maybe it had been for the best she hadn't raised two more children within the bonds of slavery.

Two more children that could be taken from her at any moment—not by Fate or Providence or God, but by those who bought and sold men.

"I ain't seen my son seven years now. Jeremy be eighteen." She shifted on the table. "His name be Jeremy Pole."

"Do you know where he is? Where he was sold?"

Her voice dropped to hardly above a whisper. "He run away from Alabama, I hear. Two years gone."

The door opened, and George didn't have to look out from behind the curtain to know Quinn had arrived because Brian Mulcahey's youthful voice was rattling on about his hen named Bessie. *Praise God.*

"Quinn," he said, his tone more urgent than he intended. "Finally."

"You back there, doc?"

"Yes. With a patient. I'll be right out." George put a hand on one of Jelly's smaller ones. "Do you know where your son is now?" He didn't ask the more worrisome question: had Jeremy been caught.

"He in New York City. Mebbe dere." Once again, there was a flash of emotion in her eyes—raw, hopeful—and then it was gone, replaced by the blank, bland expression she knew better to wear.

"All right, then. You can put your stocking and shoe back on, Mistress Jelly."

There was a rustle of movement out in the main room as Brian rattled on. "And wasn't I just waitin' for Bessie to lay her egg, but she was—"

"*Miss Lemagne.* What the *de*—What on earth are you doing here?"

That was when George Hilton realized, with a vast and instant relief, that Adam Quinn had *not* in fact sent a genteel Southern lady to draw images in a morgue. His minor irritation with the man eased and was replaced by a nudge of shock over Miss Lemagne's intrusion and bald lies.

"Why, Mr. Quinn," replied the young woman in a studiously innocent voice. "I didn't expect to see you here. I mean to say, not quite so soon." She gave a gentle laugh. "What do you think of my work so far?"

George flung aside the hanging blanket in time to see Miss Lemagne offering her sketch to Quinn, who looked over as George appeared.

"What is this?" asked Quinn.

George met his eyes directly—something he still had to consciously give himself permission to do—and pursed his lips. "Miss Lemagne gave me to understand that you requested she—"

"Now, Dr. Hilton," interrupted the lady in a sugary voice that was nonetheless lined with steel and laced with haughtiness, "perhaps y'all misunderstood. *Ah*'m here to draw a *likeness* of Johnny Thorne in order to assist Mr. Quinn in his identification of that poor young man. There's no reason to quibble about who or why that came to be. Is there, Mr. Quinn?"

She fluttered her eyelashes at the white man. They were surprisingly dark ones for a woman with hair the color of honey and skin that looked like blushing cream. "It's a good likeness, don't you agree? Of course, I've only just started, but I do believe I've captured the shape of his eyes and jaw."

"Miss Lemagne, I reckoned I made it clear that it wasn't seemly for you to, ah, to visit a place like this," Quinn said, clearly struggling to make his point without literally dragging the woman out of this mean and vulgar place—as George would have considered doing.

If he wasn't a black man and she wasn't a white woman.

"Mr. Quinn"—that steel was back in her voice, underlying the determinedly polite tone of her upbringing—"as I recall, it was you yourself who brought me to this place the first time. It was only a short month ago, when you were attempting to blame my *daddy* for *murderin'* someone. *Ah*," she said, barreling on in a softer, more explicitly Southern tone when Quinn could do nothing but gape at her, "came to offer *mah* services because y'all won't *evah* be able to find out who poor Johnny Thorne is without some sort of picture to show people. Why, to describe that poor young man would be like describing any other young man who might be walking down the street. Surely you want to find out who would do such a thing to him. Whatever it was. What was it anyhow? Did the poor boy get shot?"

"Never you mind, Miss Lemagne," Quinn replied. "I reckon you don't need to know what exactly happened to him in order to draw his likeness."

Her expression changed: her eyes sparkled, her mouth curved up, and her cheeks flushed. "I'll only need another few more moments to finish the drawing, Mr. Quinn. I can draw other copies back at the hotel."

Quinn blinked, then looked at George, who could do nothing but lift his brows in recognition of the other man being cajoled and connived, then maneuvered into a tacit agreement. But there was a reason he'd sent for Quinn in a hurry, and that needed to be attended to more urgently than a drawing.

"Miss Lemagne," he said. "I need a moment with Mr. Quinn and—and Thorne. If you could wait over there, please, miss."

She looked at the chairs he indicated, then back at him with a dissatisfied expression. "If you insist." Apparently, she knew better than to try cajoling and conniving him.

"There's something you need to see"—he told Quinn as he pulled the curtain as far over as he could to obstruct Miss Lemagne's and her maid's views of the body—"that will make a difference in your investigation."

"All right, then."

Taking care to stand between the table and the curtain to ensure the two watching females couldn't see anything even if they adjusted their position, George began to pull the blanket back from the bloodstained sheet that covered the corpse. He'd put the blanket over the lighter covering at the last minute so that Miss Lemagne wouldn't be shocked by the sight of all the blood staining the flimsy sheet—and that was even before he began a minute examination of the body, which could include cutting into it to remove organs such as the stomach or heart.

In Toronto, where he'd received his schooling, George had spent more time than most of his fellow students examining the cadavers used for their medical training. That was partly because he was a black man, and not particularly welcomed by most of the other students. But not only had he been interested in what made the bodies move and breathe while alive, and how to assess disease and injury, but he'd found himself just as fascinated by what brought them to death.

Now he had a second chance, granted by Adam Quinn and President Lincoln, to continue his somewhat morbid fascination with the story of death. He was both anticipatory and nervous.

"I haven't begun a full examination yet," he explained as he prepared to uncover the corpse. "But I can tell you what I believe about several things, including the time of death. But first, I thought you should see this."

He carefully pulled the sheet back, easing it away from the raw, angry slice across the larynx and through the carotid, down over the clavicles and torso.

"I'll be damned," Quinn breathed as he looked down.

It was only when the boy gasped that George realized Brian Mulcahey was still on the wrong side of the curtain. Before he could cover the boy's eyes, he pushed up next to them.

"*Gor!* It's a *woman!*"

CHAPTER 6

"*A* WOMAN?*"*

Adam heard Miss Lemagne's shocked exclamation, followed by the rustle of skirts—as if she were hurrying over to see for herself.

Fortunately, Hilton was quick enough to flip the sheet back over the bare torso of the person known as Johnny Thorne—but who now must be thought of as Jane Thorne. Adam felt as if his world had tilted to one side, then back again.

This revelation did, as the doctor had said, shed a completely different light on the matter.

"Miss Lemagne, please," Hilton said in a tight voice, "if you could give us another moment. Then you can finish your drawing. Brian, I'm going to need another dozen candles and a pot of kerosene from Mitchell's," he added in such a tone that Adam knew he wished he'd thought to send the boy away sooner. Hilton dug in his pocket to pull out money, but Adam was faster, and withdrew two silver dollars left over from their stop at Willard's.

"Mr. Lincoln insists on paying all expenses related to this investigation," he said when the doctor appeared ready to argue. Hilton had made it clear on more than one occasion that he was not about to be a recipient of charity—any sort of charity. But Adam had learned that, as with Brian Mulcahey's mother, employing the name of the president improved receptivity to any charitable suggestion.

After all, Adam had very few expenses other than the boardinghouse fee, and despite what had happened in Leavenworth, he was far from destitute. His fur trapping business in Wisconsin, with Ishkode, had been quite successful. Aside from that, Mr. Lincoln had assigned the salaries for both him and his newest aide, George Stoddard, as part of his budget for clerks of the Interior Department. Thus Adam would be paid a comfortable $1,600 annual wage for his jack-of-all-trades work for the president.

The number of candles and lamps Hilton required for his postmortem examinations were expensive, and there was no reason for the doctor to bear the cost himself. Especially when Adam brought the problem to him.

Brian took the money, but his eyes slid over to the shrouded corpse once more. "*Gor,*" he whispered. But when Adam gave him a stern look, he adjusted his cap and dashed off on the errand.

If only it had been that simple to get rid of Constance Lemagne.

Adam looked up and caught George's eye, and nearly grinned—for his woebegone expression indicated he was thinking the same thing.

"Brian's been helping me out a bit," the doctor said. "Running errands and such."

"I reckoned his mother might have wanted to leave the city," Adam mused. "I was surprised when he found me on the street today."

His mood darkened a bit when he remembered he'd seen Leward Hale only moments before Brian called out to him. The reminder that the man who'd destroyed his life was in the same city as he was threatened to distract Adam from the matter at hand, and it was with effort he returned his attention to the body. "What else can you tell me about Miss Thorne?"

Hilton glanced toward the curtain and, with his back to the women he kept his voice low but clear as he spoke. "She was also stabbed in the side of the kidney." He gently lifted the body to show Adam the ugly, narrow gash just above the hip on her right side. "Based on the amount of blood, I believe it was after the first laceration."

Adam let the images move through his mind as he considered this new information.

He slips out from behind the curtains and grabs her from behind, catching her as she's—probably—facing the door to the president's waiting room. Left hand over the mouth, he holds her tight and immobile as he uses his right hand to slit her throat, then, still holding her in a smothering grip, shoves the knife into her side.

"He had the knife in his hand. Wasn't going to drop it or put it in his pocket and he had to act quickly so she didn't make any sound or, somehow, struggle free. So he stabbed her again, holding the knife in her side to help keep her in place, and to quicken her death," Adam murmured.

Yes, it felt right.

Ugly, but right.

He blinked and looked at Hilton, waiting for more.

"I estimated earlier that the time of death would have been approximately eight or nine hours before the body was discovered. *Livor mortis*—the way the blood settles in the body after death, when the heart stops beating, and how quickly it does so," the doctor said, lifting a corner of the sheet to show Adam the dark reddish-purple bruiselike marks coloring the arch of the woman's back and underside of her thighs, "indicates a similar time frame.

"Of course, you understand, it's only an estimate, but between the lividity and the rigor mortis—when the body's muscles begin to tighten—from smaller to larger—and then release, I believe the time she died was between one o'clock and four o'clock this morning. The flies had time to become attracted, but, I don't think, not enough time to lay eggs. I'll do a closer look to be certain."

"That sort of wound would cause a very quick death," Adam said. "Within a few minutes. So that gives me a general idea of when the killer would have left the library." Though it was, unfortunately, a large chunk of time—and when no one would be in the corridor or up and about to witness anyone else who might be. Except Jim Lane, who'd slept in the hall.

"Yes. It wasn't an instant death, but I don't believe she suffered long." Hilton's gaze wandered back to Jane Thorne's body. "She has no other marks on her other than a few minor bruises, which would appear to be from the normal types of bumps she might get through daily life."

"She was dressed as a man. She was pretending to be a soldier. She'd purposely joined the Frontier Guard at the President's House. One of the men told me she approached him for that purpose."

"Yes. There's a bruise on the front of her shoulder where she would have taken the force of a rifle's recoil." Once again he peeled away the sheet to show Adam. "Seems to me it's fresh enough that she hasn't been firing a rifle very long. At least, regularly." He covered her up again. "Her feet are much too small for the boots she wore, but the blisters are fresh. She hadn't been wearing them long. I expect you'll want to look closely at her belongings to see if there's anything else you can learn."

Adam glanced over at the neat pile of clothing and worn boots. "I reckoned he'd just not grown into his feet yet," he said sadly. "But she never would have grown to fit in those boots."

"There's one more thing." Hilton's expression had gone bland once again. "She had recently . . . er . . . had relations." His voice was hardly above a whisper, and both of them couldn't help but glance toward the dividing curtain.

Adam drew in a long breath and expelled it slowly. His insides were in turmoil at the thought of what the poor young woman had endured. "Is there a way to know . . . was she—"

"Once I finish the examination, I'll know more," Hilton said, still keeping his voice low. "But there seems to be no indication she was forced. No bruising—at least, related to that."

They were silent for a moment, both looking at the shrouded figure.

"He wanted to make certain she died—and quickly," Hilton said after a moment. His voice was heavy with sorrow and disgust.

Adam felt the same way. "He couldn't take the chance of her

making any sounds that would alert anyone. Jim Lane—that's Senator Lane, newly arrived from Kansas—slept on guard in the hall outside the president's door all night. He didn't hear anything."

Hilton looked at him. "Either he is a very sound sleeper—which doesn't bode well for guard duty—or the killer, as you said, was very careful. Bold, but careful. But I reckon you're right—the blood marks look like a hand print right over her mouth."

"Lane's used to sleeping lightly and waking at the slightest noise. We fought against the pro-slavers in Kansas, and there wasn't anyone I'd trust more than him when it comes to security or leading men into battle."

"All right then. I can—if you like—scrape out what's beneath her fingernails, see what's under there besides dirt. Could be skin—if she was scratching at him, trying to fight him off while he killed her. Might tell us a little more about what happened."

"Skin. Under her fingernails," Adam said thoughtfully. Another form of tracks, left behind from the killer—or that she might have left on him while trying to defend herself. "That would be interesting. I reckon there might be other remnants caught on her fingers or beneath her nails too."

What if she'd scratched at the man's sleeve while fighting for her life, and there was a thread that had come loose? Or a piece of hair? He considered the body with new interest, then glanced at the pile of her belongings.

Adam had looked over the clothing of a murder victim during his previous investigation, but this time he'd do an even closer examination with an eye to finding a thread, perhaps, that could be matched to a coat—or a hair, or some other remnant left behind could help to identify not only the killer, but also the victim.

"Save everything you find—beneath her nails, or any stray hair or threads. No matter how small," he said, still musing over this interesting possibility. Animals left tracks and scat. They left remains from their kills, and residue in their dens or lairs. The distance between footprints and the height at which branches or grasses were broken or disturbed could tell the tracker an entire tale of what had gone on in a location.

And every tree, flower, bush, and grass spilled a trail of leaves, pollen, seeds—and often they clung to the feet and tails of the animals who passed by, dropping off or scattering with movement. As well, the makeup of a creature's scat or the bedding in its den could tell the history of where it had been and what it had eaten.

And the very air left dust and minute scatterings—if one knew where and how to look for it. He hadn't been exaggerating when he told Miss Gates he'd been taught to track an ant over a bed of stones. Not that it was an easy task, but he'd been able to do it on occasion.

With a rush of real interest, Adam realized the possibility was great that the killer—a far larger creature than a hare or fox—surely must have left *something* of himself behind. Not only a track and trail of his actions and movements, but also something that could help to identify him.

"All right, then. I'll save every little thing I find." Hilton glanced in the direction of the women. "What about Miss Lemagne?"

"I reckon I can't argue about me needing a drawing, especially now that we have a female victim. It wasn't my choice to have her here, but since she is, I suppose it'd be best to let her finish."

Hilton appeared to agree, though he said nothing. Instead, he turned to carefully adjusting the sheet so the body was swathed from chin to toe, hiding all evidence of violence—except for the blood marks over her face. The outlines of fingers, smudged but nonetheless obvious that the hand had been placed over her mouth before the blood splattered.

"Should I wash those marks away?" Hilton asked. "Before Miss Lemagne continues?"

Adam nodded, then brooded down at the young woman as the doctor cleaned the blood from her cheeks and jaw. Now that he knew the victim was female, he appreciated the femininity in her features. What he'd viewed as a young, beardless boy was much more recognizable as a young woman. "How old do you think she is?"

"Maybe twenty-two, twenty-three," Hilton replied, drying his hands. "Never carried a baby."

Adam nodded, still brooding. Why would a woman pretend to be a soldier? He had some ideas.

And why would a woman dress as a man in any case?

He gave a quiet sigh, then his mouth twitched a little. Well, he reckoned he knew one person he could ask about that.

The mood in the President's House was tense and sharp. Everyone seemed to be looking over their shoulders or jumping at the slightest unexpected noise. The servants moved about with worry furrowed between the brows, and the women in the household spoke in hushed whispers while casting furtive glances toward the windows—as if expecting to see lines of men marching up the hill toward the house, bayonets at the ready.

Amid this icy tension and her own fears and questions, Sophie spent almost two hours interviewing as many people as she could about whether they'd heard or seen anything the night before. She made notes to help her remember everything, and later, she would try to plot out a schedule of who was on the second floor and near the library during the night.

She began her interviews with the friends and relatives of Mary Lincoln herself, including Elizabeth Grimsley and several other female cousins who were staying at the White House. They gathered in the Red Room on the first floor, Mrs. Lincoln's favorite public parlor. Sophie could understand why it was a favorite, for the space was beautifully appointed with velvet carpet, gold damask furnishings, and ormolu clocks and statuettes. There was a large grand piano, and on the mantel were two ornate candelabra. The fireplace held only a small, smoldering fire, as the April weather was pleasant that day.

Sophie saw no sense in hiding the reason she needed to interview the ladies, for everyone in the house had heard the screaming when Leah had discovered Johnny Thorne. And although she tried to avoid answering questions about the state of the body, she knew she'd have to give up some gossip in order to get people to readily talk with her.

However, the ladies didn't have much to share. Nervous about the expected Confederate Army invasion, they'd all slept in the same large bedchamber on the second floor known as the Prince of Wales bedroom (except for Mrs. Lincoln, who'd shared her husband's bed). Sophie, who'd arrived at the White House after they'd settled in bed, had slept in one of the other, smaller bedrooms.

Although they'd talked and worried among themselves for a time, Mrs. Lincoln's guests agreed that everyone in their chamber had been asleep by midnight. Even if their slumber had been light and nervous, no one seemed to have heard anything out of the ordinary. And though Mrs. Grimsley and Mrs. Edwards didn't have any information for Sophie, they insisted on questioning her about everything related to the murder—so much so that she spent more time answering questions (or avoiding answering them) than she did asking them.

"Right here in the President's House," Mrs. Edwards, who was Mrs. Lincoln's older sister, said for at least the fifth time. "We could all have been murdered in our beds! Why, all those soldiers downstairs didn't do a *thing* to prevent it. How do they think they'll protect us when the Rebels come?"

There was discussion about whether they should remove themselves to the Willard, which would presumably be safer, until Sophie—with a bit of mischievous relish because she needed something to relieve the unbearable tension—said, "But don't you know, there was a plot to burn down that hotel last night. It was only narrowly prevented."

This sent the ladies off into other wild, conversational tangents, and Sophie used the opportunity to excuse herself. She slipped out of the Red Room and found herself in the main corridor of the first floor. A large screen made from ground glass separated the hallway from the vestibule and kept the weather from intruding on the rest of the house. There was a door in the center of the glass screen connected the vestibule to the corridor that led to the large, formal room.

She could hear raucous sounds from the East Room, where the Frontier Guard was barracked. It was the largest room in the entire mansion, taking up more than a third of the first floor, and had been the location of the single levee she'd attended at the White House. She could only imagine the state of the pale green Brussels carpeting—newly installed by Mrs. Lincoln—after sixty or seventy men camped out on it, night after night. Especially with their tobacco chewing.

How many nights would they need to be here?

Would tonight be the one when the Rebels came?

Sophie drew in a deep breath and set aside the thought. She could go back to the Smithsonian whenever she wanted—probably—but staying here meant she was not only an eye witness to whatever happened, but she could help Mr. Quinn with his investigation. Both of those options, though dangerous and unsettling, were also attractive to her as a journalist.

Surely, in some regard, the President's House was the safest place to be in a city that might be invaded by soldiers—even if it would be their target as well. Sophie would be very careful and very vigilant, but she would stay as long as she was allowed.

Last night when Mr. Quinn had brought her here, Sophie hadn't had much of an opportunity to notice the details of the president's home, dimly lit as it was—though she'd been properly breathless and awed at being inside the mansion. Though she'd been here once before, and had slept here overnight last night, today she still felt almost as if she'd ventured into a silent, most holy church: reverent and overwhelmed by the history and power of this "peoples' house."

Now, however, as she made her way along the first floor corridor, she noticed how shabby the rugs were, and how some of the paint and wallpaper peeled. There were tobacco stains on the carpet where visitors had missed the spittoons—or not cared to even find one.

When Sophie let herself through the door in the glass screen into the vestibule, she greeted the wrinkled Irish doorkeeper, Ed McManus, and asked for directions to the servant's stairs that led to the basement. He was happy to comply and directed her as requested. But before she started off, she asked, "Did you see anyone moving around last night after midnight, Mr. McManus?"

"Now, miss, sure and wasn't I off and sleeping just after eleven o'clock. But Thomas—he'd been sitting in the porter's lodge there. And wasn't he sleeping half the night, but he was in the chair and would've been the one to hear if someone come knocking. But after Mrs. Lander called at midnight, I didn't hear of no one coming anyway."

"Mrs. Lander came here? The actress?" Sophie was astonished. "At midnight?"

Old Ed had a gravelly voice that somehow fit his wrinkled face and diminutive persona. "Yes, she did. I don' know about her being an actress, like you're sayin', miss, but Thomas said as she was a fine-looking lady, and she's married to the colonel. That much I know."

Thomas Burns was McManus's assistant doorkeeper. "Do you know why she came here?" Sophie asked.

He didn't seem to mind answering her questions, though he had to pause a few times to open the door to allow more of the countless job-seekers, soldiers, or Cabinet members inside—and in such random order, some matched up with another in such a way as to be laughable. "Och, and wasn't Thomas sayin' how she had some information about a plot on the president."

"To do what—to kill him?"

"Well, that's what they're always talking about now, isn't it, miss? Killin' him, or stringin' him up or summat. Prolly ain't gonna end with jes' capturing him."

Sophie quelled a rush of apprehension and pity for Mr. Lincoln. She'd seen it countless times, but she still didn't understand such violent hatred one man could have against another.

"Where's Thomas now?"

"And ain't he off somewhere with those soldiers, watching them march with their rifles and them looking like nothing more than a pack of scraggly dogs," he replied with a shake of his head. "Don't see how they're about to protect any of us from the Rebels."

"All right then," she replied, unwilling to continue a conversation that was bound to heighten her own concerns about their safety.

It was cooler in the basement, and damp, darker, and filled with the smell of mildew and mustiness. Sophie managed to stifle a shriek—of surprise, certainly not fear, she told herself—as a rat bolted across the floor in front of her. But as she made her way from the bottom of the stairs, she heard the sounds of activity and conversation from the kitchen—along with the delicious smell of whatever was cooking.

Her stomach rumbled, and she realized her breakfast had been interrupted by the discovery of the body. Later, her task of keeping watch over the scene of the crime had also kept her from eating dinner at noon with the others. Sophie wondered if it would be permissible to ask for a piece of bread and an apple while she was speaking to the servants down here. In a way, it was strange living in such a grand house where there were servants everywhere. Especially the house of the president.

She could still hardly believe Mr. Quinn had brought her here.

And that she had slept *across the hall* from the President of the United States.

If only those condescending Knickerbockers from back home could see her now.

As soon as it came, Sophie blocked the thought of Peter and his family—the inestimable and revered Schuylers of Fifth Avenue—and the horrible scandal that had ended their engagement, causing her mortified parents to ship her off to Washington. There was no need to dwell on the past.

She found the kitchen easily. Located in the center of the ground floor of the president's mansion, it was a large, barn-like room with whitewashed walls and high, curved ceilings. There were two iron-barred windows set high in the walls, so that you couldn't see out them without standing on a chair.

When she stepped across the threshold, Sophie was shocked to find none other than Mary Lincoln herself in the kitchen, standing at the stove and stirring a large pot of something that smelled amazing. She was speaking to the cook, a light-skinned Negro who appeared to be several years older than Sophie, and two other kitchen workers. Leah, the maid who'd made the discovery of Johnny Thorne's body, was there as well.

All of them looked over at Sophie, and she had to fight the unfamiliar urge to curtsy in front of Mrs. Lincoln. *Drat.* It reminded her of the way Peter's Aunt Hildegard had made her feel.

"Are you in search of something to eat, Miss Gates?" asked the president's wife, handing her spoon to the cook. She didn't appear to be embarrassed about being discovered working in the kitchen—which was far more than Sophie could say for the snooty Aunt Hildegard.

"I don't recall seeing you at supper, Miss Gates," Mrs. Lincoln said, "but I suppose you've been busy helping Mr. Quinn and missed the meal. Mr. Lincoln told me about it all, and you were just speaking with my cousins, weren't you? What an awful business this is. All of it. *All* of it." Her voice rose to a higher, tense pitch, then she seemed to collect herself. "Cornelia, make sure this child gets something to eat."

"Yes, ma'am," replied the cook.

"Thank you, Mrs. Lincoln." Sophie still felt awkward about invading the kitchen, as well as finding the mistress of such a grand house actually cooking in it.

She didn't know Mary Lincoln at all, having merely shaken her hand at the Lincolns' first levee in March, and then met her again for another short moment last night when Mr. Quinn brought her here. And of course, there had been all sorts of gossip and tale-telling about the new First Lady: how she was a country bumpkin, how she put on airs, how she had a temper that was often punctuated by flying objects, how she was very well-read and intelligent "for a frontier woman," and more. There were also whispers that most of her family were abolitionists—including her cousin Martha Todd White. Mrs. White, who was from Alabama, had actually stayed in the White House during the inauguration festivities despite the fact that she *and* her husband had gone over to the side of the Secessionists.

Mrs. Lincoln's brothers, who had not been invited to Washington and never would be, according to Mrs. Grimsley, had already made their positions known as Confederate sympathizers and pro-slavers. Mary Lincoln's opinion was that her "brothers have made their choices—deciding against my husband, and through him, against me. Whatever happens shall happen."

But the Mrs. Lincoln facing Sophie at the moment was kind and at ease—if not a bit nervous about the impending invasion—and if the gossip about her was anything more than that from spiteful women, or powerful men who disliked her influence with the president, it was not apparent to Sophie. In fact, she could empathize with her in some ways.

The older woman was short and tending to stoutness, but she had a good-humored, round face. Her dark hair was parted in the middle and smoothed back into a sleek collection of knots and braids. Worry limned her eyes and bracketed her mouth with lines, but her demeanor was smooth.

"Thank you, Cornelia," said Mrs. Lincoln. "I don't know what we're to do about meals for all of those rough men, sleeping in the East Room. Perhaps they'll cook some of their meals over the fireplace up there. And the way they're spitting all over, staining the carpet!" Her voice rose a bit again, and she sighed heavily. "But we cannot be without them. Mr. Lincoln wants to send me away with the boys, but I *will not* go." The flash of stubbornness and fire in her eyes reminded Sophie of her own determination.

"Yes, Madam," said the cook.

"I'd best see if there is any news about the troops trying to come through Baltimore," said Mrs. Lincoln, wiping her hands on the apron she'd donned to protect her blue-sprigged lawn skirts. "Mr. Lincoln has been worried about it all the day. And those Confederates invading us here! And now this terrible thing in the library."

The mistress of the house, clearly overwhelmed by tension and anxiousness, took her leave just as one of the kitchen assistants offered Sophie a small tray. It held a small bowl of soup, a hunk of bread, and a slightly-bruised, beginning-to-wrinkle apple left over from the autumn store.

"Thank you so much," Sophie replied. "I'm hungry, but I didn't come here only for food." She looked at Leah. "As you know, I'm helping Mr. Quinn. I need to speak with anyone who had to work on the second floor yesterday or last night. Especially anyone besides you, Leah, who had work to do in the library—or who might've been around very early this morning or very late last night."

"Well, miss, there are the lamplighters who come around every evening and see to the lamps in each room, then they come through and turn them off at nine o'clock and light the candles if need be. It's Bill who does for the rooms on the second floor."

Sophie's mouth was watering as the scent of the beefy stew teased her. "If I could speak with Bill, that would be a good start. And whoever was the last person to go into the library yesterday. If you could help me determine who that is, that would be helpful. We're trying to discover whether anyone saw Johnny Thorne or his killer during the night."

Leah seemed eager to help, and, thankfully, she took Sophie to the servants dining room where she could sit and speak to each of them as she ate. It was a cramped room that held the scent of mildew, as well as that of smoke and food. Though the space was adequate, there was a scarred table so large there was hardly enough space for the chairs around it. Sophie took a seat with her tray at one end.

"I was surprised to see Mrs. Lincoln down here," she said as Leah brought her a mug of sage-and-mint steeped water.

"Oh, the Madam, she come down often. She like to cook, she says, and she misses doing for her family. Miss Cornelia says it ain't often the mistress even knows anything about the cooking or kitchen, but the Madam did so long for Mr. Lincoln and them boys that she knows all about it. She even tells Miss Cornelia how to find the best meats, and what a good vegetable looks like."

Sophie's hunger pangs had eased a bit now that she'd sipped several bites of soup and dunked a corner of the bread hunk. "Thank you. Now, you said Bill would come through and light the lamps on the second floor—about what time? And then he came back through at nine o'clock?"

"Yes, miss. The lamps get lit right when the sun is getting to the tops of the trees over yonder, and then at nine o'clock, they get turned off. That's when I draw the curtains, miss."

"And that would be the last time anyone entered the library?"

"Unless Mr. Lincoln did. He likes to sit in there with a candle and read his books. Want I should find Bill now?"

"Yes, thank you, Leah. And I do want to talk to every one of the servants." Sophie set down the sheaf of papers on which she'd been penciling notes.

"All of us?" Leah's eyes went wide. "We are thirty-four, miss."

"Yes, all thirty-four of you. Perhaps I should speak with the housekeeper and explain."

"Oh, miss, there is no housekeeper. Only a steward and butler, Mr. Brown. The Madam sees to everything herself."

Sophie hid her surprise; but that made things easier, as Mrs. Lincoln obviously knew and supported her task. "Well, then, I suppose I must rely on you to help me so that I speak to everyone. At least, everyone who works in the house."

That turned out to be only twenty-one servants, including Mr. McManus and his assistant Thomas Burns.

Bill, who was a tall, light-skinned Negro with a smooth gait, was the first to enter the dining room. "Yes, miss," he said when Sophie told him to sit. "You're wanting to know about when I was in the family room. The library."

She nodded, and he continued. "I lit all the lamps up there yesterday at half-five. That's when the shadows fall and the rooms get darker, you see. Every night, the chandeliers get lit by a gas lamp

I raise up on a tall hook. And for the small lamps, there goes a tube from the fitting in the wall to the lamp, and we light it with a match."

"But the gas lamps go off at nine o'clock, and you have to go back around to the rooms. Was that the last time you were in the library?"

"Yes, miss. The gas come from a pipe down from Capitol Hill, from the gas company. They shut down at nine o'clock, so the gas stops then. I go back to all the rooms on the second floor and light candles just before then."

"Was there anyone in the library when you went in there before nine?"

"No, miss. Only Leah, who was drawing the curtains. Only there was some blocks and a toy cart left there by Mr. Tad and Mr. Willie. I helped her put them in the cupboard so no one would step on them. Them corners of the blocks hurt your feet, even through the shoes."

Sophie smiled. "I can imagine that. Did you go back to the library at all last night? Or to any other room on the second floor?"

"Only at maybe half-ten, miss. Mr. Lincoln rung the bell. He was wanting a new candle. But he was still in his office with Mr. Nicolay and that Mr. Lane come from Kansas. He wasn't in the library, miss."

"After that, where did you go?"

"I went to bed, miss. Down here. Didn't go anywhere else till Mr. Brown roused me at dawn."

"Peter Brown, the butler?"

"Yes, miss. And he does the waiting on the family at dinner time, and other steward jobs."

"Thank you," Sophie said, and dismissed the young man. She scribbled a few notes as she waited for the next servant to come in.

The next two hours she spent in the cramped space talking to the maids, footmen, steward, and other workers. She made notes of their names and regular duties, and who had access to the second floor and who didn't. The occasional ringing of bells in the kitchen or the hallway made a pleasant chiming sound, though

Sophie admitted that it might not be quite so pleasant to the servants being summoned to upper parts of the house, interrupted from whatever task they might currently be doing—including sleeping.

One of the kitchen maids had just appeared to take Sophie's tray when the sounds of an excited conversation came in from the hallway.

"Can't know why would someone put a good piece of clothing in the furnace bin like—By the saints, Mae! Will you look at this?"

"That looks like blood. Sure is, that's blood on that coat."

"And all over it, it is. Still don't need to be throwing the likes of it in the bin when it could be—"

"Blood?" Sophie shoved back from the table and pushed her way between chairs and wall out to the hallway.

Two maids were standing there, just outside the elliptical furnace room, which was located next to the base of the curved South portico.

"I can put it in the laundry," said the one with strawberry blond hair as they inspected what appeared to be a long, weather-beaten coat. "Scrub it clean enough if I'm puttin' me elbows into it. Looks like it'd fit Tommy good."

"May I see that?" Sophie asked. The two maids—Mae, and Bridget was the Irish one with the strawberry hair—looked up.

"Miss Gates." Bridget, who appeared to have discovered the bundle, looked from the article of clothing to Sophie, and then comprehension settled over her features as she realized why the other woman was interested. "Someone tried to hide—or throw out—this coat."

"There's blood on it," Mae said unnecessarily, then her eyes widened too. "Blood. From the killer." She shoved her half of the bundle toward Sophie.

Or, more accurately, Sophie thought, blood from Johnny Thorne.

"Where exactly did you find this?" She gave the coat a shake and held it up in front of her.

It was a man's coat—not a top coat or a fancy frock like businessmen or politicians wore in the city, but a canvas one lightly oiled to keep the weather and elements off. It was the type of garment worn by the gold miners or farmers—or frontiersmen, and it would fit a man much larger than Johnny Thorne.

And sure enough, there were dark stains all over the front of it, and along the underside and front of the coat sleeves.

A cold shiver took her by surprise as she realized she was holding—she *had* to be holding—the clothing of a killer.

A killer who'd been, and likely still was, in the White House.

CHAPTER 7

*I*T WAS AFTER TWO O'CLOCK BY THE TIME ADAM RETURNED TO THE President's House from George Hilton's office.

He'd decided to leave the bundle that included Jane Thorne's belongings at the doctor's workshop. Not only did he have no place to put them for safekeeping at the White House, but he also didn't have the time to examine them as closely as he needed to. There were other, more desperate matters at the moment.

Members of the Frontier Guard were visible outside the White House in various states of marching and military drills. Adam saw some on the roof of the house, standing guard with their rifles and bayonets, and others were positioned around the exterior of the house. As he approached, giving the password when asked, he looked up and saw the much smaller heads of the Lincoln boys. They were up on the roof, marching back and forth, carrying bayonets of wood.

At least, Adam assumed they were made from wood. One never knew with Tad Lincoln—or his parents, who were surprisingly permissible with him and his older brother.

The moment Old Ed opened the door for him, Adam felt the tension permeating the very air of the mansion. The house was strangely quiet, and even the line of job-seekers—though present—seemed more subdued than before.

Twilight would soon be nigh, and with it, the fear of invasion and the reality that war was here on their doorstep.

Adam hurried up the small, informal set of stairs most often used by the servants. When he entered onto the corridor of the second floor, he brushed past the line of people waiting to see the president, ignoring the two of them who tried to catch his attention. The single guard outside Lincoln's office allowed him entrance without hesitation. Inside, he found Lane, the three secretaries, General Scott, Major Hunter, and Secretary Cameron with the president. He was mildly surprised to see Scott there, because his gout had become so painful Lincoln usually came down to meet him so the elderly general didn't have to climb the stairs.

As before, the bleak expressions of the men in the room spoke volumes and Adam wondered if there'd been some further bad news.

"The Massachusetts regiment is trying to repair the railroad so they can finish their journey here," Cameron was saying. "But the mob in Baltimore injured so many that there aren't enough able-bodied men to work quickly. The Rebels will be looking at us, sitting here without an army to speak of, and they'll come in."

"Ballycock. I told McCruder just yesterday—Washington as a city isn't easily defensible," Scott said stoutly. "Why would the Rebels risk coming in and taking the city, then have to protect it? I told him then, and I say it now. I don't believe Washington is in danger."

Lincoln was standing at one of the tall windows that over-looked the mall and the Smithsonian Castle. Beyond were visible the soft, green hills of Alexandria and its surroundings, where Southern troops were gathering. Adam could even see—so certainly the president could as well—the plantation home owned by Robert E. Lee.

Only yesterday, the brilliant Colonel Lee had been offered the generalship of the Union Army. He demurred, stating that he could never fire upon, nor lead a charge upon, his own state of Virginia—though he disagreed with the idea of secession.

His polite declination and subsequent quitting of the city was nevertheless underscored by the flag of his new commission—the

Stars and Bars of the Confederacy—which fluttered from the top of his home, distinguishable from Lincoln's office.

It was, in Adam's mind, a blunt, unnecessary smack in the face of the president as well as the Union itself.

"Well, now, if I were Beauregard," said the president, breaking in after a long silence, "I reckon *I'd* take Washington. Immediately and without hesitation. While our trousers are down around our ankles, so to speak." He turned from the window. "And so that's what we prepare for. Imminent invasion."

"If they don't let our troops come through Baltimore, by God, I'll raze the damned city," Lane said, a wild glint in his eye. "Send the Marylanders that message, sir. I've got enough Jayhawkers here to burn the city to the ground. They won't mess with us. They've got to let the regiments from the North through."

Lincoln looked at him, shaking his head. "Now, I can't let you do that, Jim. Maryland is hanging Union by a thread. If she secedes—and I reckon if there's any show of force from Washington, it'll put her over the line to the South—we're trapped worse than a rabbit in a foxhole."

Lane looked as if he were about to argue, his dark gaze flashing with fury, but he held his tongue and gave a sharp, acquiescent nod.

"Is there any news on the men who were injured on their way through Baltimore?" asked the president as if Hunter hadn't just spoken about it. Clearly, his mind was filled with far too many things. "Are we expecting them soon?"

"A scout came on ahead with the news they are traveling, but slowly, sir, due to injuries. And they bring four dead with them. They hope to be here before nightfall, as they are repairing the railroad tracks in stretches as they travel on them." Scott looked out the window as if hoping to see a sign of the troops, though he was facing the wrong direction.

"All right then. I reckon the only thing left to do is drill your men, Major Hunter, and recruit as many more as you can scrape up there, Senator Lane. You too, Adam. If the Rebels come, I reckon they'll come tonight or tomorrow before reinforcements arrive."

Adam couldn't disagree. He'd decided to save for later the brief report he meant to give the president regarding Jane Thorne when Lincoln looked at him suddenly. Eyes that had been faraway with contemplation and worry sharpened a bit.

"Is there anything of importance I should know about Thorne?"

"Only one thing for the moment, Mr. President. The rest... well, I reckon it can wait."

Wait for what, Adam didn't want to specify. Either they'd live through the attack by the Confederates or they wouldn't. And though he wouldn't forget his responsibility to the dead woman, at the moment he must help focus on the living—and keeping them that way.

Including and perhaps most important, the admirable man who'd taken on such an impossible, heart-wrenching job. Difficult enough to lead a country at war, Adam reflected soberly... but he reckoned it was beyond hell when that war was a violent rupturing of the country itself.

"What is it, then, Adam?" There was a rare testiness in Lincoln's tone.

"We've discovered that Johnny Thorne is a woman." As he said this, Adam glanced at Jim Lane. There was no flare of surprise in his expression, though everyone else in the room including the president made utterances of shock over this revelation.

He knew.

Although Lane subsequently reacted, joining the others expressing their disbelief at the idea of a woman pretending to be a soldier, it was clear that it had been no surprise to Jim Lane that Johnny Thorne was a woman.

Why didn't he tell me?

Adam answered the ensuing questions briefly, and was more relieved than he should have been when the rest of the president's Cabinet arrived for their three o'clock meeting. As Lincoln prepared to move to the large table in the anteroom where the cabinet met, Lane excused himself.

Adam did the same, and would have confronted his friend right then about the mystery of Jane Thorne and why Lane hadn't seen fit to correct the mistake about her gender, but Major Hunter strode out with them.

"There won't be anyone easily arriving on the train," said the major grimly. "The mob in Baltimore will make sure of it. Even if the Sixth Massachusetts fixes it enough to travel on, they'll tear it up again. And the Rebels have set a blockade at Harper's Ferry, so no supplies or reinforcements can come by ship either. They're gathering in Alexandria, and surely they'll cross over either tonight or tomorrow night."

"By my count, we've got the barely one hundred men we've mustered here in the White House, and Clay's other hundred at the Willard. There's nearly six hundred more at the Capitol, counting some stragglers and the Pennsylvania regiment—and that's all we've got to withstand two thousand or more Confederates." Lane's expression had taken on the feral, almost fanatic look Adam knew well. His dark eyes glittered, and the uncombed mess of his hair and two-day stubble contributed to the wild look. "Lincoln won't let us go in and teach the Rebels in Baltimore a lesson, so we'll have to do it here."

"How do you propose we do that in a city that can't be defended with a mere six hundred men?" Hunter replied warily. "Against their thousands?"

Adam hid a grin. David Hunter wasn't used to the scrappy, lawless type of war they'd fought in Kansas, and his skepticism in the face of Lane's optimism was understandable. But the Southerners who'd fought them in Kansas were familiar with the fierce Jayhawkers and their leader. If nothing else, their reputation would put the fear of God into the Rebels.

"Well, I reckon I'll go down to the St. Charles and have a whiskey, and I'll put it out that my friend General Lane is preparing to take his wild Kansas fighters and attack Alexandria tonight," Adam replied. "The pro-slavers know what to expect from the frontier fighters, and they'll spread the word."

Lane gave a little laugh. "Those Johnny Rebs'll be pissing in their pants over that. Should give them a sleepless night. You do that, Adam, and I'll get all the men moving around more in the yard, and in and out of the house here. Make it look like we've got a bigger army than we do, and impossible for anyone to count to be sure."

Hunter nodded, still wary but now displaying a little hope in his expression. "There isn't much else we can do but that, and wait for the troops to get here." He gritted his teeth and sucked in a breath. "If we get through the next two or three days, it'll be a goddamned miracle."

A little after five o'clock that Friday evening, the train finally rolled into Washington City from Baltimore. Thousands of people had gathered at the depot for the Baltimore & Ohio Railroad, excited to see the arrival of the battered regiment from Boston.

Sophie had walked to the Smithsonian in order to gather a new set of clothing and to see whether her uncle had returned. It didn't appear he'd done so, but she left a note for him in case he did. She didn't want him to worry needlessly in case he heard from Aunt Harriet that she wasn't with them.

She was on her way back to the President's House when the train whistle caught her attention as the cars approached the city. Caught up in the excitement and relief that the track was working, and that the armed troops had finally made it from Boston, she joined the crowd at the depot and found herself cheering among the smoke and ashes spewed by the engine as it rolled to a halt.

It reminded her, though on a much smaller scale, of the massive celebration a few years ago in New York City when the first telegraphic cable had been laid down across the Atlantic Ocean. Over a million people thronged the streets and were filled with excitement over the news. Unfortunately, the cable stopped working after only 366 messages, and a new one had not yet been laid.

Sophie hoped the reminder wasn't a portent of things to come here as well.

Nearly all of the two hundred soldiers of the Sixth Massachusetts were injured in some manner, and many had difficulty making their way down from the high steps of the boxcar. There were others being brought off the train on stretchers, which tilted alarmingly as those who were wounded themselves attempted to care for their comrades.

A line of hackney cabs were already filled with passengers, leaving an even greater number of injured soldiers without transportation.

"Oh, we must help them," said a dark-haired woman standing nearby. "They don't even have bandages!" She began to push her way through the crowd toward the disembarking soldiers.

Sophie followed, slinging the valise with her clothing over an arm.

The next thing she knew, she had put aside all thoughts about the murder of Johnny Thorne and the bloody clothing that belonged to his killer, and was helping a young man who'd been hit in the thigh by a heavy piece of scrap metal flung at him during the riot. His trousers were torn and stained with dark blood, some of it still shiny, and he could put little weight on his leg because a horse had also stepped on his foot during the melee.

Without hesitation, Sophie wrapped her arm around his waist and said, "Lean on me, soldier." She looked over and saw the woman who'd started the effort assisting another man to walk. "Where do we take them, miss?"

"The infirmary is on E Street," replied the dark-haired woman who somehow had taken charge. "Near City Hall. This way."

"I never thought to see the day when I'd need to lean on a pretty woman to get where I was going," said the man as he allowed Sophie to help him along. His voice was tight with what she realized was pain, and she felt his muscles bunching as he tried to keep himself from putting too much weight on her. "I'm sorry about this, miss."

"Not at all. What's your name, soldier?" she asked. "And you mustn't injure yourself further. I'm stronger than I appear; you can lean on me more heavily."

"Thank you, miss," he said. "My name is Heath Eldritch, and though I don't want to crush you, I'm much obliged for your help."

"It's the least I can do to thank you for your bravery in Baltimore—and for supporting the Union. I'm Miss Sophie Gates. I'm only recently here from New York City." She thought it might be best for her to talk so he didn't feel obliged to make conversation as they paced their way north on New Jersey Avenue up to E Street.

"Good for Massachusetts!" shouted someone as they trudged past. "Long save the Union!"

"Bunker Hill is not forgotten!" cried another relieved soul.

"Thank God Massachusetts has not forgotten the Union," said an elderly man as Sophie and her charge passed nearby. "Thank you, sir!"

Those of the regiment who were able to marched south to the Capitol in neat rows, carrying whatever weapons and supplies they'd been able to retain during the riot. The people who'd greeted the soldiers at the depot now spilled along either side of New Jersey Avenue, cheering and waving them on as the bedraggled soldiers made their way two blocks and up to the Capitol. Their troop's military band had been lost during the riot—their instruments stolen or destroyed—and it was an odd, almost eerie experience to see a conflagration of soldiers marching without their band.

Sophie assisted Mr. Eldritch, walking with the other injured men and those assisting them, as well as the six who were carried on stretchers. They made their way northwest to the Washington Infirmary instead of to the Capitol, but received no less an enthusiastic welcome from those gathered to watch.

"I've only been in Washington for about eight weeks," she said, working to keep her voice from sounding out of breath as he leaned more heavily on her. Blood from his injury now stained her skirt, and with every step, she felt the young man grimace with pain. She gave up trying to talk, focusing on taking as much weight as possible while managing her small valise with the change of clothing she'd gone to fetch from home.

Mr. Eldritch, who she guessed was about the same age as she—twenty-one—was neither a particularly slender man nor a stout one. He was dressed in black pantaloons and a civilian cap, but like a handful of others in his regiment, wasn't yet wearing the official uniform of a dark gray coat. He carried a rucksack over his shoulder that had shifted and settled in the crevice between their torsos so that Sophie felt its weight bump against her with every labored step.

By the time they reached the infirmary, she was out of breath and damp with perspiration, and her corset felt even more tight and restrictive than usual. She'd managed not to trip over her skirt and crinoline, but the hems were dark with mud. And her valise had bumped against her hip the entire way. She'd surely have a bruise by tomorrow.

Nonetheless, Sophie was happy to have been able to assist Mr. Eldritch, for he could not have made it on his own. And what sort of welcome would it have been to these loyal troops if they'd been left at the depot waiting for a conveyance to return—or, worse, each had been required to make his own way? She was filled with admiration for the dark-haired woman who had taken the initiative and organized the crowd to step in and assist.

Inside the infirmary, they were directed to an empty bed in the long line of white-sheeted cots in the ward. The place was loud with activity and bustling with movement, as this was the first significant influx of wounded soldiers to arrive—of what Sophie realized would likely be many.

Because she read a vast number of newspapers from a variety of cities, in both the North and South, she was not of the opinion shared by so many that the war would be over in a month or two. Each side was determined—and assumed—to be the victor, but yet cloistered by its own certainty that it would easily raze the other.

"I'm much obliged, Miss Gates," said Mr. Eldritch as she placed her valise on the floor, then helped settle him on the cot.

The infirmary was sufficiently lit with gas lamps on the walls, and Sophie wondered briefly whether they, like those at the White House, would go out at nine o'clock when the gas company shut down for the evening. The ward to which they'd been directed smelled of antiseptic and the scents of unwashed bodies, blood, and other bodily fluids.

She looked around and saw that there weren't enough attendants to see to each soldier immediately, and that no one would be available to examine Mr. Eldritch soon, as his injuries weren't as severe or life-threatening as some others. The dark-haired woman who'd organized the effort was assisting her charge onto the next bed over, and Sophie heard her say something about getting bandages and water.

She turned back to Mr. Eldritch and said, "I'm going to remove your boot so when the doctor comes, he can take a look at it." He nodded, then gritted his teeth as she carefully adjusted his injured leg flat on the bed, then expelled a rush of breath as she carefully began to loosen the boot from its lacings, gingerly working around his smashed foot.

"Where are you from?" she asked, hoping to distract him from the pain.

"Lowell," he grunted. "Massachusetts." He hissed out a breath as she finally pulled away the boot, revealing a gray stocking and a misshapen foot.

As Sophie well knew, in any other circumstance, it would have been highly improper and somewhat uncomfortable for her, a young, unmarried woman, to be removing clothing from a man—especially one she didn't know—but this was an extenuating situation. And as Sophie kept glancing covertly at the female organizer, she saw that the other woman was doing the same thing in assisting her charge to be comfortable. She didn't seem to give a thought to what anyone might think or whether it was scandalous; she just did it.

And so Sophie willingly followed suit.

There was no blood staining Mr. Eldritch's stocking, and although Sophie wasn't a trained medical professional, she had had some experience with treating injuries during the course of her life. She glanced at the bloody wound that still seeped and realized she would need to find a clean bandage.

"And what do you do in Lowell, Mr. Eldritch?" she asked, carefully rolling down his stocking.

"I work at the livery my father owns," replied her charge. His voice wasn't quite as tight now, likely because his poor foot was no longer compressed by its boot. "Twenty years tending to horses day in and day out, and never had my foot stepped on a once." He tried out a smile, and it worked as a wry comment on the situation. "Are you a nurse, Miss Gates?"

The stocking was removed, revealing his broken, mottled skin. She'd never seen a man's bare foot before, but it wasn't particularly shocking—except for the dark, purple-blue bruising over a third of it. The flesh was hot and taut with swelling, which was part of the reason removing his boot had been helpful in relieving the pain.

"No, I'm not a nurse," she replied. "But even I can see that you're in need of a bandage, and some washing away of that blood."

She wasn't certain whether she should go so far as to completely cut away the fabric of his trousers in order to fully expose the wound, which was high on his thigh. But she could at least clean it up and pull away the blood crusted material that had begun to dry against the wound. Looking around to see where to get a small basin of water and bandages, Sophie stood, then made her way down the row of beds to fetch the supplies.

When she returned with a small bowl containing a bare half-inch of water—all that was available, for so many needed it—a small bandage, and a cup of water for him to drink, she said to Mr. Eldritch, "Do you want to talk about what happened in Baltimore?"

The journalist side of her was curious, and it would keep his attention fixed while she dabbed away at the injury on his thigh. She handed him the mug to drink, then turned her attention to his torn leg. The wound was raw and glistened with dark blood, and she fancied she saw the white marble of bone revealed deep within the striations of red flesh, muscle, and whatever else was beneath the skin.

Feeling a little ill, Sophie averted her eyes and thoughts from the possibility that she was seeing *bone* down in there, and tried to ignore the stench of blood as well as other smells—waste, sweat, fear—that filled the room. She'd seen the remnants of violence and injury, but she wasn't immune to it.

"We got to Baltimore on the train from Philadelphia, and then we had to transfer to the other station in the city for the train that would take us here to Washington." Still gripping the cup she'd given him, which was now empty, he closed his eyes as he settled back on the cot. "Normally, the train cars get pulled by horses through the streets for about a mile from one station to the other, and the first several cars managed to get through before the mob waiting for us became too big and violent. But by the time ours came up—we were in the seventh rail car—the horse masters had given up and the mob was getting more excited, and so we had to march on foot.

"We could ignore the name calling and the jeering and even the spitting, Miss Gates," he said, his hazel eyes earnest. "It wasn't that. It was when those Seceshes in Baltimore started pulling up bricks and stones from the street and throwing them at us that it got worse. Calling us traitors!" He shook his head on the flat pillow, his eyes shocked and angry now. "*They* were the traitors—attacking government soldiers as they were! And crying for secession!

"Then someone from the crowd fired a shot into our regiment, and then some of us fired back. Next thing, there was everything being thrown—stones, pieces of metal, horse shi—beg your pardon, miss, horse dung—and so many of us were hurt. On both sides." His voice faded away as he settled into silence. "I reckon that was only the beginning of it."

"It must have been terrible," she said, dipping the cloth into what was left of the stingy water in the bowl. Both the cloth and the water were now tinted pink, but his wound looked a little better. She'd pulled the torn pieces of trouser away from the injury, using the water to dampen the blood that had crusted the fabric to his skin over the last few days. "And frightening."

"Not so much frightening," he said stoutly, "but shocking. How can men and women attack their own countrymen like that?"

Sophie shook her head. That was a question that would likely be asked countless times over the next days, weeks, and months. Surely it wouldn't be years.

"The infirmary needs more bandages," said the dark-haired woman who'd been working next to them. "They've run out already. And they don't have enough blankets."

She'd helped her charge take off his shirt to reveal an ugly, circular wound in his arm that appeared to be from a bullet, and now looked at Sophie and Mr. Eldritch. "I'm going to go get some from home. And some food and water for these men. Mr. Martin says they've hardly eaten since yesterday."

"I'll go as well," Sophie said. There were many supplies she could get from the apartment at the Smithsonian. No one was there, and whatever was useful could be brought here to the infirmary. She turned to Mr. Eldritch. "Is there anything you need?" New stockings for one, she guessed, and trousers as well.

"No, miss, I'm going to be just fine," he said stoutly. "Won't be long before I'm lining up to go fight them Rebels."

Sophie smiled and bid him farewell, then caught up with the dark-haired woman as she left the infirmary.

"Thank you for organizing everything as you did," Sophie told her as they walked out of the place. The Capitol rose on its hill ahead of them to the south, a proud and dominant symbol of what those soldiers were fighting for. And yet its state of partial construction made a poignant statement—as if to remind one that the Union itself was imperfect and in disrepair.

"Every time I see that unfinished dome, I think it looks like a hoop skirt frame only half covered with crinolines and skirts," said her companion with a short laugh. "I look at it every day on my way to my job."

"Where do you work?" Sophie asked, expecting her to give the name of a shop or private household.

"I work at the Patent Office," she replied. "I believe I was the first woman ever hired there. And even now there aren't many of us women with jobs in the government."

"Why, that's amazing! However did you manage to convince them to hire you?"

She smiled, revealing a few charming dimples. "I'm not quite certain. Persistence, I suppose. But when President Buchanan was elected, my position was eliminated and I moved back to North Oxford, Massachusetts, until the job came back. North Oxford is my family hometown, and that's why I knew some of those soldiers who came in on the train. I just couldn't leave them there struggling," she said, sobering. "Incidentally, I'm Clara Barton. And I want to thank you for stepping in and helping me right away. Once you did, some of the other ladies did as well."

"Of course. I'm Sophie Gates. I live at the Smithsonian Castle. Joseph Henry is my uncle."

"It's a pleasure to meet you—is it Miss?—Gates."

"Yes it is." Sophie paused, gesturing toward the spires of the castle, which rose from behind the hotels, shops, and houses they passed as they walked down E Street. "I'll go back to my family's apartment and get whatever I can find. They've all left the city, so they won't miss anything. What do you think is most needed right now, Miss Barton?" She wasn't certain whether the title was correct, or whether the woman was married (that was why it was helpful when someone was there to make introductions, Sophie thought). Clara Barton was about twenty years older than Sophie, but she wasn't wearing a wedding ring.

"Bandages and food, I expect. I heard the matron say that there were provisions enough for the soldiers who made it to the Capitol, where they're to sleep, but not enough there in the infirmary. But I would expect some of them will also need clothing to replace that which was damaged, and more blankets as well."

"Then that's what I'll gather up to bring," Sophie replied. "Would you like to come with me? It would be far easier with two carrying supplies than one."

Miss Barton gave a shy smile. "I would very much like to. I have always been fascinated by the Smithsonian Institute, and although I've been in the public areas, there is obviously much more to see. It must be quite strange and exciting to live in a castle."

"It is the most interesting place I've ever lived," Sophie replied as they began to walk together. "I've been here in Washington only since late February."

"Where did you live before?" asked Miss Barton. "If it's permissible for me to ask."

Sophie smiled. "Of course it is. New York City."

"Such a busy place. Did you like it there?"

Although Miss Barton didn't ask what had brought her to Washington, Sophie found herself elaborating. "I did. It was a very exciting city; always something happening. And so many people! But there was a bit of a . . . well, a—a disruption in our plans, I suppose one could call it . . . and my parents thought it might be a nice change for me to visit my uncle." Sophie's cheeks warmed. "Disruption" was a very mild word to describe what had happened. And her parents had been trying to save *their* reputation more than giving her a "nice change" by sending her off for a "visit."

Banishment was probably a better term.

"How long do you plan to be here in Washington, with the war coming, then?"

Sophie gave her a little smile, though she had a twinge of sadness inside. "Indefinitely, I hope. At this time, I've no desire to return to New York—even if my Uncle Joseph is a Southern sympathizer and I am a confirmed Loyalist." That, at least, was the bald truth.

And Miss Barton seemed to appreciate her position, for she smiled back and gave her an affirmative nod.

Somewhere, a clock struck seven. The sun had just set, and although there was still a comfortable glow spilling over the patch of land called the National Mall, the shadows were long and Sophie knew it would soon be dark. But the street lamps had been lit, and it seemed as if the arrival of the regiment from Massachusetts had brought many people out from behind shuttered doors and windows, enlivening the city once more.

Still, as they made their way across the Canal to Maine Avenue, Sophie couldn't help but look toward the Long Bridge. When she noticed several patches of flickering firelight on the Virginia shore, she felt the nervousness she'd suppressed for a time return.

As if reading her thoughts, Miss Barton said, "Are you fearful of an attack on the city? And you—surely you aren't staying in the Castle all alone?" Her voice rose with concern. "You said your family had gone."

"Everyone says it's only a matter of when, not if, the Confederates come," Sophie replied. "So, yes, I suppose I'd be foolish not to be a little fearful. Or more than a little," she added. "I'm not staying at my home right now. A—er—friend invited me to stay with them, and I'm safe with many other people."

She wasn't certain whether she should mention any of the details about Mr. Quinn's invitation, or about the happenings at the White House. "I went home to get a change of clothing," she added, gesticulating with her valise. "And then I got caught up in all of the excitement with the arrival of the train."

By now, they were nearly to the red sandstone building. It had eight towers, and between its flagrantly gothic architecture and the fact that it was not constructed of the same white marble as every other governmental building in the city, the castle certainly drew the eye—some more appreciative than others. Beyond, the Long Bridge arched across the Potomac, and the sounds of tromping feet and jangling bridles filtered through the twilight.

Miss Barton slowed. "The Rebels . . . is that them? Coming across the bridge?" Her voice, though soft, lifted to a higher pitch.

Sophie hesitated, then continued on. They were nearly to the private door used by the Henrys to access their tower apartment. "I believe those are Union men. See, they are gathering at the edge of the bridge and marching back across now. They did that much of the night last night. But the sooner we're inside, the better, I think."

She unlocked the door and stepped into the foyer of the East Tower, where she took up the lantern hanging by the doorway. After lighting it, she led the way up the stairs to the five-room apartment she shared with Uncle Joseph, Aunt Harriet, and their three daughters.

It didn't take long for the two women to pack up some old petticoats and handkerchiefs, along with a sheet, that could be used for bandages. Sophie also found several blankets that had been packed away for guests. She considered her valise for a moment, then upended its contents on her bed and used the satchel to pack the donations for the soldiers. She could always come back later for her clothing.

"There's another place I intend to look for clothing and bandages," she told Miss Barton, handing her the bulging valise. "You said you wanted to see some of the private areas of the castle—well, follow me."

Sophie led her mystified companion down to the main floor of the institute, then, still shining the way with the lantern, she took them up another set of stairs to the North Tower.

"This is where the naturalists who catalog all of the specimens for the institute stay when they're in residence," she told Miss Barton as she opened the door to what was obviously the realm of multiple bachelors. "Uncle Joseph allows them to board here free of charge between their trips, in exchange for their work for the museum."

"That's very kind of him." Miss Barton was looking around the apartment, which consisted of a large sitting room that sprawled into a second chamber.

Sophie gave a little chuckle. Considering how much work the naturalists did for the Smithsonian, only in exchange for a place to sleep, she thought her uncle probably got the better end of the deal.

From the doorway, one could see four of the beds lined up in the second chamber. In both rooms, books, bottles, papers, and half-burned candles littered every surface. An inkwell had been knocked over on a nearby table, but it must have been empty, for there was no accompanying stain. Several pencils and sketches had accumulated on another table's surface, and there were two pairs of boots on the floor.

The chamber, though messy, and with its windows closed didn't smell particularly fresh, wasn't so much dirty as disorganized and cluttered. And more than a little dusty.

Sophie cast a grin toward Miss Barton. She'd been up here only once before, when her uncle had sent her to fetch a book from one of the men—Stimpson, it had been. The condition of the place had been the same—although at that time, three of the naturalists and explorers had been sitting around arguing with each other about the specifics of some genus or other.

"Where are they all now?" asked Miss Barton, stepping farther into the room. "Did they evacuate the city? Or are they at the public rooms at the hotels?"

"Mr. Stimpson and Mr. Kennicott went on a short visit to Philadelphia, but I expect they'll be back any time now—at least, as long as the railways are open.

"Some of the others have left to go on expeditions. As a rule, they come and go as they please. Usually there are four or five living here at a time, but they rotate among about a dozen of them, coming and going for months at a stretch. It just happens that the place is empty at the moment, though any one of them could return any day." She was particularly aware of the comings and goings of the young men because of the regular meetings of the Megatherium Club—which was what the group of scientists called their informal fraternity. Their weekly meetings, which took place in lieu of visiting a gentleman's club, were held downstairs in the display rooms after the museum was closed.

Out of curiosity and boredom—and because, well, she'd already caused one scandal; why not another?—Sophie had actually infiltrated one of their meetings in March when she was dressed as a man. It still tickled her that none of the naturalists, who saw her nearly every day, had recognized the quiet Henry Altman as being Dr. Henry's niece.

Except Mr. Quinn.

He'd just *had* to show up for that particular meeting—she still didn't know why or how that happened. The luck of the fates *never* seemed to be with her. But at least Mr. Quinn hadn't betrayed her real identity—and for what reason, she couldn't fathom.

Sophie walked briskly toward the back room. "I'm sure there are some things here that can be donated to our Union soldiers. Although they might need to be washed."

Miss Barton gave a short laugh of agreement, then followed her into the bedroom area. It was a bit of a treasure trove when it came to potential clothing donations: they found several flannel shirts, some stockings, and even a pair of trousers that had been left behind. Sophie ruthlessly dragged blankets from three of the beds, commandeered two feather pillows, and finished her thievery by folding up a large piece of canvas. Surely it would come in handy for some purpose at the infirmary.

"I'm so grateful to have met you," Miss Barton said as Sophie locked the door of the Smithsonian behind them.

It was left to bring their loot to the infirmary—a task which they now learned would be easier said than done, having realized the four bundles they had to manage were heavy and awkward. As it was now well gone an hour after sunset, night had come and it was dark but for a splinter of moon and the few streetlights. Sophie looked around, but she didn't see any hacks. Drat.

Miss Barton valiantly tottered along as she managed two of the bundles. "Certainly I could have found some items at my boardinghouse and surely some of the other boarders there might have donated something—but I doubt I could have scared up this much in one trip."

"I'm very happy to have met you as well." Sophie said, struggling to sling one of the bundles over her shoulder. "Otherwise, I might have been merely sitting around and—"

Her voice choked off as a large figure detached itself from the shadow of the building, stepping menacingly into their path. "And where might you ladies be going?"

CHAPTER 8

"M R. QUINN! OH MY GOODNESS, HOW YOU STARTLED ME."
Miss Gates had sucked in her breath when she saw him, but her companion had gasped and reeled backward, holding up a large parcel as if to ward off attack.

Thank the Lord. Adam felt a rush of relief that he'd found her safe and intact, followed immediately by a rush of irritation. He surreptitiously slipped his revolver into its holster and did his best to keep his voice even. "Miss Gates. It's not advisable for a woman—or two women"—he nodded at her companion—"to be going about at night in a city soon to be invaded."

He had to grit his teeth to keep from saying more that might not have been so polite. Had he not had a similar conversation with her just last night, when he'd come over to find out who had a light on in the Smithsonian? Why didn't she understand it simply wasn't safe for a woman—or anyone, truthfully—to be about alone in Washington right now?

And it had happened again tonight, as he was watching a loud troop of men march strategically across and near the Long Bridge: he'd seen a flickering light in the castle. And it had moved around between at least two towers, arousing his suspicions.

This was after he'd spent too much time attempting to find her by searching throughout the Executive Mansion. He'd originally wanted to talk to Miss Gates about the discovery that Johnny Thorne was a woman, and to find out if she'd learned anything by talking to the servants and ladies of the household.

But his concern mounted when the exasperating woman had been nowhere to be found. Nor had she been seen by anyone since before supper—which she'd definitely missed, according to Mrs. Lincoln. When he saw the light in the towers, he'd vacillated between worry that it wasn't her, exasperation over her risk-taking if it was, and the hope that she had, in fact, just gone home and was safely there despite how risky it might have been.

Miss Gates, whose bonnet was crooked, straightened up to her not-very-threatening full height and appeared to be ready to argue. But then she surprised him. "Perhaps it was a bit foolish, but the soldiers were in need. I knew we could retrieve some things for them from here, and I wasn't thinking about what time it was or the fact that it was getting dark. I was thinking of their comfort."

"All right." How could he argue with that? "I reckon you'll need an escort wherever you're going. Are you taking all of that with you?" He eyed the four large bundles they were slogging between the two of them. "To the soldiers? Which ones?"

"The Sixth Massachusetts." The other woman spoke up for the first time. "Many were injured during the riot in Baltimore, and Miss Gates and I helped some of them to the infirmary after their train arrived. Then we discovered their lack of bandages and other supplies, and Miss Gates offered to obtain some from her home. Incidentally, my name is Miss Clara Barton," she added with a firm tone—clearly expecting an overdue introduction.

"I'm sorry, Miss Barton," Miss Gates said hastily. "This is Mr. Adam Quinn. He works for Mr. Lincoln."

Despite the introduction of the president's name, Miss Barton still seemed wary of him. Or perhaps she was simply shy, Adam amended, noticing how she hung back a bit so that her face was obstructed by her bonnet. Nor did she join the conversation as they began to walk.

He'd swung up two of the bundles, slinging one over his left shoulder where he maneuvered to clamp and anchor it with his false hand, then held the other by the strings used to tie it up in his right. This left him unable to reach his revolver quickly and easily, but he certainly wasn't going to allow them to struggle alone with the awkward packages. How on earth had they expected to make it all the way to the hospital with them? Women were so nonsensical at times.

"Thank you, Mr. Quinn," said Miss Gates in a prim voice, as if she could read his uncharitable thoughts. She lugged the valise she'd brought to the White House yesterday, but it appeared much heavier tonight.

As they walked, she described in more detail the arrival of the soldiers and what had happened at the infirmary. By the time they reached the hospital, he could tell she was tiring because of the way her sentences slowed and shortened, and the pauses between each thought.

"Thank you for your assistance, Mr. Quinn," said Miss Barton as they stepped into the infirmary. "And for the escort."

"I'll see you home as well, Miss Barton," he said. "It's not safe for anyone to be out at this time of night with the Rebels breathing down our neck."

"Miss Barton! Oh, Miss Barton, they said how you was here."

She looked over at a tall, spindly man who looked like he was barely twenty. Her face—flushed from the exertion of their walk—brightened with a smile. "Kenneth! Mr. Norton told me I might see you." She turned back to Adam. "Thank you for your offer, Mr. Quinn, but I believe I'll stay here for a while. I know many of these men—and Kenneth is the son of a family friend from North Oxford. I'll find someone to bring me to my boarding-house, or I'll locate a cot here. If the city is invaded, I venture to say I'll be safer here amongst a troop of soldiers than at my boarding-house. Thank you again. Miss Gates, it was a pleasure to meet you. Have a good night, and pray the Confederates are stayed."

Before Adam could speak, she swept off to speak to the young man. He looked down at Miss Gates, whose face seemed too pale and the skin under her eyes shadowed. The shallow bonnet she wore had been knocked even further to the side—he guessed because of her exertions with the bundles of donations.

"I reckon I'd best get you back to the house. You look tired on your feet, Miss Gates."

"Yes, but just one more moment. I want to check on Mr. Eldritch."

Adam chafed a bit as she went off, then looked around the infirmary with a wary eye. Having spent far too long in one, he'd discovered he didn't care for hospitals—even as a visitor and not a patient. The very smells of laudanum and other medicinals made his stomach flip like his mother's flapjacks. One of the patients was groaning in pain from somewhere, and that sound along with the familiar smell of an abundance of bodily fluids and the sight of a long row of cots made his throat dry. An ache began in what remained of his left arm, then moved like a phantom into the missing part below his elbow. His head began to throb.

"Mr. Quinn?"

Adam started a little when he realized Miss Gates had caught him just before he slipped into that dark tunnel of the past. But he was seasoned at collecting himself quickly, and he just said, "Are you ready to leave at last?"

"Thank you for waiting," she said in that voice of hers that made him think she was somehow teasing him. "Yes, I believe I am quite ready to go home—well, to go back to the—er—house."

The White House was only about ten blocks west of the hospital, nearly straight down E Street. The alphabet streets weren't nearly as busy or well-lit as the broad, diagonal avenues that radiated out from Capitol Hill—Pennsylvania being the busiest of course. But despite the fall of night and the imminent threat of invasion, there was a smattering of bystanders along the way.

Many of them spilled onto the narrow street from public houses or smaller hotels and boardinghouses. Most every person Adam saw was a man—and many of them drunk and rowdy, clearly expecting some sort of military activity—though there were a few prostitutes leaning against random buildings. He was even more relieved that Miss Gates hadn't attempted to walk back by herself at nearly ten o'clock. This thought lodged in his mind, and he couldn't keep himself from speaking it.

"How on earth did you think to manage getting back to the mansion alone, Miss Gates? Safely?" he said after a particularly drunk man tottered into their pathway and leered at her, making a clumsy swipe as if to take her arm as he called her "Daisy-Lou."

Adam dispatched him with a sharp word, and took possession of her arm himself.

She sighed wearily, curling her fingers around the crook of his elbow. "I admit, I didn't think far beyond the moment of helping the soldiers. If it came to it, I suppose I would just have done what Miss Barton intends—to sleep at the infirmary."

Adam gave a rough laugh. "I reckon a ward filled with wounded men in various states of injury and consciousness isn't going to be much safer than E Street, filled with drunks and bravados."

He paused to maneuver her to his other side, using his good hand to curl her fingers around his false forearm. This left his right hand free to settle over the butt of his revolver.

Men anticipating war—a battle, either victorious or no—were not predictable. And from the snatches of conversation he heard, many of those celebrating were doing so in anticipation of a Southern victory in the city tonight or tomorrow. Thus, he kept sharp eyes scanning the street from both sides as they made their way along.

That was the reason he saw Leward Hale an instant before the other man saw him. Adam's stride hitched, and his hand went to the revolver as he met the other man's eyes.

Hale was in conversation with three other men—not great odds, Adam noted immediately; especially since he was short an arm and had Miss Gates with him—and they all appeared to have had a few drinks if the giddy light in their eyes was any indication. But the glint of pistols stowed in each man's holster were a cold warning that he would have to take care.

"Adam Quinn," said Hale, swaggering out of his group just far enough that they couldn't pass by. "Last time I seen you was back in Lawrence. When you was hiding behind a lady's skirt." He snickered, and his friends joined in.

"Leward Hale," Adam replied, curling his fingers around the

butt of his gun, fighting back the nauseating fury that rose in his throat. "Last time I saw you, you were using what little ingenuity you own to kill a three-year-old boy."

His words were sharp and filled with disgust, but came nowhere near expressing the loathing he had for the man in front of him. He was aware of Miss Gates stiffening next to him, and actually felt the way her attention flitted back and forth between him and Hale, but he couldn't spare a look at her. He was too busy keeping his eye on the four pro-slavers; two of whom he'd seen earlier today on the street corner.

The lean, carrot-haired Hale laughed, displaying a misleadingly charming dimple. "Sorry about the boy, but at least he won't grow up to be a nigger lover like you and Crazy Jim Lane. I heard'at Lane's been trying to round up a few old men to protect that nigger-kissing ape in the White House." He settled both hands on his hips, his fingers fluttering toward the butt of his pistol.

Adam held the other man's eyes as he withdrew his revolver. He didn't lift it, didn't aim it, but the sharp click of the hammer cocking beneath his finger said all he needed to say.

"That's all right," Hale replied, his eyes gleaming as they swept over to Miss Gates, then back up to meet Adam's. He might have been in his cups, but his gaze was hard and gleaming with fanaticism. "When the White House burns and our kinsmen come over the bridge, we'll be here to cheer them on . . . and help collect the spoils of war." He looked at Miss Gates again, this time more slowly.

Adam's breath caught at the audacity of the man, and he heard his companion's shocked gasp. Then she tensed more, drawing in a breath, and he was afraid she was about to speak—good Lord, that would be *all* he needed—so he pressed in his left arm hard, trapping her hand against his side in warning.

"I reckon we'll see about that," he told Hale coolly. "You know the Jayhawkers better than your Virginia brethren do. You know what your kinsmen will be facing. You know Jim Lane's men offer no quarter—especially to woman- and child-killers." He held the other man's eyes, boring into them with his own as he blocked away everything but the two of them: the other men, Miss Gates, the fact that he was now one-armed, and the roaring hatred that threatened to send him leaping at the bastard and taking his chances anyway. "Step aside."

Hale looked up at Adam just long enough so as not to appear too easily cowed, then turned abruptly away to join his friends. He said something and the group rumbled a derisive laugh, but no one made a move toward Adam and Miss Gates.

Nonetheless, Adam met the eyes of each of the men as he walked past, giving them the same silent warning he'd given Leward Hale: mess with me and live with the consequences. He kept his pace easy and steady, neither hurrying nor dawdling, and when Miss Gates's curiosity got the best of her and she drew in a breath to speak, he merely gave a sharp jerk of his head and compressed her hand tightly against his side once more.

He couldn't speak even if he'd wanted to, for his throat had gone to dust now that the moment had passed, and the wave of grief made his eyes sting. Just seeing Leward Hale and his smug, ugly face brought him straight back to that day in Lawrence.

That sunny, bloody day.

Not until they were several blocks away, when he was certain no one had followed them and he felt he could trust his voice, did he permit Miss Gates to speak. And then he immediately regretted it.

"Who was that? What an odious man! What was he talking about? I've seen one of those men before, I'm sure of it. Is he the one who—who took your arm?" And then, more hesitantly but no less nosily, "Was the boy your son, Mr. Quinn?"

"Leward Hale. An incident in Kansas. In a matter of speaking. No." He paused, then gentled his voice. "My godson. Carl. Along with his parents, who I was very close to."

"I'm so very sorry." Her fingers tightened around his arm in a heartfelt squeeze.

They walked another block in silence, approaching Pennsylvania Avenue. The Treasury Building rose to the right, its marble blocks cool and bone-white in the moonlight. The President's House was just off to the left where the Avenue intersected E Street at a dog's leg angle, and it too reflected pristine in the moonlight. A single hackney trundled by, and someone shouted in the distance. The earthy, mucky scent from the swampy land down the slope from the White House filled the air, along with wood smoke. It was, in spite of everything unpleasant hanging over the city and filtering through Adam's thoughts, a beautiful, balmy spring night.

He wondered what tomorrow would bring. A city overrun by soldiers, filled with gunfire and heavy smoke . . . death, violence, victory?

Or another quiet, tense dawn, with the city and its inhabitants holding their collective breath and waiting for what was surely inevitable?

Now they passed the Treasury and were close enough that he could see—because he knew where to look—the guards posted on the White House roof. And as they started up the curving drive to the mansion, a voice called out from the darkness.

"Who goes there?"

"It's Quinn. Is that you, Benson?"

"What's the password?"

"Springfield."

"All right, then. Evenin' Quinn. Yes, it's me, Benson."

"All is well, then?"

"Yes it is. So far."

They walked past the guards and Miss Gates murmured, "There's a password?"

"It changes three times a day," Adam replied, then chuckled. "The first night the Frontier Guard was settled here, before they all went to bed, Mr. Lincoln meant to go in and greet them. He walked up to one of the men stationed at the door to the East Room—James Cody, it was—and Cody stopped him with a bayonet and demanded the password. As it turned out, no one had told the president what it was . . . and Cody wouldn't let him through."

"Oh my," Miss Gates said in a shocked voice. "What happened? Was it possible he didn't realize it was the president?"

"He knew. I reckon he was just demonstrating how serious he

was about his post. But I don't think the president was suitably impressed," Adam said with another little laugh. "Finally Cody let him through."

"I should hope so."

They were approaching the house now, from which two windows on the top floor—Lincoln's office and that of the anteroom—glowed softly, and Miss Gates said, "Mr. Quinn, I don't know whether you're as tired as I am, but I doubt I'll get much sleep tonight. Waiting. Watching." She drew in a heavy breath. "And . . . I have things to tell you about Johnny Thorne."

"You missed supper," he replied. "And I reckon it was a challenge to help a lame soldier walk all the way from the depot to the hospital. It's no wonder you're tired." *And that your bonnet is crooked.*

"Not to mention lugging that bundle of blankets back to the infirmary," she said with a strange sort of giggle. It almost made him want to smile—the sound of that little, light bit of laughter that he reckoned came from her being overtired and nervous. "If you hadn't come along, I truly don't know what we'd have done."

"It's finished and over," he replied. "All worked out for the best. I reckon I need to hear what you've learned, but it needs to wait until morning—depending what happens tonight. I have the eleven to two o'clock western watch, and I reckon it's getting near time for it by now. I'll need to speak to General Lane and Major Hunter first."

"And so by tomorrow morning, Johnny Thorne might not be relevant?" She stopped, forcing him to do the same, and looked up at him. "If the Confederates come?"

"No," he replied, a little stung that she would think so. "But if the Confederates *do* come, I expect we'll all be busy trying to keep *ourselves* alive."

"That's what I meant," she replied a little defensively; then she gave a short laugh and flapped her hand. "Forgive me. I *am* tired—I didn't sleep a wink last night, I think, what with listening and waiting for something to happen—and I missed both dinner and supper today. Thank you again, Mr. Quinn, for helping me and

Miss Barton tonight. And for walking me back here." She gave a little shiver as if just realizing what sort of danger she might have been
in, had he not been available or come looking for her. "I hope
your watch is uneventful, and that you do get some sleep when
your shift is over."

"Thank you, Miss Gates." He wanted to say something more,
but nothing seemed right. His mind was filled with so many other
things.

They'd reached the front door, and Old Ed was there to let
them in.

"Miss Gates," Adam said as she started off to, presumably, the
second floor. "In the future if you leave the property here—at
least for the time being—I reckon it would be a good idea for you
to at least tell someone—*and* even to take someone with you."

"I reckon you're right," she replied with a tired smile, and then
she started up the grand stairway—sagging shoulders, dragging
steps, cattywonker bonnet and all.

*The day was sunny; so bright it hurt the eyes. Adam wore a hat low on
his forehead to keep the glare from blinding him as he scanned the never-
ending prairie of dry, straw-colored grass. It swooned and shimmered with
each breath of breeze, like the waves of a dun-colored ocean.*

*It was a beautiful afternoon. His heart was full. His grandfather's fid-
dle sat in its case, roped to the back of his saddle, ready for tonight's
shindig. He couldn't wait to see Tom, Mary, and little Carl and all their
other friends.*

*The Skilltons' house was a neat log cabin on the edge of cleared land
Tom meant to farm. Wheat, he said. Some oats, and he reckoned a bit of
alfalfa too. A winding brook cut through a stand of willow trees. It was
just down a small incline from the house and its stable so Mary could easily get water until the well was dug. And the stable, Adam remembered
with a grin, had been built even before the house because Tom's precious
horses and cow needed shelter.*

*As he drew near the dirt track that led to Tom Skillton's cabin, he heard
the sounds.*

Shouts. Screams. Gunfire. Whinnies.

Then a roaring noise that somehow filled the ears, though he could see nothing to cause it.

And smoke. Thick and choking, it suddenly enveloped him. Everything became a blur, and black and thick, and Adam's world was suddenly hot and bright, filled with a fire, laced by screams and terrified whinnies. Shots. More cries.

Pain. Searing, blazing.

And suddenly, there was Leward Hale, dancing and laughing in his face. He held Adam's left arm, and he waved the limb along with his rifle in wild victory as he mounted his horse. He rode down Pennsylvania Avenue toward the White House, leading a group of men carrying rifles.

Blood spun and splattered on the street behind Hale and his cronies, and it splashed against the pristine white of the President's House . . . dripping down the sides as if buckets of red paint had been spilled from the roof.

And Jane Thorne was there, dancing and twirling in a skirt and crinoline as the slit in her throat yawned like a wide, ugly grin. It came closer to Adam, bright red and shiny, thick with evil and heavy with rust, until it overtook him: wet, dark, thick, smothering—

Adam clawed awake, his eyes bolting wide, his chest heaving, his body damp and tight. His missing arm screamed with remembered agony, and his mouth was parched.

He lay there, panting, fighting himself back to normal as he focused on his surroundings. On reality.

The world was gray with light as dawn spilled through a tall window of the East Room. Thankfully, Adam slept on the floor near the wall. He'd chosen a corner just inside the door, but away from the two long rows where the Frontier Guard slept, bisecting the room. No one was near enough to feel him struggling and shaking in his dream. He hoped he hadn't cried out . . .

Adam cradled the elbow of his left arm, holding it and the stump angling from it, against his abdomen and tried to slow his breathing. Tried to fight off the pain from a limb that no longer existed. Wisps of the dream still caught at his mind, and he willed them away.

It had been months since he'd had a nightmare so violent and gripping—one that had taken him back to such detail of that day. Most often, he merely dreamed of fire and pain and screams.

But he'd come face to face with Leward Hale yesterday. It was no wonder he'd fallen into such an ugly nightmare.

Adam pulled to his feet just as the clock struck six. The man standing guard at the door—it was Garland, he thought—gave him a brief nod as he slipped through to find the water closet.

It wasn't until he splashed cold water on his flushed face that the last remnants of the nightmare faded. Only then did the realization struck him: another night had passed, and the Confederates hadn't come.

Saturday April 20

They didn't come, was the first thing Sophie thought when she realized it was past dawn. Her eyes were gritty and there was a crick in her neck, but the house was calm and the noises from beyond were the normal ones of servants and residents.

She had slept only slightly better than her first night in the White House, but that was to be expected considering the amount of physical activity she'd done yesterday. She and three wives from members of the Frontier Guard shared the same small bedroom and had slumbered fitfully.

When she woke, Sophie was a bit sore from her effort helping Mr. Eldritch limp his way to the infirmary, along with his rucksack and her valise—and she did, in fact, have a bruise on the side of her hip from the latter—not to mention the second trip she'd made, carrying a heavy bundle of donations back to the hospital. Yet, despite the fact that she was hungry and a layer of exhaustion settled over her like an ever-present cloud, she was also relieved the night had passed without incident.

But that meant they had another long day and night of wondering and worrying ahead of them. Would any reinforcements come from the North? Would *tonight* be the night the Secessionists crossed over into Washington with their rifles and determination?

Aside from all of that, Sophie realized that it had only been yesterday morning that Johnny Thorne had been found in the oval library.

It seemed as if much more time had passed than a mere twenty-four hours.

And another long, anxious day loomed.

The bedrooms in the White House each had a marble sink with running water, a luxury Sophie took advantage of to wash up and clean her teeth. Then, her stomach growling, she collected the bundle of clothing that presumably belonged to the murderer. With a last bit of regret that she hadn't brought the fresh clothing for herself from home last night, she left the room in hopes of breakfast—and finding Mr. Quinn.

A clock struck eight as she made her way down the main staircase—already filling with the never-ending line of job-seekers and self-proclaimed Union loyalists. Her crinoline, though not nearly as wide and stiff as it could have been, brushed over the rows of walking sticks, shoes, and boots as she descended. At one point, it snagged on a buckle, and she nearly tripped when the hem was yanked backward and caught under her foot.

"Drat," she muttered, grabbing the railing to catch herself. The owner of the boot bent to unhook the lace edging. "Thank you, sir."

"Of course, miss," he replied, but another man further up the stairway—well-groomed and dressed in fine clothing—said, "Blasted skirts are more trouble than they're worth. Ought to be outlawed!"

Another man spoke up. "I've pleaded with my wife not to wear them, but she insists. Her hem almost caught fire when she stood too close to the grate one night."

This began an energetic discussion among the men in relation to the dangers and inconveniences of crinolines and hoop skirts—with which much Sophie had to agree, although she knew men caught their clothing on fire at times as well. Even the blood-stained coat she currently carried had a small burn at the back hem.

But despite the fact that the comments followed her all the way to the first floor, she declined to engage. And fortunately, she didn't catch her crinoline on anyone or anything else on the way down, for that would have been a mortifying underscore to the men's argument.

As Sophie reached the bottom of the stairs and came through the glass screen's door into the vestibule, she stumbled to a halt. Mr. Lincoln was standing there speaking to three men she didn't recognize, along with General Winfield Scott, whom she did know based on his crusty age, towering height, and impossible girth. Fortunately, none of them seemed to take notice of her, and she edged into the shadows so as not to disturb their conversation—and because she felt odd interrupting the president during a meeting, even though he was standing out in the open.

"It's not possible for us to allow more Union soldiers to pass through Baltimore," one of the men was saying in an arrogant tone. "Unless *you*, Mr. President, are willing to bear responsibility for the bloodshed that will follow. And there *will* be bloodshed."

Mr. Lincoln looked down at him, for he was much taller. "Very well. You may return to Baltimore and advise Mayor Brown and Governor Hicks that I've received their message."

"And there will be no other response at this time," General Scott added gruffly. He nodded at Ed McManus, who opened the door for the three men from Baltimore.

No sooner had they gone and Mr. Lincoln fell into conversation with the general than the front door was opened again by the elderly doorman. Sophie, who'd begun to step out from the corner, eased back in an effort to stay out of their way—but also because she was curious.

"Mr. President, sir. General Scott. Major Thomas Cole sends news from the War Department." The uniformed man who came in was out of breath as he stood ramrod straight and saluted.

"What is it then?" growled the general as he snapped a return salute. "Report, Private."

"Yes, sir, General. All the bridges on the rail lines to the north and west of Baltimore have been destroyed by the Secessionists. They're burned up and torn down and completely impassable. And the telegraph lines that run alongside them have also been cut. The mob has pulled down many of the poles as well, so it will take that much longer for the telegraph to be repaired."

General Scott and Mr. Lincoln exchanged looks. "Is there any other news, then?" asked the president.

"Yes, sir. There's also word that the militias in Maryland are gathering up to attack any Union troops that try to move through Baltimore or Annapolis. There won't be any reinforcements coming through without a fight—if at all."

Sophie's fingers opened and the bundle of bloody clothing nearly fell from her hands.

We're trapped.

There was no way in, and no way out of the city for people, food, or supplies. Or soldiers.

She'd heard enough murmured discussion since her arrival at the president's home to know that with the city cut off by rail, telegraph, and river, it wouldn't be more than a week or so before Washington would starve due to lack of supplies. And in such a weakened state, and with no military reinforcements, it would be ever so simple for the Southerners to take it.

And that would be the end of the United States of America. The Confederacy would permanently break the Union.

The Rebels would take Mr. Lincoln, and surely they would kill him.

CHAPTER 9

S OPHIE'S HANDS WERE COLD AND HER INSIDES TIGHTENED SO SHE FELT nauseated. Yes, she'd been afraid of invasion. But this news made the situation even more dire. More real.

Especially now that she saw the long grooves lining Mr. Lincoln's face, and the dull weariness in his kind eyes.

He was just as anxious as she was. More.

Before Sophie could decide whether to slip away before she was noticed, or to boldly walk across the corridor to try and locate Mr. Quinn, none other than the man himself stepped through the glass door from the main corridor.

"Mr. President," he said, striding past without seeming to notice her. "I heard there's news from Cameron at the War Department."

"I reckon it can't be much worse," replied Mr. Lincoln, sinking Sophie's stomach even more as he confirmed her direst fears. "We're completely cut off from every form of communication and transportation from the north and west. And Baltimore threatens bloodshed if we attempt to bring any reinforcements through there, the devils!" His voice rose a little. "How *dare* they place the blame for bloodshed on *me* when they mobbed and stoned our men from Massachusetts. Traitorous devils!"

Sophie could see how sober Mr. Quinn's unshaven face had become. "I'll get with Lane and we'll scare up some more recruits. Ed McCook arrived yesterday from out west, and he's a good man. We fought in Kansas together. His father's here in Washington already—" He stopped and shook his head. "I reckon you don't need the details, sir. You need the men."

"As many men as you can muster," the president replied. "Anyone who can manage a rifle. And as many rumors as you can spread."

"Yes, sir," Mr. Quinn said, and just as he turned to leave, he caught sight of Sophie. His step hitched and she stepped away from the corner, still holding the bundle of clothing. "Miss Gates."

"I was looking for you," she said in an attempt to forestall any comment he might make about her eavesdropping. But fortunately, Mr. Lincoln seemed not to notice, for he was in deep conversation with General Scott and yet another arrival who'd just been given entrance via the front door.

She heard the word Gosport—which she knew was a naval yard in Norfolk—but could discern nothing else.

Mr. Quinn shook his head. His eyes were dark and veiled with weariness, and he too had deep lines in his face. She noticed he wasn't wearing his prosthetic today, and his sleeve hung empty from just below the elbow, instead of being pinned up as men often did. "I reckon I don't have much time to talk with you now, Miss Gates."

"Of course not," she said briskly, unaffected by his tone, which was much more clipped than his usual drawl. She struggled to keep pace with his long stride as he was obviously so distracted he didn't think to slow for her shorter legs. "I heard what Mr. Lincoln said."

"I need to find Lane," he continued in that terse tone. Then suddenly, as if remembering she was there, he stopped. "Miss Gates, don't leave this house unless you take someone with you."

"I'm going back to the infirmary today," she told him firmly. "Miss Barton needs my help gathering up more donations, and there's nothing else for me to do but sit around here and worry. There aren't even any newspapers coming in for me to read. I'm not going to be useless. But I doubt there's anyone who can accompany me; I'll not take any of the Frontier Guard from their duties."

He drew in a breath, hesitated, then expelled it. "All right, then. I reckon I can walk you over there because I've business on the Avenue. At Willard's," he said, more to himself than her. "And if I stop by the St. Charles, I reckon I . . ." He stopped and looked at her as if seeing her for the first time again. "Is that blood on those clothes?"

She clutched them tighter. "Yes. It's a coat that was found yesterday, and I'm certain it belongs to Mr. Thorne's killer. I was hoping you'd look at it to see if you agree."

He shook his head, and she fairly saw his thoughts slow, settle, then organize as his eyes focused on her with clarity. "Not *Mr.* Thorne. Johnny is a woman. Or so Dr. Hilton discovered yesterday."

"A woman?" Sophie blinked. "That's . . ." She couldn't think of a word to describe her shock and fascination.

"I reckoned if there was anyone I knew who'd have an opinion about a woman dressing as a man, it would be you, Miss Gates." A flicker of humor flashed in his dark eyes, then was gone and replaced by that worrisome gravity. "I meant to get something to eat from Miss Cornelia in the kitchen, then take care of my business in town. Can you be ready to leave for the infirmary in thirty minutes?"

"I'm ready now. I wanted to show the coat to you and ask where I should keep it, then I was prepared to leave."

"Will you bring it? I reckon I can look at it while I eat. Have you eaten this morning?"

"Not yet."

They went to the kitchen where Mr. Quinn was greeted by the cook as if he were a long-lost son who'd been starved for years. Obviously, he'd come scrounging for food in the past.

More quickly than Sophie had imagined, she and Mr. Quinn were situated in the servants' dining room at the same table where she'd interviewed the staff yesterday. They'd hardly sat down when a scullery maid appeared with a tray of fried ham, toasted bread, and baked apples. She also had cups of coffee and a small bowl of peanuts.

Sophie, sensitive to the fact that Mr. Quinn wasn't wearing his prosthetic, laid out the coat on one end of the table while he worked quickly but awkwardly to make up his plate.

"It's not of particularly good or expensive quality," she said, mostly to herself. "I suppose that tells us something about him."

The amount of blood on the coat made her empty stomach want to turn, but she steeled herself. There would be much more bloodshed before the year was over, and, thanks to Miss Barton, she'd already realized she'd be doing something about the war effort.

Mr. Quinn moved to stand next to her. He held a plate balanced on what remained of his bad arm, and, without any appearance of self-consciousness, fed himself with his right hand.

"Blood on the sleeves as expected if it belonged to the killer," he murmured after a moment. "And down the front. If he stood behind her and grabbed her by the mouth . . . Otherwise she'd have made noise. And then he held her very tight and cut her throat. One quick slice." He paused, picking up one of the sleeves to reveal a long, dark stain on the bottom of it.

"See, there's a great deal of blood staining the bottom of the left coat sleeve . . . and it would have seeped through to the shirt beneath it. Hmm." He paused as if to think over that possibility, then continued. "That large amount of blood was from when he held her there, hand over the mouth, and the blood spurted up and over the bottom of his sleeve from the fresh cut. We know for certain he sliced with his right hand and held her with his left because of the marks on her face. It bears out."

Mr. Quinn didn't seem to recall that Sophie was there, and she stood quietly, nibbling on a slice of ham laid over a piece of crusty bread. Both were spread with baked apples. The fruits were soft and slightly sweetened, sprinkled with cinnamon and sugar, and their juices soaked into the edges of the bread just enough to flavor it without dripping through. Though he was talking about blood, she was somehow surprisingly hungry enough to eat without hesitation.

As long as she didn't picture the scene he was describing too closely in her mind.

"He held her in place, hand over her mouth, until she died. He had to," he muttered, "or she would have woken the house. So there was more blood on his right sleeve from when he stabbed her in the side."

Sophie blinked at this bit of information, but again chose not to speak. It was rather fascinating to watch Mr. Quinn's face as he told the story, for he seemed to actually *see* the events happening in front of him. He spoke as if he were actually there.

"The killer was calm—and yet desperate to have the strength and ability to hold her while she struggled and fought and died. He stabbed her, and used the knife in her body to help hold her immobile. What did he do with the knife after?" he muttered. "Where did he put it? He must have taken it with him."

Mr. Quinn reached for his coffee and drank it without slurping while continuing to contemplate the clothing. From the hallway came the chimes of different bells, calling for servants to the upper floors, and the sounds of them passing by on the way upstairs to their various tasks.

"He was quite taller than she. At least five inches."

"How can you tell that?" Sophie asked when he lapsed into silence again. "His height?"

Mr. Quinn looked at her in surprise, and she tried not to be amused or offended that he seemed to keep forgetting she was there. "His height? Ah, yes. Look at the way the blood stained his left arm—the one that held her over the mouth. It's all along the bottom of the coat sleeve, and under the armpit. Shows that the angle of his arm was coming down to cover her mouth and hold her still because his arm was more open from the shoulder, due to his greater height. It gave more area for the blood to spray. See how it's not the same on the other sleeve?"

"What if she was sitting down and he came up behind her? He'd be taller then, no matter what. Oh, right. There'd be blood on wherever she was sitting. And there isn't."

He nodded absently, still staring down at the clothing. Then suddenly, he turned to look at Sophie. "Where did you say this coat was found?"

"In the furnace room, in an empty trash bin. Bridget, one of the chambermaids, found it. She was surprised someone would throw away good clothing, so she was going to clean them up for her husband."

"He threw it away—or hid it—because he couldn't be caught with bloody clothes. But what did he do after he took them off? Where did he find new clothing? Where did he change? And when did he find the time to hide these clothes?"

"I spoke to Bridget and the two men, Larriman and Tool, who see to the furnace room. Based on their duties and schedule— she cleans it, and they keep the furnace running, of course—the clothes would have had to have been hidden sometime yesterday between eight o'clock and ten o'clock in the morning. That's the only time that room was empty."

He looked at her again, this time with a glint of admiration. "Well, that's quite helpful, Miss Gates. Thank you."

"Did you see Dr. Hilton? Did he tell you when he thought Johnny—er, Miss—Thorne was killed?" Sophie began to stack their empty plates on the tray. "Where shall I put the coat when you're finished looking at it? Oh—I didn't get to look in the pockets."

"Questions. Always questions, Miss Gates," he murmured, bending over so as to anchor the coat with his half-arm while he dug in the pockets with his hand. "I reckon I should put this with the other—"

The way his voice cut off had Sophie looking up sharply. He'd turned the coat over during the process of digging in the pockets, and his expression could only be described as stricken.

"Did you find something important?" She moved toward him in hopes of seeing.

He looked at her as he flipped the coat in half to bundle it back up, then in half again. "A few coins and a button. Not much else."

She tamped back the urge to question him further, mainly because the look on his face wasn't one of subterfuge, but one of arrested thoughtfulness. And shock.

He'd found something that bothered him, and, true to form, he was being reticent about it.

For now.

Pennsylvania Avenue was even more deserted than it had been yesterday when Adam left the White House. Nonetheless, it was another beautiful spring morning that belied the unease that had settled over the city's occupants.

Or, most of them at least.

There were those who proudly wore their Secessionist cockades, overtly waiting for the Confederate army to come. Leward Hale was certainly one of them.

Although he had much on his mind—and Jane Thorne's murder, along with the unpleasant theory that was beginning to form, was only part of what concerned him—Adam remembered to maintain a pace slow enough for Miss Gates not to have to run along to keep up with him. It also helped that she'd slipped her fingers around the crook of his elbow.

"So Johnny Thorne is a woman," she said as they passed the Treasury building. "Therefore, one must consider why she would dress up as a man and pretend to be a soldier."

He cast her a look. "I reckon you've got some opinions on the matter, Miss Gates."

She smiled up at him, her gray eyes dancing from within the shelter of her bonnet. "Well, you did ask me for my thoughts."

"I allow I did." He smiled back, permitting himself to push away the burdens of the day for just a few minutes. After all, it was beautiful weather and he was in the company of an intelligent and interesting—if not challenging—companion with an infectious smile. And she was quite nice to look at as well.

"A woman might dress in man's clothing for several reasons," she began in a tone that reminded him unpleasantly of a schoolteacher. In general, he much preferred his learning to take place outside, among the elements of nature, or by doing things on his own—rather than to be talked at.

Nevertheless, Miss Gates, however much she might remind him

of a teacher, was clear and concise in her thoughts and reasoning. "She might want to be mistaken for a man in an effort to go about doing business that women don't do—or aren't *allowed* to do. Such as being a soldier."

"Or a journalist."

"Or a journalist," she replied, smiling again. "Or, she might want to go about some activity or business simply without drawing attention to herself—thereby blending into the crowd as a man, and being less likely to be noticed if she were in feminine clothing. Or," she said, tightening her fingers on his arm for balance as she hopped aside to avoid a swampy, smelly puddle on the walkway, "she might want the comfort and ease of not wearing eight layers of restrictive clothing."

"*Eight* layers?" Adam had never actually counted, but he supposed it was possible.

Her cheeks turned slightly pink, making him grin even more. "I could enumerate them for you, Mr. Quinn, but I don't think that would be strictly proper. Perhaps you could simply trust that I am aware of the number of articles of clothing the average woman is required to wear."

"Most assuredly, Miss Gates, I'll take your word for it." He became serious again, mulling over her points.

"Oh," she said after a few more steps. "There's one other reason I can think of for a woman to dress as a man—and that would be in order to remain near her husband or some close male relative when he went away. To go with him, I mean."

"Away—as in, to war. Or joining the army." He chewed on that as they walked another block. A woman who wanted to stay with her husband—or some other man she was close to. A brother. A father. A lover. He was beginning to feel an unpleasant sense of inevitability.

"And if that's the case, at least one person must have known she was really a woman," Miss Gates added unnecessarily. "The husband, of course."

Based on Hilton's revelation that Miss Thorne had had sexual relations near the time of her death, that meant someone *definitely* had known Johnny was a Jane.

Dammit.

Adam did not like the way his thoughts were going. It was possible Jim Lane knew Johnny Thorne was a woman in disguise because the husband—or lover, he reckoned he'd best be open to all possibilities—had told his commander about it, for some reason. That could be true.

He might have been able to dismiss his growing concern if he hadn't seen the burn on the back of the bloodstained coat. If anything, that made him even more determined to speak with Lane at the earliest possibility.

But he'd been unable to talk to his friend since yesterday afternoon, when he'd informed Lincoln and the others about Thorne's masquerade. They'd both been too busy and working on too many different tasks in order to keep the president and his family safe.

And he'd made no progress in discovering Miss Thorne's identity—although Adam was beginning to fear that Jim Lane might be the one to help. Even so, he intended to stop at the St. Charles to see whether Miss Lemagne had finished her drawings.

"I don't know how you're ever going to discover her real identity," Miss Gates was saying, uncannily following his train of thought, "unless there *was* someone who knew she was a woman. If she's not from the city here, how would you ever identify her?"

"I reckon that's one of the things that's been keeping me up at night," he said wryly. He felt her attention slip to his empty sleeve, and wondered if she'd somehow guessed that was why he wasn't wearing his prosthetic today. The pain from his amputated arm had nagged at him, lingering from last night's dark dream, and he'd decided not to buckle on the false limb this morning. Instead, he'd rubbed his favorite lavender-scented balm on the end of the stump and gave his arm what he considered a refreshment.

Despite missing the utility of the prosthetic, Adam also felt a little lighter and a little less restricted without all of the Palmer arm's straps and ties that fit around his torso and over his shoulder.

"I don't know how you'll ever find out who did it," Miss Gates said. "With all of the people who walk in and out of the mansion, and so many rooms where anyone could hide . . ." She shrugged, looking up at him with those big gray eyes. "It seems impossible. Unless you can somehow trace the owner of the coat."

Adam's mouth tightened, but he replied, "I reckon that's a good start. And I haven't yet been able to examine the clothing she was wearing. Hilton gave it to me yesterday, but I left it with him." That was another thing worrying at him—another thing he'd had to set aside due to the current military operation in which he was involved.

"Mr. Quinn! Mr. Quinn!"

He and Miss Gates turned to see Brian Mulcahey flying down the street toward them, his face flushed pink from running. He wore his boots and a tweed cap that appeared new.

"Mr. Quinn, mister-doctor sent me to find you again," he panted as his feet slapped to a halt on the cobblestones. "He's been done with the examination."

Adam, who still held Miss Gates's arm, felt her interest and curiosity blossom as if a sign had been painted on her face. Submerging a sigh, he reckoned he'd soon have another female invading Dr. Hilton's office—or at least thinking up reasons to do so. But first, there were manners to attend to. "Brian, you'll want to bid Miss Sophie Gates a good morning now that you've come up and interrupted her on her way." He looked pointedly at the boy's cap, then watched with amusement as Brian realized his error.

The boy's face turned darker red and he yanked off the head covering, twisting it in his hands as he stood up straight. Adam could almost imagine Brian hearing his own mother's voice, reprimanding him over his rudeness.

"Begging your pardon, Miss . . . uh . . . Gates?" He glanced at Adam for confirmation and received an encouraging nod. "And top o' the morning to you, miss. I hope you're about having a nice walk today." He seemed to struggle for what to say next, and

Adam, exchanging glances with her as she smiled at the boy, took pity on him.

"Miss Sophie Gates, may I introduce Brian Mulcahey. He has been a very useful aide and runabout to both me and Dr. Hilton, as well as for Mr. Lincoln."

"It's a pleasure to meet you, young sir," she replied, inclining her head. "Am I to understand that Dr. Hilton has finished his examination and there might be more information about our murder victim?"

"He's a *she*," Brian informed her as Adam winced over her use of "our" in relation to the murder victim.

But he supposed he had no choice at the moment. Miss Gates had been involved almost since the body had been found, and she had provided some much needed assistance.

Brian was still describing his experience effusively. "Yesterday, we didn't know he was a she, but when doctor-mister showed Mr. Quinn, I saw her b—"

"*Brian*," Adam choked out just in time, and felt his own face grow warm. Blast it. He didn't dare look at Miss Gates, who seemed to be shaking with—he hoped—suppressed laughter, and instead focused on the boy . . . who'd just realized his near mistake. Now *his* face was bright red, and even his freckles seemed to be blushing. "Did Dr. Hilton say whether it was urgent that I come, Brian?"

"No, sir, Mr. Quinn. He said I was to tell you to come when you can, but if it's tomorrow that's all right, too. He's put the body on some ice to keep it fresh. Are the Sech—Seck-sess—the She-*sesh*-onists," he finally managed, "really going to attack us tonight?" His green eyes were wide. "Miss Lemagne said so. She said they're going to take over the whole city."

"Miss Lemagne?" Adam didn't know why, but he was compelled to glance at Miss Gates, who by now had gotten her giggles under control.

"Miss Constance Lemagne?" she said, sweeping a look from Adam to Brian and back again. "Is she still in the city then? I thought she might have evacuated with the rest of the Southern sympathizers. Isn't she from Alabama?"

"She's still here, miss," Brian said, still with his most polite demeanor. "She was at Dr. Hilton's yesterday, drawing a picture of the body." His voice was rich with relish that Adam wished he could eradicate.

"Was she?" Miss Gates's voice was strangely devoid of inflection. "At Dr. Hilton's, was she?"

Adam rushed to speak, realizing he needed to fix something . . . but he wasn't exactly certain what needed fixing. "Miss Lemagne's maid was in need of a doctor, and I reckon she felt Dr. Hilton would do a fine job seeing to her." He congratulated himself on his quick thinking to explain the inexplicable. "And while she was there, Miss Lemagne suggested that a drawing of Thorne's face might assist with the identification—so I would have something to show around."

"How enterprising of Miss Lemagne," replied Miss Gates in that same tone that *seemed* normal, but there was something about it that made the hair on the back of his neck want to prickle.

"She's very pretty and very nice," Brian said helpfully. "Even though she likes the Sesh—those rebellious traitors!"

"I'd be happy to show around Miss Lemagne's drawing," said Miss Gates. "While I'm at the infirmary this morning, and possibly Miss Barton would help as well. She's been living here in Washington for longer than I have, or Miss Lemagne has. Or even you, I suppose, Mr. Quinn. Of course, Miss Thorne—I *do* wish we knew whether that was her real name or not—might not even be from Washington."

"If she was here because she wanted to be near her—er—husband," Adam said, without giving an explanation as to why that was very probable, "and she was in the White House with the Frontier Guard, then I reckon it's most likely she's not from Washington. Most of the men garrisoned there are from Kansas or other places out west."

"So perhaps Miss Lemagne's drawing won't be all that helpful after all," Miss Gates said with a bland smile. "Oh, and speak of the devil. Miss Lemagne!" She released Adam's arm in order to wave. "Wasn't she staying there at the St. Charles? It looks as if she's packing up to leave town."

He looked over and saw Miss Lemagne standing next to a barouche in front of the hotel. Her maid Jelly was there as well, and Miss Lemagne was supervising the driver, who was loading trunks onto the luggage shelf on the back of the carriage.

"I didn't realize you knew Miss Lemagne," Adam said as the Southern woman looked over. She spoke to the driver, then began to make her way down the block toward them.

"Oh, yes. Recall that we met briefly at the levee at the White House—on that awful night when you and Dr. Hilton caught Mr. Billings's murderer. And I've seen her several times since then on a number of social occasions—dinners, salons, even once at the theater. She's very amiable."

"Mr. Quinn! And Sophie Gates. Oh, and young Mr. Brian," said Miss Lemagne gaily as she arrived in a vacillating swirl of broad yellow skirts and a tall, arching bonnet adorned with green leaves and yellow flowers. Its matching ribbon fluttered in two untied pieces over the front of her bodice, and she wore a pair of pale yellow gloves.

"I was so hoping y'all would call today, Mr. Quinn. After I saw you yesterday, I got myself right to work and I've completed two more copies of my drawing of the poor woman's face. They're very good likenesses, I think, and I'm certain it will be helpful when we begin to show them around the city. The poor woman," she said, looking at Miss Gates. "What a terrible thing to happen—or perhaps y'all hadn't heard about it, Sophie, darling?"

"Unfortunately, I was there when the discovery was made," replied Miss Gates in a very smooth voice. "Right there in the White House, it was. Such a horrific thing—to have one's throat slit—"

"Her throat was *slit?*" Miss Lemagne turned a shocked look at Adam that had a hint of accusation in it, leaving him uncertain whether her reaction was because of the nature of the violence, or because Miss Gates had been permitted to know the cause of death but she had not.

"Thank you very much for making those drawings, Miss Lemagne," he interrupted quickly. He sensed there was some sort of unspoken communication happening between the two women, but exactly what it was eluded him. He just knew he needed to take control of the conversation before—well, before something uncomfortable happened, like the two women deciding to walk over to Hilton's to look at the body again. He subdued a shudder at the thought. "I reckon you must have worked very hard to get them finished before you had to leave town."

"Leave town?" Miss Lemagne gave a light laugh. "Why, Daddy and I aren't leaving Washington." Her Southern accent became more pronounced and drawn-out. "We're moving into Mrs. Billings's house. We're goin' to be stayin' here *permanently*, because Daddy has asked Althea to marry him." She gestured toward the barouche, where the driver and her maid waited.

Her smile revealed a dainty dimple in one cheek and was accompanied by a sparkle in her eyes, and before he realized it, Adam was smiling back.

"That's wonderful," Miss Gates said in a slightly too-loud voice, and Adam blinked—realizing he'd been lost in Miss Lemagne's smile for a moment. "But aren't you nervous about staying here with the war going on, Constance, darling?"

"Why, whatever for? Our boys are coming across from Alexandria tonight. That's what my daddy says, and he knows everyone," she replied. "There aren't enough Union men here to fight them off. Two hundred? Three at the most? Against Beauregard's thousand?" Her blue eyes glittered with excitement.

Her comment jolted Adam back from what had been a light and pleasant conversation to the reality of war and the predicament the Union was in. His smile faded, but before he could respond, Miss Gates spoke up.

"Only three hundred? Heavens, no, there's over a thousand—" She stopped abruptly and clapped a hand over her mouth. Her eyes had gone wide and appeared very innocent and shocked.

She looked up at Adam as if she'd just spilled some great secret, and that was when he suspected what she was doing.

"Miss Gates," he said firmly, as if embarrassed by her runaway mouth, "I believe you said you needed to be at the infirmary as soon as possible. Perhaps we should be on our way so you aren't late."

"Yes, Mr. Quinn," she said in the meekest voice he'd ever heard from her; and that was when he knew for certain she was playacting. "It was very nice to see you again, Constance. Now that you're staying in town, I'm certain I'll see you again soon. Mrs. Carpenter holds such pleasant salons."

"Miss Lemagne," Adam said with a brief bow. "I reckon I'll need to get those drawings from you. When would be convenient?"

"Why don't y'all call on me at Mrs. Billings's house after you get Miss Gates to the infirmary. I'm on my way to the house now with my things—surely you remember where it is, Mr. Quinn?"

"I do, yes, thank you. I'll be there as soon as I am able." He nudged Brian, who'd become distracted watching a fine set of bays trotting by, pulling a sleek, shiny landau.

"Top o' the day to you, Miss Lemagne," said the Irish boy, still looking at the horses. "*Gor*, look at them! They couldn't be any more the same color if I painted them!"

As they walked toward the barouche loaded with the Lemagnes' trunks, Miss Gates took Adam's arm and began to speak breathlessly, "I'm so very sorry, Mr. Quinn! I hope I didn't say anything completely untoward about all those extra men at the White—" She stopped herself as if realizing her voice was pitched loud enough for Miss Lemagne to hear, then, looking guilty once more, she waved at the Southern woman as they walked on past.

"Well done, Miss Gates," he said when they were out of earshot and he'd sent Brian off to tell Hilton he'd be there no later than tomorrow.

Assuming he was still alive tomorrow. And not captured.

"Thank you," she said in her normal voice, which was far less light and giddy than a moment ago. "Now when you see Miss Lemagne to pick up the drawings, you can dig those seeds in a little deeper by hemming and hawing about what I said. You know she'll rush off to tell her father, and possibly some other people as well. And since he 'knows everyone,' I'm certain Mr. Lemagne will help spread the word."

"I reckon you've got it all figured out, don't you?"

"Just consider it one of my contributions to the Union's cause. One of many, I hope. I did hear Mr. Lincoln say he wanted you to muster up anyone who could handle a rifle." She gave him a side-wise look.

"I don't reckon he meant women," Adam replied, a grin tugging at his mouth.

"Well," she said as they reached the steps of the infirmary and she released his arm, "I could always dress up as a man."

He laughed as he walked away, a little startled that even on a day filled with so much anxiety and danger he could still manage to do so.

He just hoped there would be something to laugh about to-morrow.

CHAPTER 10

Sunday April 21

MIRACULOUSLY, THE SUN ROSE THE NEXT MORNING OVER AN OMInously quiet, tense Washington. Another night had passed with no sign of the Confederates.

It was, Sophie thought, almost worse than actually being invaded: the waiting. The stretching tension. The constant unsettling of her stomach.

She was still staying at the President's House, though she'd seen little of Mr. Quinn since he left her at the infirmary yesterday. He'd made arrangements for one of the Frontier Guard to escort her back when she was finished at the hospital last evening, but she hadn't seen him except for a brief passing in the corridor after she returned. Then Sophie spent another near-sleepless night sitting with the other women, talking about what might and might not happen and what they would do if it did.

This Sunday morning, the streets were silent and empty except for the few brave—or unfortunate—souls who remained in the city as they went to church services. Since the railways were down, the only way evacuees could leave now was by wagon or cart, which made for limited options.

She heard whispers that there was a shortage of food, and that if the rail lines didn't open soon, or if the blockade of the river wasn't ended, they could starve. This fear was evidenced by the smaller, simpler meals coming up from the kitchen downstairs.

Sophie had managed to stop by the Smithsonian yesterday

while she was out with Miss Barton seeking donations, and she'd retrieved clean linens for herself. But it wasn't until late afternoon on Sunday that she finally had the opportunity to wash up and change into the pale pink dress. She put on a lace collar, tucking its underside edges beneath the neckline of her dress bodice, and pulled on two matching cuffs.

As most women did, Sophie had far more collars, cuffs, and removable sleeves than she did skirts, bodices, and dresses. For day-to-day wear, those removable and easily washed parts helped to keep the actual dresses unsoiled, for they couldn't be changed nearly as often and were more difficult to launder.

Sophie was contemplating this fact as she smoothed the points of her collar into position over the buttoned-up front of her bodice. Clothing was very dear to everyone but the wealthiest, and even they didn't have unlimited articles of clothing. It continued to bother her that whoever had killed Jane Thorne had thrown away his bloody coat—a more expensive article of clothing than even a shirt or trousers.

None of the members of the Frontier Guard had more than one change of clothing with them, with perhaps an extra pair or two of socks and under linens. And surely there were very few of anyone here in this house—save Mrs. Lincoln, perhaps—who had more than one coat that he could spare by throwing it away.

With the amount of blood on the coat, however, what option did he have? He could try and wash it off, but he'd have to hide it until he had the opportunity to do so. Any of the servants doing the laundry would surely notice and comment on bloodstained clothing, especially in light of the murder.

Still mulling over these thoughts, Sophie stepped out of the bedroom and found herself in the corridor with Mr. Lincoln. He was facing a wiry, dark-haired man who was clearly beseeching him for a position—and had obviously been doing so for some time.

"Please, sir, if you'd just take one moment to reconsider—"

"Go away!" exclaimed the president, dragging his arm from the grip of the insistent job-seeker as he reached for the doorknob to the anteroom. "I cannot attend to all these many, small details! I could as easily bail out the Potomac with a teaspoon!"

He pulled away at last and ducked into the waiting room of his office, leaving the undaunted position-seeker standing in the corridor looking after him. Nicolay, who'd also witnessed the incident, turned on the man and sent him scuttling away.

"We've more important things right now. Take you—all of you," he growled, waving a hand at the ever-present line of men waiting for Mr. Lincoln. Although this was the shortest lineup Sophie had seen, there were still at least two dozen people in the corridor and on the stairs. Some of them she even recognized from having seen them over the last several days. "All of you go, now. It's Sunday, for pity's sake! And don't come back!"

Sophie hurried toward the stairs, unpleasantly aware that even the most patient of men, Mr. Lincoln, was exhibiting tension and impatience during this siege of sorts. That knowledge confirmed her worst fears of how dire the situation was.

As she started down the stairs, she saw Mr. Quinn along with Senator Lane and a man named Mr. Arick speaking with Major Hunter. They were standing at the base of the stairs and didn't seem to notice her.

She paused halfway down the steps, partly because she didn't want to interrupt their conversation, but also because this was the closest she'd been to the famous and fascinating (and maybe a little mad) Jim Lane, and she was curious about him.

He was very tall, probably as tall as Mr. Lincoln, who towered many inches over everyone except Mr. Quinn and General Scott. He was over forty, and his hair was terribly long and uncombed. He looked as if he hadn't shaved in weeks. The new senator and war hero had a long, gaunt face and intense, dark eyes that held a gleam that was almost fanatical. She supposed that sort of fierceness was important for a general in war, but it made her feel a little wary of the man despite his heroic reputation.

And now, faced with him in person for the first time, Sophie couldn't help but be reminded of the case when Lane shot Gaius Jenkins. Lane had been charged with cold-bloodedly murdering him over some sort of land dispute in Kansas, but during the trial he'd been acquitted for the reason of self-defense. Still, there was something about the man that bespoke of madness.

"There's no word where the New York Seventh is," Major Hunter was saying as Sophie paused on the steps only a short way down. "And when they might arrive. We've got to hold off until they get here."

"The Confederates across the river—they're all saying we've got a thousand men here, ready to go," Arick told him in a sort of wry, wondering voice. "Somehow they got word we're four times bigger than we are. And there's rumors you're going to lead them over and attack Alexandria," he added to Lane. "They're pissing their pants afraid of your Jayhawkers."

Senator Lane grinned (and so did Sophie, knowing she'd contributed to the rumors), and, scratching his unshaven chin, looked at Mr. Quinn—who was also unshaven and appeared more scruffy and uncivilized than Sophie had ever seen him. But Mr. Quinn didn't have that wild light in his eyes.

Could he truly track an ant's path over stones? She thought he *had* to be teasing her about such a thing.

"I reckon we should send more of our men out to see what they can find. Two each to Baltimore, Annapolis, and Alexandria," Senator Lane said to Mr. Arick, who Sophie had learned was responsible for keeping the roster and schedule of the Frontier Guard members.

"Ask ones who know their way around and won't get lost. They might get taken for Secessionists if they know the terrain and seem to be locals," added Major Hunter.

"Yes, sir," said Mr. Arick. "I'll talk to Hoban and Walton, for certain." He made an about-face and went off toward the East Room, from which Sophie could hear the sounds of male voices and activity. Major Hunter accompanied him, and Sophie decided it was safe to continue her descent.

"Jim," said Mr. Quinn. His voice stopped Senator Lane as he started toward the steps. "Where's your coat?"

Sophie had just reached the bottom of the stairs and she hesitated, loathe to walk between the two of them as they were still conversing.

"My coat?" Lane stilled, then he saw Sophie. "Good afternoon, miss," he said with a smile. "We've been doing a fine job holding off those Rebels for the last few days, ain't we? And don't you worry—we'll keep'em away. You have nothing to fret about. Those Confederates'll have to go through my Jayhawkers to get to anyone here in the White House." And he bounded up the stairs on his long, long legs.

Mr. Quinn muttered something and looked up after him. Sophie couldn't quite read his expression, but it didn't look pleased. She noticed he was wearing his prosthetic today, but that the lines on his face seemed more pronounced. Or maybe that was due to the dark stubble covering his jaw and cleft chin.

"Good afternoon, Miss Gates," he said politely, but his mind seemed elsewhere.

"Good afternoon, Mr. Quinn." She felt compelled to say something further, but his expression seemed so remote and blank that she felt uncharacteristically hesitant to continue. She wanted to know whether he'd visited Constance and retrieved the drawings, but something told her now was not the time to mention it.

Yet she had the urge to reach out, to cover his flesh and blood arm with her hand in a steadying sort of way. Instead, she spoke. "Is there anything I can do to help, Mr. Quinn—anything? At all? In any way?"

"Stay safe," he said as the sound of the soldiers taking up their arms and lining up for drills came from the East Room. "That's all, Miss Gates. Only stay safe, and pray that we get through this."

And before she could respond, he gave a short incline of his head, then started down the corridor to where the Frontier Guard waited.

CHAPTER 11

Monday April 22

ADAM'S EYES WERE GRITTY FROM LOST SLEEP, BUT HE OPENED THEM to yet another dawn in which Washington still slept safely.

They still haven't come.

Four days, and they still *haven't come.*

Although he certainly didn't want the Secessionist soldiers to descend on the poorly armed and frighteningly unprepared city, Adam reckoned the waiting for the battle seemed nearly as awful as the invasion itself would be.

As before, he'd settled near one of the walls in a far corner in the room to sleep. He preferred the relative privacy for putting on and taking off his prosthetic, as well as his reaction to any nightmares that might disturb his sleep. Now, he looked around to make certain none of the women staying in the White House had entered the East Room—which now held more than 110 men as a result of his and Lane's recruitment. When he saw none, Adam felt it was safe to pull off his shirt in order to don his false limb.

Adam didn't need assistance strapping on the Palmer arm, though it had been easier when he shared a hotel room with his uncle Joshua and he'd given him a hand. But he'd been wearing the prosthetic for nearly two years—after first having a leather-covered Selpho arm, which smelled like a dead carcass after a few months—and had worked out the process of fastening the complicated buckles and ties on his own.

The Palmer—which was considered the most realistic and useful of prosthetics currently available—was made from willow, hollowed out so it was strong, light, and cured, and it was covered with a fine stretch of lambskin. The lambskin made the hand look almost like flesh, and it was soft and natural to the touch. With a complicated set of straps and gears, the forearm and its hand allowed Adam to use the muscles in his shoulder, upper arm, and elbow to maneuver the hand, wrist, and even pinch the fingers.

There were other options for false limbs—metal, pincerlike fingers, or a rudimentary sort of stub into which different implements (fork, knife, screw, pencil) could be inserted, or even an immobile hand carved of wood—but Adam had been fortunate to be able to acquire the practical Palmer.

He'd worked diligently over the last two years to learn to use the arm, and he could do nearly everything he used to be able to do—except play the fiddle. In spite of that—or perhaps because of it—Adam still carried the instrument and its case with him, for the fiddle had belonged to his grandfather. But he wasn't certain he'd want to play it again even if he could. It carried too many memories—as well as a bullet from the pro-slavers that attacked them at Tom and Mary Skillton's place on that terrible day. He saw no reason to remove the lump of lead that was lodged in the back of the violin.

Now, as he settled the false arm over his stump, he couldn't help but think about Leward Hale and wonder what had brought him here from Missouri. Hale, like his cohort Orin Bitter and many of the pro-slavers who'd fought for Kansas to be a slave state, hadn't even lived in the territory. Instead, bands of like-minded men had crossed the state line from Missouri to terrorize the Free-Staters and fight for the right to make Kansas part of the extension of the "peculiar institution." They also voted fraudulently in the territory's elections for government and statehood.

But what had brought Hale and his friends here, to Washington? Was it simply because they—as everyone—had known war was imminent, and they came to fight for the South?

That was the reason most of the men who made up the Frontier Guard had traveled here: enthusiastic with the prospect of protecting the capital, their president, and the Union. Some of them had been in Washington since the inauguration in early March, hoping to get positions in the army or government.

Adam finished buckling on his arm and reached for his shirt. In the process, he got a good look at the floor of his spot in the East Room in full daylight for once.

When he saw the dark smudge and the drops of pale candle wax there on the carpet—right near the wall where he'd slept the last two nights—he stilled. That stain looked a lot like blood that had soaked into the carpet. And it was accompanied by a few small drips of wax.

Just like there had been upstairs, in the doorway passing from the oval library to the president's anteroom.

Adam looked down at the marks on the floor, considering. If he could determine whether the stain was, in fact, blood, that would be helpful. And, yes, he reckoned there had to be a lot of candle wax drips around the East Room . . . but the drips were on *top* of the stain, meaning they came after the blood. Aside from that, the Frontier Guard didn't have much use for candles with all the gaslights in the room, and the fact that when they were actually in the room and not drilling or marching, the troops were either sitting around talking, cleaning their guns, or sleeping.

Not really a need for candles.

Nor were there any around that Adam could see.

But what he *could* see was how it might have happened . . .

The killer had left the second floor, carrying the bundle of his bloody coat and the candle, and he'd sneaked into the East Room. A smudge of blood and a few drips from the extinguished candle which had not yet hardened could easily fall on the floor here. And this location was just far enough inside the doorway, and near the wall—away from the others in the room but easy to get to without bothering anyone—which was why Adam had chosen it for himself.

It would have been simple for the killer to slip in, put the bundle on the floor and either sleep here or join the ranks of the other men in their neat lines down the center of the room. Probably no one would have noticed—thinking someone was merely returning from taking a piss or guard duty.

Adam had slept in the East Room Thursday—the night of the murder—but he'd chosen a spot closer to the window that night because he'd been discussing strategy with Major Hunter in that section of the room.

He shook his head, pulling on his shirt, still looking at the stains. He reckoned he didn't much like what they implied.

Not at all.

And as if his very thoughts had conjured it, the double doors to the big room opened and Jim Lane walked in. It was the first time he'd seen his friend since yesterday, and since he'd hardly talked to him since Sunday, Adam couldn't help but wonder whether Lane had been avoiding him.

Especially since he wasn't wearing the coat he'd been sporting when he first came to the White House. The coat he'd showed Adam a week ago—with a burn on the back of it.

But Adam thrust that unpleasant thought away. Jim Lane was not only his close friend, but he was no coward to avoid talking to him. Both of them had been busy doing what they could to shore up the protections of the White House and the city, and the mansion and its grounds were large and everyone was busy, anxious, and determined. It was no wonder they hadn't often crossed paths.

Nonetheless, Adam rose quickly and started toward the Kansas senator, who strode right down the center of the room to the middle so he could speak to some of the guard.

Adam reckoned it would take one simple question on his part to remove the niggling uneasiness that had lodged in his mind. And then he could put the worry about Jane Thorne's murder away until things were decided here in Washington—one way or another.

By the time Adam got across the room, Lane had turned and started to make his way out again, deep in conversation with Major Hunter. Adam followed, joining Lane and Hunter as they climbed the stairs to the second floor for a meeting with General Scott and Colonel Stone.

Nicolay met them in the corridor. "Another contingent from Baltimore is in there," he said in a low voice as he opened the door to Lincoln's office and nodded them to go in. "They want the president to guarantee that no troops will come through the city or even travel *around* it."

Hunter scoffed disbelief and fury as Lane growled, "He's got to bring troops through. I told him we'd go to the city and raze it if Baltimore needs to be taught a lesson."

Adam, Lane, and Hunter entered the office to find Lincoln out of his characteristic patience, and freely scolding the messengers from Maryland as General Scott and Colonel Stone looked on.

"You gentlemen express great horror of bloodshed, and yet would not lay a *straw* in the way of those who are organizing in Virginia and elsewhere to capture this city." The president's eyes flashed with intensity. "I must have the troops to defend this capital! It lies surrounded by the soil of Maryland. Our men are not moles, and can't dig under the earth; they are not birds, and cannot fly through the air! There is no way but to march across Maryland, and that they *must* do."

All of Adam's concerns about Lane faded away when he saw the president's face. Grave, dark with gloom and doubt, and oh, so sober.

Lincoln had turned to pace across the room and added in a lower but no less vehement voice, "Those Carolinians are now crossing Virginia to come here to hang me. I *must have those troops.*"

"Well, you've received your message," General Scott said brusquely to the three men from Baltimore. "Take it back to your governor and your mayor, and know that the Union *will* have the troops through Maryland."

Nicolay closed the door behind the trio and Lincoln turned back to his advisors. "Have you anything further to report, General?"

Scott, whose gout often prevented him from climbing the

stairs, had taken a seat. It creaked now as he moved his large, bulky frame in an effort to find a comfortable position. He sighed and pursed his lips. "Word is a force of up to two thousand troops are preparing to attack Fort Washington. There are another two thousand coming from Harpers Ferry to join the attack on Washington."

The room was silent for a moment, then the president said, "Can no one bring me any news other than gloom?"

"Some, sir," Hunter said. "We have reports from our spies that the Confederates in Virginia are in dread of James Lane and his bloodthirsty horde—those are the exact words. That's surely why they haven't come across the river yet."

Lincoln nodded at the Kansas senator. "I reckon you don't mind keeping that sort of reputation."

"Not if it makes the city safe." Lane grinned and his eyes danced with a light that Adam recognized as fervor for battle.

"The Confederates also believe, according to Millard Thompson, who just crossed back over from Alexandria before dawn, that you've been planning this defense of the President's House for months, Senator Lane. They think you've been secretly assembling the force here since before the inauguration."

Lane gave a bark of laughter, crossing his arms over his woolen vest. "It's working, then. The lies we've planted are working. We've got less than two hundred men here, and less than a thousand more elsewhere in the city. And they're afraid of us. That's why they haven't come."

"Yes, the lies are working. In fact, they believe you've got enough men to fight off five thousand troops—they just don't know where you're hiding all of them." Hunter's mustache lifted in a slight smile. "I wager there's spies all over the city trying to find them."

Even Lincoln laughed a bit at that, but Adam heard the strain under it. "I reckon the news could be worse, then. But I begin to wonder if there is even any help coming. If our only help is those who are here now, and no more who will come to our aid," the president said.

"No, sir," Colonel Stone said. "More will come. *I* believe it. The response to your request for troops throughout New York and Maine, and Ohio, Indiana, and Michigan was of great excitement. All are proud, patriotic loyalists. They'll come."

Lincoln turned from where he'd been contemplating the view from his window—a view that included the sight of smoke from enemy camps and the Confederate flag fluttering from the rooftops of Alexandria. "And yet we hear that the Seventh regiment from New York has been attacked, cut up, and driven back." He sighed, twirling his spectacles around between two fingers. "Perhaps there *is* no North, after all."

"That's a rumor, sir," Hunter said. "We don't know that to be true."

He stopped twirling his spectacles. "Then *why don't they come?*"

The president's words hung there, low and anguished.

Scott glanced at the others, then with an abrupt gesture, sent them all from the office except Colonel Stone.

Adam, though shaken by the dismay and doubt from the president, seized on the opportunity to speak to Lane once they were in the corridor. "Jim, I reckon I need a word with you."

"If this is about that damned Thorne matter—"

"It is," he shot back, suddenly out of patience with all of it. "I need a word with you, Jim. Now."

His expression and tone must have warned Lane, for the other man gave a curt nod. As there was a group of job-seekers waiting for Lincoln—a much diminished number now that attack was imminent, but listening ears nonetheless—Lane slipped past the sliding door that led to the private side of the corridor, then opened the door to the oval library.

Adam followed, closing the door behind them. He glanced at the spot where Jane Thorne's body had been found, and saw that the bloodstains hadn't yet been cleaned. In fact, the room had an air of hesitancy and neglect—as if no one had ventured in since the tragedy. He wasn't the least bit surprised Mrs. Lincoln hadn't wanted to use the chamber. He was surprised that it appeared even Tad and Willie had been kept out.

He faced Lane, who was standing near the door wearing a dark glower.

"You knew Thorne was a woman," Adam said. "Why didn't you tell me? Why did you let me believe otherwise?"

Lane shrugged. "You'd find out soon enough, and I didn't have the time to have this sort of conversation. But here I am."

"A woman is *dead*," Adam shot back. "She was brutally murdered. Someone has to take the time to find out what happened."

"Look, Quinn, I know you're doing this for Abe, but we've got a goddamned *war* going on. We're going to be attacked and invaded—and we none of us might even be *alive* tomorrow. Why in the hell are you worried about one damned body? Tomorrow, there could be *hundreds*. There'll be *thousands* before this is all over. Ours included."

Adam, who generally had a long strand of patience, barely managed to hold back his rage at Lane's nonchalant dismissal. Instead, he remained focused and spoke in a cold, even voice. "Did you know from the beginning—when she joined the Frontier Guard—that Johnny Thorne was a woman?"

Lane cut his eyes away, took a deep breath, then looked back at him. "Yes."

Adam, knowing the power of silence, waited for more. He kept his gaze fixed on Lane, steady and cool.

"Her name is—was—Pamela. She and I were . . ." He looked at Adam blandly, apparently unwilling to put the truth into words.

"She was your mistress." Adam didn't attempt to hide his disgust. He remembered what Hilton had told him—that the young woman had recently had relations. *Christ Almighty.* "You had a rendezvous with her that night. In here. *In this room.* When you were supposed to be guarding the president."

Good God. He could hardly believe it.

No wonder Lane had insisted on taking the duty to sleep in front of Lincoln's door—and without allowing anyone to spell him.

Pursing his lips, Lane nodded. Then his eyes went dark and flat. "I didn't kill her, Adam."

"Where's your coat? The one you told me on Sunday at Willard's that someone had tried to set you on fire? You showed me the burn." Adam's voice was steely, partly to hide the disbelief that a man he'd admired and befriended could have done such irresponsible—and worse—things. The woman had been his mistress—surely he'd felt at least *something* for her. But thus far he hadn't expressed even the slightest bit of grief over her brutal murder. All he cared about was the impending war.

And then there was the sad fact that Lane's wife—the one he'd remarried after she divorced him over previous infidelities and abandonment—had been betrayed once again.

Lane scrubbed a hand over his face, the bristles rasping in the taut silence. "I don't know."

Adam's mouth twisted with derision. "I do. I have it. It's got the blood of Pamela Thorne on it, Jim."

Lane's eyes widened. "What in the hell are you—Adam, I didn't kill her! *Christ.* I swear it."

"It sure looks like you did."

"Are you calling me a liar, Quinn?" The other man was more than an inch taller, and had full use of all his limbs, but Adam wasn't the least bit concerned by Lane's suddenly murderous expression and the wild violence in his eyes. Even if the older man attacked him—which wouldn't be unexpected; Jim Lane wasn't called "crazy" for no reason—Adam would handle him.

"I'm telling you the facts: your coat has Pamela Thorne's blood on it. You hid the fact that you knew her, that she was your mistress, *and* that you'd been with her in this room the same night she was killed. I reckon that doesn't make you seem very innocent at all."

Lane stared at him for a long moment, and Adam saw the way his jaw moved as if he were contemplating what to say—or do. His fingers opened and closed into tight fists. "I didn't kill her," he said again.

"What time did you have your rendezvous with Miss Thorne? What time was the president's door unguarded?"

"Mrs. Thorne. She was married, all right? At least she wasn't an innocent." When Adam continued to spear him with his eyes, Lane spoke reluctantly, "Two o'clock. Or thereabouts. We'd made arrangements for her to meet me in here. When I did my perimeter around the mansion that night, I spoke to her then and told her to come up here when she was off her shift."

Good God. Adam still couldn't believe it. "No wonder you didn't hear anything that night," he said bitterly. "I reckoned it was impossible not to hear someone being killed in the next room, but now I know why."

Lane started to say something, but Adam pressed on. "So she was alive when you—finished. How long was your rendezvous?"

"Dammit, of course she was alive. And my coat—I took it off when—er—when we were together." Lane had the grace to look a bit abashed. "I must have left it in here." He glanced around the room as if hoping the article of clothing would manifest itself. "I—wasn't paying much mind when I left her at the door."

"And somehow you didn't hear her having her throat slit a short time later, while you were in the hallway next to the room? I don't reckon that's very believable, Jim. Your coat's covered with her blood and you were with her around the time she was killed."

"How do you know when she was—Christ, Adam, you know me better than that. I didn't kill her." His voice was tight with anger. "I don't kill people in cold blood—and not like that."

Adam looked at him, but was unable to voice agreement. After all, there was the situation of Gaius Jenkins.

"I'm going to find out what happened, Jim. Whatever it was." He made certain the implicit threat was in his eyes: *And if you're guilty, our friendship won't stop me.*

It was well past the ten o'clock curfew of the Black Code when George Hilton stopped his wagon on L Street. After a look around to be certain no one was watching, he pulled his hat lower to shadow his face and tucked the rifle beneath his long coat. Then he climbed down, tied up his horse, and gave her a feedbag to keep her busy, and quiet, for a while. Only then did he approach the neat, wood-frame home numbered 1806.

This well-kept neighborhood on the northwest outskirts of the city was composed of whites and free blacks. Nevertheless, the scents of coal smoke and refuse filtered through the air, for waste always seemed to collect in the low areas along the walkways and roads.

All along the street, during this night of anxiousness and gloom, the windows were shuttered and dark. Many of the houses had been boarded up when their owners evacuated in advance of the coming Confederate army, and for those who couldn't leave—or chose not to—they simply remained behind closed doors and prayed.

Except for the contingent of men at 1806 L Street.

George went around to the back of the house where the prohibited comings and goings wouldn't be so noticeable and rapped quietly. There was a long moment before the door shivered slightly in its moorings, and the peephole slat opened to reveal a faint glow of light.

"The night is dark," said a quiet voice.

"But dawn, like hope, will always come," George said, finishing the passcode in a murmur.

The peephole closed and the door shimmied again, then opened into a small anteroom. Beyond was a shadowy kitchen, its windows shrouded to keep the meager light hidden from outside. George could see men gathered in there, and he smelled the remnants of a meal of boiled cabbage and potatoes.

He stepped inside, the rifle still swathed beneath his coat. "Sorry to be late," he said. "I had a medical call that delayed me."

"Thought you might have been picked up by the constable," said Paul Jennings, a Negro who'd bought the house in 1854 when it was just built. He proudly told anyone he could that he'd paid a thousand dollars for it, brand new.

For more than a decade, Jennings had been a free man—ever since Senator Daniel Webster had bought him, then immediately given him his independence. Prior to that, he had been a slave owned by Dolley and James Madison since he was nine. He'd lived in the President's House with them during the war with England in 1812.

"Wouldn't be the first time I've been stopped by the constable," George said with a low rumble of laughter as he followed Jennings into the kitchen. "But usually I can convince them I'm a hack, and they let me alone."

Driving a hackney cab was a lucrative job, and was one of the few allowable positions for a black man. It was also one of the only excuses a Negro could have for being out past ten o'clock.

"Just so's they don't see what I got under my long coat," he added, flipping it open to reveal the rifle he held tightly along his side. He grinned at the others in the room.

Paul Jennings's kitchen was packed with over fifty men—all of them black, and all of them free. And all of them were determined to protect themselves, their families, and their city from the Confederates. The very fact that they were meeting after ten o'clock at night, and that many of them were armed, would have sent the lot of them to the whipping post—and then to jail.

If they were lucky.

If they weren't lucky and some greedy and enterprising Southern sympathizer had other ideas, any of the free men could be kidnapped and sent off into slavery in places like Alabama or Mississippi. It happened far more often than any of them cared to think.

Just as slaves who ran away to freedom were there one day, then gone the next, a free man could be going about his business one day here in Washington, then be snatched off the street and sold down South the next.

"I done lived through an attack on this city once," Jennings said, though he'd told the story many times before—but George allowed there were new faces in the group who mightn't have heard it. "Back in 1814, when I's fi'teen years old and them British come.

It was me and the doorman and the gardener—we all took down that big ol' painting of Pres'dent Wash'ton and saved it from when the English soldiers fired up and burnt down the pres'dent's house. Pres'dent Madison's house it was then."

"Now do tell, Paul . . . was that the paintin' was done by . . . what was his name, now . . . was it Gilbert Stuart?" asked one of the men with a hearty chuckle. Clearly he'd heard the story before and knew his lines to prompt it going on. "The one likeness as big as the general hisself? The famous'un?"

"It shore was, and heavy as a dead cow it was. Took the three of us to save it away for Miz Madison. We put it on a cart with some o'them fancy silver vases, yea big," he said, measuring with his hands, "and saved it from the British. An' that's why we's here tonight, men. But tonight our enemy ain't the foreigners of another country, but it's them who would enslave us all again. An' our wives an' our chillen. I din't save and save to buy my chillens' freedoms to see any of 'em taken up by them Southerners."

Low murmurs of agreement filtered around the room, and George found himself nodding along. He might not have a wife or children, but he had patients and friends—and of course his own liberty that was at stake. Every man in the room knew that if the Confederates took Washington, they'd be shackled and sold off whether they had papers of manumission or not.

"I writ a letter to Mr. Cameron," said one of the men standing near the corner. Jacob Dodson was tall and lean and his eyes were bright with intelligence. He had his own Sharp's rifle leaning against the wall next to him. "And he writ me back."

"The Secretary of War?" asked George.

"Yes, sir. That's him. I work as a footman in the Senate Chamber, and so I got the name of who to send to, and how to get it delivered. Then I writ Mr. Cameron to tell him I knew of some three hunnerd, very *reliable* men who would desire to enter the service of the city to protect it. And I signed my name so he knew I was a colored."

"Even though they don't want no blacks in the military, you got paid for your service from before, din't you? When you was with Mr. Frémont out West?" said Jennings for the benefit of those who might not know. Some of these men had joined the meeting tonight without knowing many of the others.

But they all had the same reason for being there.

"Yessir, you know I did, but it was special from Congress, 'cause they wouldn't let me join the army. Officially. And so I sent a letter to see if they'd join us up now." He shook his head. "But Mr. Cameron writ me back they don't got no intention to call up any colored soldiers."

Though a little stung by the continued rejection of his race, George could do nothing but shrug. "Well, that doesn't much matter, does it—since we're already here. And we're already armed."

"No, it sure don't," Jennings said vehemently, and the fifty other men in the room nodded soberly. Though they were each risking imprisonment or worse for owning a gun, that was far better than the possibility of being unarmed and helpless when the Confederates ran over the city.

"And I bin storing up foods, too," said Marcus Teller, who wore an eyepatch due to one of his eyes being burned away by his former owner. "In the cellar."

"And I tole Missy she need start saving all the leads and metals she can. We can make our own bullets if we need to," added Brownie Bixley.

The others nodded, murmuring agreement. All were stockpiling food as well as every bit of ammunition they could. The only thing they couldn't do was march in the sorts of drills the likes of the other militias, and the Frontier Guard, were doing. It was too risky.

"Since we can't march," said Jennings—who was the self-appointed leader of the ragtag militia—"we can at least be organizin' where to meet when the Confederates come."

"And a watch schedule," added Jacob Dodson, "to call the alarm. Using the communication we already got."

With the far-reaching and tight tentacles of the black community—both free and slave, connected both locally and also throughout the country, from Mississippi to Maryland to Ohio and Pennsylvania—information was spread quickly, news was shared, and warnings were given. All by word of mouth.

By the time the fifty-odd men had agreed on a rudimentary meeting place for their militia, as well as where to take their families for safety in the event of an invasion, it was past one o'clock. Even though the meeting broke up then, they couldn't all disburse at the same time for fear of being noticed.

"I've got room for five in my cart," George said as he replaced his hat and hoisted his rifle. "Under the canvas in the back. I'm going back into the First Ward. Whoever wants to ride with me." He shrugged and gave a small grin. "I got papers saying I'm a hackney driver if I get stopped."

"A hackney?" Golly Best, a young man with eyes that always seemed to be popping wide with interest or astonishment, shook his head. "There's bad times in this city now, specially with the war coming. But you hear there's a driver was found, his throat cut open? Was a hackney driver too. Mebbe you best be watching your back, driving around like a hack yourself. Stick to doctorin', there, Hilton. Be safer, mebbe."

"But at least I get paid in copper and silver when I drive them rich folks around, instead of the eggs and bread, maybe a sweet potato pie even, I get for doctoring people," George jested. "Or, worse is when I get pickled beets. Man, I *hate* pickled beets."

The others laughed.

"Well, you can save your pickled beets for me then, doc. Arissa's in the family way again, and she's got a taste for anything sour like that."

"Why, that's good news," George replied with a genuinely pleased smile as he extended his hand for a shake. The others slapped Golly on the back or gave him little congratulatory shoves of affection.

The younger man accepted his handshake. "So I reckon if I take all the pickled beets off'n your hands, you'll see that baby into the world, there, for us doc?"

"I sure will. I'd be honored to, Golly." When the congratulatory talk died down, George asked, "Now, who's going to ride with me?"

"More likely get stopped tonight, now the streets are clearer and the militias patrolling," said Dodson. "Be careful. All of you."

Moments later, George and his friend Brownie Bixley, along with three others who wanted rides, slipped out of Jennings's back door and made their way quietly to his cart. He made short work of tucking them all beneath the heavy canvas covering, then climbed up and started off.

They weren't stopped by anyone. In fact, this, the northwestern part of the city was unnaturally quiet. The moonlight filtered through some clouds, but it was only a half-moon and it didn't cast very much light at all.

George dropped off the three other men at the beginnings of the alleys where they lived, and that left only Brownie Bixley. He climbed out from beneath the canvas and joined George on the front seat of the cart. They'd kept up the charade in sight of the others because the fewer the connections between the two men, the fewer the questions that might come up in the future.

"Looking for information about a man named Jeremy Pole," said George as they drove along. Bixley lived in the Third Ward, and it was a little risky driving him all that way this late at night—them being two black men. Though Bixley had light enough skin, with a hat on he could maybe pass for white with George as his driver.

"He's eighteen years old and ran away about two years ago. His momma's name is Jelly, and she's from down near Mobile. She thinks he might be in New York. She's looking for news of him."

Bixley nodded. "I'll send word up and around. Maybe the general's heard of him. That Miz Tubman . . . she's a little mad, but she shore knows what she doing."

"Much obliged, Brownie. I'll ask Wormley next time I see him too. Sorry he wasn't here tonight." George navigated past a carriage parked in front of a wood-frame house, keeping a sharp watch for anyone who might stop them. But the street was silent and empty, and whoever was visiting the house wasn't coming out.

"I heard tell there was a man kilt up at the president's mansion."

"There was. Throat was slit clean across, then he was stabbed in the back. Right there in the house, two doors from where Mr. Lincoln was sleeping." George made a disgusted noise, but kept the rest of the information about Thorne to himself—including his involvement in the investigation.

He'd finished his examination of the body on Friday, and here it was just before dawn on Tuesday and Adam Quinn still hadn't come by to see him.

George knew Brian had given him the message, so he supposed Quinn was busy trying to figure out how to protect the president and Mrs. Lincoln in case the Confederates came. And everyone said they would come—maybe even tonight. George didn't know how Adam Quinn had come to be so trusted by Abraham Lincoln, but he'd seen with his own eyes the affection and respect between the two men.

That day, walking into Mr. Lincoln's office, had been one of the proudest days of his life—second only to the day he received his degree from the Toronto School of Medicine. Mr. Lincoln had thanked him for his help in capturing the man who'd killed Mr. Billings, and he stood in the office of the man who would— George believed it with every fiber of his being—free all the Negro slaves. Someday.

"Miss Lizzie tell you anything else about it?" Bixley was still talking about the dead body, and he assumed Elizabeth Keckley would be telling George all of the gossip since he drove her around a lot.

"Not very much." George couldn't reveal to anyone that he'd taken both Mr. Billings's and Johnny Thorne's bodies and cut them open to try and find out everything there was to know about how they died, and who they were. He was a black man. A doctor—something impossible for a Negro to be here in the United States. And he was mutilating the bodies of white people.

That was not something he wanted others to know about.

And that was part of the reason he'd been so shocked when Miss Lemagne had showed up at his makeshift office in the basement of Great Eternity Church.

"There's a passel of soldiers staying there," George said so Bixley wouldn't think he was holding out on him. "Right there in the president's house."

"And some at the Willard too, I hear," replied Bixley. "Almost got blown to smithereens Thursday night. You hear 'bout that?"

"Not much." Thursday night was the first night the Frontier Guard had been at the mansion, and Mr. Clay's men had been barracked at the fancy hotel. It was also the same night Thorne had been murdered.

"There was fifteen—maybe it was fifty—bundles of rags all over the hotel. Soaked in kerosene. Tucked in corners all over, with a long wick leading to each one so's they could light it and get away before it all caught up and came down."

"How'd they find out about that?"

"You know Birch? He the old doorman there, always in his white uniform, ever'day, all day? Nosy old bastard, but damn good thing he was. He was poking around and found one of them bundles. And then he found another, and the next thing you know, he's got all the footmen and grooms and maids looking all over the place. He's been telling that tale to whoever would listen. Surprised you ain't heard it."

George gave a short laugh as he pulled up near Bixley's street. "I've been damned busy. But good on Birch, then. Yeah, I know him. They catch the men who did it?"

"Not that I know. Ask Birch next time you see him. He'll be glad to tell you all, and more." Bixley slid off his seat. "Jeremy Pole. I'll put out the word. You got anything else coming?"

"I might. Soon. You hear of anything, you send to me. You know I got my office underneath that Great Eternity Church, over on Ballard's Alley. There's space there."

"I sure will. Same to you." Bixley squinted up at the moon, which had been waning last week and was nearly gone tonight. "Should be darkest tomorrow or Wednesday."

They looked at each other, nodded, then Bixley slipped off into the night.

Dark nights were an invitation for invasion or attack.

And for moving cargo a man didn't want to be seen.

* * *

At the White House that night, Mrs. Lincoln refused to dress for bed.

Instead, she and her companions—including Sophie Gates—remained in their clothing, sitting up, anxious and awake, prepared to be captured.

CHAPTER 12

Tuesday April 23

"**I** DON'T UNDERSTAND *WHY* THEY DON'T COME!" CONSTANCE HAD to force herself to remain seated, even though frustration and excitement trammeled through her limbs and tempted her to pace the room. "Where are the soldiers?"

She was sitting in the small but elegant parlor of her friend Rose Greenhow, along with several other ladies. They were all Southern sympathizers—at least, as far as Constance knew—and they ranged in age from seventeen to forty, which was the handsome and popular Mrs. Greenhow's age.

All of them had been expressing, in a more restrained fashion than Constance, their disappointment and concern over the fact that it was Tuesday morning—almost ten days after the war had started—and the Confederates *still* hadn't invaded the city.

"They need to wait for more men," Mrs. Greenhow replied, leaning forward to pour coffee into her china cup. "Now that the Union troops from New York have arrived in Annapolis, they'll be here sometime today. It was you who told me there were over a thousand men in the President's House, Constance. And there are even more hidden throughout the city. We don't want our men to be taken by surprise and outnumbered." Although she spoke calmly, Mrs. Greenhow's dark eyes were shrewd and thoughtful. "It's better that General Beauregard should wait, so he can be thoroughly prepared to take the city. Because when he does, the war will be over."

She had a mysterious smile that caught Constance's attention. "General Beauregard? But I thought he was in Charleston."

That smile curved into something more feline. "He's not. He's in Alexandria."

Constance almost asked how Mrs. Greenhow knew that particular information, but Mrs. Burnside interrupted. "And once General Beauregard takes the city, we will all celebrate at Mrs. Davis's levee in the Executive Mansion!" Her eyes danced. "Once that rail-splitting ape is chased out and *civilized* people are living there once again."

The ladies agreed with a round of applause, beaming at each other.

"It's so lovely that you've been able to stay here in Washington instead of moving back to Mobile," Mrs. Greenhow said to Constance. "You're quite an addition to our salons. And even though you must excuse me for the stingy repast"—she gestured to the simple corn muffins and tiny pot of cream on the table—"once our boys come, there will be flour and sugar and oranges for all!"

"Miss Lemagne, did you say you wanted to show us something?" asked Mrs. Wagner. "A drawing?"

"Oh, yes." Constance withdrew from her small drawstring bag a copy of the likeness she'd done of Miss Jane Thorne. "A friend of mine is looking for this woman. Do you recognize her?"

Mrs. Wagner took the paper. "Did you say you drew this? Why, you have quite some skill, Miss Lemagne! I'm thoroughly impressed. But, no, I don't believe I know her."

She passed the drawing around the small circle.

"Why is your friend looking for this girl?" asked Mrs. Greenhow, refilling all of the coffee cups that had gone low. "Is she gone missing?"

Constance hesitated, then plunged into a careful explanation. "She was killed. Her body was found, but we don't know who she is."

"She was killed? How terrible! What happened?" asked Miss Bettie Duvall, the youngest of the group at sixteen.

"I'm not certain how she was killed," Constance admitted. "I only saw her face when I was drawing it."

"Do you mean to say you saw her *dead body*? And you drew a picture of it?" Miss Duvall was aghast. "I declare, that's the most ghastly thing I've ever heard!"

"It certainly wasn't very pleasant," Constance said agreeably. For some reason, George Hilton (she still couldn't think of him as a *doctor*) and the memory of his quiet and confident person invaded her thoughts.

He was far too outspoken and commanding for being a black man, and she didn't like it. And whatever he was doing with the dead body of Miss Thorne made her insides queasy. He'd done something with Mr. Billings's body as well, after he'd been murdered, and she couldn't understand why Mr. Quinn had involved that Negro in any of these processes.

In fact, Constance was beginning to regret that Jelly had gone with her on Friday to the man's office—if you could call a cold, dark, damp cellar an office; which Constance couldn't—for now her maid wanted to go back to have her *foot* looked at by the man again.

"Who is this friend of yours who's trying to find this out?" asked Mrs. Burnside, still looking at the drawing. She frowned at it. "Perhaps she looks a bit familiar to me, but I can't place her. Rose, do you know her?" She gave the paper to their hostess.

"Yes, Constance, do tell us who your friend is," replied Mrs. Greenhow. "No, Alice, I don't believe I know the poor girl." She handed it back to Constance.

"His name is Adam Quinn. He's a friend of Mr. Lincoln's," she said, and the other ladies hissed their displeasure. But Constance smiled as she tucked the paper away. "It was because of him that I learned the true number of men barracked at the President's House."

Or, more accurately, because of that Sophie Gates's thoughtless tongue. She'd only met the woman twice, but both times, she seemed unable to control the thoughts that came right from her brain to her lips. But the fact that Miss Gates seemed to be staying at the President's House did give her pause.

"Ah," said Mrs. Greenhow. "So he's the one. Yes, the handsome Mr. Quinn is a friend of Constance's *and* a friend of Mr. Lincoln's. She introduced me to him—was it Sunday, Constance?—and you said so at the time. I do believe if I were you, I'd do my best to keep your Mr. Quinn close."

The other ladies tittered, and Constance smiled in agreement. Despite his rough frontier clothing and uneven manners, keeping the intriguing and handsome Mr. Quinn close would not be the least bit of a hardship.

As she had done ever since the Sixth Massachusetts regiment arrived on the train Friday evening, Sophie helped Clara Barton collect and deliver donations to the infirmary once more on Tuesday.

Each day, they visited the soldiers they'd assisted that first night, then went on to visit with some of the other members of the troop. After that, they went door to door, from shop to shop, also visiting as many households of people who were left in town, asking for donations of bandages, socks, and food to help the hospital.

"People have been so generous," said Clara, as she'd told Sophie to call her. "At least, the Loyalists have been."

There'd been a few Southern sympathizers who'd turned them away, often with barely concealed glee about the upcoming invasion. It seemed everyone expected that tonight—whatever night it was—would be the night the Confederates would come.

Sophie, who'd sat up for the last two nights, fully clothed, with Mrs. Lincoln and the other women, was almost ready to say "let them come"—just to get it over with.

But of course she didn't really feel that way. Yet, it was almost like a dream every morning when dawn came and the city was still quiet and secure. Only then did the ladies feel it was safe enough to close their eyes for a few precious hours of sleep.

And then when they woke up later in the morning, it was to yet another long day of anxiousness and gloom. Waiting.

Late yesterday, however, there'd been some news—finally—on the Seventh New York regiment and another one from Massachusetts. According to rumor, those two sets of troops had reached Annapolis. Those who were the most optimistic hoped the reinforcements might arrive in Washington sometime today. Even so, every person inside the White House was tense, sharp, shadow-eyed, and grim, for the threat to any Union men trying to move through Maryland was well-known.

They didn't want another mob attack or riot like there had been in Baltimore. And Sophie knew, from being at the White House, that General Scott had sent *eight* different riders to Annapolis late yesterday to get news, and to bring pleas for the soldiers to hurry to Washington. As of this morning, none of the eight had returned.

That was an ominous sign, and it made the mood in the mansion even darker.

Thus, Sophie was glad to leave the house, as she did most every day. And although most of the time she had a member of the Frontier Guard as an escort down Pennsylvania Avenue, she hadn't caught more than a glimpse of Mr. Quinn since their conversation on Sunday.

"Let's put up the target here," Clara said, setting down the painter's easel that Sophie had "borrowed" from the naturalists' supplies in the North Tower.

They were near in an empty lot next to the wide open—but muddy—space of the National Mall, in the shadow of the stub of the unfinished Washington Monument. The abbreviated marble column was surrounded by scaffolding and building debris as it had been for seven years, since the construction had paused in 1854.

"Do you think they'll ever finish it?" Sophie asked, looking up the small hill toward the stunted monument as she rested an old canvas painting of a barnyard (also "borrowed" from the North Tower) in place on the easel for their shooting target. Near the

Mall was the perfect place for target practice, as it was wide open with several empty lots and, with the city so empty, very devoid of people.

Clara raised her dark brows. Although she was generally rather shy, the two of them—along with Clara's sister, Sally Vassall, who also lived in the city—had become quite comfortable and outspoken friends. "If we win the war, I think they'll *have* to finish the monument. Don't you think? If we don't . . ." She grimaced as she stepped away from the easel, putting twenty paces between her and the target as she untied and removed her bonnet. "They'll tear it down. The Confederates."

Sophie stood next to her, removing her own bonnet (it got in the way when one was managing a firearm; and her gloves, also, had been eschewed so as not to stain them with gunpowder). She watched as Clara expertly cocked her revolver, then fired at the target. The ball ripped through the canvas painting in the center of the upper right corner, replacing half of a bright yellow sun with a dark hole.

"But if they do finish it," Clara said, nodding in satisfaction before she stepped back to allow Sophie a shot, "I fear there will always be a line showing where the construction stopped and then started again. The blocks will be different shades of white, for the bottom half will have been much longer aged."

Sophie lifted her shotgun, settling it against her shoulder, and aimed. *Boom!* The butt of the gun kicked against her in the same place it always did, and the shot scattered into small holes at the edge of the painting. "So much for Madam Cow," she said. "Next time I'll try for Mr. Rooster." He was closer to the center of the painting which was, quite honestly, an eyesore. Mr. Stimpson, Sophie decided, should confine himself to drawing diagrams of clam species instead of painting idyllic barnyard scenes.

"Beef is better than eggs, if you can get it," Clara quipped, then took her turn while Sophie reloaded.

They went back and forth like this several times over the next hour. Although both of them needed improvement, eventually, the barnyard scene was riddled with black holes and torn canvas.

"The last time I did shooting practice here," Clara said as she expertly reloaded the revolver's cylinder, "one of the constables tried to stop me. That was last week, just after the news came about Fort Sumter." She closed the chamber and looked up. "It seems that this week the constables either don't care, or have left the city."

"Or else they've recognized the importance of proper shooting skills," Sophie said with a giggle, struggling to reload her shotgun. "I *live* on the National Mall and I've never thought about doing target shooting here. But you're right, dear Clara—we must be prepared to protect ourselves for when the Rebels come." She stepped back as her companion positioned for another shot.

"We are going to need another painting, I think," Clara said as she cocked her gun. "Perhaps one not quite as poorly rendered as this one? Those goats have a canine look to them, if you ask me."

"But that just makes using it for target practice all the more satisfying." Sophie was still chuckling as she caught sight of an open carriage crunching along the road toward them. It didn't look fine enough to be a private vehicle—which might have given a clue to its occupant—so she presumed it was a hackney.

When it pulled up next to them and the female passenger looked out from the side opening of the barouche, Sophie didn't immediately recognize her.

"What an enterprising idea," said the woman, looking pointedly at their arrangement. She was quite beautiful, and was dressed in fine clothing with a tall, arched bonnet of dark blue. A wide white bow tied under her chin matched the ribbon on the bonnet and the yellow and white daisies decorating it. "There's no sense in sitting back and doing nothing while we wait, is there?"

Clara had just taken her shot when the carriage stopped, and now she turned. "Why, Mrs. Lander, how good to see you. And that is quite the truth you speak."

"I thought that was you, Miss Barton," replied the woman with a smile.

"Thank you again for your donations to our soldiers," replied Clara.

The lovely woman's face sobered. "My husband the colonel is one of 'our' soldiers, and I would hope that he and his men will receive the same care and attention no matter where they are during these troubling times."

By now, Sophie realized this was Mrs. Jean Lander, the famous actress—and, she realized with a flash of excitement, the woman who'd visited the White House at midnight to warn Mr. Lincoln of an assassination plot.

"Would you care to take a shot?" Clara asked with a smile. "I believe it's important for women like us not to settle for waiting to be saved and protected, but to be prepared to do so ourselves."

Mrs. Lander seemed delighted with this idea, and she called to the driver for assistance.

"Thank you—what was your name again?" she asked the man as he helped her and all of her skirts, hoops, and petticoats safely to the ground.

"Isaac, ma'am." Beneath the brown bowler hat, which he tipped politely, his face was tanned from the sun. His hands were the capable, worn ones of a man who'd used them often.

"Thank you, Isaac." Mrs. Lander followed Sophie and Clara's example, removing her bonnet. She handed it to the driver, who set it inside the carriage.

Mrs. Lander took the revolver Clara offered her, and seemed very comfortable with it. "As if it's not enough that the Rebels are breathing down our necks, now people are being killed outright in the city. My favorite hackney driver—his name was Louis—was murdered right here on the street last week! He always knew to wait for me outside the Willard or my house every day—the Colonel refuses to bring our carriage to the city from home, and so I quite relied on Louis to be driven from rehearsal to the theater, and to every other event in town. His landau was always clean and neat, so my hems didn't get dirty and I didn't get tobacco stains on my skirts—unlike most other hacks. Not his though," she added in a stage whisper, glancing toward Isaac. "It's just as clean as Louis's was. I looked inside before I engaged him, of course, and I was pleasantly surprised.

"Anyhow, I was quite devastated when I learned that poor Louis had been found dead—he was such a friendly fellow. Reminded me of a wizened leprechaun—small and wrinkly like an old apple, but very quick and efficient. He knew how to manage horses."

She faced the target, checked the weapon, and prepared to fire. "Someone cut the poor man's throat, if you can believe it." She paused, drew a breath, then took aim and slowly pulled the trigger. *Boom!*

"That was a very nice shot, Mrs. Lander," Sophie said when the ball hit one of the few sections of the painting that was still intact. *Good-bye to the canine-like goat.*

"Thank you." She looked at Sophie questioningly.

"I'm so sorry," said Clara. "Mrs. Lander, this is Miss Sophie Gates. She lives in the Smithsonian Castle with Dr. Henry and his family—she's his niece—but she is currently staying in the President's House. She's been helping me collect donations for the infirmary."

Mrs. Lander gave Sophie a surprised and perhaps even envious look. "How incredible. The President's House? As it happens, I was there very late on Thursday night. I suppose it's very . . . anxious there at this time, isn't it?"

Sophie seized upon the opportunity to do some further investigating. "Yes, it is rather . . . gloomy at times. And, incidentally, I heard that you had called at midnight last week. Terribly enough, a man"—she chose not to share the details about Jane Thorne for fear she'd have to give a long explanation—"was found dead the next morning in a room on the second floor."

"The second floor? The next morning? Why, that's where I was! That young, quite amiable assistant to Mr. Lincoln—Mr. Hay, I believe his name is—took me and Millicent up to the second floor right that night. We sat in the waiting room and I told Mr. Hay what I knew about the plot. I'd heard a man talking about doing a thing that 'would ring throughout the world'—and I knew I must warn Mr. Lincoln.

"It was so quiet up there on the upper floor. Mr. Hay told me he didn't want to wake the president, and that I should tell him whatever I knew, and he would make certain to tell Mr. Lincoln. I'm certain he did." She looked at Sophie questioningly, as if she would somehow know what transpired between the president and his secretary.

"Millicent? Is that your maid?" Sophie asked. "She came inside with you? What about your driver?" She realized the questions were tumbling out almost rudely, but she didn't care. She knew the answers might be important. And Mrs. Lander seemed to be the type to enjoy being the center of attention—even an interrogation.

After all, she *was* an actress.

"Yes, of course, Millicent is my maid. I wasn't going to come out without a chaperone—and the colonel is out of town." Her expression sobered. "That was the last time Louis drove me anywhere. I was looking for him, as I expected he'd be waiting outside my home the next morning—rather later than usual, due to a lack of sleep on my part," she added with a wry lift of her brows, "and he never arrived. And then later, when I sent around to Willard's looking for him, I learned he was dead."

"Louis drove you to the President's House. Did he come inside with you?"

"No, of course not. Whyever would he do so? He remained with the carriage while Millicent and I went inside. That tall Irish man called for Mr. Hay, and showed us to the stairs to meet him."

Sophie felt a sudden rush of excitement. "Are you quite certain Louis didn't come in with you? Mr. Burns—that was the tall Irish doorman—said that your driver came inside."

Mrs. Lander appeared astonished by this information. "But, no, of course he didn't come in with me." She thought for a moment. "Perhaps he was merely curious about the great white house, and wanted to take a peek inside whilst he was waiting. There is something about that mansion that feels so very important—just stepping over the threshold it makes one draw in such a deep breath of awe. . . . Although, I venture to say, it's looking rather shabby as of late. Like a worn-out hotel."

Sophie nodded. "Perhaps that was it. He was just curious to see the inside." She hesitated, then went on, "And he was there when you came out, and drove you back home?"

Mrs. Lander gave her a strange look, as if just realizing how invasive Sophie's questions were. "Yes, of course. Miss Gates, you seem inordinately interested in all of this."

Clara, who'd been listening to the exchange while cleaning her black powder revolver, answered. "They're trying to find out who murdered that poor man up at the President's House, and Sophie is helping with the investigation."

"Is that so?" Now Mrs. Lander's astonishment was laced with admiration, if not a bit of skepticism. "Do you fancy yourself a Pinkerton, then, Miss Gates? Like that Kate Warne? And what on earth does my driver have to do with all of it anyway?"

"I don't really know, Mrs. Lander. But the man was killed sometime between midnight and half-past five that night, and so Mr. Quinn—that is, the man who is helping the president with this problem—is trying to determine who was in the house and where everyone was at the time in order to narrow it down. And"—Sophie added as she picked up her bonnet—"I can't help but find it interesting that your driver turned up dead the very next day after he drove you there."

The other woman shook her head. "As sad as it is, I see no connection, Miss Gates."

"Perhaps you'll change your mind when I tell you that the person who was killed in the President's House *also* had his throat cut."

Mrs. Lander's eyes went wide, almost completely round, as she tilted her head thoughtfully. "Well, that is quite interesting. Still, I see no reason for there to be a connection. However . . . I suppose now I'll be thinking about that all of the rest of the day." She turned and summoned Isaac, who'd brought his carriage over to one of the rare trees on the mall and was feeding his horse. "I suppose that's preferable to stewing over when the Confederates are going to come. And whether the New York regiment will get here first."

Sophie couldn't disagree with that sentiment.

Later that day, after Sophie had returned the remains of their shooting practice to the Smithsonian and walked another block collecting donations, Clara suggested that she and her sister Sally, who'd helped them on the latest round of knocking on doors, along with Sophie, should visit the rest of the soldiers of the Sixth Massachusetts regiment—the ones who didn't need to be in the hospital—at the Capitol.

By now, it was just after four o'clock, and the tension that seemed to overtake the very air of the city as evening and night drew near, was palpable. The hoped-for arrival of the New York regiment hadn't happened, and it seemed as if perhaps it had been only a rumor that they'd gotten to Annapolis. What had been a spark of hope had burned out and become dull and gloomy once again.

Sophie thought she might want to return to the Executive Mansion soon, but she hadn't yet been inside the Capitol since coming to Washington, so she agreed to go with Clara and her sister—mainly out of curiosity. But she also was reluctant to return to the President's House any sooner than necessary, knowing how short-tempered and anxious Mrs. Lincoln and the other ladies would be.

"I'm certain I'll know several of the men," Clara told Sophie as they approached the steps to the majestic domed building. Even with its scaffolding around the partially finished dome, the structure was the grandest, most awe-inspiring building Sophie had ever seen—and that was saying quite a lot, for New York City was filled with many opulent, grand buildings. And, thanks to Peter and his family, she'd been inside many of them.

"My goodness, look at this," said Sally as they were stopped by a sentry who stood in front of a pile of sandbags that rose nearly to Sophie's shoulders. These blockages had been placed around the perimeter of the building at the base of the stairs, leaving only two small passages.

The guard used his bayonet to block their progress, which would have taken them through a small passageway between the sandbags and up the steps to the arched entrances to the Capitol.

"Excuse me, misses," he said, standing there in the gray uniform coat of the Sixth Massachusetts, "but you cannot proceed without giving the password." Although he was polite in tone, the steely expression in his face indicated he was quite serious about blocking their passage.

Of course they didn't know the password, and the three women stood there for a moment, discussing their next move—within the sentry's hearing. Despite their obvious distress, he was not inclined to allow them entrance. Clearly, he'd been given very strict orders.

Just as they were about to leave in defeat, someone called from across one of the arched entrances. "Miss Barton? Miss Clara Barton? Is that you? And Mrs. Vassall, too!"

"Mr. Jones! Oh, excuse me, *Colonel* Jones," amended Clara with a shy smile as she smoothed her skirt. "One must remember protocol now that you're officially in the army."

Indeed, for yesterday, the men of the Sixth Mass had taken their oaths to the United States Army for ninety days.

The colonel grinned and bowed in acknowledgment. "Miss Barton, I'd heard you were visiting our men at the hospital. And you've been bringing blankets and stockings and more to them." The colonel turned to the sentry, who'd gone to stand at attention at his officer's approach. He saluted his man, then said, "At ease, Triplett. These young ladies may pass in with me, for Miss Barton and her sister have been keepin' our boys comfortable in the hospital. What brings you here, Miss Barton?"

Clara quickly introduced Sophie, and the three of them walked up the broad expanse of steps and into the vast, colonnaded portico in his company. Sophie couldn't keep from gawking at the high arches and the frescoed ceilings as their footsteps echoed across the marble floor.

This, she thought with a swell of pride and hope, was what the war was truly about: maintaining the solvency of the Union, governed here within these massive walls and inside the two new lavish wings for the chambers of Congress. *This building represents our country, our government, and what the Founding Fathers built. What our ancestors fought England for.*

To her shock, tears stung her eyes as Sophie trailed along behind Colonel Jones, whom she'd learned was the commander of the Sixth Massachusetts.

We can't let our country fall, she thought. *We must keep it together.*

"We had to remove the portrait of President Tyler that was hanging in the corridor," the colonel was saying as he saluted a sentry guarding one of the doors. "Or I wager it would have been shredded with the tip of a bayonet."

"I can sympathize with their disgust," Miss Barton replied with heartfelt emotion. "After all, he acted no less than a traitor when he presided over the secession convention in Virginia last week. Imagine, a *president* of the nation assisting a state to secede!"

"Mr. Buchanan's painting is put away as well, for the same reason," Jones said. "Because he did nothing to prepare the Union for the inevitable after Mr. Lincoln was elected."

Now as they made their way down the marble-floored corridor, Sophie heard the sounds of men marching in drills, their boots ringing in echoes somewhere in the building. There were voices and the clicks of ramrods loading from other parts of the wing. But most of all, heaven help her, she noticed the *stench.*

Obviously, although there was plenty of room for a thousand men to barrack here, there had not been any attention given to the problem of sanitation for so many.

The rank smell was incredible.

And she didn't even dare to guess what was in those buckets and troughs lined up along the hallway . . . but from the look and odor, she suspected it was the obvious.

They passed boxed-up marble statues standing next to their pedestals, and rough planking that had been nailed over life-sized paintings and portraits—all in an effort to protect the contents of the building should the worst occur.

As Colonel Jones opened the door to what Sophie realized was the Senate chamber, there was a sudden spurt of loud cheering and shouting from inside.

"What is going on in here?" Jones demanded as a group of men fell back from where they'd been gathered around one of the large desks that lined the room in a semicircle.

Still relatively new to military protocol—for they'd been mustered from a militia back in Massachusetts—the men were slow to stand at attention at the arrival of their commander, and rather sloppy as they did so.

"Leavy, what is going on in here?" Jones asked again as Sophie and the Barton sisters followed him into the chamber.

"Sir," said the man, standing at attention. "We were cutting that damned traitor's desk to pieces!"

Sophie could see that was the case: several bayonets had been thrust into one of the desks, and the red leather chair had been cut open.

"That's Senator Jeff Davis's desk," murmured Clara, who was close enough to see. "Er—*former* desk."

"Mr. Davis doesn't *own* the desk," replied Jones tersely. "The government that you are protecting does. You are meant to protect the property here, men—not to destroy it!"

Sophie stepped aside as Jones moved forward to finish admonishing his troops. She looked around the elegant, high-ceilinged Senate chamber, relieved that the smell of human waste had been replaced, at least in this room, by that of food. When she looked closer, she saw the grease stains on the leather chairs and the marble floor. There were scattered everywhere trays and plates with ham bones and bacon leftovers, along with stewed potatoes and gravy slopped on the walls, furnishings, and floor. Tobacco stains colored the walls and floor, where the juice had missed the spittoon—or hadn't even attempted to find the vessel.

She'd peeked in to the East Room at the White House, currently bed and board to over a hundred men, and the mess the

Frontier Guard made there wasn't nearly as severe as that here in the Senate Chamber. Still, the ill caretaking of the chamber, as with the half-finished Washington Monument, was yet another symbol of the destruction and threat to the American democracy.

Suddenly, she was tired and anxious. It was time to leave. If she went soon, she'd make it back to the Executive Mansion before the sun set.

Sophie bid farewell to Clara and Sally, and as she was escorted out from the Senate Chamber (for she never would have found the way herself), she toyed with the idea of just returning to her own home at the Castle. If she kept the lights off, no one would know she was there and thus she'd be in no danger.

The idea was very attractive—especially since she'd hardly given a thought to writing a newspaper story since meeting Clara Barton and joining her in the efforts to provide for the soldiers. Between the murder investigation and working with her new friend, Sophie hadn't even picked up a pencil or paper except for the notes she'd made for Mr. Quinn.

As well, she might get a quiet night's sleep without having to listen to Mrs. Lincoln, Mrs. Grimsley, and Mrs. Edwards talking about what would happen when the Confederates came. Those conversations only made everything worse. She might even sleep better knowing the Smithsonian wasn't a target of the Rebels, and that she was out from beneath the roof that was.

Outside once again, where the air was fresh and didn't stink like an outhouse or a banquet room, Sophie paused at the top of the hill. She looked left, down toward the red-orange brick of the Castle—which was in closer proximity—and then to the right, along the broad Pennsylvania Avenue to where the president and his family were. The sun was preparing to set directly in front of her, tinting the sky pink and red like a watercolor wash.

She counted five flickers of campfires across the Potomac and shivered. They were there. Waiting. Waiting to come across the Long Bridge and seize the city.

If she walked home—back to the Castle—she'd be there before darkness set in. Sophie was tempted. Very tempted. She could send word to Mr. Quinn, somehow. Maybe one of the men here would take the message. So at least he wouldn't worry about her.

Sophie flushed at the thought. Clara had made some comment earlier today about "your Mr. Quinn"—it was after Mrs. Lander had left their shooting practice and they were discussing the conversation about her driver Louis.

"He's not *my* Mr. Quinn," Sophie had replied tartly. "If he's anyone's Mr. Quinn, he's Constance Lemagne's."

And that was fine with her—as long as he didn't try to keep Sophie out of the murder investigation while allowing the pretty, simpering Southern belle *in*—such as to draw pictures and visit the makeshift morgue.

But Clara's comment had lodged in her mind, and it stuck there as Sophie began to make her way down toward—sigh—Pennsylvania Avenue. The idea of being courted by a man, or even having a man being *interested* in courting her—not that she believed Mr. Quinn had the least bit of consideration toward doing so—made her stomach feel tight beneath her stays and her mouth dry. Almost as much as when she sat there politely listening to Mrs. Lincoln and her relatives wail on about the impending invasion.

After what had happened with Peter, Sophie didn't think she ever wanted to get married, let alone have a courtship with a man. Even with a man as radically different from Peter Schuyler as Adam Quinn.

Maybe she would be like Clara Barton—unmarried at the age of forty, and *happy* about it.

George whistled softly as he approached the dark house. It was past ten o'clock, and the moonless night was still. The city was more than four miles behind him, so there was nothing here but all shades of gray and black shadows.

And, he hoped, nothing else.

A maple just beginning to burst into leaves buffeted gently against the overhang of the roof, making soft, skittery, scraping

noises. The faint scent of wood smoke hung in the air, telling him
someone had burned a fire recently.

But other than that, the house that was tucked into a pair of
small, gentle hills appeared abandoned. Even the scent of horse
dung was absent.

He whistled again, low and smooth, so that it melded with the
breeze and the softly clattering branches in a gentle announce-
ment of his arrival.

He'd not been to this house before, but Brownie Bixley had given
him the directions. Brownie had meant to come tonight, but George
told him to stay home with his wife and boys. If the Confederates
came, he'd need to be there to get his family to hiding. And to help
protect the city.

George knew Beauregard was in Alexandria, and that he was
amassing men with amazing speed compared to Mr. Lincoln's
mustering his army—thanks in great part to the state of Maryland's disagreeability in allowing any of the Northerners through.
That was the thing about the network of communication among
the Negroes: there was little information to be hidden when
slaves and servants lurked everywhere and no one paid any mind
to them. So they heard everything, they spoke to each other in
their own coded ways, both free and slave, and therefore George
had learned the city was still at great risk. Beauregard needed to
attack before reinforcements arrived from New York and Massachusetts, and that meant he had to act soon.

That was why George had risked coming here tonight. And why
he was particularly thankful even the stars were swathed in the
darkness of clouds.

He edged into the shadows by the maple and waited, listening
and watching, pressing himself up against its trunk. He felt the
roughness against his temple and the palm of his hand, and he
smelled the fresh, loamy scent of damp bark.

The ride beyond the city in his trundling wagon had seemed
even longer and darker than his usual journeys because he knew
Confederate soldiers lurked all throughout the hills surrounding

Washington. They spied and waited and watched, and because of that, he was putting himself at risk more than he'd ever done. Even here in the middle of nowhere, in the dark of night, someone could be watching and waiting around any bend in the road or beyond any stand of trees.

Spies, scouts, traitors, slavers, soldiers.

Escapees.

He'd left the wagon and its cargo parked in a throng of thick pines and tall brush some ways back. Then he unhooked his mare, leading her along with him for another half-mile. He tied her up—Blaze was her name—and left her tucked in a different stand of trees and brush with a nosebag of oats and prayers that no one would hear or see her. George not only couldn't afford to lose her, he didn't *want* to lose her. She was a smart and gentle mare.

Then he'd walked the last quarter of a mile to this meeting place. If someone heard the whuffling of his horse, he'd be too far away for them to instantly connect him to Blaze, and the horseless cart, almost a mile away—if it were noticed, hidden as it was—would appear abandoned.

By now George estimated it had been at least ten minutes since his last whistle. There'd been no sign nor sound from inside the house—although shack was a more appropriate term. It looked as if it might blow over in a strong wind.

With one last look around to be certain he was alone, he slipped from the relative safety of the tree and melded into the shadow of the shack. Around he went to the back, careful to avoid tripping on or knocking into debris from the decrepit building. As he moved toward the center of the back wall, where the door was, he heard a faint whistle coming from inside.

The sound was hardly discernible, but it was enough to have his muscles relax a bit in relief. He was a free man, *born* a free man thanks to his mother's determination and cunning, but the awareness that that could change in the breath of a moment always lived with him.

He whistled once more, putting his mouth next to the place where the door appeared to be, so he could keep the sound as quiet as possible.

Something creaked on the other side of the rough wooden slats that made up the wall, and then it slid away. The angular shape of the opening was pale yellow, and, heart pounding, George stepped inside.

CHAPTER 13

BIRCH REMOVED HIS GLOVES—PRISTINE AND WHITE AS ALWAYS, LIKE now, even at the end of his shift—and folded them neatly. Though his hands were old and gnarled, dark as walnuts, a little crusty at the knuckles, they still worked just fine.

Sure, he might have some days it was harder to get up before the dawn and dress and come down the Avenue to the hotel to get shaved before his shift—with more aches and pains than he had only a few years ago when President Pierce was here—but he still mostly worked just fine.

And if it weren't for *him,* the Willard—that blessed, beautiful place that give him so much happiness over the years since he was freed—well, that stately ol' hotel would be burned to the ground. Woulda gone up in flames last Thursday night if ol' Birch, he hadn't seen it all going on.

Damned Secessionists.

Ol' Birch—yessir, he nodded to himself—he's a man who saw *ever'thing.* He noticed ever'one, and nothin' went on around the Avenue he didn't know about.

And he remembered it all, too. All o' it.

He might be almost seventy, but ol' Birch, he got eyes like a hawk. An' his ears work just fine too. And bein' at the front door of the Willard Hotel—don't care what no one else tried to argue, it was the fanciest, most import'nt meeting place or eating place or business place or politicking place in all o' Washington, even more than the Capitol or the pres'dent's house—and Birch, he bein' at the front door of the Willard ever'day meant he *saw* and *heard* all of it.

Ain't never a face or a person or a carriage passed by that front door he didn't see or notice. No, sir.

Birch tucked the folded gloves into a pocket of his dark coat with the big silver buttons, the uniform he wore every day to manage the comings and goings at the Willard, and smoothed down the front of it. Though his shift might be ended—and late, it was, tonight that he was finally making to leave—a man hadda take pride in his appearance, black or white or red or yellow, and Birch, he did make sure of that. Even when he was off-duty. They din't pay him much at the Willard, but that Lizzie Keckley, she help keep him in *style* just as she kept Mrs. Lincoln in her fancy dresses. He smiled and shook his head. Imagine that—him bein' dressed by the same seamstress doing the *president's wife!*

If he were twenty, thirty years younger . . . well, he might be considerin' courtin' on Miz Lizzie. She sure had a good way with a needle and thread, and she was as kind a soul as they come.

Though servants were relegated to using the back entrance of the hotel, Birch—well, he was the exception. How could they keep *him* from goin' in and out the front door when that was what he *did* all day?

He chuckled to himself at the thought as he walked from the back near the kitchens up through the lobby of his beloved Willard. He adjusted a large pot of ferns in the hall because its fronds threatened to block the entrance to the ladies' eating room—though it was nearly empty now with everyone gone out of the town, sad as it was—and paused to straighten one of the spittoons near the hotel's entrance. He *tsked* at the sight of tobacco juice sliding down the side of it and hollered for one of the boys to come clean it up. Couldn't have a dripping spittoon be the first thing a man saw when he come in the door to the Willard, now, could he?

Then Birch couldn't resist opening the door for a late arrival; hell, it was half-past eleven o'clock—two men in top hats and expensive frock coats; that was Mr. Elmer Garrett and his brother—because probably Wally was standing around jawing with the hackney drivers like he allus did instead of payin' attention to the work.

That was why Birch was there bright and early at six o'clock every morning, even on Sundays—apologies to the Lord—and why he stayed till ten o'clock at night, sometimes as late as eleven or even midnight. That was because there was no one but Birch who opened the door with such grand welcome, who saw everything and noticed when somethin' was goin' go wrong even before it did.

Didn't he catch Mrs. Blair's valises before they fell off the back of the coach last time she come to town? Or rescue Mr. Peltham's walking stick before it rolled into the Avenue and got crushed by a carriage wheel? He even snatched up a pretty bonnet just as it blew off the head of Miss Chase and tumbled into the street. Miss Chase—now she was a pretty, fine lady, wasn't she?

No, there's no one but Birch who could be the doorkeep at the Willard. Old Ed McManus, he up at the President's House—well, he might be a doorkeep, but he didn't have the notice Birch did. No sir. Wasn't nearly as much comings and goings down there at 1600 as there was here. And Old Ed could stay there, at that end of the Avenue, and Birch here, and that old Bassett—good man, he was but still he wasn't no Birch—up to the Capitol.

They ought to have a guild for doorkeeps, Birch thought as he finally stepped outside and stood there on the corner of Twelfth and Pennsylvania and drew in a breath of the evening air. Sun was long down and there was only a new moon tonight. He'd be walking in the dark the way home, but there was no one in Washington who'd bother him being out so late even though him being a black man and all.

He was too damned old to be kidnapped and taken down South to work in the fields, and alongside of that, ever'one of the constables knew Birch. None o' them would bother him if he was out past curfew.

Birch watched a few hacks go by, all the while spying on Wally to see if it was really safe for him to go on now and that his re-placement would do right for the rest of the night. Shouldn't be so busy that even Wally could handle things—though here was Birch, just now leaving and it was going on to midnight, so it was time things quieted down.

But everyone was saying Beauregard was gonna come over that river tonight and take the city. That it was gonna be tonight, be-fore them troops from up north ever got here. Birch didn't like that thought, but there warn't nothing a nigger could do about it.

Damned Secessionists.

Reminded him of that night—Thursday night, it was, the night Senator Lane's frontiersmen was all rallying around out in the street—and all the other comings and goings that happened that night.

That was the night them Secessionists almost blew up his hotel, and well, it was just by chance Birch was there till midnight that night, because it wasn't till then he noticed them bundles of rags stuck in the corner of the lobby and beneath the curtains. They was gonna set them bundles on fire—they smelt of kerosene, too, some of them—and burn the place down.

Damned Secessionists.

The Good Lord was surely looking out for Birch and the Willard then, keeping His favorite doorman on till far too late in the day.

It was because of all the excitement with the soldiers marching to Mr. Lincoln's house that he had to stay so late *that* night. And the fear the Rebels was gonna come across the Long Bridge.

Who was goin' stop them? It was gonna fall to them rough, scruffy frontiersmen with their rifles and pistols, their worn can-vas coats and heavy boots and wide-brimmed hats didn't belong in the likes of the gold and brass Willard—exceptin' that rough looking Mr. Lane, who's still got a room here—though he ain't been around much, helping the president as he done. And even now, Lane got that flag just now hanging there outside his bed-room window—the one his men jest brought back from beating up some Secessionist devils over acrossed the river coupla hours ago. You could see it from down on the Avenue, that flag, and it had been torn up and shot through by the Loyalist men and brought back like a trophy to show the might of the United States.

Yah, Birch liked that. All the rest of his duty, he kept walking out just far enough away from the door so he could see that flag fluttering in the breeze up there, remindin' him that there's men who's fightin' for the Negroes and the city and the president and the country.

That Mr. Quinn, he gone with them today and helped bring back that flag. Birch liked that man—he sitting in there now at the drinking counter with the other mens who brought back that trophy, and they having some ale and whiskey to celebrate. And maybe to spread some more rumors to keep General Beauregard from coming acrosst the river tonight. Oh, yes sir, Birch knew how it was, he thought to himself with a grin. How Mr. Lane and Mr. Quinn and some of the others was putting jest the right information into the ears of jest the right peoples. Birch warn't no fool.

That Mr. Quinn's momma raised him right, sure did, and he polite and look a man in the eye no matter what the color his skin or the age of his body—old or young—or whether he be whole or partial. Was a shame about his arm, that, and how his wooden one even got broken last month when there was all that about the murder of Custer Billings. But he was wearing it again, and seemed to be all fine.

Well, now, Birch figured it was time to walk on home now. Wally seemed to be doing some of his work at least some of the time, and today—well, it was a day Birch's knees were a bit on the tryin' side, and he was really wanting to lay his head on that pillow of his because it was ver' nearly Wednesday mornin' already, and he hadda be back at six o'clock.

As he started up Fourteenth Street, he took one last look over the hackneys waitin' there outside the Willard, and was put in mind of that old Louis who drove the dark blue landau, God rest his soul. Now who'd wanta hurt a shriveled old man like Louis, anyway? And cut open his throat?

What'd he ever do to no one? Not even a black man hisself—just a short little German man with a soft voice.

Last time Birch saw Louis was that same night Thursday—seemed like everything happened that night, too. He shook his head, unbelieving of it all. Mrs. Lander come out of dinner here at the Willard, half-past eleven it was, and she was bound and determined to go up the Avenue to the President's House. On a night like that, imagine! When the Confederates was expected to come any time!

But Louis was gonna take her, as he allus did, and Birch himself helped Mrs. Lander get into his carriage and her maid too. And before they started off, he remembered seeing a man climb up to sit next to Louis, and he rode off with him on the carriage on the way to the President's House.

They rode off and left Birch go on back to the door, opening it for Mr. Seward and Mr. Blair. And that was when he saw them rags piled under the curtains. When he smelt the kerosene, and he saw the long wick leading from it along the wall to a corner there, he knew what it was all about. Right away, Birch knew.

And he knew just when they got put there, and he was sure'n all he knew who put them down there, too, bein' someone who never forgot a face or a person and who saw everything. Talking about frontiersmen, with their rough coats and dirty boots . . . he'd seen them.

Them damn Secessionists.

They found more than fifteen bundles of rags on that main floor of Willard's before dawn come—it took all them hours to search the whole place, and they locked the doors so no one could come in and set 'em afire while they was searching.

Birch, he looked in every corner and alcove, under every sofa and chair and the footed spittoons too, and even in the trash bins—where he found another pile of kerosene-soaked rags.

Even now, as he trudged down the dark street up toward the north side of town, he got angry all over again. How dare those white devils try and do this to his hotel! Burn it down! All those peoples inside it too, sleeping—why that woulda been murder, it was!

Cold murder.

Just as bad as was done to poor Louis.

He heard the scuff of a shoe on the hard-packed dirt walkway. It was behind him, and Birch—well, he warn't no fool, and something told him to turn and look there in the shadows.

But just as he did, something dark and heavy swung through the air. He cried out just before it crashed into the side of his skull.

Pain exploded in his head and that was the last thing he knew.

George's shadow threw long and broad inside the small, decrepit shack. It was lit by one stingy lantern, and the windows were covered with thick blankets to keep the light hidden.

The floor was dirt and the walls were rough planks of wood. A few lumps in the shadows were too small to be people—he hoped—and more likely old furniture. A faint rotting smell indicated some leftover food, or a disintegrating rodent. George wagered on it being the latter.

There was no one in the room but the man who'd opened the door. He was about fifty, of average height with fair, blotchy skin and hair going to gray and white at the mouth of his beard.

"I got cargo for you," George said, a little wary because the man was white. Not that a black man wouldn't betray another black man—oh, it happened all the time, especially slaves who betrayed others trying for their freedom—but there was still more likely to be danger with a white man.

Still, Brownie knew him, and George trusted his friend.

"Where is it?" asked the man. They gave no names and both instinctively tried to stay in the shadows. The less either of them knew about the other, or anyone else involved in this secret transportation system—and especially about the cargo being delivered or exchanged—the safer they were. All George knew was the man was a Quaker who lived near the Pennsylvania border.

"Back a piece. Thought it was safer. I'll bring it along. Do you have anything for me?"

The man grunted and gestured to the darkest corner. George hesitated only a moment before walking over there to look, and the back of his neck prickled with awareness as he turned his back on his contact. Even though he was several inches taller than the other man, broader in shoulder and younger in age, he was still black and the man was still white.

But there in the shadows and beneath a dark canvas, George found ten Enfield rifles and two large boxes of ammunition. He exhaled silently, then turned to face his companion, who was watching him with a calm yet arrested expression. Perhaps he, too, was wary of a large black man he didn't know who was here to retrieve weapons.

"All right," said George.

It didn't take long to make the exchange. George jogged back to get Blaze, then hooked her up to the wagon and drove the mile back to the meeting house.

Admittedly, he felt that prickle of caution as he approached the shack again—it wasn't out of the realm of possibility that his contact had called in some hidden reinforcements who were now waiting to ambush him . . . but all went well.

He pulled his wagon behind the shack. Only then, when they were so close to the house and bathed in shadow, did he remove the false back to the wagon that made a hidden compartment beneath the bench seat for the driver.

His contact whistled softly, but this time it was in admiration. "Never seen anything so clever before."

George smiled warily and nodded. He'd thought hard to design something that wouldn't be an obvious false front, and he knew it was one of the best of its kind. He hadn't intended the other man to see it, for, again, the fewer people who knew his business, the safer he was. But it was too late.

And unless one really knew where and how to look, the false front was perfect. He'd fashioned it by laying down three barrels on their sides—barrels that would fit tightly under his bench seat, protruding only three or four inches from there into the back of the wagon, and wedged in tightly so they didn't roll or move. Then he carefully cut off the round front of each barrel, and then the top third of each of the sides of the containers—right where they bumped against the one next to it.

He pegged the parts together with wooden plugs so that it made one piece that appeared to be the fronts of the three barrel heads lying on their sides, wedged under his seat. The tops of the barrels were intact so if anyone looked closely, they'd see the curves of the barrels extending into the shadows beneath the bench, giving the illusion of three round vessels tucked under the seat. But the sides and bottoms of the horizontal barrels were missing, which left room for one or even two people to secret themselves fairly comfortably beneath the driver's seat.

He set the false front aside and said, "All right. It's safe to come out now, Freddy."

He offered a hand to assist the spindly man of twenty as he rolled out carefully from beneath the seat. Then, with a soft groan of pain from unmoving muscles held in a small area for several hours, he turned back and helped his wife struggle free.

"I'm sorry you had to be in there so long," George said.

The man nodded, then looked nervously at the white man standing there, waiting. But when the Quaker offered his hand to help the woman—whose name George never learned—down from the wagon, Freddy seemed to relax. "Thank you, sir."

His wife groaned softly as she maneuvered herself to the ground, then smoothed her skirt and hair as the man poured them some water from a small jug. He also offered the couple a piece of jerky and a heel of bread.

"I've got some papers for you." George went back to the wagon and removed a small piece of wood from the bottom of the hidey-hole. Inside were their false manumission papers. Such documents were ignored as often as not, but having them at least gave Freddy and his wife more of a chance of making it to freedom.

"Thank you, Doc—" Freddy cut himself off, obviously remembering the warning of no names.

His wife's eyes went wide as they went to the other man, but he'd turned to go into the shack. "Thank you," she added in a whisper.

When the Quaker came back out from the shack, George said to all three of them, "I'm also looking for any word on one Jeremy Pole. Ran away from Alabama, near Mobile, four years ago. Send any word back for his mother Jelly. She's waitin' to hear."

In the soft spill of lantern light from the shack, the woman's eyes glistened with emotion. She nodded, then straightened and went about tucking her papers into just about the safest place a woman could have: the hidden pocket underneath her skirt. Freddy did the same, hiding his inside the back of his waistband.

George helped his contact load up the last of the rifles and the ammunition in the hidey-hole. Then he replaced the false front and turned back to them. "Thank you, sir. Take good care of my friends here. She's got a bun in the oven and an ache in the toe."

They laughed softly there in the darkness, for an aching middle toe was one of the many varied codes slaves used to ask for help to escape or freedom.

George had done his part; now it was out of his hands, and the compassionate Quaker would take on the task.

"Good luck with your baby," he said. He tipped his hat to the man, who then turned away to rig up his own horse to a small cart.

Then without another word, having exchanged one form of contraband for another just as dangerous one, George drove off into the night.

Somehow, the ride back into Washington felt longer to George, and filled with more apprehension and anxiousness.

Maybe it was because now he carried rifles and ammunition, and if that cargo were found it would be the end of him. Guns were illegal and forbidden to blacks whether they be free or slave, and he'd have no excuse for being in possession of them.

Maybe it was also because it was even darker, even quieter, even more threatening as midnight came and went. Beauregard, if he were to bring his troops over tonight, would wait until everything was closed-up and quiet before sneaking into the city.

Any way he looked at it, George was admittedly a little spooked as he navigated Blaze down the unrelieved darkness of the deserted road. The only sound he heard was the quiet jangle of her harness and the soft clop of her hooves on hard-packed dirt. The closer they came to the city, the more houses they encountered, the fewer empty lots, and the smaller the spaces between them.

The more chance of being seen or heard.

On the one hand, *he* didn't see or hear any sign of lurking Confederate troops—and he expected if they were about and saw *him*, there'd be no reason for them to hold back stopping a black man driving around at midnight. So that eased his mind a bit.

Yet, as he turned Blaze down N Street, which would take him southeast to Ballard's Alley, George felt that prickle of foreboding climbing up his spine.

He felt as if there were eyes everywhere, watching him. He reached next to him, touching for comfort the rifle he kept there on the bench seat. If he were accosted, he'd probably use it. He'd *have* to use it.

George didn't like the thought of that, and even less the idea of war coming to his doorstep, for he was a doctor. He'd taken the Hippocratic Oath and his responsibility was to save lives or at least better them whenever possible.

Not to take them.

As he spotted Great Eternity Church's cross, mounted on the front of its low roof and only visible when close enough that the other rooftops weren't in the way, George thought he saw something move in the shadows . . . or something shift ahead.

Some*one.*

Someone near the church. Going around toward the back, where his place was.

He blinked, and the impression was gone—but the lingering apprehension remained. He realized his mouth had gone dry and he gripped the reins tightly. He had to unload the wagon tonight and put the contraband weaponry in the safe place beneath the church because he didn't dare wait until daylight.

But if someone was around to see him now . . .

He drew back on the reins and waited for Blaze to still. He tried to slow his pulse to normal as he listened, attuned to the light shift of the breeze. The smells of smoke and sewage buffeted upon the air, and the night was silent. He heard nothing.

Damn it.

George despised the fact that he had to control this fear every time he moved about at night.

No, this apprehension was with him whenever he encountered a white man—especially a group of white men—day *or* night. Whenever he entered an establishment owned by a white man that he didn't know, or walked in a deserted area, or even attempted to treat the illness of a white person.

It wasn't so much the underlying (and sometimes blatant) disregard most whites had for blacks—the belief that George and his dark-skinned, African-born people were less intelligent, capable, sensible, and *human* than they were.

It was the fear that anyone at any time could take him, and he'd be abducted and sold off into slavery. For any reason, and he would have little or no legal recourse.

This was a constant, though subtle, worry, and one he felt mortified over having to battle every time he interacted with a white person with whom he was unfamiliar. And it made him feel weak and like less of a man.

He climbed down from the wagon and quietly led Blaze to the post near the side of the church where he could tie her up.

What would it be like to go anywhere and do anything without that fear?

It hadn't been like that in Toronto, where he'd studied medicine. But here, he—

George stilled. The door of his office was slightly ajar. His heart surged into his throat and he froze. He heard movement inside: someone was in there, digging through his belongings.

Or looking for something.

A cold sweat sprang free all over him, sending a trickle down his spine. Giving Blaze a pat on her soft nose as much to comfort her as himself, he moved to withdraw his rifle from its hiding place on the seat.

With that heavy, illicit comfort in his hand, George moved quietly to the steps that led down to the door, listening carefully.

There were no voices, but there were more sounds of clinking and movement from within. Gripping the gun, George nonetheless kept it close to his side, out of sight. He'd prefer not to use it, and prefer even more not to be seen with it—but not enough to leave it behind and himself unarmed.

At the bottom of the steps, he eased open the door with his foot. His breathing seemed far too loud in his ears, his heart thudded in his ears as more cold sweat made him feel clammy and ill. The scents of tobacco smoke and whiskey reached his nostrils, fighting to be noticed over the smell of Jane Thorne's warming body.

As George stepped into the doorway, the figure inside turned sharply.

"Where the hell have you been?" it demanded.

CHAPTER 14

"WHERE THE HELL HAVE *YOU* BEEN?" GEORGE HILTON REPLIED. "I sent word to you more than three days ago, Quinn."

Adam grimaced, peering at him in the dim light thrown by a single candle. "I'm sorry. We can talk about that later. Right now, I reckon I—or he—needs your help more'n you need my explanation. I think he's going to die."

"Who is?" Hilton rested the rifle—which he wasn't supposed to have—against the wall and hurried over to the examining table behind the curtain. The arrested expression he'd been wearing was gone, replaced by one of calm efficiency, and his shoulders had lowered and widened.

"It's Birch. The doorman at the Willard." Adam had only lit the one candle, and that was so he could get inside and settle his burden without falling on his face and hurting the man any more than he already was. Then he'd turned to trying to stanch the blood pouring from the back of Birch's head, and cursing the doctor for not being there when he damned well needed him—discounting the fact that it was after midnight, and the man had a bed in a rooming house elsewhere.

George swore under his breath, but he'd snatched up the candle and was already examining the bloody, inert form of the wiry old man that Adam—one-armed and half-drunk—had managed to bring here. "What happened?"

"Got hit from behind. I didn't see it, but I was leaving the

Willard with some of the men barracking at the White House—
we had a few whiskeys—"

"You don't say," Hilton replied dryly as he used his finger to
peel open one of Birch's eyes, then shined the candle on it. "I
could smell you the minute I walked in here. Quit breathing it on
me and get some damned lamps lit. Don't look to me like he's
gonna die."

Adam huffed a relieved laugh and sprang into action. As he
found lamps and set them up nearby, he frowned. "Speaking of
smells . . . what on earth you got rotting back there?"

Hilton paused in his ministrations and fastened a gimlet eye on
him. "Among other things, Jane Thorne's body. The ice keeps
melting and I didn't know what you wanted me to do with it because you haven't been here."

"Right." Adam grimaced again. "I've been trying to keep the
damned Confederates from coming in and tearing up the city."

"By drinking whiskey?" Again, the doctor's voice was dry as
dust. "That's one tactic I've not heard of."

Adam sighed and ran a hand through his hair. "We were celebrating—a few of the Frontier Guard men and I took a Confederate flag right from the middle of the town square in Falls Church."

He almost smiled as he remembered the exhilaration of galloping into a crowd of Confederate men and scattering them like
buckshot. Stockton grabbed the flag, and with a few whoops and
rifle shots into the air, Adam and his companions wheeled their
horses around and barreled off. That was the first time he'd felt
free and filled with such energy since he'd come to Washington.

It was the first time in over a week he'd felt any hope to speak of.

Unfortunately, now that the effects of the whiskey were wearing
off, that sliver of hope was disintegrating.

"We brought the flag back to the Willard, and Lane hung it
from his window—then he bought us a few rounds." And Adam
had joined his colleagues at the bar counter, all the while feeling
disloyal because of his suspicions over Jim Lane.

It was due to concern over his friend's possible guilt that, over
the last few days, he'd allowed himself to think less about the murder investigation. He justified the inattention because Lincoln

and Major Hunter needed all of his head-power focused on keeping the city and White House safe, but Adam knew it was really because he didn't know what he would do if it turned out his friend had killed Pamela Thorne—or how to prove it if he had.

"Well, now why didn't you say so? A shot-up, tattered Confederate flag hanging from the window at the Willard is definitely goin' keep Beauregard from invading the city and tearing it up," Hilton said.

Once again, Adam stifled a laugh. "Things've been damned tense and anxious up at the White House, and two whiskeys—well, I reckon it was three—took a little bit of the edge off. By the way, I found out her real name—it's Pamela Thorne. I'll explain after I tell you about Birch.

"I was leaving the hotel and saw him in front of me, and I reckoned I'd catch up to him and say hello. He was the one who realized what was going on that night the Secessionists tried to burn down the hotel. Birch was walking along, then turned a corner, and when I finally did too, I was just in time to see someone attack him. Jumped him from behind, then smashed a heavy stick over the back of his head. The bastard took off running when he saw me. I went after him, but he was too far away and it was too dark to see which direction he went.

"Then I went back to see to Birch. All that blood—at first, I thought he was already dead. He's an old man, you know. You sure he's not going to die?"

"He might if you don't get me some more lanterns lit," Hilton said mildly.

Adam looked at the three he'd done so far. "Well how damned many do you need?"

"More'n that if I'm going to stitch him up. That's a nasty laceration there on the back of the head. Those kind bleed a lot, but that doesn't mean he's going to die. His pulse is nice and strong and he's moved a few times now too. I expect he'll come to soon. And you'll need some light too, I'm guessing, so you can look over some of Jane—I mean Pamela Thorne's things while you're at it. I can't keep her here much longer."

Adam couldn't disagree, but he felt a little disconcerted about deciding what exactly to do with the poor woman's body—and whether to bother Lincoln about it during such a crisis. He supposed he could ask Lane, as it was because of him she was there at the White House anyhow, but that didn't set well with him either.

Not until he knew whether Lane had murdered her. And the uncomfortable truth was, he *did* know what he would do if it turned out Lane was guilty. He just didn't want to have to.

The thing that he just didn't know was the answer to why—and that was a fact in Lane's favor. Adam couldn't think of a reason the man would kill his mistress—especially after bringing her into the president's residence with him. Unless . . . Adam frowned. What if Pamela Thorne was in the family way? And she'd told Jim about it, and he didn't want news to get back to his wife Mary.

"Brian said you had information for me," he said to the doctor as he set a fourth lamp on the table next to Birch's head.

Now that Hilton had cleaned away the blood, Adam could see how the gash had split the skin at the back of the old man's skull. Still looked lethal to him, but Hilton was actually whistling a little under his breath as he threaded a needle, so he reckoned the doctor wasn't worried.

"That's right," said Hilton, pausing in the middle of a tune about "deep down in my heart." He looked up. "I finished looking her over. I didn't see anything that made it look like she was interfered with unwillingly."

Adam nodded grimly to himself; he already expected from his talking with Lane that Pamela Thorne was a willing partner. His apprehension grew, for if Hilton revealed something that would convict Lane—at least in Adam's mind—that would be very unpleasant.

So he decided to put the question out there right away. "Was there any chance she was in the family way?"

Hilton glanced at him as he finished knotting the thread. "She wasn't. And how did you find out her name? Do you know anything else about her?"

Adam hesitated. But, dammit, Hilton trusted him—and had helped him out many times in the last month. And he reckoned it wouldn't be a bad idea to have someone he could talk things over with besides Miss Gates.

"She was Jim Lane's mistress. I don't know anything else about her—where she's from, who her family is. I got him to admit they were together, and that they'd had a rendezvous in the oval library that night she was killed at two o'clock." He gave the other man a wry smile. "Your estimate on the time of death was pretty close, because it had to have happened after two and, I'd wager, before four."

"If Lane was telling you the truth about her still being alive when they were finished—or when he left her."

Trust Hilton to speak so pragmatically.

"Yes. I do believe him—well, about that at least. But there's a snarl in his story that's been bothering me. We found his coat. The killer was wearing it when he cut her throat."

The doctor was no longer whistling, and although he was paying attention to his needle and the precise stitches he was making, he nodded. "That ain't good for Mr. Lane. And the fact he claims he didn't hear anything from that room when he was sleeping in the hall outside and he's supposed to be on guard duty? A good sentry wakes at the smallest sound. I've been wondering about that since the beginning."

Adam nodded reluctantly. "Unless he heard something, but just thought it was her leaving the room after their—uh—engagement." He looked at Hilton. "I reckoned from the blood and some tracks and footprints in the room that the killer hid behind the curtains. It appears he was there for a while."

"How do you know that? And how do you know the coat was Lane's? He admit it?"

"After a fashion." Adam went on to describe how he knew the coat belonged to the Kansas senator because of the burn on the back, and then shared their conversation about it in the library on Monday. Then he explained how he'd determined where the killer hid.

"Didn't Lane kill a man back in Kansas? Just up and shot him over something silly like a well or some water?" Hilton pulled the needle through, raising his arm as he drew it tight, and Adam fancied he could hear the sound of thread sliding through flesh. Between that, the whiskey he'd had some time ago, and the knowledge that Pamela Thorne's unpleasant-smelling body was behind the other curtain and beginning to decompose, Adam wasn't feeling particularly steady.

"Gaius Jenkins was his name. Yes, Jim shot him, but it was self-defense—and the judge on the court case agreed. Jim came here to Washington to argue for the Kansas legislation, and during that time, Jenkins took over Jim's homestead land. He squatted there and planned to farm it—what Jim had already begun to clear. But the worst part was his daughter's grave was there—Annie, who was only six when she died. Jenkins actually tilled up the field and the gravesite where Annie was buried." Adam shook his head and pursed his lips—as if it would protect him from the horrific image of a poor girl's body being torn up by a plow, and he wholly understood why Jim had been devastated by grief and blindly furious with Jenkins.

"That's awful," Hilton murmured.

"Yes. When Jim found out . . . well, the only way to describe it is he went mad. But he didn't kill him outright. It wasn't until Jenkins came—he'd been drinking—and brought some friends. He provoked Jim—who I reckon I have to admit can be easily provoked—and one thing led to another. Jim shot him when Jenkins pulled a gun on him."

"So you don't believe your friend killed Pamela Thorne." Hilton's skepticism should have rankled Adam, but he understood why the doctor felt that way.

Yet, he couldn't say whether he thought Jim was innocent or not. Too many things pointed to him. "What else did you find out?"

Hilton glanced up at him as he tied off the thread. "Killer had dark hair."

Damn. "How do you know that?"

"Found some in the top of her hair that didn't belong to her—probably got there when he was holding her from behind and cutting her throat."

Adam nodded, already seeing it in his mind. "When she struggled against him, and that part of her head would have hit his chin and probably rubbed against his beard." Then a thought struck him. "Jim doesn't wear a beard. He doesn't shave often enough, but he doesn't have a beard. So his hair there wouldn't be very long. How long was the hair?" For the first time, a small bit of hope filtered through him. "And Jim's too tall for the top of her head to rub against his chin like that."

Hilton nodded thoughtfully. "That's a fair point. I'll show you the hair when I'm finished here. You ever look over her clothes and all? I don't have room to keep all that stuff here. And it's not good, me having a white woman all cut up here in my office. You've got to get that business out of here."

Adam nodded. "I reckon you're right about that. Let's wrap her up tonight in a sheet, and I'll send someone for her tomorrow." He could figure out what to do then, or maybe just send Pamela Thorne to the real morgue, where they kept bodies until someone claimed them—or they decomposed too much and needed to be buried. Which it seemed as if, ice notwithstanding, Mrs. Thorne was at that point.

Birch gave a soft groan as Adam began to lay out Pamela's clothing and her shoes on a table so he could look them over closely. Hilton brought four lamps over and placed them around to offer the best light.

"So we know that the killer surprised Pamela from behind, stepping out from the curtains. He had to have been hiding there—I reckon while she and Jim were—uh—otherwise engaged. Oh, yes, and Jim said he took off his coat during all of that. He says he must have left it in the library, and I reckon the killer took it."

"He put it on and then attacked Miz Thorne?" Again, Hilton's skepticism was obvious.

Adam nodded. "I can see how it happened—the coat was over the chair next to the curtains where the killer was hiding, or even over the sofa. But when Jim was ready to leave, he went out the main door to the hallway where he was on guard. It's across the room from the windows. And I reckon Pamela Thorne walked him to the door, so her back was to whatever was happening in the room. They might even have spoken for a minute, or embraced. She wouldn't have gone out that way herself just in case someone saw her.

"By then, the killer knew he was going to kill her—but why?—and he also knew he couldn't go around with blood all over him. So he snatched up the coat—or maybe he even did it *while* they were—uh—distracted and that's why Jim forgot to take it with him because he didn't see it. He would have had plenty of time to think it through—the fact that he'd need a way to hide the blood on him."

Hilton was nodding as he seemed to absorb what Adam was saying. "I still don't know how you could tell the killer hid behind the curtains, and that business."

Adam shrugged. "It's like tracking an animal outside—there are signs and marks of movement inside as well. And part of it is . . . well, I call it 'knowing.' It's as if I become the animal—or in this case, I become the man—and can see through his eyes and understand what he did." He felt strange putting into words what Ishkode, and his grandfather Makwa had taught him about there being a spiritual part to tracking. Once one learned the basic skills, that element of "knowing" made the tracker exponentially better.

Instead of being derisive in regard to Adam's explanation, Hilton appeared interested. "*I* don't understand it, but I have to believe it, I suppose."

With a nod of acceptance, Adam continued talking through his theory. "When Pamela came back, she was probably going to leave by the side door near the windows, and then go out through the anteroom or the president's office. Everyone was asleep and those rooms should be empty.

"The killer waited until she passed by, then stepped out from the curtains, grabbed her over the mouth, and *sliced*. He was wearing Lane's coat, so all of the blood went there—and on hers as well." He gestured to the one laid on the table. "Then he held her until she died so she'd make no sound—or no loud enough sound—for Jim to hear. And even if he did hear something from the room, he'd assume it was her getting dressed again or something.

"After she was dead, the killer picked up the candle she'd brought with her—"

"You didn't mention a candle," Hilton said with a grin.

"She had to have a candle; it was pitch dark in there otherwise with the windows closed and the lamps off for the night. The killer took it with him, and spilled a little wax and dripped some blood on his way out. Then he sneaked down and went into the East Room and curled up on the floor near the wall, where he slept the rest of the night—but that was after he'd removed Lane's bloody coat. He probably kept it in a wadded bundle next to him."

"The East Room? Where the Frontier Guard is? So he must be one of the frontiersmen."

Adam nodded soberly. "Possibly. Or, if he wasn't, he knew enough about where they were sleeping to reckon he could use the East Room and all the men as concealment overnight. In the dark, no one would notice an extra person huddled by the wall, and in the morning, he could slip out without anyone seeing him.

"The next day," Adam said, thinking about all of the facts he'd learned from his own interviews and Miss Gates's as well, "while everyone was distracted by the shock of finding a dead body, he hurried down to the basement and put the bloody coat in a trash bin." As he spoke, Adam remembered that Jim hadn't been there at the door of the library when the body was found.

Another point against his friend.

"What about that dark hair you found in hers?" he asked. If he could somehow prove that hair couldn't belong to Jim, that would go a long way in exonerating the senator. But how on earth could he do that?

Just then, Birch shifted on the table next to them. "What happened?" grumbled the old man.

"Easy there, sir," Hilton said, putting a gentle hand on him so he didn't roll off the table. "Your head hurt at all?"

"Hurt like a sum-bitch."

"It's going to be that way for a while. Do you know your name?"

"Of course I know my damned name," snapped Birch as he struggled to sit up. Hilton assisted from behind, and the older man's feet dangled off the side of the table.

"Well, sir, why don't you tell me what it is then?"

"Well, it's *Birch*. Who asking?" He said, trying to angle around to look behind him. Then he caught sight of Adam. "Mr. Quinn! What you doing here?"

Once he explained, Birch's irritation faded. "I remember you now," he said as Hilton came around to the front. "You's the one who wanted to take Louis's body. Why'd you want that for if he's already dead?"

"I wanted to . . . examine it." The doctor seemed a little abashed.

Adam gave him a jaundiced look. "Is it fair to say you have *two* bodies back there, and not just Pamela Thorne's that's causing the smell?"

"S'pose it is."

Adam was glad he hadn't gone back there to look around before Hilton showed up home. That would have been an unpleasant surprise.

"What you want with poor Louis, anyhow?" Birch said. "Last time I saw him he was driving Mrs. Lander up to the President's House at *midnight* of all things, and then next day he turn up his throat cut. Still don't know why anyone would want to do that to poor Louis."

Adam stared at the old man, then looked at Hilton, who nodded gravely and said, "And he was also stabbed in the back right side, just like Miz Thorne was."

"It's the same killer."

"I reckon you're right."

Adam narrowed his eyes at Hilton. "I suppose that was part of what you wanted to tell me?"

"I didn't know if it would help your investigation, but when I heard another man's throat was cut, it seemed important to take a closer look. Anyways, I like the practice."

"And poor Louis, he ain't got no family neither," put in Birch. "So they ain't gonna bury the body right away. And half the city gone—well, I told George here I didn't figger anyone cared if he took care of Louis. But he didn't say he was gwine *examine* him."

Adam hardly heard what Birch was saying, for he was thinking about the implications of this new information. "So Louis drove Mrs. Lander up to the White House, and the next day he's dead in the same way Pamela Thorne was killed. Why? What's the connection?"

"It were Mrs. Lander *and* her maid Millicent went up the White House," Birch said firmly, "and I saw when Louis brought them back. But when he come back, the other man got a free ride—he wasn't there."

"The other man?" Adam said sharply. "Tell me about that."

"Well, he sit right up there with Louis—climbed up next to him just as they were driving off. When he din't come back, I figgered Louis was jes' givin' him a ride to the mansion. Mebbe he was part o' them soldiers up there and wanted a ride, and Louis—he a good man and he wanted to help a soldier, mebbe."

"Did you ask Louis about him?"

"Naw." Birch shrugged. "Only saw him when he come back at fi'teen afore one, and I was ready go home then. But then I found them pile of rags they was gwine use to burn down Willard's, so I din't get home till near dawn, looking for all them other ones."

Adam was still looking at him, a disturbed inevitability sliding over him. "And tonight you were attacked. Why? To be robbed?"

Birch gusted out a laugh. "I ain't got two coins rub together. No one gwine rob me. But—my gloves!" With a panicked expression, he began patting the pockets of his frock coat.

"That's what I reckon too—no one would have any cause to rob you," Adam said. "So there's another reason. Were you talking to anyone about how you saw this other man riding with Louis that night?"

The old man produced his spotless white gloves with an exclamation of relief. "Not one drop blood on them, too." Then, realizing Adam had spoken, he tilted his head and winced as if caught by surprise with the pain. "Mebbe I said something to someone. I don't recall."

"Do you recall anything about what that man looked like? The one who rode up next to Louis? Was he tall, short, dark, light? Did he have a beard or sideburns?"

Birch seemed a little taken aback by Adam's rapid-fire questions. "Well, how'm I supposed to know? He was sitting next to Louis, so how do I know how tall he was? His hair was dark. He had a beard, I remember that."

"Louis was a small man," Hilton commented. "So did the man sitting next to him look taller or the same size?"

"Hmm." Birch screwed up his face, wrinkling his eyes closed. "He was prolly taller than Louis by yay so." He measured a good five-inch span with his hands.

"So that would put him about five feet, maybe nine inches? Or ten." Adam could picture it.

"Be about the right height to get his beard hair in Miz Thorne's when he was cutting her," Hilton said agreeably.

Adam nodded. "Suppose it's time I looked at her things. And I reckon I should take a gander at Louis too, and his things as well."

"I noticed something interesting about them. The way they were cut."

He looked at Hilton. "And?"

"Miz Thorne—the beginning of the cut was a little shallower, a little more jagged. Like he maybe hesitated. But for Louis, the cut was smooth and deep all the way across."

"So I reckon he might've been a bit spooked about actually killing a person in cold blood—though he did it anyway," Adam said.

"Yes, and by the time he did Louis, he was easier about it."

Adam thought about that for a moment, then looked at Birch. "Where did they find Louis's body? And who found him? When was it, do you remember?"

"Well, it were late in the day next day. I remember, because Mrs. Lander were asking out for him, and I ain't seen him—and that was strange. So they found him cut up and dead mebbe two o'clock?"

"Could you tell whether he'd been dead for long?" Adam asked, then looked at Hilton. He didn't know how soon the doctor had learned about the body and got involved.

"He couldn'ta laid there long, Mr. Quinn, because it were right there in the vacant lot next that boardinghouse on L Street. On the 400 block of L Street it was, and peoples pass by there alla time. He was in his carriage, and summat found him there on the floor of it." Birch *tsked*. "He allus kep' it so clean in there, and now look at it—all bloodstained and all."

"What do you reckon they did with his carriage?" Adam said.

"It still there, far as I know. Got blood all over't and all the peoples are gone from the city right now. Who would take it? Now, his horse I say summat took him, but I don't know where that went."

"Four hundred block of L Street. All right." Adam wished he wasn't so tired, but he was. "I'll have a look over there tomorrow when it's light out."

Adam insisted that he would drive Birch home, telling him to rest for a while longer while he looked at the belongings of Pamela Thorne, and then at Louis's wizened body.

"There's hand prints on her coat," he said, laying it out so he could bring a lantern over to examine it closely. "I reckon they have to be from him. The killer."

Then he caught his breath. "George. You see this?"

The doctor came over, and Adam pointed. "What do you see on that handprint?"

"A handprint. Got cut off a little, I think, at the edge there. Looks like maybe he took her by the hip and rolled her over."

"That's what I think. She was in the way; maybe she fell on the floor in front of the door." Adam could picture it in his head. "And he couldn't open it, so he had to move her. He grabbed her by the hip, and shoved . . . but see the first finger?"

When George drew in his breath, Adam knew he'd seen it too. "It's like his forefinger isn't as long as the others."

Adam was nodding, looking at the handprint from all angles. "It may be. But it could also be the way he grabbed her—the way the coat folded beneath his fingers, because he was moving in a hurry. But it's possible. I reckon it's possible we're looking for a man who's missing the top knuckle of his finger. Maybe there's another, better print."

He and Hilton used the expensive kerosene lanterns to closely examine all sides of the clothing, but there weren't any other discernible full handprints.

Adam sighed, looking at the coat again. He carefully tested it with his own right hand, and saw how it was possible to grab it and not have the full length of each finger connect with the fabric.

Inconclusive. The print was inconclusive.

Damn. He thought he might have had his best, clearest track—so to speak—so far.

Scrubbing a hand over his face, blinking his bleary eyes, Adam finally decided it was time to try and get some sleep. Though the whiskey had long worn off, he'd had a long day, and tomorrow—if it came peacefully—would be just as tense.

And if it came in the midst of war, then it would be even worse.

CHAPTER 15

NO TRAINS—NO TELEGRAPH—NO ANYTHING
—The Washington Star
Wednesday, April 24, 1861

ON WEDNESDAY MORNING, THE RESIDENTS OF WASHINGTON AWAK-
ened to dark, frustrated headlines.

The tension was particularly unbearable for both the perma-
nent and temporary residents of the Executive Mansion, and the
slight hope that came with each new day and no invasion had
begun to wear off into brittle awareness that the days slogged on
with no end in sight.

There was no news from the New York Seventh, or the Massachusetts Eighth—both regiments of which were rumored to have
landed in Annapolis. Of the eight riders General Scott had sent
up there to find out, none had returned to confirm this, and
more and more people began to believe it wasn't true.

As Mr. Lincoln said when he visited the Sixth Massachusetts
early that morning: "I don't believe there is any North. The Seventh Regiment is a myth. *You* are the only Northern realities."

Having sought his spot on the floor of the East Room well past
two o'clock last night, Adam woke later than usual. He was
groggy, and the remnants of his dreams clung to him like black
cobwebs: a murky swirl mixed with the dry-mouth effects from a
good portion of whiskey the night before, the shouts and thudding sounds of galloping into a cluster of Rebel soldiers and the

whirling of the flag they'd captured, dead bodies with their throats cut open, and Leward Hale's wild eyes as he screamed threats at Adam's nocturnal self.

By the time Adam shook the sleep from his eyes and sat up, most of the large room was empty of the Frontier Guard. The scent of bacon and eggs—which had been cooked over the two fireplaces—lingered, and he heard men drilling on the lawn outside.

He longed for a bath or a dunk in the river, and it was nearly warm enough to do the latter without shriveling his balls up to his insides. But he'd have to suffice with a quick wash up at one of the sinks. Or, he thought with a smile, if he went down to the basement, Miss Cornelia might let him use a pan of warmed water.

As it happened, the cook was happy to do so—as well as to feed him. Adam was on his way back upstairs to the second floor after these small comforts when he encountered Miss Gates.

"Oh, Mr. Quinn, I'm so glad to have seen you! I heard you were with the scout group that captured the Confederate flag yesterday in Virginia. That must have been quite exciting." Her eyes, though underscored by dark circles, danced. She wasn't wearing a bonnet, which was an indication that she had no plans to leave the mansion soon.

Although he knew he was needed up in the president's office, and that he had a myriad of things that called to him, Adam discovered he was in no hurry to rush off. Instead, he smiled down at her. "I reckon it was quite exhilarating, if nothing else. And what have you been doing with your days, Miss Gates? Writing news stories or visiting the infirmary?"

Her nose wrinkled a bit as she replied ruefully, "I've not thought about writing a newspaper story for days, Mr. Quinn. And have you heard—they've begun to run out of paper to even print them on! All of the newspapers in town are running short. The *National Republican* was asking for the return of their newspapers from Friday so they could reuse the paper and print on the back. But I have been collecting for the infirmary, and I've visited the Capitol—which is an utter disgrace with all those soldiers there!—and yesterday, Miss Barton and I did shooting practice on the National Mall."

Adam blinked. "On the National Mall? You were shooting at things?" He couldn't keep the horror from his voice.

"Not precisely *on* the Mall," she amended quickly. "And yes, we were shooting—at a very poor attempt of a barnyard portrait. I do believe we might have put a few spindly painted cows and one ca-nine-like goat out of their misery."

"I see."

She lifted her brows. "The point is, Mr. Quinn, that we were hit-ting the *painting*, and nowhere else. In other words, Miss Barton and I are quite good shots." She sobered and he saw a flicker of worry in her eyes. "Do you think they're going to come tonight? Beauregard and his men?"

Adam hesitated, then he decided there was no reason to pre-varicate. "With reinforcements from the North in Annapolis, and close enough to arrive within a day or two, God willing . . . I reckon Beauregard has to act sooner rather than later if he wants his chance. If the New York Seventh doesn't get here today, I be-lieve it'll be tonight that the Rebels strike."

Miss Gates was nodding. "That was my thinking exactly. Oh, and Mr. Quinn, about that other matter."

"I haven't forgotten about it," he replied, a bit sharply.

"No, of course not, Mr. Quinn. I merely wanted to tell you that I learned something interesting. I believe there was another man in the carriage when Mrs. Lander came here at midnight, the night of the murder, and that he came into the mansion."

"It's very interesting you say that, Miss Gates, for I have recently come to that conclusion myself. Why do you believe this?"

"Miss Barton and I spoke with Mrs. Lander yesterday, and she said that her driver absolutely did not come inside with them. But Thomas Burns, the doorman, said that the driver *did* come in— just a short while after Mrs. Lander and her maid, as if he meant to bring something to them.

"When I asked him what the man looked like, he said he was

certain he'd seen him before, and that he had a dark beard and mustache. He couldn't tell me much about his clothing, but he did say he wasn't dressed like an important person; that is to say, not in a nice frock coat or top hat—and that he didn't even have a hat. Can you imagine that? He also said," she added breathlessly, "that the man was about thirty years old, and of average height. Mrs. Lander's driver, Louis, was over forty and he wasn't—"

"Average height," Adam finished for her. "In fact, I reckon he was hardly taller than you, Miss Gates. Thank you—you've now helped to confirm something I suspected."

She beamed up at him and he found himself smiling back. "I shan't ask how you came to know that," she added. "But you could tell me if you like." Her eyes danced with amusement.

Adam capitulated and gave her a brief description of what he'd learned last night from Birch.

"So the person who killed Jane Thorne—"

"Her name is Pamela," Adam told her, realizing it had been that long since he'd actually spoken to Miss Gates.

"Who is she?"

Ah. That was where Adam didn't really want to get into details. He felt his cheeks warming a bit, for he knew the moment he told her about Pamela Thorne's connection to Jim Lane, there would be more questions and they would lead into a realm of topics he didn't wish to discuss with a proper young lady.

Although he supposed Sophie Gates didn't precisely fit the "proper" mold, going around dressed like a man as she had done, and shooting at paintings on the National Mall. . . .

"I don't know much else about her but her name," he equivocated.

Her expression portrayed a healthy skepticism, but, thankfully, she had another bone on which to chew. "So do you think the man who killed Pamela Thorne also killed Louis the hackney driver?"

"I am certain of it."

"And that the killer is the extra person who rode in on the hackney? The man with a dark beard and mustache?"

Adam nodded. "I reckon so."

Her eyes fairly sparkled. "Then I suppose we are getting much closer to identifying that man. And Thomas says the man looked familiar to him—which means he must have been here before. Or comes here often."

"I reckon that's so." Adam hated to think that the killer was a member of the Frontier Guard, but it was becoming more likely that was the case.

"Is there anything else you know about him that might help? From your tracking knowledge?" She gave him a pert smile at that last part, and he wasn't certain whether she was teasing him a little, or whether she was breathless with anticipation.

He considered, then decided to be honest. "It's possible he's missing part of his finger—the right forefinger. There is a handprint on Miss Thorne's coat, but I'm not certain the finger appears to be missing because of the way he gripped the edge of it, or because he truly is missing a knuckle."

Her impish smile widened. "What is this, Mr. Quinn? Your tracking abilities are being called into question?" She was clearly teasing him, and he couldn't resist a smile. "Surely not!"

He shook his head. "Well, I reckon I might have more information about him later today, Miss Gates."

"Wait a moment." She held up a hand, and her eyes went vacant as if she were concentrating very hard. "A man missing part of his finger . . . with a dark beard. I'm certain I saw someone like that. Not very long ago, it seems . . . I think." She frowned, closed her eyes, then opened them again. "Yes, I saw someone meeting that description, Mr. Quinn—and recently. But I don't remember where or when. It could have been at the infirmary, or on the street, or even here . . ." She looked around nervously. "It could have been someone here, Mr. Quinn."

He refrained from telling her it likely had been—all indications pointed to the man being in the White House. "If you remember where or when you saw him, please send word to me as soon as possible, Miss Gates. As soon as I speak with Mr. Lincoln and he releases me to do whatever tasks I'm assigned by Major Hunter, I'll be examining Louis's carriage—and the crime scene where the poor man was killed. I reckon there might be some-thing helpful there."

At least, he hoped so.

"Oh, that sounds quite interesting. May I come with you?" she asked. "It would be a fine break from going door to door and ask-ing for bandages and whatnot."

Damn. He should have known better than to tell her of his plans. "I—"

"Adam! The president has been calling for you."

He did his level best not to show vast relief when he saw Cliff Arick coming toward him down the corridor. "Excuse me, Miss Gates," he said.

She gave him a look that indicated she knew exactly why he was rushing off, but said nothing other than, "Good luck, Mr. Quinn. I'll send word if I remember anything else."

Adam hurried up the stairs to the second floor, noting that al-though the line of job-seekers had thinned considerably, there were still a dozen or so men waiting for their chance to speak to Mr. Lincoln.

The mood in the president's office could hardly be any more gloomy and anxious. As had become usual, Mr. Lincoln was sur-rounded by his secretaries, General Scott, Major Hunter, Secre-tary Cameron, and another man Adam didn't know. Jim Lane was noticeably—at least in Adam's mind—absent.

"Adam Quinn, this is Lieutenant John Dahlgren from the Navy Yard," said Mr. Lincoln grimly. "He's the commander there and was just advising us that he discovered sabotage at the shell house. Proceed, Lieutenant."

"There is a whole supply of shells we'd recently made that have been filled with sand and sawdust instead of gunpowder," said Dahlgren in disgust. "And a battery of cannon has been spiked."

Scott swore, and Major Hunter's epithet was much clearer and no less crass.

"Traitors. Damned traitors," Cameron said. "They're every-where in this godforsaken city."

Lieutenant Dahlgren turned to the president. "I will continue to sleep in my office because the attention demanded by all of these matters is incessant. I wish to be ready for a Confederate attack at a moment's notice, Mr. President."

"Thank you, Lieutenant."

"You should also know, Mr. President, sir, that should the Confederates attack, I will blow up the shell house—and perish in it, if need be—rather than give up the Navy Yard to those Rebels."

Because he knew Abraham Lincoln far better than any other man in the room, Adam recognized the glimmer of emotion in the man's deep-set eyes as he replied again, "Thank you, Lieutenant.

"I've just received a letter from Mr. Spinner," said Nicolay. "Mr. Corcoran has made the United States Treasury an offer."

"An offer of what sort?" Lincoln replied flatly.

William Corcoran was the wealthiest man in Washington, and Frances Spinner was the U.S. Treasurer.

"He's offered to loan five hundred thousand dollars' worth of gold to the government in the event we need it, and will accept a bank draft on our account in New York."

Lincoln stared for a moment, and then he laughed harshly. "I see. And so when the city is overrun by the Confederates, Corcoran's gold will be confiscated—but he will rush off to New York to cash his bank draft. So even Corcoran believes we are to fail, and fall to them."

The tense humor faded from his expression as Nicolay replied, "As Mr. Spinner believed. He intends to decline the offer for that reason, but of course wanted your consent."

"He's got my damned consent." Lincoln pivoted sharply and stalked to the window where he could see the river. The river which remained horribly empty of steamers carrying troops.

Someone knocked on the door and Stoddard rushed to open it. A Frontier Guard messenger rushed in.

He barely saluted before allowing his news to tumble out. "Mr.

President. General Scott. Ed McCook has returned. The troops are in Annapolis. The Seventh and the Eighth."

A gentle hiss of exhaled breath and tension eased the room slightly.

"Then why don't they come?" Lincoln said flatly, turning from the window.

"There are militia all over the countryside of Maryland, determined to fight them back should they try to march. Generals Butler and Lefferts are trying to reckon the best route to take and remain safe."

How long would the generals argue and discuss, leaving Washington vulnerable? Although Adam wanted to curse aloud, the president was more contained. "Very well. Thank you."

"If they leave Annapolis today, they'll arrive tonight or tomorrow," said Scott. "Depending how hard they have to fight to get through."

"Tomorrow will surely be too late," Lincoln replied. "The food is nearly gone—I've just had word that flour is selling for *fifteen* dollars a barrel—it was just six last week. And most of the shops have been shuttered. Beauregard knows we're surrounded and weak. He's gathered his troops. Surely they'll attack tonight."

Adam wasn't free to visit Hilton until much later in the day. Only then was he able to walk up to Ballard's Alley to help the doctor transport the bodies of Louis and Pamela Thorne to the city morgue.

By the time they finished swaddling the corpses and loading them into the doctor's wagon, it was nearly half-past four. The day was hot, and they were both a little sweaty—though not as rank as the bodies were. Adam was just climbing into the cart when he heard a familiar voice.

"Mr. Quinn! Mister-doctor! Where you goin'—what *stinks?*"

Stifling a smile, Hilton replied, "We've got some smelly cargo for sure. How's your mam? And your sister? And where's Bessie today?"

"Can I be ridin' with you?" Without waiting for permission, Brian climbed aboard, then made a point of holding his nose.

Adam couldn't disagree—the stench was unpleasant. No wonder Hilton wanted to get rid of the bodies. Then he looked more closely at the young boy, and saw that his face seemed paler and more drawn than usual. "Dr. Hilton and I reckoned we might scare up something to eat at the Willard today, as most of the shops are closed." *And there's not much food left anywhere else.* "Are you hungry, there, Brian? Would you care to join us?"

"*Gor*, and I ain't been eating for two days, so, aye, Mr. Quinn!"

"Two days?" Hilton replied, his shocked eyes meeting Adam's. "What did I tell you about coming to me if you and your mam needed anything?"

"Well, me mam was poorly and I had to watch Megan and Ben—he's crawlin' around and don't you know he's just always about gettin' into the coal bin. And then I got to feed Bessie, and I don't know how to cook and I can't leave them, and—"

"Your mam was sick? Why didn't you—oh, never mind. I'd best get over to see her right away."

"I'll take care of this," Adam said, jerking his head toward the contents of the wagon. "Go on with Brian and see to them." He would have given the doctor some money to help pay what would surely be exorbitant prices for food, but he knew George would refuse.

"Thank you, Quinn. Let me get my bag, Brian, and then we'll go take a look at your mam."

"I'll bring some meat pies for you too," Adam said, making the decision to add that to his tasks before looking at Louis's carriage. "We can't have Bessie starving."

"Remember Megan don't like peas," Brian told him earnestly as he scrambled down from the wagon. "So Bessie can eat hers."

"Right," Adam said, scruffing a hand over the boy's hair. That made it stand up more, and he had a rush of worry over what would happen to the poor Irish family—and the others who were left here in Ballard's Alley—if the Confederates came.

Yet another thing to weigh down his mind.

He wondered if Mrs. Mulcahey had any sort of firearm. Even if she did, could she afford ammunition? That pit in his stomach dug deeper as he considered their plight and what he could do to help.

Besides keep the Confederates from coming.

By the time Adam took his cargo to the morgue and brought back some food for the Mulcahey family and Hilton, it was almost six o'clock, and his mood had gone to deeper gloom. A dismal inevitability hung over the city, and though he knew he was expected at the White House, Adam wanted to get over to look at Louis's carriage before it got any closer to dark. Thus, he didn't dawdle other than to determine—via Hilton—that Mrs. Mulcahey, though weak, was on the mend.

And it made him feel mildly better when he saw the shiny new rifle leaning against the wall in the Mulcahey home. He had a feeling Hilton had something to do with that.

From Ballard's Alley, it was only seven blocks to the houses at 400 L Street, and Adam made good time with his long legs—and the fact there was hardly anyone on the street. He patted his pocket to ensure he still had the drawing of Pamela Thorne there. He thought if he had the time, he might show it around to anyone who was still in town on that block.

As he walked, aware that he had less than an hour before it became too dark to see, he noodled over what frustratingly little he still knew about the killer and his reasons for murdering Pamela. The reason Louis had been killed was surely because he'd seen—and perhaps recognized—the extra man who rode in on Mrs. Lander's carriage that night. And noticed that he didn't return.

But had the man ridden in on that carriage with the express purpose of sneaking into the White House to kill Pamela Thorne? Why on earth would anyone take such a risk? What had Pamela known or seen that had endangered her life?

It had to have been something.

And Adam didn't even know whether her killer realized he was slitting the throat of a woman, or just believed it was a man who knew something dangerous.

But, he reckoned as a thought struck him, if the man had sneaked into the White House that night, *he must have known Pamela was there.* How had he known that, unless he were a member of the Frontier Guard?—or, he supposed, a member of the household staff.

But if the killer was a member of the Frontier Guard, why did he have to *sneak* in that night? He would have been admitted freely—and the same was true for any member of the staff or anyone important whom Lincoln knew.

And why would he risk killing Pamela so boldly—on the first night of the troops staying in the mansion?

"It must have to do with the timing," Adam muttered as he reached the 400 block. "She had to die *that night.* But why? What was happening—or what had happened—or what was *going* to happen that she could have stopped or ruined, and so had to be snuffed out like a damned candle?"

He thought again about the difference Hilton had pointed out in the way the cuts had been made over the two victims' throats. Pamela's had been a bit jagged at the beginning—indicating a hesitation—and Louis's had been smoother all the way across. Adam had attributed that to the fact that the killer might have been nervous over cutting someone's throat for the first time, but what if it was more than that? What if the killer had known Pamela, and *that* was the cause of the hesitation?

At that moment, he saw the empty lot where Louis's landau sat, forlorn and forgotten in the half-abandoned city. Adam didn't hold out a lot of hope that he'd find anything important—after all, it had been five days since the hackney driver had been killed. Even though the carriage was still there, that didn't mean it hadn't been disturbed.

He was mildly surprised that some enterprising soul hadn't taken it and utilized it to escape the city, but perhaps the blood put them off.

Because there was a *lot* of blood inside.

He'd opened the door and looked into the carriage. It wasn't difficult to determine where the body had been when it was found—the pattern of bloodstains made it obvious: in a heap on the floor as if tossed into the carriage.

Adam was delighted to discover a lamp hanging inside the carriage door, and lit it so as to provide more illumination within the vehicle.

And then he took his time, looking over the scene.

The spray of blood made it obvious the killer had cut Louis's throat from behind while the driver was standing at the door of the carriage, looking inside. So the killer had somehow manufactured a reason for Louis to look inside, either before or after driving his fare, then had come up behind him.

The killer had done the same as he'd done to Pamela: after slitting Louis's throat, he stabbed the driver's lower back, and held him there until he died. By that time, Adam imagined, the killer had shoved Louis at least part way into the carriage.

Once Louis was dead, the killer pushed him all the way inside so he could close the door.

And that was how he'd left a bloody handprint.

Adam exhaled softly when he saw it on the seat on the right side: a perfect handprint, as if the killer had had to catch his balance, and he'd used his right hand for leverage.

But what made his pulse kick up was the print itself. The hand was about the same size of his own, but it was clearly missing the first knuckle of the forefinger.

He whistled softly. A man of thirty, of average height and build, with dark hair, beard, and mustache—and missing part of his finger.

Despite that remarkable confirmation of his suspicion, Adam continued to examine the inside of the carriage to see if there was anything else that could help identify the culprit—or give an indication of his actions.

Understanding the activity, Grandfather Makwa had impressed on him, was just as important as reading and following the tracks—for without that element of placing oneself in the mind of the animal, it was easy to make mistakes and to miss important elements.

Adam had learned that lesson well, quite early on in his outdoor education. He'd been tracking a bear over a difficult terrain that included a small river and its shoreline, which was made up of large, flat boulders the size of wagon wheels interspersed with beds of pebbles. Nonetheless, he'd managed to follow the bear for miles through the woods, across the river where it fished for food, then along the shore over the stones, and then back into the forest where the ground became hard and overgrown.

But Adam had become so engaged in simply looking for the next track that he forgot to be aware of the *meaning* of the movements—the subtle signs that indicated the bear's action and reaction, along with mere movement.

It wasn't until he was following the track which had circled around behind him that he realized his mistake: he'd been so engrossed in following the trail that he'd unwittingly positioned himself between the bear and her cubs.

By the time Adam understood how he'd missed the entire element of the bear keeping watch over her cubs while hunting and fishing for herself, and how she was about to respond to a threat to her cubs—which was Adam—it was too late.

The bear was there, roaring as she barreled down upon him from a small incline. He hardly had time to fling himself to the ground and lay there, stiff, silent, heart thudding like mad as the furious female launched toward him. Chances were, he'd die a very unpleasant death at the clawed hands of the mother, and he had no one to blame but himself.

Makwa had impressed on him the importance of the "knowing," and Adam had lost it.

But just as the bear laid her claw over his shoulder, a loud disturbance nearby drew her attention. She finished her swipe—cutting through his buckskin vest and shirt—then roared again. With great relief, Adam recognized the noise as Ishkode and Makwa distracting the bear, and as they drew her away and closer to her cubs, he pulled to his feet.

Makwa didn't have to tell him what he'd done wrong. They never talked about it after—there was no need, for the lesson had been learned. And Adam still had the reminder of it in the form of scars on his right shoulder.

Now, with that in mind, he looked through the carriage thoroughly, but there was nothing else he could find of importance—especially since dusk was beginning to darken the world.

When he was finished, he eased out of the carriage and, taking the lantern with him, shone it around on the ground. The sun was just above the horizon—he did a quick measurement and figured another three-quarters of an hour before it was gone. Full darkness would fall shortly after on a city ill-defended and prepared to be invaded. He needed to return to the White House before then.

The lantern revealed little outside the carriage—too many footprints from people removing Louis's dead body, as well as a bit of rain overnight on Monday, had obliterated most of the tracks.

But Adam had a unique handprint to work with now, and he was grateful for that. While there were many men who'd lost hands, fingers or parts of fingers due to farm machinery, misfired guns, or other mechanical accidents, it certainly eliminated the majority of men. And if Miss Gates could remember where and when she'd seen the dark-haired man with the missing knuckle, that could help him along even further.

Replacing the lantern, Adam extinguished it and closed the carriage up once more. He was just beginning to walk down the street when he noticed the house number of the building next to the vacant lot where Louis's barouche had been abandoned.

430.

430 L Street.

The number that had been on the scrap of paper in Pamela's pocket.

He dug the drawing of her out of his coat and walked up to the front door. A sign hung next to it:

ROOMS FOR LET

Then below, a hand-lettered addition read:

NO ABOLISHUNISTS NEED APPLY

With a grimace, Adam jangled the bell. Heavy, lumbering footsteps from inside made their way to the door, and it swung open to reveal a large woman with a rosy pink face and a bust that jutted through the doorway whilst the rest of her was inside the threshold. The very strong aroma of onions accompanied her, and her greasy brown hair was pulled back in a tight bun.

"Good evening, ma'am," he said.

"You lookin' for a room? I'm all full up but one on the top floor. It's small but it's all I got. You ain't no *Northerner* are you?"

"Thank you, ma'am, but I'm not looking for a room."

"Well what—" she began in a huff, then clamped her jaws shut when Adam handed her the drawing of Pamela Thorne. "What about it?"

"Have you seen this woman?"

"And what if I have?" she barked. "What you want with her?"

"I'm only trying to find out if she was here, and if she was visiting anyone, that's all, ma'am." If it had been anyone else, Adam would have dug out the placard Lincoln gave him—but he sensed if he did so here, it would end up in pieces on the ground again, or worse.

"Well, she might have been." The woman peered at him through narrowed eyes as if she expected a snake to jump out at her. "You stay here."

She turned in a swirl of skirts and a fresh gust of onion, and lumbered off into the depths of the house. Adam waited at the door, watching the street and looking around. He supposed he could knock on all the doors in the block and see if anyone else had noticed Pamela—and perhaps a man with a dark beard who was missing part of his finger.

When he heard hurried footsteps coming toward the door, he turned just in time to see Leward Hale fairly running down the hall.

"*Quinn?* You *bastard!* What in the *hell* have you done with my sister?" he shouted, and lunged at Adam.

CHAPTER 16

SOPHIE GAVE A LITTLE SIGH. SHE'D RETURNED TO THE PRESIDENT'S mansion shortly before dusk—after another day visiting the soldiers and helping out at the infirmary by washing bandages and writing letters for the wounded—and here it was: the same glum, impossible evening. And although she'd racked her brain, she couldn't remember where or when she'd seen the bearded man who was missing half a finger.

After dinner in the Family Dining Room on the first floor, she and the ladies tried to play faro in the Red Room, but no one seemed to be able to concentrate. Every time there was an unusual noise, all heads pivoted in that direction until an innocent explanation for the sound was discovered. Then they returned to their cards, but with a lack of gusto and attention.

At last, feeling stifled and nervous, she rose and excused herself. Perhaps she could find Mr. Quinn and see whether he had any news from his examination of the hackney cab.

"Good evening, Private Ewing," she said to the sentry guarding the door to the East Room. "Could you tell me if Mr. Quinn is in there?"

"No, Miss Gates, I can't say he is. I ain't seen him some time now."

She started to turn away, then noticed the sliver of light from beneath the dining room door. "Is he in with the president in the dining room?" She certainly wasn't going to look inside herself.

"No, miss. Only Nicolay and Hay, General Scott, Major Hunter, and Mr. Lane are in there now."

"Thank you," she replied, and turned away. She peeked in the Green Room, which was dark and silent even though it was before nine o'clock. The household had learned two days ago that the gas supply was dwindling, so the decision was made that only the most necessary of chambers would have their lamps lit as a matter of course. The Blue Room was also vacant, which Sophie had expected, and so she went out to the corridor.

As she passed through the vestibule, she noticed the stairway leading to the second floor was, for once, empty of people waiting to see the president or someone else with supposed influence.

"And rightly so," she grumbled to herself. "The poor man needs a break from all of those cloying, demanding people!" Even those from his wife's family—like the man who'd waved his letter of recommendation from a distant Todd cousin of Mrs. Lincoln the other day as Sophie came by. As if she would be able to make any difference in the president's decisions. And besides, weren't Mrs. Lincoln's relatives all slave-owners and Secessionists—including her brothers?

"And what is it you're muttering to yourself, then, Miss Gates?" asked Old Ed as she approached the front door.

"Oh, nothing important," she said. "Have you seen Mr. Quinn?"

"No, miss, I can be sure I haven't, not since he left earlier today at two o'clock or there'bouts to go down to the Willard for Mr. Lincoln. And then he was about going on to the Treasury, I was hearing, and then some other places."

"All right then, thank you. But I would like to get some air."

"Sure thing, Miss. But don't go far, now." He opened the door for her and she stepped out into the evening. "Them Confederates are bound to be coming tonight."

The day had been unusually warm and humid for late April, but now the night air was cooling a bit and it was far more comfortable. She drew in a few clean breaths and wandered alongside the front of the house until she reached the sentry at the corner.

Then she turned around and walked back.

After a few times of doing so, with no sign of Mr. Quinn, Sophie decided to go back inside. She didn't know why she was so restless . . . well, that was wrong. She knew *exactly* why she was so restless, and she wished she had something interesting to focus on. Even working on writing a newspaper article didn't appeal. She seemed to have lost interest in journalism—at least, for the moment.

If she was home, she could find a book to read, or go wander through the museum and look at the exhibits—the mummies were a favorite—or any number of other occupations. When Mr. Quinn came back, she might be able to nudge some more information from him, or at least a rousing discussion about the investigation.

Anything to keep her mind off tonight.

"Thank you, Mr. McManus," she said when the old man let her back inside. "If you do see Mr. Quinn, would you tell him I'm looking for him?"

"Of course I will, young colleen, but in my day, it was always the man who was doing the chasing after of the bonny lass, and not the bonny lass doing the chasing."

Sophie's cheeks warmed, but she knew better than to protest. She knew her Shakespeare, and was well-versed in the implication of protesting too much. "Thank you, Mr. McManus, for thinking of me as a bonny lass," she said with a smile that her disapproving mother would surely have described as cheeky.

She thought about going down to the basement to see if Miss Cornelia would let her have some tea, but changed her mind when a thought struck her. She could go up to the library and see if there was a book that interested her—and while she was there, maybe some new inspiration about the murder of Pamela Thorne, or the man who'd killed her, would strike.

Even though Mr. Quinn had agreed that the library could be cleaned and used again—at least, once the carpet was taken up and the bloodstained furnishings replaced—no one had ventured inside. The family had ceased using it for their evening gatherings for a number of obvious reasons. And Sophie knew the maids, especially Leah, had no interest in going in the chamber. Changing that was not on anyone's list of priorities, so she expected there would still be the bloodstains and those minuscule wax drops Mr. Quinn had pointed out to her.

Perhaps she could spend some time studying all of that in an effort to see at least some of what he'd discerned from his examination.

To her surprise, at first it seemed the door had been locked. But she jiggled the knob and discovered it had only stuck for a moment, and she was able to turn it with a little effort. Now it opened and she looked inside.

The chamber was still, as if arrested at some point in time and frozen there forever—abandoned and forgotten. She'd thought ahead and brought a candle, and its meager light cast only a small circle around her as she stepped in and closed the door.

The scent of blood still hung in the air, though it was faint—or perhaps even a figment of her imagination. And there was also the aroma of wood smoke from the fireplace—though it hadn't been lit for several days—and the faint smell of kerosene. The curtains on the far wall were closed, flanking the two armchairs that graced the small table with its writing implements, and everything else seemed just as undisturbed.

Despite the gruesomeness of the space and what she knew had transpired within, Sophie found she wasn't as affected by it as she had been when the scene was fresh. However, she discovered that, regardless of her plan to reexamine the space for the clues Mr. Quinn had noted, she felt a little less eager to do so now that she was there, inside, alone, in the dark, and with all those bloodstains—and the spirit of Pamela Thorne surely hovering about somewhere.

With a little shiver that she told herself was *nonsense*, Sophie set the candle on a table near the long sofa and chairs in the center of the chamber, and began to peruse the bookshelves for something that might interest her.

Edgar Allan Poe. . . . She hadn't read his stories in quite some time; perhaps they'd be a nice diversion. She'd particularly enjoyed "The Purloined Letter" and "The Cask of Amontillado."

Although . . . his macabre tales tended to be about dark and stormy nights, and sometimes even about murder . . . so perhaps that wasn't—

Sophie paused. There was something on the ground over there, something on the floor near one of the chairs by the curtains.

It hadn't been there the last time she was in the room with Mr. Quinn, and since no one had come in (that she knew of), she was, of course, curious.

For some reason, she took up her candle—as if its small, singular flame would somehow banish the ghosts or unpleasant thoughts that might accompany her to the spot where Pamela Thorne had been murdered—and brought it with her. Strangely nervous, she nudged the object with her toe. It seemed to be a bundle of clothing.

She crouched carefully, using the hand not holding the candle to ease herself into position while her corset restricted her torso in protest. Then she reached for the bundle.

There was nothing inside of it—just clothing.

No, they were more like rags.

Rags.

Rags that smelled like kerosene.

Sophie gasped and lost her balance, tumbling onto her rump . . . and that was when she saw the silvery blade of a knife.

Right by the side of her throat.

CHAPTER 17

"Y OUR SIS—" ADAM DODGED JUST IN TIME TO ALLOW LEWARD Hale to tumble out the front door of the boardinghouse.

"What the *hell* have you done with my sister?" bellowed the other man as he swung around. He was holding a revolver. "I'll shoot your other arm off, Quinn, if you don't tell me where Pamela is."

Adam's shock had already begun to dissipate, but he didn't have a weapon in his hand and he was looking down the short barrel of one in a wild-eyed, spitting fury. "Put that down, Hale, and I'll tell you what you want to know."

Although he deeply loathed the man and despised the mere sight of him, Adam forced himself to set that aside—just for the moment; *only* for the moment—in order to deliver what must be terrible news.

"Where is she, Quinn?" Hale had lowered the revolver, but he was fairly shouting through his clenched teeth. "What have you done with her, you bastard? Is that how you exact your revenge, then? On an innocent woman?" His voice had gone high and tight, and his expression was filled with the same hatred and disgust Adam felt toward the other man.

He had only a moment to consider his next move, and decided there was no simple way to put it. "If Pamela Thorne is your sister—which it appears she is—she was killed last Thursday night."

"*Killed?*" Hale screeched, the revolver up and pointing at Adam once again. "Why, you—"

"*Wait.*" Adam held up his hands—including the false one that the bastard in front of him had *given* him—in a possibly futile effort to calm his adversary, but he couldn't just stand there and get shot in cold blood—which Leward Hale was more than capable of doing. "Just wait a damned minute, Hale."

The revolver trembled in the pro-slaver's hand and his eyes were wild, but he didn't shoot. And the weapon wasn't cocked, so Adam figured he had a fighting chance—a moment to make his case.

"Tell me," Hale demanded. "Tell me *now.*"

"If Pamela Thorne is your sister—"

"My sister's name is Pamela Buckthorne, but she's in that drawing you have there. Did you kill her or not, Quinn? I'll put a ball in you right—"

"I didn't kill her. I'm trying to find out who *did*," Adam replied, keeping his eye on the finger at the trigger and the thumb that was prepared to cock the hammer. He fidgeted a little, using it as an opportunity to put more space between them.

Hale spat a long stream of tobacco, and it landed on Adam's boot. "Why should I believe you didn't kill her? You hate me, and the feelin's mutual."

"I don't kill people in cold blood," Adam replied evenly. "Especially not women and children," he added without hiding his disgust, "and certainly not by slitting their throats."

The gun wavered again. "Someone cut her throat? Is that what yer tellin' me?" Hale's eyes were wide with shock and grief, and for a moment, Adam almost sympathized with him.

"Yes. I'm telling you, someone cut her throat in one of the rooms at the President's House."

Hale's expression went blank for a moment, and then a rush of black fury came back into his face. "*Lane!* Goddamn that bastard! I told her—" He steadied the revolver, which was pointing once again at Adam's chest. "He cut her throat, that goddamn bastard. Nothing's too bad to happen to him. When the Confederates come in, I'll be right there, first in line to cut him to little pieces." He glanced west, where the pink sky was rapidly turning dark. "It won't be long now."

"Lane didn't kill her."

Hale barked a rough laugh. "He sure did, that goddamned nig-ger lover—sure as he killed Gaius Jenkins and got off scot-free. Paid the damned judge, I know he did."

Adam didn't like the way the gun was wavering about as Hale ranted wildly, and as he spoke, he shifted again to put more space between them. "Hale, I reckon I despise you more'n I despise any other person on this earth for what you and Orin Bitter did to Tom Stillwell and his family, but I'm telling you right now—Jim Lane didn't kill your sister. I *know* he didn't because it was a man who's missing a finger on his right hand. And he's got a beard and mustache."

Somehow, those calm words penetrated Hale's madness. "What did you say?" Even in the dim light, Adam saw that his blue eyes went from crazed to icy marbles. "*What did you say?*"

"The man who killed your sister has a black beard and mus-tache, and he's missing part of his right forefinger."

"You're lying. Goddamn you, Quinn, you're *lying.*"

"You know him? Who is he? Hale, he *killed* your sister—he put a hand over her mouth, then cut her throat in cold blood—and then he stabbed her in the back and held her there while she died. He muffled her voice, held her in place with a damned *knife in her back* while she *died.*"

"He wouldn't. No, he wouldn't do that—no matter what she—"

Adam dived at the man, ramming into his torso with such force they tumbled to the ground. He landed on top and jammed his left arm under Hale's throat—having a wooden limb was handy for that sort of movement—then shoved his knee into the elbow connected to the hand holding the revolver. He reached behind him and slammed the side of his fist down into Hale's knee, which was just coming up to ram into his back.

Hale cried out as Adam's furious blow stopped—and possibly cracked—his pistoning kneecap, and used his free arm to wallop Adam in the side of the face with a fist. He took the blow, his head jolting to the side as pain crashed over his temple and cheek.

Then, wound tight with fury and hatred for the man beneath

him, Adam shoved his arm farther up into Hale's throat, using the point of his elbow to dig in on the side. The pro-slaver coughed and choked beneath him while struggling to hold onto the revolver.

"Drop it," Adam said, dodging another punch, which was aimed a little wildly and only glanced off his shoulder. He couldn't quite reach the revolver, and he didn't want to shift his position and give Hale any leeway. "Drop the gun." He put more weight into his arm and knee, pressing into his adversary's throat and elbow, and at last the man's fingers relaxed.

Adam snatched up the gun, rolled off, and pulled to his feet. His ears still rang, and his head hurt. He was a little out of breath, but he was in much better shape than the coughing, wheezing Leward Hale.

As he looked down at the man, that rush of bitter hatred and violent fury returned. He pointed the revolver at Hale and used his thumb to cock the hammer. The sound—an ominous click— caused Hale's harsh breathing to catch.

Adam *needed* to pull the trigger.

He needed to put the ghosts away, he needed revenge and peace.

He wanted to squeeze the trigger slowly, to watch the man's eyes fill with realization and fear . . . and to see that Leward Hale knew he could take from him even more than he'd taken from Adam . . . and so much less than what he'd taken from Tom and Mary and little Carl. Tears stung his eyes as he thought about those innocent lives lost—all the innocent lives already destroyed due to this conflict.

By God, he *wanted* to put a ball into the man who'd fought a bloody war to keep other men enslaved. Who'd hanged innocent men simply because they'd disagreed with him. Who'd tarred and feathered farmers and other settlers in Kansas in an effort to scare them away from the land so he and his fellow pro-slavers could have their way.

His hand trembled with emotion. His breathing roared in his ears.

Instead, he spoke. "Who is it? Who killed your sister?"

"Robert Buckthorne," Hale rasped, never taking his eyes from the barrel of the gun. "Her husband."

Husband? Hadn't Lane said she'd *been* a wife? Damn. Another lie, or a prevarication? "I thought her husband was dead."

A spark of spirit came through in Hale's rough voice. "He will be soon's I get my hands on him. Pamela, she left him—wanted to divorce him—back in Kansas. She left him and took up with that bastard Lane." He spat. "Don't know what got into her head. Then Buckthorne took it into his head to have a 'talk' with her when she was here in Washington with that bastard *Lane*. Thought he might talk her back into his bed—but you're tellin' me he did more than talk to her?"

Adam shook his head. "Where is he now—her husband?"

To his surprise, Hale's mouth split into an ugly smile. "He's finishing his job. Up at that nigger-loving rail-splitter's fancy house." His laugh was a little mad.

Adam's heart skipped a beat. "What do you mean? What job?" When Hale remained silent, he began to squeeze the trigger, nice and slow, so the man could see it.

Hale stopped giggling, his eyes snapping to the trigger. "I told you that house was gonna burn. It's going up tonight. And soon's Beauregard and his men see the flames across the river, they're coming. They know." He grinned, viciously this time. "They've been waiting."

Christ.

Adam spun away, then thought better of it and turned back with a sharp pivot. Hale had just crawled to his feet, and the blow from the revolver—which carried all of Adam's grief and fury and disgust—caught him right at the side of the head.

Hale dropped like a stone, but Adam didn't see him hit the ground. He was already running to the White House.

CHAPTER 18

S OPHIE STIFLED A SCREAM AND FROZE, HER BREATH CUTTING OFF sharply. The organs inside her turned to ice, and her stomach was doing horrible things.

From the corner of her right eye, she could see the hand holding the knife—the forefinger was partially missing; Mr. Quinn had been right about that. But that was small consolation at the here and the now.

Was the killer going to slice her throat too? Her vision wavered and her stomach pitched. Well, drat it, if she was going to die, she wanted to know who was going to kill her. But she dared not turn to look with that blade *right there*.

She'd seen what it could do. Sophie swallowed hard as her vision wavered into a swirl of terrified white light and sudden black shadows.

"Stand up slowly, now, miss," said a voice that was vaguely familiar.

Sophie could hardly breathe, for her stays felt frighteningly tight—as if her cousin had pulled the laces too far. "I'll . . . I'll try," she whispered. "It's difficult with a . . . with a cors . . . et . . . you know," she said, both terrified and shocked that somehow through that terror, she was babbling.

She still held the candle on its metal stand, and its flame shivered not so much from her rising to her feet, but from the trembling of the hand that carried it. Her palm, which she levered against the armchair to help with balance, was slick, and her fingers felt like ice.

As she rose, she maneuvered carefully—and slowly, due to necessity—so that she could face the man who'd killed Pamela Thorne and the poor hackney driver.

And who, it appeared, intended to set the White House on fire.

By the time she'd risen to her feet—it felt as if it had taken *hours*—she could see his face. And she recognized him.

"You . . ." Words failed her for once, but she didn't have to speak it aloud. She was right. She *had* seen him—several times over the last week of living here, for he was one of the men waiting every day for Mr. Lincoln to grant him an audience. A job-seeker.

Some days he'd been on the second floor. Other days, he'd only been on the stairs. He was there the day she caught her crinoline and nearly tumbled down. She gasped. *He'd been here the morning Pamela Thorne's body had been found.*

Right there—in the corridor just outside the very room in which he'd killed her.

Talk about "The Purloined Letter"! The man had been hiding in plain sight—and because of the lax security in the White House, he'd been able to go wherever he wanted whenever he wanted.

"You . . ." She swallowed and tried again. "You were one of the ones talking about the—the plot to burn Willard's. You said you were Mrs. Lincoln's r-relative." She remembered seeing him stroke a hand over his beard—and how she'd absently noticed the missing finger.

"Well, now I lied about that part," he said with a cold smile. "About bein' Mrs. Lincoln's relative. But the rest—that's right."

Her maneuvering had positioned her slightly farther away from him and that wicked knife, and she was facing him, with the armchair and table behind her. Now that the blade wasn't nearly touching her throat, and she could see him, her terror eased a bit. Her scattered thoughts began to settle. And she still held the candle.

In its metal holder.

That could be useful.

Was it her imagination, or had the knife lowered slightly? It was still there, pointed at her—and he could slice her in an instant—but at least she would see it coming.

"The *failed* plot to burn Willard's," she said, her voice a trifle steadier. "Were you part of it, or did you just get the idea from them for—for tonight?" She glanced at the bundle of kerosene-soaked rags. Over the last week, he must have had plenty of opportunity to wander around the house and plot where to put the rags so they wouldn't be noticed.

His mouth twisted behind his beard; it appeared she'd hit a sore point. "Was my idea first—burn down the fancy hotel. Had some friends to help me—Hale and some others. But I had to come here—take care of Pam so she wouldn't squeal. She heard us talking when she come to see her brother at the boarding-house."

"You were part of the plan to blow up the Willard?" Sophie thought if she could keep him talking, maybe she could figure out a way to escape this mess.

"I knew the minute word got out what happened, Pam would flap her big mouth to Lane. Lane don't know me from Adam, but I knew she'd tell him everything. Even her brother too. And any-how, the hotel didn't blow—Hale and the others were too damned sloppy. That's why I'm doing this one myself. Can't rely on no one else to do it. Want to see that bastard Lane and the rest go up in flames. And you're going to help me. Stroke of luck you came in here like this." He smiled coldly.

"There are others joining me at any minute," she said rashly, re-fusing to let her insides squiggle into wild snakes of fear. "They'll be here any time now."

He laughed. "I don't think so. They're all downstairs, hiding and waiting for the Southerners to come. Won't be waiting much longer. It's going to be tonight. They been waiting for this place to go up in flames—they'll see it from across the river. That's their signal."

Sophie had been edging slightly toward the table, and she dropped her free hand to her side. If she could reach back without him noticing . . . "So you killed Pamela Thorne. In this very room. Why? Because you thought she'd know it was you who blew up Willard's?" she asked desperately, trying to think of a way to distract him. And how exactly did he think *she* was going to help him, anyway?

His eyes bored dark and furiously into hers. "Her name is *Buckthorne*, not Thorne, goddammit. Woman needs to respect her husband. Take his name, she *keeps* it—till death do us part."

"You're Pamela Tho—Buckthorne's *husband?*" she said, seeing no reason to hide her shock. That wicked knife blade had flashed with his agitation, and she didn't put it past him to lash out at her. She swallowed hard at the thought of the blade slicing through her throat . . . or torso . . . or over her face—

"I sure as hell am, goddamned *whore* she is." Spittle gathered at the corners of his mouth, and his light blue eyes were filled with a wild, unholy light. "She deserved it—taking up with that bastard Lane. The whore *left me* for him, and I followed them here all the way from Kansas. She's *my* wife, dammit. Made a vow before God, and now look what she done. Cuckolding me with a nigger-loving madman! How *dare* she!"

Sophie could feel the edge of the table directly behind her, and she began to inch her fingers backward. *Please*, she thought. *Let me just . . .*

"You—you were mad at her that night. Did you just hide here all d-day?" she asked, emphasizing the tremor in her voice. If he thought she was terrified—which she *was*, but she was *also* thinking—he wouldn't suspect she had plans for her candle, which by now was sitting in a deep gutter of hot wax.

Just another inch . . .

"Sure *was* mad at her," he said, lowering his voice menacingly. "She deserved to die. Saw her marching in the street—dressed indecently—in *trousers* like a *man*! Stay at home with her rightful husband, she'd be in her skirts like a lady should be. But joining up here at the rail splitter's house so she could stay with her lover? I wasn't going to allow that. Letting her take up with that Lane bastard . . . telling him all our secrets."

"Your secrets?" Sophie exhaled softly as her fingers touched the edge of the pen stand. "What secrets?"

"I *told* you, dammit! Ain't you listening, you damned bitch? The minute the Willard burned down, my wife—she'd go rushin' off tellin' everyone. I had to stop her before she did. I had to take care of her that night, because the next morning, it'd be too late. The Willard. I *told* Hale she couldn't be trusted, but he didn't believe me. She was his sister, he said. Let her come see us, and maybe I could talk her into coming back home."

"But how did you know she'd be here—in this room?" Sophie asked, trying to picture the impossible.

"I heard her—talking to Lane. I saw her marching with the soldiers when they come up here on Thursday night—walking along like she had a right to be with all them men, leaving her husband behind. I knew why she was doing it—to be with her *lover*." His sneer was ugly, and madness danced in his eyes. "I got a ride up here that night, figured I might be able to talk to her—talk some *sense* into her, get her to leave with me, get away from the place— but when I heard her talking to Lane about their *meeting* later that night, I—"

"When did you hear her talking to Lane?" Sophie asked, momentarily distracted from plotting her escape by the story. "How could you, when there were guards everywhere?"

He seemed pleased with himself, and the knife blade dropped a trifle more. "I slipped off the hackney into the shadows—no one noticed me. Wanted to walk around the house and see how I could get in, and I *saw* them. There was my wife, standing guard and there was that cuckold *Lane*—right there, planning their tryst for later that night! I heard them talking, and I knew right then I was going to kill someone. *I was going to kill someone that night.*" His eyes blazed now, and Sophie's pulse skittered.

"And so you w-waited?" Her mouth was dry, but with the table behind her now, it felt like an anchor in a storm. "H-here?"

"I had to listen to them here in this room—I had to *hear* them together!" His eyes were wild again. "I wanted to *kill him*. But I had to wait—couldn't take both of them without someone hearing. And his coat fell on the ground, right off the sofa, right in front of me—like it was a sign. Bastard didn't notice, and she walked him over to the door—giggling and buttoning up her clothes the whole damned way—and I grabbed that coat. I *knew* what I was going to do then, I knew—*what are you doing?*" His face was thunderous as he brandished the knife.

Sophie gasped, and it was more nerves than bravery that had her whipping the candle up at him. Hot wax flew everywhere, and the metal edge of its stand hit him in the face.

She screamed as the blade swung toward her, and grabbed the table to swing it at him even as she closed her fingers around the ink pen.

The table didn't do much to stop him, but it slowed him enough that his blade was on the downswing when she jabbed the pen into his face.

Sophie choked back shock and horror as the sharp metal point penetrated his eye, puncturing it like a small tomato. He shrieked with pain and fury, clapping a hand to his eye as blood poured down his face. She stumbled back, tripping on her dratted skirts, and nearly fell into the armchair, all the while staring at the sight of the pen sticking out of his eye . . . the blood and innards of the orb draining down his face—

By now, she could hear shouts and pounding feet. *I'm safe. I'm safe.*

And she was, for two different doors burst open at the same time. But it was Adam Quinn she saw as he exploded into the room, and she drew her first easy breath when she saw he had a revolver pointed at the agonized Mr. Buckthorne.

"Find the rest of the rags," Mr. Quinn ordered, heaving for breath as if he'd run a far distance, as he spoke to the cluster of men and women crowding in behind him. "I reckon they're in all the unoccupied rooms." He looked at Sophie. "You all right, there, Miss Gates?"

All she could do was nod, because she was pretty certain if she tried to speak, she'd burst into tears.

And that was something she absolutely, positively would *not* do. Ever.

EPILOGUE

Thursday April 25

*I*T WAS NOON WHEN THE CHEERS CAME UP FROM THE CAPITOL.

The Sixth Massachusetts men, who'd been at watch on Capitol Hill, had at long last seen the train coming from Annapolis. The Seventh New York had finally arrived, and shortly behind them was the Eighth Massachusetts.

The Confederates had lost their advantage.

Washington was saved.

Amid the joyful ringing of church bells and firehall toll bells throughout Washington, Abraham Lincoln had a relatively quiet moment in the room he called "the shop"—his office, which looked out toward the river that would not, at least in the near future, be breached by the rebellious pro-slaver Confederates.

Cheers had been ringing all over the city for the last thirty minutes. The sound reached his ears even up in the recesses of this sanctuary, and the relief over the entire town was so palpable it seemed to waft up from the Mall below and embrace the mansion itself. Transportation, medical needs, and telegraph lines were open, and more reinforcements were on their way from Ohio, Pennsylvania, Maine, and more.

When Hay admitted Adam and his two companions, Adam could see immediately how relief had eased the dark tension in the president's expression, and that at least some of the light and humor that had long lived in his mentor's face had returned. If not as robustly as before, at least enough that there was returned the warm sparkle in his eyes and a more relaxed slump to his shoulders.

"I think we might go down to Charleston and pay her the little debt we are owing her for the skirmish at Fort Sumter," Lincoln said with a wry smile. "Now that the North has, in fact, arrived."

Adam smiled, and though he nodded and replied, "I think that's a fine idea, Mr. President," he knew far too well that it wouldn't end there. That more blood would be shed and far more lives would be lost before all was settled.

The president seemed to know this reality as well, but he had no choice but to act accordingly as the Commander of Chief of a country at conflict with itself. The decision to maintain the Union at all costs was, Adam and Lincoln both believed, the right decision—but it would be a long, difficult, and heartbreaking one.

"The Seventh will be marching up Pennsylvania momentarily for me to greet them," said Lincoln, twirling his spectacles in the relaxed manner he'd adopted in the past. "So I've only a right short moment to thank you, Adam. And Miss Gates," he said giving her a grave nod. "And Dr. Hilton." He nodded at the third member of the group.

"Yes, sir," Adam replied more formally than he would have done if he and Abe were alone.

"The case of Johnny Thorne—but it was actually Pamela Thorne, was it not?—has been concluded then?" Lincoln asked, getting down to business.

"Actually, her name was Pamela Buckthorne. She was using the name Johnny, and a shortened version of her last name, in case someone might recognize it. Jim might have known the name Robert Buckthorne from his days in Kansas—although it sounds as if they'd never actually met—and Pamela, for whatever reason, had decided she no longer wanted to be with her husband, and chose to . . ." Adam studiously avoided looking at Miss Gates as he pushed on, "be in an affair with Jim Lane. It started back in Kansas, some months ago."

"But Buckthorne knew this, is that correct?" Lincoln asked, still twirling his spectacles. "And he was displeased about being cuckolded—and not only cuckolded, but by one of his loathsome enemies, Jim Lane—an anti-slavery proponent."

"That's what I understand," Adam replied. "He knew she'd come to Washington with Lane, and when he saw her marching with the Frontier Guard on the day they came from the Willard to garrison here, he was furious—"

"Because she was wearing trousers and dressed as a man," Miss Gates said with a definite bite to her tone. "He called her some inexcusably crass names, Mr. President."

"Yes, I can see how that cuckolding business might make a man testy," replied Lincoln. "But then he went on and killed her over it? Right down the hall from here. I'm not hesitant to say that I hope the man burns in hell for what he did, and how, and why."

Adam couldn't agree more. "He killed her partially because he was furious about her relationship with Lane, but also because she knew about their plans to burn down the Willard. He realized the moment the news came out that the Willard had burned down—which was planned but didn't actually happen—Pamela would know who was responsible, and she'd tell Lane or someone else. And then that would ruin their real plans to burn down the White House.

"That was why she had to die that night—because Buckthorne and Leward Hale and their other men expected the next day to dawn with the hotel nothing more than a heap of ashes."

"And, no doubt, a number of dead bodies," Hilton said in that mild, low voice of his.

"Murder and the great destruction of property," Lincoln said with a dark look. "And the doorman Birch is responsible for stopping it."

"He is. He would have been here today to meet you, sir, but he's still recovering from the beating he took Tuesday night," Adam explained.

"He was a fine man," Lincoln said. "Very polite, and with amazingly white gloves. I look forward to thanking him in person when he's recovered."

"I know he was upset at missing his chance to meet you today, Mr. President," Hilton said, a wry smile tickling his lips. "And he intends to return to his post as soon as he is able to stand readily. He wanted to go back today, in fact—said he never knew when there'd be another plot he had to stop, and that was 'right important, all things considered.' But I convinced him he'd best stay in bed for one more day, even if he had to miss a day of work— which seemed to bother him more than missing a meeting with the President of the United States."

Lincoln looked at him for a moment as if uncertain whether to believe him or not, then began to laugh heartily. "Well, that is a man with loyalty and dedication. I believe I'll need to make a visit to see him at his door someday instead of requiring him to come all the way up here." He was still chuckling when someone knocked on the door. "Yes?"

Nicolay poked his head into the room. "Mr. President, the Seventh is on their way here."

"Yes, I'll be there in one more moment."

The door closed, and Lincoln looked back at the three of them. "Just a few more things and then we can put this matter to rest, I believe. First, Adam, the library can be cleaned up and refurnished? The boys have been nagging to get back in there to retrieve their toys, and the bloodstains—well, I wouldn't want to give them any ideas. Especially Tad."

Adam chuckled. "Yes, there's no reason I can think of to keep the oval library closed off any longer."

"And it was just by chance that you went up there last night, Miss Gates, and encountered Buckthorne—interrupting his scheme?"

"Yes, sir," she replied. "I was looking for something to read. I was thinking Poe might be a good option—"

"Ah, yes, 'The Purloined Letter' or 'The Murders in the Rue Morgue'?"

"I thought perhaps either of those might be too macabre . . . especially the Rue Morgue," Miss Gates replied with a smile. "But then I saw what looked like a bundle of clothing on the floor, and it hadn't been there before. When I got close enough to look at it, I realized it smelled like kerosene—just like the bundles of rags at the Willard—and then . . . and then he was there. With that awful knife."

Her shudder was noticeable, and Adam felt another rush of relief that he'd made it back to the White House before anything worse than a bad scare happened to her. He'd never have forgiven himself if something had happened to Miss Gates.

"As I recall, you came bursting through the front door without even waiting for Old Ed to open it," Lincoln said to Adam.

"I'd just been in the Second Ward, and Leward Hale, the man who—"

"Gave you that arm," the president said, looking soberly at him. "Among other horrendous things."

"Yes. He'd just confessed to the plan of burning down the White House, and I was hoping to get here before any of the plot was put into play." He glanced at Miss Gates. "I got here and was looking around for signs of where the fire was to be set, and I—and half the house—heard you scream."

"You threw a candle at him?" Mr. Lincoln asked with genuine interest.

"It was on a small metal holder with a sharp edge, and there was a good portion of hot wax collecting there," Miss Gates explained. "I was waiting for the right moment, but then he startled me and I just . . . threw it at him." Her eyes were wide, and Adam noticed her face was pale even now. "And then I managed to grab the ink pen off the table, and I jabbed it at him, and . . ." She broke off and swallowed audibly.

The president was nodding. "Yes, Miss Gates, you did a right brave thing. And I believe you saved us from this great white house burning down *and* the signal to Beauregard to march across the river. Although my wife might be slightly disappointed in not being required to start from scratch on the outfitting of a presidential mansion," he added with a deprecating laugh, "I think all around, it turned out well."

He turned to Adam. "What of Leward Hale?"

"He's got a large knot on his head, but he'll recover—in prison, most like, for his attempt to explode Willard's."

"And Jim Lane? What was his involvement?"

Adam shrugged. "A few falsehoods to hide his infidelity, sir. I believe that's the extent of it."

"That's a relief. Now," said the president, "let us all go out and celebrate the saving of the city. There's to be a band playing and a march on the Mall, and later tonight, I'm told, there will be more music and revelry on the square. As for the three of you— once again, I thank you all for managing all of the other tasks set upon you as well as this one—and doing it so well. Not one of you, I think, could have finished this problem without the help of the others."

Although he said the words, and clearly meant them, it was Adam on whom the president's eyes rested the longest. It was as if he knew that, for Adam, the effort and time, and the very point of being here in the city, was the most trying and difficult of them all. His deep gratitude and understanding was reflected in his gaze, and Adam nodded with acknowledgment in return.

"Oh," said the president as they turned to go. "There was one other thing that became clear to me now that this debacle has ended."

The three of them paused at the door.

A smile played about Lincoln's mouth as he looked at Miss Gates. "Buckthorne was brandishing a terrible knife at you, wasn't he? And in the midst of it all, you managed to stay him with a mere ink pen."

She began to giggle, clearly anticipating what he was about to say, as the president, also fighting a chuckle, went on: "Which just goes to prove that the pen *is* mightier than the sword, doesn't it, Miss Gates?"

A NOTE FROM THE AUTHOR

The twelve-day span between the firing on Fort Sumter—the "official" start of the Civil War—and the influx of reinforcements from the North was an extremely tense, anxious time for the City of Washington. I've done my best to depict with accuracy the main course of events and general mood during this time period in *Murder in the Oval Library*.

Although the resources I tapped while researching this book are numerous and could never be itemized in this limited space, in particular, I found *The Siege of Washington* by John Lockwood and Charles Lockwood and *The 116: The True Story of Abraham Lincoln's Lost Guard* by Charles Muehlberger particularly invaluable to me for filling in the details, and understanding on a day-to-day basis what was happening in Washington from April 13 through April 25, when the Seventh New York did, in fact, *finally* arrive to great fanfare and wild relief. Additionally, *Lincoln's White House* by James Conroy was also invaluable for my understanding of not only the plan of the mansion in 1861, but also the details of the household itself.

I chose to depict Senator Jim Lane in this book as a close friend and confidant of Adam Quinn's, and although there were many who loathed the man and considered him mad and ruthless, there is no doubt he was a brilliant and bold military tactician, and an excellent statesman for Kansas. His reasons for fighting to abolish slavery were related more to the economic impact of the "peculiar institution" than that for social justice, but regardless, he was a tireless advocate for the free statehood of Kansas.

His experience fighting the pro-slavers during Bloody Kansas, and the fact that he and Abraham Lincoln had much in common and had met during Lincoln's visit to Kansas in late 1859, made him the perfect leader for the Frontier Guard—which was installed in the White House on April 18 just as I've described in this book. Lane was a philanderer and had a rocky marriage (as indicated herein), and a personality that bordered on unstable. Many historians believe he suffered from depression or bipolar disorder, and unfortunately, Senator Lane died in 1866 due to a self-inflicted wound.

While one cannot attribute the fact that the Confederate Army didn't descend on Washington solely to Jim Lane's guerrilla warfare tactics, it's clear they most certainly had an impact on keeping Beauregard from invading. Lane had fought the pro-slavers in Kansas, and he knew how to manipulate them and their collective psyche. But aside from Jim Lane, there were other men in Washington working to spread rumors about the number of troops and militia in the city—and as the city was overrun by Southern sympathizers, it wasn't a difficult proposition.

Whether the Confederates muffed their chance to take the capital because of administrative military issues (which is part of the explanation in *The Siege of Washington*) or because of the careful spreading of rumors and visibility tactics, we won't ever know for certain. But there is evidence in letters and reports to support the fact that every time the Rebels thought they had enough men to invade, more information (usually false) came out that spooked them. Either way, the fact that the Confederate Army did not take Washington when it had the opportunity is likely one of the most important lost-chance military operations ever—and would surely have ended the war almost before it began.

Clara Barton came on the scene in this book in much the same way she began, in real life, what would be her iconic career as the woman who founded The American Red Cross: by helping the Sixth Massachusetts men when they disembarked from the train after the Baltimore riot. And, yes, she actually did conduct shooting practice in an empty lot near the National Mall (although I'm fairly certain her target was not a poorly rendered barnyard painting).

The British-born actress Mrs. Jean Davenport Lander did, in fact, visit the White House at approximately midnight on the night of April 1819, and although the "extra" rider on the hackney carriage is a product of my imagination, the details about her visit are truet

Additionally, there was a foiled plot to burn down the Willard Hotel on that same night of April 18–19, and although I have no idea who discovered the bundles of rags throughout and was able to stop the plan, it certainly seems reasonable that someone as dedicated as my fictional Birch would have been the one to do so.

Although Leward Hale and Robert Buckthorne are also fictional characters, and what happened to Adam Quinn and Tom Stillwell's family in Kansas is also fictional, they are all based on actual people and events related to the horrific Bloody Kansas war during the last half of the 1850s. There were numerous instances of ballot-box stuffing, tarring and feathering, murder, kidnapping of free blacks, ambushes, and the wanton and random destruction of Free State families and their homesteads. Unfortunately, none of the descriptions I provide in this book are exaggerated in relation to that miniature "civil war."

The garrisoning of soldiers in the White House, the Willard Hotel, and the Capitol Building did happen just as described—up to and including the awful sanitation problems and the tobacco spots, grease stains, and destruction of the desks and property of Southern Senators in the Chamber.

As strange and dangerous as it seems to us today, the depiction of the job-seekers being a near-constant presence in an executive mansion during wartime is also shockingly true. Although Nicolay and Hay eventually helped to limit the hours that the president— or as they nicknamed him, the Tycoon—would be available to meet with those pressing for positions, the house was open and accessible during this time to anyone and everyone. It is more than probable that someone like Robert Buckthorne could have been there every day, ostensibly waiting for the president while casing the place—and even hiding his bundles of rags—in preparation for the plan to send the mansion up in flames. And it's quite true that anytime anyone stepped out of the bedchambers or any of the rooms on the second floor, they could easily encounter a stranger or the lineup of people waiting to see Lincoln.

Finally, a word about Adam's tracking abilities and approach. My presentation of tracking in such a way—by employing not only the mechanics of looking at shapes, angles, the movement of ground, etc., but also the spiritual sense of "seeing" and "understanding" what the creature is doing—is taken directly from traditional Native American teachings. I find it not only fascinating, but also extremely intuitive that the best trackers—of which I hope Adam continues to be—use not only their five basic senses, but also the natural connection to their world and the perception of a broad consciousness in order to succeed in following and understanding the actions and movements of an animal or man.

I hope you enjoyed reading *Murder in the Oval Library*, and have come to agree with my take-away from the vast amounts of reading and research I've enjoyed with this project: that truth is, really, truly, stranger than fiction.

—C. M. Gleason, September 2018